TESTIMONIALS...

"If escape is a reason for reading, *Change Me Back* is the vehicle. Lynne Anders' first paranormal book brings new life to the vampire genre. You'll recognize legendary characteristics, but plenty of updates and accommodations to modern life make the story fresh.

Once 'changed' by Zach at her senior prom, Emma, now undead, is on a mission to regain her mortal self. Her goal is challenged by her attraction—rather, *addiction*—to Zach and countered by an evil ancient whose designs and desires thwart both the mission and addiction. The action starts immediately and moves—erratically, erotically, enthrallingly—to an ending that explodes in a force of nature, plot twists and, ultimately, fulfillment."
—**Jean Erickson**

"What an exciting love story. I can't remember reading a story that kept me on the edge of my seat as this one did, anxious to turn the page to see what happened next. I also enjoyed the way Lynne told the story from each character's point of view. It brought added life to the main characters.

Is it possible vampires really live? After reading this story, what will you believe? I now look at people differently wondering if they are really who or what they appear to be."
—**Mary Christensen**

"Lynne is brilliant in her first foray into the paranormal world with this portrayal of vampires. *Change Me Back* brought out emotions that surprised me. It is a unique love story about giving, protection, and eternal love. Now if I see someone in a restaurant ordering a rare steak, I may wonder, are they..."
—**Bernie Christensen**

"*Change Me Back* is an exhilarating vampire story complete with villainy, betrayal, and love. One wonders if Zack, because of his hope for the future, will choose to become the circle leader or leave it to others? Will Emma remain a vampire or leave the immortal world to reestablish contact with her human family? This story will keep you guessing. I highly recommend this great read."
—**Barb Lunsford**

BOOKS BY LYNNE ANDERS

THE FORREST SERIES

Samantha's Hope
Samantha's Love
Samantha's Heart

THE LURRY SERIES

Time for No One
The Result of Time
Will Time Change Anything?

THE CHOSEN CIRCLE SERIES

Change Me Back

NEW SERIES COMING IN EARLY 2021

Forever Love

Find all books on Amazon.com
or visit her website:
LynneAnders.com

CHANGE
ME
BACK

CHANGE ME BACK

THE CHOSEN CIRCLE SERIES
BOOK 1

BY LYNNE ANDERS

Andrea Kerner Publishing
Phoenix, AZ
Author_LA@lynneanders.com

CHANGE ME BACK
THE CHOSEN CIRCLE SERIES, BOOK 1

Andrea Kerner Publishing
Phoenix, AZ
Author_LA@lynneanders.com

ISBN: 979-8645968052 (paperback)

Library of Congress Control Number: 2020913768

Cover design by Jena Brignola
Cover image by DepositPhotos.com
Photo by David Miller
Chapter icon created by Ayse Muskara from Noun Project
Book Shepherd, Ann Narcisian Videan, ANVidean.com

DEDICATION

To my husband. Thank you for your encouragement, for your continued love, and especially for creating the name of the special drink my vampires ingest. You rock!

Acknowledgements

This book is one for the ages. I never considered writing a paranormal romance, but when Emma and Zach began to whisper in my ear, well, the results are contained within the following pages.

To those who are always in my corner:

My beta readers: Mary, Bernie, Jean, and Barb. Please continue to push me to be better.

My friends who read the stories and encourage me daily: Marsha, Aileen, and Sandy. What would I do without you?

My Book Shepherd, Ann Videan, who, once again, helped craft this book into a much better read, and who also holds my hand each step of the way through the editing process. Even though your suggestions and insights appear unattainable for me at times, I eventually find a way to muddle through and have improved my craft because of them. Thank you.

My cover artist, Jena Brignola. I am once again amazed. The cover portrays Emma and Zach to perfection. Thanks for fitting me into your busy schedule.

For those who follow me, whether through my website, book signings, or because you're a family member I force to read my work, I hope this new adventure proves to be the positive challenge it was to create.

Becoming a member of the Desert Rose RWA Chapter changed my life. I will always be grateful for the many hours of questions answered and pointers shared. You all rock!

CHAPTER 1

EMMA

Senior Prom Night

Ayres Bridges, considered a computer geek to many, focused solely on his hobby instead of on girls and dating. From the same neighborhood as me, we'd become friends during elementary school and remained so throughout high school. When he asked me to prom, I thankfully accepted. Wasn't it better to attend than to wish forever that I had? Besides, he told me, how else could he show off his dance skills? Now, how does a girl say no to a man who can dance? My friend promised he held no hidden agenda, only friendship and a shoulder to lean on, knowing full well I wished someone else had invited me, and who that someone was. His understanding of my situation filled my heart with mixed joy.

Sorrow doesn't cover how I felt when we passed through the stars and moons archway at the entrance into the gymnasium. Not twenty feet in front of us, Zachary Matthews, the basketball jock I was in love with, stood smiling at that blonde bombshell, Michelle Markum, who was all decked out in a designer strapless dress made of chiffon tulle in one of our school colors, green. Typical, little miss cheerleader.

My dress, although strapless as well, was fashioned from one of my older sister's well-worn formal gowns. Long, purple, and sparkly, it complimented the theme of our prom perfectly, even though the dress itself was long past its prime. We continued in after the standard first picture was snapped, bypassing Zach and Michelle without a word. I purposefully held my head up and walked with a grace I sometimes possess, my dress swaying gently with each step taken. My long light-brown ponytail hung in waves and stopped mid-back, but was nowhere near the sophisticated up-do *she* wore. Over-the-top makeup, applied at the insistence of my sister, felt alien on my face, too. However, it accentuated my golden-flecked brown eyes and high cheekbones. Damn, I looked good, even by *my* standards. But then, I'd prepped for *him*.

Our eyes met when I turned my head back, checking to see if I'd made an impression. I tried to smile, but my heart wasn't in it. At least he gave me the once-over. When we glimpsed each other the last time, I saw regret. He attempted to pull away from Michelle. But, she looked over her shoulder toward me and grabbed his arm to stop him. I hoped he'd pull away to follow us. He didn't. I glanced back at Ayers and gently smiled, hoping he hadn't witnessed my deflected gaze toward Zach.

The tall computer tech and I continued past the rest of the athletes gathered near the entrance and located his friends on the other side of *The Starry Night*-themed room. Twinkle lights, intertwined with silver stars, hung low over most of the room including the dance floor. Dark-blue Mylar balloons showcasing crescent moons rose high above each dark-purple tablecloth adorned with stars and moons glitter. If not for my emotional upheaval, I'd be whisked away into the sparkling sky and rocketed toward the moon and stars. Dreams of what's to come create such thoughts. My dream crumbled behind me to my left.

Our table, with only two empty seats, sat near the stage. We greeted Ayres' best friend, Seth and his girlfriend Kim, and lowered into the two vacant chairs. As Ayers held my seat for me, I peeked back once more at the handsome basketball player, still wishing I was on his arm tonight. My sigh was internal. The lights dimmed and dancing began. My attention refocused on my date and I buried myself in his world.

Ayres and I danced to several songs, took a break, ate cake, and drank spiked punch with the rest of our group. I'd tossed aside all thoughts of what could have been, that is, until a hand clasped my shoulder from behind. When my head turned back, I looked into the dark-blue eyes of "my" ballplayer.

"May I have this dance please, Emma?"

The curl of his lips and the glint in his azure eyes caused my heart rate to surge instantaneously.

"Ayres? Do you mind?" I waited for my date, who also knew I was hopelessly in love with that guy, to keep me from more pain. It didn't happen.

"Not at all, Emma, as long as you come back with that smile still in place." He squeezed my hand before I stood.

I kissed Ayres' cheek and then clasped Zach's proffered hand. The six-foot-three jock led me to the dance floor, surrounded me in his arms, and leaned in. I thought he meant to kiss me. Instead, his nose nestled in my hair and he inhaled heavily. I couldn't see his expression, but I heard his sigh.

"What are you doing? You know what shampoo I use." My hand flew to the side of my head to make sure hair hadn't been pulled from my ponytail.

"You smell... almost too good to be true. You've never worn perfume before. What is it?" He inhaled again, this time next to my ear.

Nerves moved my mouth, which could barely keep up with my gushing words. "Oh, that! I don't wear perfume to school. Some people are allergic to scents and I've never wanted to put someone off because of how I smell. Guess I decided to walk on the wild side tonight." My mind raced around like a hamster on a wheel. *Calm down, Emma. Just talk to the guy*, I chastised myself. "In answer to your question, I wear Opium. It's been my favorite for years." Why am I nervous now? We've been close friends all year. I relaxed, somewhat, when he didn't appear to notice my shaky voice or sudden blush.

"It smells delicious."

When I looked up into his eyes, they twinkled from the glimmering lights above our heads. It was his smile that melted my heart, though. I so wanted it to be only for me, but I knew differently now and couldn't allow myself to get caught up in the moment.

"Thank you." Additional words formed in my head, but nothing more came out.

The second the dance ended, I released my hold on him and almost ran from the gym. It was the only time I'd be in his arms, and I wanted so much more. Mom had told me schoolgirl crushes ended after graduation. But, this wasn't a crush. It was love. An unrequited love now.

I stepped out into the parking lot and shivered from the chill in the air. Indianapolis can be downright cold in May and tonight it was. My arms wrapped my shoulders. Why didn't I think to bring a jacket or cloak to wear with my strapless dress?

The shadowed sidewalk that led me away from him also reinforced my sorrow. With my head bowed and arms wrapped against my sides, I strode toward the math building where Zach and I had spent so much time discussing everything. When I stopped beside "our" bench, my hand gravitated to the top rail and I held on while tears filled my eyes. When the first one fell, someone's hand clasped my shoulder. That's the last memory I have of the night.

CHAPTER 2

ZACH

E mma walked through the door on Ayres' arm and spotted me. Her eyes accused me and I immediately regretted my decision. Both of our evenings were ruined and it was all on me. Attending another prom, especially at my age, was not on my agenda, but when Harley begged me to ask Michelle, how could I tell my teammate no? He had covered for me last season when I showed up late for practice, or when my system was in need of blood and I left to grab a Crimson from the nearby Steak 'n Shake. He threatened to out me to Coach. Not to explain how I am a two-hundred-and-fifty-seven-year-old vampire, but rather that I am not trustworthy or loyal, and disappear occasionally for no apparent reason. So, with Michelle as leverage, I had no recourse but to ask my colleague's girlfriend's friend to be my date.

Now, the girl of *my* dreams believes I have ditched her for this whimpering idiot. A beautiful slender blonde may have been my ideal when I was much younger, but I outgrew women who spoke only of their vain wants and needs, and neglected to even pretend to be interested in mine. Emma is not like them. She is intelligent, concerned with the environment, outspoken on women's rights. She volunteers at the local humane society and continually helps those less fortunate. My sorrow rings me like fifteen hula hoops circling my body at the same time.

The attempt to intercept her when she strode by was thwarted by Michelle, who grabbed my arm to stop me. Again, my bad. I should have brushed her hand off and spoken with Emma, who came to the prom primarily because I asked Ayers to bring her. I figured I could explain why I changed my mind to attend and why the cheerleader was on my arm instead of her. However, my chance evaporated in a nanosecond. I promised myself I would dance with her this evening to explain and, hopefully, quell her anger and hurt. Some other unsuspecting fool could dance with the blonde, who was now hanging all over me like Spanish moss on a live oak tree in the south.

Maybe if I focused on my date for a few minutes, it would appease her. "Can I get you something to eat or drink, Michelle?"

Her insufferable giggle tortured my ears. This stuck-up sampling of what teenage girls strive to become in today's world annoys me. Also, pretending to be eighteen again wears me out. If not for Emma...

She slapped my arm before responding. "No, silly. My cheerleader skirt won't fit if I eat cake."

"Then, how about dancing? You do dance, do you not?" If she declined and I had to sit next to her all evening and attempt to carry on an intelligent conversation, I might have resorted to feigning illness and taken her home early. My only reason for dancing was to check on the girl in the purple gown, anyway.

"Of course, I do." Her eyes sparkled with expectation while her lips curved into a sensuous smile.

Her response settled me momentarily. I could do without the "promise for later" smile, though. I stood, buttoned my suit jacket, and took her hand.

As I walked Michelle toward the dance floor, she took time to reprimand me. "You know, it would have been nice if you'd picked me up instead of meeting me here. Now, how can you take me home?"

"I will either call for a taxi or ask one of my teammates to assist us."

"Call a taxi. Then I can have you to myself for a few minutes." Her voice became throaty and the promise-for-later smile returned.

We made it to the dance floor, which ended her admonishment. I chose not to respond to her last comment. I did not intend to escort her home. I would call a taxi, but for her only, if necessary.

Unfortunately, the slow tempo encouraged my date to snuggle far too close for my comfort. Her heavy application of perfume assaulted my senses. I wanted to distance myself, but she pressed closer while I led her around the floor.

Emma occupied a chair on the opposite side of the room at a table comprising most of the computer club members. My body relaxed momentarily. She was clustered by Ayres and the guys, and safe from other lecherous boys obsessing on her beauty. She did not observe my wistful gaze either. I watched her eyes, how her lashes fell against her rose-colored cheeks, then fluttered open projecting her twinkle-eyed smile. I closed my eyes and sniffed the air to draw in her scent. My body, already attuned to her, thrummed with desire. If I was not careful, my date would believe I was in her thrall, when it was Emma who unsteadied me. My eyes opened and I forced down the desire that possessed me when the girl I love fixed her gaze on me. My impulse was to capture her in my arms and make away with her, take her someplace we could be alone.

Instead, when the music stalled for a few moments, my date shook my arm, which brought me back to the moment. I escorted her from the dance floor and back to our seats at the basketball team's table. "Excuse me a moment, Michelle. I need to use the restroom. Can I bring you anything? Punch… or maybe a bowl of pretzels?"

Confusion skated through her eyes. "I already told you I don't want anything to eat. Did you not understand?"

I swallowed back the retort I wished to provide and simply smiled. "Just checking."

When she sat, I turned for the restroom but left through the back door. I had to hurry. I needed to calm my body before my fangs extended. My reaction to Emma and this entire predicament sapped more of my energy than I realized.

Sated by the drink and further energized from the moonlight, I reentered the gym and glided toward the table where my date spoke with another of her kind, another skinny cheerleader-type. I switched direction and searched for the girl of my dreams. At the moment, she and Ayers sat alone at their table. Deciding it might be my only chance to speak with her, I grasped the opportunity.

I rested my hand on her bare warm shoulder. When her head rotated back to see who stood behind her, I smiled into her golden-flecked brown eyes. "May I have this dance, please, Emma?"

It did not surprise me when she asked Ayres for his approval. Actually, it would have been rude of her not to ask. Satisfied that he accepted my request, she stood and allowed me to lead her to the floor and spin her into my arms.

The closer I held her, the more my body thrummed. If I had a regular heartbeat, it would have been off the charts by then. This young woman's essence consumed every pore of my body. Never have I felt the draw, the immediate desire, to mate with a mortal. That it had occurred more often than I would have liked this past year further propelled my decision. I needed to explain first, though. She must understand and be willing... Unsettled by this craving, I knew I must quell the urge before my thirst overpowered me and I did something I would regret.

The more I attempted to engage her, the more her gaze focused somewhere else. The song ended long before I was able to speak my mind, and the young woman fled the room without a backward glance. Even though I wanted to follow, I was resigned to return to my date, who flicked a fake diamond ring on her finger as I approached.

"Were you just dancing with *her*? You told me she meant nothing to you. Why did you lie, Mr. Bigshot?" Michelle stood and stared me down in an attempt to intimidate me, I suppose.

Does that kind of theatric work on humans?

My body, on fire for the gorgeous woman in purple, struck a threatening pose. "I should escort you home, Ms. Markum." My gaze lowered to hers and I forced my intent into her psyche, which prompted the appropriate result. She visibly wilted and nodded.

The smooth texture of my voice coaxed, "Please gather your things."

With no time to spare, I carried the charmed cheerleader home, dashing through the shadows to remain unseen. I deposited Ms. Markum at her door, expanded on my charm that a headache ended our evening, and verified she was inside before I checked my watch. I would have to hurry.

I arrived back on campus in less than fifteen minutes. As I approached the gym, I sensed her near, but not inside. I raced toward the aroma of the fair Emma and found her at the bench where we used to share our private thoughts and desires. The purple dress sparkled in a halo provided by the illuminating overhead light as I slowed my pace to a walk. My hand clasped her shoulder again. She flinched at first, but her head slowly turned.

Tears streamed down her face and smeared her mascara. Knowing I was the cause ripped me to shreds. Involuntarily, I skimmed my thumb under her eyes to wipe at the moisture.

"Do not cry, Emma."

Her hand grabbed for mine. I should have stopped her. I did not. The cooler temperature of my skin popped her eyelids open wide and she blinked rapidly. I decided to relay my standard speech. "The night air is cold and I left my gloves at home. Here, clasp my hands in yours to warm them."

She backed away with a suspicious glance, but charming her was out of the question. I would not do that to her. I loved her. I wanted her to understand me before I shared my true identity with her, hoping against hope she would accept me for what I was. But, I have been a coward amongst cowards. This entire year passed and I did not divulge it to the one I want with me throughout eternity.

I gestured toward our bench. "Sit with me for a few moments. I would like to explain."

Emma, though reluctant, lowered onto the bench, but kept her distance.

"I am sorry, Emma. I should have accompanied you to your prom, though I did not wish to attend in the first place."

Her gaze raised to mine. "Why not? Isn't prom night a rite of passage, a final goodbye to our high school years?"

I internalized my chuckle. If she only knew how many proms I had attended through the course of my existence.

"I require no goodbye. What I do require is your forgiveness." I managed to grasp her hands in mine and hold them gently but firmly as she resisted. "I need to discuss something else with you, Emma. I hope you will listen before you make a final judgement."

Her gaze showcased her beautiful eyes again, though they opened wide with obvious dread. How I longed to pull her to me, kiss her the way I have wanted to kiss her, and make her mine for all eternity.

She shivered, not against the cold, but clearly with her fear of me.

"Emma. What is it?" I willed her to stay with me, to allow me to explain.

"Zach, your eyes are black. Where'd the blue go? Or is it the darkness that makes them look evil?"

The love of my life abruptly stood, but I could not allow her to run. She had seen into my soul and it frightened her. I tried again. "Please. Do not run away. I can explain."

Her head shook slightly, her lips pressed together in a straight line, and tears once again chased down her cheeks.

When she pulled her hands from mine and spun away, I grabbed her arm to stall her. "Emma!"

Before I realized the action, I drew her to me and did the unthinkable. I sank my fangs into the tender skin of her neck. She attempted to jerk free from the attack, but I held her tightly while her sweet nectar poured down my throat. My body trembled from the instant infusion of human blood, a feeling I have not experienced in decades. Euphoria greeted me at the doorway into oblivion. I grasped her closer and continued to drink from the woman I am meant to spend the remainder of my existence with.

Her body finally relaxed while encased in my arms. The moment her heartrate slowed to a few beats per minute, I withdrew my fangs and kissed away the puncture wounds. Her eyes opened briefly and I smiled into the most beautiful pair of golden brown eyes on the face of the Earth.

"Do not be afraid. You are part of me now, Emma. I will protect you for all eternity." Before she fell into the deep slumber of change, I needed to charm her, to wash away the past few moments so she could assimilate into her new life without remembering my deception. I would explain once she recovered and was willing to listen.

"Emma, my love, please listen." My gaze focused on her worried eyes. They calmed almost instantly. "You will call Ayres in the morning to apologize for your early departure. Tell him you left the prom to think things through. You will remember nothing past your approach to our bench, and will awake in the morning happy you chose to attend."

Her nod was the confirmation I required.

Emma, reeling from the loss of blood, fainted into my arms. She was light, a mere feather, as I drew her against my chest. My urge to bed her tonight, as I had been directed, increased. Instead, I carried her home. Her age. She was still a child for all intent and purposes, and I had just committed her to a life she did not ask for because of my maker. If not for his demand... damn. What had I done?

In my haste to get her home safely, I skirted residential areas with lighted streets and moved quickly toward Emma's home through the shadows, as I had done with Michelle. I worried my actions tonight would create difficulties I had not imagined. For one, Francisco's demand that I commit this lovely young woman to a life as my mate. Maybe he would understand my reluctance to bed her now in order to share our blood, and allow some flexibility before I must complete the process. His inability to acquiesce to anyone's request was legend, though, if it was not in line with his directive. I had to find a way to make him understand, to grant me—and her—time. I drew her face close and kissed her lips while memories flooded me.

The moment I met Emma, I had fallen head over heels in love with her kind and generous heart. I had spoken nonstop about her to the others in our circle for the past two years and promised she would be the one to share this life with me. Francisco, intrigued himself with the stories I shared, followed me one night and witnessed for himself the beauty in the young girl. Without a thought for her human life, he ordered me to change her immediately and integrate her into his circle.

As my maker, I must do his bidding or pay his price. His threat tonight was clear. If I did not change and bed her, he would ban me from his circle, change her himself, and I would have to watch as my love drifted away from me. That option... If it came to be, I would end my existence.

I, once again, thought of myself as a coward. I granted her no choice in the matter. And, now? Now that it was done, regret filled my soul. I should have waited. I should have tried more ardently to explain first. How will she accept this fate I have forced upon her? Will she cope? And, will my motive be enough for her to understand why I took her humanity from her?

As I made my way down her street, I wondered who in our circle I could call upon to assist my love into her new existence. Someone gentle with knowledge and sympathy to the situation. Only one name came to mind, only one I could trust. That also filled me with dread.

Emma's home was quiet when I deposited her in her bed. I half expected her father to be sitting in the living room, but he was snoring in the room down the hall. After a quick reconnaissance, I found her mother lying next to him. She was off into dreamland as well, as were her siblings.

With no other choice or help, it was up to me to remove her gown. My fingers fumbled at first, but the back-zipper slid down effortlessly and the entire concoction settled on the floor at her feet. My body twitched as my gaze observed her delicate skin for the first time. I drew her to me and carried her almost-naked form to the double bed against the far wall. As I laid her down, desire flooded me, but I withheld my craving for another time. Only my age kept me from taking what I considered to be mine. If I had been younger in this existence... I damned myself. I would not take her against her will. I could not! As if she read my thoughts, her eyes slowly opened and her gaze captured mine.

"Go back to sleep, my love. We will speak later."

Rolling to her side, her eyes closed again. My mind tumbled as I swallowed down my longing once more. Will she remember I was here? Hopefully not.

I gathered the dress and hung the purple raiment in her closet. When I turned to check on her, my gaze flowed around the room. This was where we studied for tests, so I knew it well. However, on my way to her bed, I knocked over a stack of books from her desktop when my shoe snagged on the foot of one of the oversized chairs. I caught the ones that tumbled before they hit the floor and placed them on the bookcase shelf next to her desk. I waited a moment to make sure she did not stir.

Now I needed to rush. One of her parents might wake and wish to check on her. A tank top and corresponding shorts lay across her chair. I grabbed them and, although she remained out, I managed to complete my task. Once she was nestled on her side in bed again, I sat down next to her and caressed her cheek. Her skin glowed with a dazzling luminance from the moonlight as it filtered in through her shear window coverings. She appeared as the angel she is: soft, delicate, a pure beauty.

My desire to bed her pushed to the surface again, but I stalled it one more time. I would not harm her. I must wait until she understands who and what she has become before I truly make her mine, and me hers. Francisco will have to be satisfied with my decision this time.

When I stood, I covered my love with the comforter and kissed her forehead. That feeling of remorse shrouded me again. I should not have changed her. I only meant to tell her how I ended up with Michelle Markum. That it was *her* I should have asked to prom. My fingertips brushed her hair away from her shimmering skin.

"I will be watching, my love, and waiting for you to come to me."

The front door closed quietly behind me and I rushed back to my apartment on the outskirts of town.

12

My front door lock clicked into place at the same time keys clattered into the bowl on the side table under the front window. I turned and gazed out that window. My humble dwelling felt lonely. I thought maybe Emma might have accompanied me home after I explained my decision to invite that airhead to the prom. Now, she will be in pain for two or three days while her body assimilates into its new form, and I will not have a chance to speak to her until then.

"She will not want to talk with you, stupid. Damn, Zach. What have you done?"

I flopped down on my sofa, picked up the friendship ring I purchased to present to her tonight, and twisted it in my hand, regretting the past two hours and the pressure placed upon me by Francisco.

When I picked up her faint scent, I crossed to my desk and grabbed the pamphlet outlining ways to donate to the Humane Society of the United States. A faint essence of Emma resided on it.

My lips twisted down when thoughts of the future, our future, dissolved. Together, Emma and I could have expanded our interests into reality and helped make this world a friendly place for all who exist here. My wish was, one day, for humans to accept vampires without hesitation. We will not be considered the deadly creatures people currently believed us to be.

I slumped down on my sofa again. But, I *was* that creature. I just killed the girl of my dreams.

Lynne Anders

CHAPTER 3

EMMA

When I woke Sunday morning, chills and heat both permeated my body. I believed I'd contracted a cold or the flu as achy pain and muscle cramps persisted all day. I briefly spoke with Ayres, when he called to check on me. I apologized for leaving the prom and relayed my current dilemma. He was sweet and told me to rest. But, I couldn't. I couldn't eat. I slept through most of the day, and awoke in the wee hours only to writhe in agony again. Mom did her best to comfort me, but none of her home remedies worked this time. She wanted to call the doctor, but I told her I'd be fine, to give it a couple of days. That appeased her. She still fed me chicken soup and crackers, which were tasteless and didn't infuse my body as it normally would. In fact, nothing worked. I resigned myself to suffer through whatever malady consumed my body, unless it became unbearable.

Wednesday, when I woke, the muscle cramps had ceased and my aches were tolerable. My mouth tingled, though, like your arm feels when you sleep on it and deprive its circulation. Even though I wasn't one hundred percent, I dressed for school anyway, tried to eat the tasteless breakfast cereal placed before me, and walked to the bus stop in time to catch the city bus I took most mornings. For some reason, noise from the traffic, birds chirping incessantly, and the bright sunlight amplified my headache, which roiled my stomach. So much for feeling better.

When I boarded, Phyllis, a young girl from my business ed class, beckoned me to sit with her in the back. Glad to have some diversion from my malady, I strode to the rear of the bus and plopped down beside her.

"Hi, Emma. I haven't seen you this week. Had a cold or the flu or something?"

The way her words spilled from her mouth sent chills up my spine. Her lips moved faster than the words came out. I shook my head and blinked trying to keep up. "Stop, Phyllis. You're making my head spin."

She paused, caught her breath, and began again. "Sorry. I get excited and my mind takes off and leaves my mouth minutes behind. Anyway, since we don't have lots of time now, let's have lunch together. I have something I want to discuss with you, if you feel up to it."

Since I hadn't been to school in two days, I wasn't certain what work waited for me, but I agreed and we decided to meet at the cafeteria, then go outside somewhere to talk, if it didn't rain. "Twelve fifteen sounds good. See ya there."

The bus slowed as we neared our stop.

"Perfect." Phyllis collected her books and we stood to leave.

Carbon monoxide fumes permeated the air the instant we stepped off the bus outside our campus gate. Strange, I hadn't noticed the overpowering odor before. It dissipated quickly, while we walked through together, but was replaced by the sweet smell of fresh cut grass. My head turned swiftly, searching for the reason for the odor, even as I waved to Phyllis, who had turned toward the science building. As I headed off to English Lit, I realized the only mowers working this morning appeared quite a distance away. Interesting. With an "oh well" shrug, I loped along toward class while trying to put my headache and upset stomach out of my mind.

Since Zach would probably be too busy to have lunch with me today, I was happy I had plans. I didn't feel like talking to him anyway. My feelings were hurt, especially since he didn't have the decency to check on me when I missed school Monday or Tuesday. I supposed he was too wrapped up with that blonde.

Morning progressed rather well, although tempered by my sluggish body. However, when dozens of mumbled voices and distinctive fragrances attacked my senses, I worried I'd developed some adverse sensitivity issue. Or could it be a consequence that would pass from the flu I'd had? Maybe I just needed to eat.

Classes sped by with ease, I retrieved what work I missed, and met my new lunch friend at the cafeteria with five minutes to spare. We purchased our food, exited the building, and traversed the stone path leading to the botany enclosure. It was one of my favorite places on this seventy-six-acre campus. So many unique trees and plants grew in that special place. Something was always in bloom and cast out a fresh scent throughout the circle. That day, it was apple blossoms. Before I sat, I inhaled deeply with my eyes closed. Other fragrances filled the air. What were they? Lilies of the Valley. And peonies. And lilacs. My sense of smell picked out each of them. Pleased I'd identified four individual scents, I lowered to the bench with a smile. Mr. Scott, my botany teacher, would be pleased.

Phyllis started by discussing our plans for college and what major we'd chosen. I wondered at her deflection. She skated around whatever subject she had on her mind this morning until she finally placed her half-eaten sandwich on the wrapping paper in her lap and grasped my arm. Not sure what she wanted to discuss, I followed suit.

That's when she brought up my illness.

By the end of our lunch period, logic was replaced with horror, confusion, and fear. I was reduced to tears. In few words, I was told I didn't have the flu, I'd been *changed*. The night of the prom, someone had changed me into a blood sucking, evil, twisted creature. I was no longer human, I was... Oh my God, could this actually be true? I was a *vampire*.

I stood to run, but Phyllis grasped my arm to stop me. My agitation grew. She was wrong. She had to be wrong. I felt like me. I ate my sandwich like a human person would, right? I remember looking in the mirror this morning. I saw my reflection and my eyes weren't red. I'd have remembered if they looked red.

My gaze spun to her. Why would she lie to me? I jerked my arm from her grasp. Instead of running, though, I paced in front of her. She'd concocted this story to hurt me. Why? I stopped in front of her and glared.

"Who put you up to this, Phyllis? And why a story about me being a vampire? That's just... insane. So, tell me now. Who wanted to hurt me?"

I leaned over and grabbed her arms to shake the truth from her. Her sorrowful gaze met mine and I recoiled when reality hit me square in the face. This wasn't a lie! I released my grasp on her and stretched my arms in front of me, rotating them to look at my skin. Nothing had changed. This must be a dream, then. When I pinched my flesh and felt no pain. I pinched again, and again. Nothing.

Tears welled in my eyes. "It can't be true. I won't accept it. It's a trick, right?"

Again, her facial expression told me differently. "I'm so sorry, Emma."

Panic replaced my disbelief. "There must be something that can be done, Phyllis. Tell me, tell me what I can do to stop this... this change, from taking place. I'll do anything. Please. Just tell me." Still weak from the weekend, I caved into the emotion. All I could do at this point was to stare at her and gasp for breath.

Phyllis pulled me down next to her and stroked my arm to soothe me. "A couple of vampires from my circle apparently witnessed the deed and, since I at least knew you, asked me to clue you in on the dos and don'ts."

My eyelids flew open. She's one, too? Surely, she was pulling my leg. My mind would not accept she was a vampire. She couldn't be. Could she?

My head shook as I laughed at her. I *have* been pranked. "Vampires aren't real. They're made-up creatures just like werewolves and demons. They're a figment of some amazing minds that created the many books I've read." I allowed her to ponder that remark, then something she'd said niggled at me.

"What do you mean by 'my circle?'"

When she didn't laugh or respond, something inside me shivered. I began to suspect my belief was incorrect. The longer she spoke, and from the questions she answered, I knew deep down she spoke the truth. I began breathing hard again.

But... why me?

"I didn't want to do this here, but you need to know, Emma. Your existence has changed drastically and, before you do something you'll hate yourself for, you need to understand."

"If I am what you say, why didn't I attack my parents when I woke up? Everything I've read about young vampires suggests they're bloodthirsty from the beginning."

I was horrified. I could have killed everyone close to me.

Phyllis chuckled. "*Those* are made-up stories, Emma. Trust me. You could have awakened desiring blood, but you wouldn't have known what you craved at first. Besides, I've been at your house all weekend, mostly at night, observing your change. I would have intervened if your cravings took over. I promise." She grasped my hand in sympathy.

"So, that's a myth. I will crave blood, but can control the... cravings?"

My instructor nodded. "For the most part."

Nevertheless, I pressed my lips together and squeezed my eyes closed. I could have... I could have. Why was this done to me? I wanted to die.

Though Phyllis noticed my dismay, she continued her explanation. Thankfully, her words stalled images of my parents' bloodied bodies lying on the living room floor at my hands. My eyes opened and I listened more intently.

"To answer your first question, a circle is a group or family of vampires. We're overseen by a leader and, typically, a second-in-command. We must abide by the circle rules to remain in good standing, or be tossed out and left to forage on our own. My circle lives primarily in Noblesville. We're small compared to most, hosting only twenty. It's vampire law that you must become part of your maker's circle. It's mandatory you follow the one who changed you."

"Who changed me? How can I follow when I don't know who did this to me?"

She must know. Someone asked her to discuss this life with me. Maybe someone from her circle? She did say one of those members watched the beast who did this to me.

"I don't know, Emma. I only know one from my circle observed from a distance and told me your maker carried you off when you fainted into his arms."

"So, at least I know it was a man. And, your friend knew *me* but, didn't know the creature who did this?"

She shook her head, but I doubted her. Maybe the creature planned to come forward himself. My mind spun with confusion while she continued.

"Please don't worry about that right now. Let's find a way for you to move forward."

I nodded, but with reluctance.

"You are considered a hybrid vampire, as am I. Your body assimilates regular food as long as you feast on blood two or three times a week, more so if you place yourself in highly emotional situations. Your body won't overcome its craving for blood ever and if you don't keep that thirst quenched, you could possibly hurt, more probably kill, someone."

Phyllis produced a tall plastic tumbler from her backpack and asked me to drink. She said I'd feel better instantly. I couldn't see what was inside, but trusted she spoke the truth. The sip I took from the straw lay in my mouth for a moment before I allowed it down my throat. A syrup, but not sweet, coated my tongue. She was correct. My stomach felt more settled than it had since Sunday morning. The strange sensation in my gums quieted, and my dull headache diminished. I took a long draw on the straw and felt the concoction's infusion begin in my toes and expand to the top of my head. Before I knew it, the cup was empty and I desired more.

"What is this?" I licked my lips to capture any remaining liquid.

"It's called a Velvet Crimson. It's an animal blood concoction we can—"

"This is blood? Oh, my God, Phyllis. Why didn't you tell me? That's sick!"

I grabbed my throat as my stomach roiled at the thought of animal blood. I expected to lose whatever liquid I drank in record time. When my stomach heaved, I turned away. Nothing came out, though. I had to swallow several times to calm the upset.

Phyllis watched and shook her head. "Mind over matter, mind over matter. You feel better, don't you?"

How could she trick me like that? "Yes, but animal blood? Like cows or horses or whatever? That's disgusting." I wanted to toss the container as far from me as possible.

"The issue is, your body requires it to exist now. It won't be as disgusting the next time. Actually, it tastes great once you get past the idea that it's blood." She laid her hand gently on my arm. "It comes from vampire-owned businesses. I'll get into that a bit later. But, now that you feel better, let me continue."

Wondering what more I could absorb during this first entry into my new life, I sat quietly to listen pondering the change in my body after I consumed the drink. I still trembled, but felt better than I had in days.

Phyllis smiled encouragingly. "Your skin will not burn in the sunlight. That's pure myth. However, sunlight will sap your strength the longer you're exposed. But moonlight will infuse you with energy beyond anything you've ever experienced."

Although I love the sun, I've always been a night person, much to my parents' dismay. However, the dilemma behind the message struck me again. I wanted to run away, hide, until I woke from this nightmare.

I willed myself to stay and listen to her explanation. When her voice changed to a whisper as other students passed by, I was amazed I understood every word as if she spoke them out loud. When those students passed, I held up my hand to stop her.

"How will I know when I require this blood drink?"

"First, you'll sense a tingling in your gums, stronger than you felt this weekend. Then your fangs will extend. This occurs when you're in desperate need of blood. If you keep quenched, they'll stay put. Go ahead, feel your incisors. They're longer than before already."

Great. I didn't realize I had fangs, but when my shaky thumb stroked my right incisor, I could tell it was longer and more pointed. My mouth clamped shut immediately.

Phyllis's expression told me she understood. "A fresh start will help you, too. After graduation, move out west. Maybe try Phoenix. You'll have lots of sun but even more cloudless nights. You can apply to Arizona State or the University of Arizona if you still plan to attend college."

College? How could I attend college now? How can I hide what I am from everyone? My life, the one I had planned since I was small, evaporated Saturday night.

"I can't attend college now. Are you mad?"

My instructor clasped my hands. "Yes, you can. Once you're more accustomed to your new existence, you'll fit in with everyone else. Look at me, Emma. Would you know I'm not human? And would you believe I'm one hundred and fifty-six years old?"

Her grin was priceless and also heartwarming.

My mouth opened when I sucked in a breath. "No! You don't look older than eighteen, maybe twenty. Why is that?"

"My body, though yours may be different, ages one year in twenty. I look maybe twenty-five if I don't dress like a teenager or style my hair this way. I've also moved around, changed jobs, become a high school student even, in order to conceal my identity so I can remain in my current home."

Moving a lot? Changing jobs? Aging? My mind stopped on aging. She ages one year in twenty? What about me? Will I appear as I am for twenty years before the first subtle change? Won't it be obvious to my parents?

My eyelids sprung open. "My parents!"

That's when the waterfall began. My family. I will not be able to spend their golden years with them. They'll never have grandchildren from me, I'll never see my siblings or my nieces or nephews. I'll outlive all of my family and be alone. Why? Why would someone, or rather *something*, do this to me? For what purpose? Why subject me to this life? Or death actually? Hybrid, my ass. I'm no longer a living human being. I'm death on steroids.

My new friend consoled me, speaking softly to slow the flow of my tears. She described her life as happy and content, but admitted the first fifty years were the worst because of her family.

"Time passes slowly for us, Emma. We watch while our families pass on with the realization we won't see them in the hereafter. I've never asked, but believe our souls are lost as part of our rebirth. I don't think I've entered a church or holy place since."

Saddened again, I dry my face. I have no choice but to accept my new fate. Accept, not enjoy. I'm damned now. I will forever live this existence. Unless…

A thought entered my mind. Is it feasible? Could someone change me back?

"Phyllis, has anyone ever asked to have this predicament reversed? I mean, it's only been a couple of days. It shouldn't take much to make me human again, right?"

She appeared stunned. "Why in the world would you want that life back? Think about it. No illness will claim you, you're faster and stronger than any human, and you'll have an eternity to enjoy this Earth. Why would you want to go back to being human? Trust me, Emma. You'll love your new existence in no time."

She didn't answer my question. "So, you don't know of anyone capable of changing me back?"

Her harrumph to my question spoke the truth. "No. But, I've never asked."

"So, maybe?"

Phyllis' shoulders raised up in answer, which gave me hope. I intended to pursue this quest no matter the outcome.

Hope provided me with a little renewed confidence, but I did have concerns about where I'd live in the meantime.

"What about my kind? Is Phoenix someplace where I'll fit in? And, what about living in my maker's circle? You said I had to exist in it."

"Until he makes himself known to you, you won't be required to live within that circle. Besides, Phoenix has several communities that will welcome you. There are a few farther south, too. I'll check them out for you if you wish."

My head bobbed while I processed her words. Out west? I know nothing farther away than Indiana.

Phyllis' narrative continued for another fifteen minutes. My skin was tougher, denser, than previously. The texture felt the same, but it could withstand minor abrasions and would also heal rapidly from a major injury. My body would remain as it is today. No more yoyo gains or losses from eating habits of old. I decided to think about that much later. Food didn't appeal to me at the moment.

Phyllis consoled me for the few minutes we had before our next class. I thought about ditching, but I'd already missed two days.

"You'll get used to it. And, wait until the first full moon. It isn't just for werewolves. Our kind blossoms in the moonlight, remember?" She patted my hand. "Don't worry. I'll be with you all the way through until you leave for college. I'll teach you all I know."

Werewolves were real, too? My head shook. My life, as I'd known it, was gone. My hopes for a future with Zach or any man, raising a family, living and growing old with him, were ancient history. I nodded, picked up the remnants of my mostly uneaten lunch, tossed it in the trash bin, and trudged back to class. I had three more to work through before I could go home and absorb everything Phyllis had disclosed. I wasn't me and never would be me again… unless.

Damn. My family. How will I hide my new identity from them?

Throughout my afternoon classes, I pondered my new existence. I supposed it could be worse. After reading most of the vampire books written and believing them to be pure fiction, I half expected I'd be running around with my fangs hanging out in search of my next victim. The fact that I could survive without drinking from a live person or animal relieved some of my pent-up anxiety.

23

However, alone in my room that night, I sat crossed-legged on my flowery print comforter pondering my new life, or death, if you will. My friends would all be dead to me soon, my family, everyone I knew would disappear from my life forever.

I climbed from my bed and slowly stumbled toward the window. As I looked out over the dark lifeless street, tears pooled in my eyes. Why? Why do this to me? How could I find comfort knowing how lonely my life would become? My head dropped into my hands. I wept for my youth and for all the stolen moments lost to me forever.

CHAPTER 4

EMMA

Ten Years Later

The back two wheels of the Southwest jet stagger their landing as the plane lowers to the runway and rolls along the wet pavement, braking slowly to keep from skidding. It's been a bumpy ride, which is not unusual for a flight into Indianapolis. I can count on one hand how many smooth landings I've had over the years when I've returned home, which is just another reminder I lived in tornado alley once upon a time.

The rain-spattered window next to me showcases the lush airport grounds in the dim late-afternoon light while the aircraft creeps onto a taxiway. I live in the desert now, colorful only during the short months of winter and spring, and brown the remainder of the year. However, this is where I grew up. I miss the green, but not the humidity it takes to keep everything this luxuriant. I'd still live here if…

My eyes close and I whisper a silent prayer, "Lord, if you will, help me find a way."

I'm ready for the saga that's become my life to be over.

My mind tumbles with the reason for my return: my tenth high-school reunion. I promised Stephanie Foster I'd come home. How could I say no to my once best friend, even though I've kept our friendship at a distance? She doesn't know the real story behind why I left and hopefully never will. She'd ditch me in a heartbeat. Heartbeat. The irony of the term makes me chuckle wryly.

The plane slows to a crawl as it turns into the gate. Passengers, eager to depart, rise as one the moment the motion subsides. I stay seated. I don't wish to move just yet. This is where it all began and I've come home this time to find out who did this to me and why. The years have been kind, but torture, too. I'm not close with my family any longer, and dread the day I promised to see my parents this trip. Will they welcome me or will they run for the hills? I can see hate filling my mom's eyes, which brings tears to mine.

When it's my row's turn to exit the plane, I grasp my purse, haul out my carrier from under the seat in front of me, and stride quickly up the aisle.

The flight attendant's scent is thick with a musky fragrance. It almost makes me gag and I want to turn away, but I smile to be friendly.

"Thank you," I mention quickly.

She's already picking up debris from around the seats, but nods, "Thanks for flying with us today."

When I step out into the waiting area at gate B-16, I check my watch. It has updated to four o'clock. Great. I should be on my way in less than forty minutes. I thread down the long corridor—through travelers, both going and coming—and hurry toward baggage claim, already searching my phone for a restaurant.

The car rental agent eyes my driver's license and then me. "Ms. Christensen? Looks like you won't need to renew your driver's license for a very long time."

I grin, "You're correct. Arizona licenses are good until we're sixty-five." Her comment reminds me I'll have to do something with my appearance in a few years. I'll probably still look like that photo when I'm sixty-five.

The young lady smiles when she hands my credit card and photo ID back to me.

"Thanks."

Once I connect with Interstate 70, my pace slows the closer I progress to downtown. Friday rush hour traffic is to blame for the snarl. My body, tense from sitting four hours on the flight from Phoenix, aches for a run, but I resign myself to relax and follow along with the rest of the travelers. When the pace slows to a crawl, I shake my head and try to find something to occupy my mind with anything other than why I was forced to leave my home. It doesn't work. Returning home brings back the reality of it all.

It's too bad I didn't know what was in store for me back then. I still had a life, had choices regarding my future. "My future," I mutter as I continue to creep. "No choices and al-l-l-l the time in the world."

It began the night of my senior prom. I hadn't intended to go. The one boy I wanted to accompany didn't ask. His name trapesing through my mind brings his image into full view. Zachary Matthews. Tall and slender, he played point guard on the high school basketball team, had aspirations to become a physician, and his dark blue brooding eyes could pierce my heart in an instant. I was smitten.

We shared several classes our junior year, but he sat next to me senior year in calculus class and we often chatted about the music of our time. I think he loved Alicia Keys almost as much as I did. A memory of one afternoon while studying at my home finds its way into my mind.

After two hours of math problems, I decided to switch on my iPod to allow us a break from the monotony. The song, of course, was *Girl on Fire*. I stood up, pretended to vamp like Alicia Keys, and belted along with the music. Not to be outdone, my friend also stood and accompanied me until our voices could be heard down the block. The groove of the song ended, but our antics didn't. We danced and laughed around my room to the next song, and the next, until Mom knocked heavily on my door and asked us to quiet down. That caused us to laugh even louder, until he kissed my cheek.

I'd forgotten about that kiss.

He loved the Indianapolis Children's Museum. I remember he took me there at least twice that I recall. He told me he enjoyed sharing his knowledge of science with me, and mentioned I had an inquisitive mind like his.

We also attended a couple of the Indianapolis Colts football games with several friends and threw popcorn at each other when the opposing teams scored. Then there were the baseball games and, most definitely, the Pacers basketball games. Most of the time we were together in a group but, once in a while, it was just Zach and me. Sports created a deeper connection for us. I suppose most teenaged girls weren't interested. But, I was. And, I was spending time with him. My silver lining.

We developed a bond, a kindred spirit, which surpassed the trivial idealisms of most teenagers. Even though we didn't date, per se, we shared lunch hour often during our senior year, studied together, traded class notes before tests to make sure we had everything covered, and occasionally sat on a bench near the math building to reflect on what our teachers attempted to drill into our heads. We laughed and teased and, in general, were comfortable in each other's company.

I thought our bond was solid, I thought he cared about me as much as I cared about him. I was proven wrong that long-ago May when my friend betrayed me. He asked one of those blonde cheerleaders to prom instead of me. Our friendship died a silent death that day. Oh, we continued to share stories, trade notes, and pretend everything was the way it had been. But, it wasn't, at least for me. The last few weeks of high school turned out to be the worst of my life, especially since I was no longer me and had to hide what I had become from my friend and other classmates. Actually, a few showed bitterness toward me when I wouldn't engage with them as much as I had in the past. How could I? One little slip...

Ten years have passed and I haven't seen Zach since graduation. Steph, who knew I cared for him, once mentioned to me he'd become a doctor. I intend to ask more when I see her. But, he broke my heart back then and, if I run into him at the reunion, I may or may not speak to him. Hurt feelings churn inside me even after all these years.

Tingling gums drag me back to the here and now, and I exit the highway on Illinois and drive to the White Castle parking lot on South. It's on my list. It's a place I can trust. I still check the parking lot before I exit the rental. When I feel safe, I slip out the door and lock the car.

The restaurant has few customers when I pass through the glass door, so I advance to the counter and wait for the cashier. The odor of frying onions permeates the room, which also brings back special memories of my dad. Whenever we'd have a free Saturday afternoon, we'd make the trek to our local White Castle to fill up on our favorite delicacy. Mom wouldn't eat them, which made the trip singularly unique to us. So may memories of my human life parade through my mind, which also reminds me to call home when I reach the hotel.

The cashier approaches, stares into my eyes, and grins. "What can I get for you?"

"Um, four with fries and a Crimson to drink."

The young female employee stalls for a second then regains her balance. She smiles and blinks twice in recognition. She's like me. She's a vampire, too.

My bag of food is placed on the counter alongside my special drink. "That'll be twelve sixty-five.

I gladly hand over the cash. The drink alone is worth twice the price right now.

When I step away, the clerk mentions, "Have a nice night."

I merely nod. I know what she's insinuating, but I'm not like most young vampires. I don't prowl the streets at night trying to hook up. It's not who I am. Maybe it's because I'm still in denial about my identity and what I've become. At home, I have my circle and a few unsuspecting human friends, but I spend my free time, mostly alone, studying anything I can put my hands on about my kind.

Reading one detail chilled me. At any time, my craving could overpower me and cause me to lose control, which means my fangs will elongate and I'll sink them into the first unsuspecting human in my path. The thought is enough to make me want to end my existence. That's why I need to find out who changed me. He has to fix this. I want my life back. There has to be a way to change me back.

I quietly consume my burgers and fries, and suck down the sweet thick liquid while I shake the dread that encompasses me. It's been a little more than ten years since the night I was changed into this creature. Ten years is ten too many.

I mentally revisit that night often. Was there a sign or a clue I missed? Did someone or something follow me around and I didn't notice? No matter how often the images converge, the result doesn't change. Whoever did this to me, or maybe it's *whatever* did this to me, remains a mystery.

The drive to the hotel from White Castle takes ten minutes. I pull up to valet, climb out, and check my surroundings. The JW Marriott is new to Indianapolis, at least for me. Adjacent is the Indianapolis Indians Victory Field, where I took in many a baseball game over the years I lived here. Funny how communities continue to morph into something else while you're away. Indianapolis has done just that. The downtown prospers now. That wasn't always the case.

With an "oh well" shrug, I drop my rental car key into the hand of the young man with a smile, grab the valet ticket, and follow my bag into the lobby behind a doorman. He doesn't appear to be a day over twenty himself and I know I appear to be a teenager still, even though my driver's license attests to my current true age of twenty-eight. I often chuckle when I'm carded at bars or when I order a glass of wine or some other stiff drink. I wonder how many years it will take before I look older than eighteen. Fifty? One hundred? I shiver at the thought. Over a hundred. Damn.

Once in my room, I unpack what little I brought and sit down to call Steph. She's the only person, other than my parents, who could lure me back. Well, except for my desire to find out who my maker is. When her voicemail picks up, I leave a message I'm in town and to call me. I also place a call to my parents and agree to see them Monday evening for dinner, since Steph mentioned her plans for us included both Saturday and Sunday. With nothing else to do, I change into running shorts and t-shirt, and jog down the Canal Walk.

Running for me is therapy. I'd add healthy, but, well... not necessary for this body. It provides time for me to work through issues I've collected since becoming what I am. One of the things that took a while to absorb was drinking blood and where to find it. That's where The List comes into play. It's a collection of locations throughout the world where vampires can purchase a drink made with animal blood known as a Velvet Crimson, or Crimson for short. Most vampires I've met don't wish to harm humans or animals and, with the ability to curtail our craving by simply purchasing this drink, our identities and lifestyle remain hidden from the general population. Once this information was compiled and made available, death by savage animals dropped significantly worldwide.

I asked Phyllis once where the blood came from to create this concoction. I was flabbergasted. Vampires work with slaughter houses around the world to collect blood from the animals, transfer it to their factories and, once it's purified, store it away underground. Decades ago, a special protein was also developed to add to the animal blood, which makes it more palatable for us and provides the nutrients, if you want to call them that, to sustain our cravings. I couldn't believe the enormity of the process, but was glad for it.

More idle thoughts, which hit closer to home, drift through my mind during my run, like, what does my sister look like now? I haven't seen her in five years. Same for my older brother. He's married, has a couple of kids, and lives in Cincinnati. Just a couple of hours from here, I thought about driving down, but decided against it. What would I say? I didn't attend birthday parties, the wedding, bridal or baby showers. I simply fell off the face of the Earth as far as they're concerned, which is how it has to be for now. It doesn't make missing them any easier, though.

Steph is the only friend I stayed in contact with, especially after her divorce. She needed me and I couldn't deny her, ever. And, Ayres. Even though we talk on the phone occasionally, I've kept hidden from him, too. When he invited me to his business's grand opening three years ago, I wanted to attend, but fed him some story about not having enough time off from my job, which was an outright lie. Saddened by thoughts of ditching the people I loved, my mind spins, wondering how I'll explain once I'm changed back.

By the time my mind shuts down, I'm near the turnaround. I decide to call it a day and return to the hotel for a cool down and shower. Room service will be sufficient tonight.

Steph's home in Lawrence, Indiana is located farther northeast than her parents' home off 38th and Saddle Drive. I'm there with plenty of time to spare and still feel bright eyed and bushy-tailed after ingesting my drink yesterday.

The instant I step out of my car, Steph rushes from the front door screaming to high heaven. "You're here! You're really here! I can't believe it took you this long to come home. Come here and give me a hug."

Steph wraps her arms around me while tears fill my eyes. She was my best friend in high school. We did everything together until she got pregnant just before prom. She and Max married right after graduation, and divorced a year or so later. But, her handsome son is the apple of her eye. Lucky girl. At least I can share him for a few days.

"It's so good to see you." I pull back and look at her face, which has aged a bit, probably from being a single mom. She's still beautiful with her long dark-brown hair and eyes. We're almost eye level, too, which I find odd. She used to be two inches taller than me. Have I grown or has she shrunk? Maybe I stand taller now that I'm a vampire. I gulp before my mouth spits that out for everyone to hear. "So, where's Tray? I'd love to see him."

"Oh, you know kids. He's off playing soccer this morning. My neighbor, Judy, took him to practice so you and I could catch up. Come in, come in. What can I get you to drink?"

My chuckle stays hidden. I was about to ask for a Crimson, but withhold that request and ask for a Diet Coke instead as I follow her inside her one-story brick home.

Steph and I spend a couple of hours filling each other in on our lives. I try to be as truthful as possible, and relay that my job in Arizona as a medical facility office manager keeps me busy most of the time. When I tell her I'm not dating anyone, that opens the door to her promising to fix me up at the reunion.

"I know someone you really like is going to be there." The sing-song in her voice sweetens the air. "Remember Zach? I heard from Marge he promised to attend."

Zach. The mere mention of his name storms my thoughts with his dark-blue eyes. My mind conjures what he will look like now. Will he appear the same or be more dashing? It's too bad I can't act on my impulses, even for one night. How I would love being in his arms again, if only for a few minutes. Minutes? Hell, days, months, years, centuries. I repress the desire that suddenly blooms and respond the best way I can.

"He must be married and have several kids by now, too, don't you think? It's been ten years since high school." I hide my unrestrained curiosity behind the glass of soda.

Steph shakes her head. "I don't think so. He did go away to college. Um, Stanford? He lives on the west coast somewhere, from what I've heard. He's unmarried, but married to his work... a cardiologist, I believe."

My heart clutches at the thought. Unmarried doesn't mean unattached. "Well, if he shows, I'd love to say hello. Now, what can I do to help prepare for tonight?"

While Steph discusses the night's agenda, my mind conjures another memory of the one who got away.

I had difficulty writing an essay for my History class. I mentioned this problem to Zach while we sat on our bench during lunch one day. He asked me the topic of my story and I told him the Nineteenth Amendment, woman's right to vote, which passed Congress in June of 1919 and was finally ratified August 18, 1920. My story began in the 1800s when women organized for the first time to attain this right. However, I felt I didn't have enough meat in the piece to garner an A. Zach read what I had written so far, then discussed it with me in great detail. I sat mesmerized by his voice and words. It was as if he'd lived during those times, the way he spoke. I took massive notes and rewrote the essay that night. Needless to say, I received an A for my efforts. When I showed him my graded paper, his eyes lit with happiness. I hugged him that afternoon and promised I'd return the favor one day. Interesting. He never asked me to help with his classes. He always coached me through mine.

Steph's remarks about the throng of returning students draws my attention again. With a graduating class of more than one thousand, four hundred are expected for this first reunion. Steph and I go over the agenda one more time and I promise to arrive at six tonight to help with the finishing touches to the gym. I'm reticent to return to the location where I was changed. However, I need to find out who did this deed and why.

With a final wave, I drive off toward the hotel. If Zach is supposed to be there tonight, I must look my best, and that takes prep time.

The decorating committee transformed the gymnasium into a glittering silver and gold play land complete with helium-filled balloons standing tall from each white cloth-covered table. That was my job. Add balloons where needed.

Enlarged images from our senior yearbook of many of the clubs and activities hang throughout the hall, including some photos of our favorite teachers. The front check-in table displays a name badge for each classmate who registered to attend, which incorporates our senior picture and name. When I find mine, I chuckle while I pin it to my dress. I have not changed one iota since that photo was taken and wonder if anyone will notice. One name badge I look for, but don't find… Phyllis isn't coming. I still have many questions, but one in particular. Who can change me back? Disheartened, I step away from the table and stand lost in thought. I have to find someone who has the answer to that question. With no one to ask at present, I decide to check out the enlarged pictures to see if I remember anyone while I add balloons on the final two tables.

As I pass by photos of some of the clubs I participated in, somehow a memory of the day the photo was taken tumbles through my mind. The light conversations, the happy sharing of time with my friends. They each rush through in a nanosecond, but pain from the loss of my youth stops me in my tracks when the next photo comes into view. It's the 2008 basketball squad and I gaze at the tall figure of the handsome Zach Matthews. Even though my heart no longer beats regularly, it still feels the emotion created by this fine specimen of a man. My gaze captures him head to toe. He, like the rest, wears his uniform. My fingers reach out to touch him, but I withdraw them instantly. My audible sigh reminds me he's off limits. I can't get involved with him or any other human. And, now, I'm almost too afraid to see him.

I spin away from the enlargement, wondering how I'll react if he does show. How will he react when he sees me? We used to be friends, good friends. Will he remember all the conversations, the shared notes, the last time he held me close? Impressions from ten years ago may have blurred in his mind. He may not even remember my name. Saddened by that thought, I walk away before tears manifest themselves.

Out of the corner of my eye, I watch as classmates arrive. One catches my attention immediately, and I return to the entrance to greet him and his date.

"Ayres! Hi! How are you?" The man before me is no longer a high-school senior. He appears to be a successful businessman, dressed in an expensive suit, and holds the hand of a lovely raven-haired woman who gives me the once over.

"Emma Christensen as I live and breathe. You did come." He releases the beauty's hand and reaches for me, circling my waist with his arms. "It's wonderful to see you again. Are you alone or do you have a significant other?"

"You know I don't have a plus one. But, look at you, Ayres. All grown up."

My friend hugs me tight.

"I'm sorry I missed your grand opening. I wanted to come, but…"

"Not a problem."

When he releases me, happiness shines his eyes.

"You've heard me speak of Rachael. Well, Emma, this is my fiancée, Rachael Meyer. Rachael, this is Emma Christensen, one of my friends from high school."

I reach my hand to her hoping she doesn't feel the cooler temperature of my skin. "It's very nice to meet you, Rachael. Ayres told me you're planning a wedding, what, next year? Congratulations."

Her smile almost reaches her eyes. "It's nice to meet you too, Emma. Ayres told you, did he? I thought we were keeping it a secret. Well, please don't tell anyone. We're planning a save-the-date party for later this year."

"No one will hear it from me, I promise."

I attempt to convey I'm no threat, but I don't think it registers with her. Instead, she grabs Ayres' arm, pulls close, and holds tight.

That's my cue. I decide not to ask him to dance with me later. "It was great seeing you, my friend. Please keep in touch once I'm back in Arizona. I enjoy our discussions immensely."

Rachael relaxes somewhat when I mention Arizona. Did she not know I live almost seventeen hundred miles away?

"I promise. And you must promise to come to our wedding, Emma. I, we, won't take no for an answer this time."

My friend smiles when I nod. He and his fiancée saunter past me toward the name-badge table.

I circle back to Steph and our group of girlfriends and their husbands. I asked for the table next to the wall on purpose. It's the perfect vantage point to watch everyone. I can also escape quickly if I feel pressured to speak with someone I'd rather not. Not everyone from high school remained friendly in the months before I left home. I don't need a revisit of the animosity they conveyed when I withdrew from a couple of my after-school programs. My need for blood caused me to rush to the Steak 'n Shake after my last class. And, since I didn't wish to return appearing high or under the influence, I typically went directly home. How could I explain the truth? Again, one little slip…

My attention reverts to the stage when our principal, Mr. Hoffmeyer, taps the microphone.

"Good evening, Class of 2008." His voice, still familiar, at first stalls my schoolmates from talking. A moment later, loud applause, whistles, and catcalls reach a thunderous pitch, which stops his speech. Once the boisterous noise dies down, he continues. "I'd like to welcome you home to enjoy your ten-year high school reunion."

Once again, the crowd goes wild and interrupts our principal. He raises his hands to calm the crowd.

"Okay, okay. Let me finish so you can enjoy your evening reacquainting yourselves with your schoolmates." He waits while the racket dies.

The crowd remains quiet. "I knew you'd learn to listen!" He chuckles at his own joke and resumes. "We want to thank your Reunion Committee for their hard work tracking you all down, which in several cases was not an easy task. To the Decorating Committee and the overhaul of this gym in such a short time… you must thank your Creative Arts teacher, Mrs. Allen, for her input and advice. She's attending tonight and would love to speak with you. And the Clean Up Committee, who promise to put everything back tomorrow the way it was.

"Several of your teachers chose to join us tonight, too, so please find them and thank them for their continued hard work. Now… sit back, have some hors d'oeuvres, cake, and punch, and listen and dance to some of the music you grew up with. Thank you all for returning to Warren Park High School. We're happy you're here."

The high school class of 2008 erupts into applause one more time while Mr. Hoffmeyer exits the stage. He's replaced by a five-piece rock band, who immediately begins playing a Lady Gaga song. It's fast and upbeat. The dance floor is covered in no time with high school friends rocking to the beat of our lives. Steph, the only one left with me at our table, accepts a friend's offer to dance and leaves me sitting alone. The room darkens suddenly and I watch as spotlights capture faces of students from my school. Many seem familiar and a few close by wave as they gyrate to the rhythm. A smile curls my lips when two members from my debate team hustle through to the floor with a quick nod my direction. So many people I'd forgotten about when I left home to attend college out west. Hopefully, I'll be able to catch up with some of them tonight.

My gaze stays focused on the dance floor, so I don't sense him until he plops down in the chair next to me. My quick head turn shifts me in my seat and I gasp.

"Zach! Hi." I force down the wave of desire that courses through me. He can't see me in this state. It'll undo me.

"Fancy seeing you here. Last I heard you were out west somewhere in the hot desert. How are you, Emma?" His eyes, still a sobering dark blue, focus on mine.

My breath catches in my throat.

I can't force my gaze away from his. His eyes dance in the light much the way they did the night of our prom. He doesn't look a day older, either, or is my mind remembering ten years ago? When my legs begin to tremble, I push my fingertips against my knees to keep them still. I want to touch his face, I want to know the feel of his skin beneath my fingertips, but I can't. It would only lead to ruin. My ruin.

I calm my mind. In a voice lacking emotion, my words sound lifeless. "I'm doing great, Zach. So, how are you? Married with a bunch of basketball-playing kids? Are you still with Michelle?"

I know he isn't, but I need to diffuse this conversation some way.

His deep-throated chuckle tears at my walls. "Michelle? I haven't seen her since prom night. She went with me because her friends were dating my teammates. I had *my* eyes set on someone else, but didn't think she wanted to go."

My dry swallow covers my immerging anxiety. "Why?"

Does he mean me?

He focuses on his hands in his lap and shrugs. "I didn't have the nerve to ask her. I just figured her answer would be no."

He *does* mean me. "You should have tried. I'll bet she would have jumped at the chance back then."

That comment draws his face up again. However, his squinted eyes appear confused. "You think so?"

Damn. Why would he think I'd say no after all the time we spent together? I have to divert this conversation before I'm in his lap. "You'll never know since you didn't ask."

He nods and looks toward the dance floor. "Will you dance with me now?" His hand shifts and covers one of mine on my knee.

My mind whispers *no, no, no*. My heart sings *yes! Yes! YES!* I must get this over with if I'm ever to move on.

"Sure."

I wanted to say what first came to mind. Yes, please, so I can be in your arms again, if only for a few moments.

We stand at the same time and the handsome man grabs my hand with his long slender fingers and pulls me toward the dance floor. After a few steps, the music changes. It's a slow one. I get my wish to be in his arms, but draw my lower lip into my mouth when my gaze is drawn to his smile. What if my desire draws out my fangs?

Before I can stop him, Zach wraps his arm around my waist and clasps my right hand tightly. While he waltzes me around the floor, he doesn't speak. He pulls me close and breathes into my hair.

My nose presses against his crisp white shirt and captures the faint aroma of a cologne and soap mixture. My body trembles with recognition. It's the same smell from ten years ago. I'd know it anywhere. But, why do I know it? That was before… Fear seizes me and I tense. I remind myself of my heightened awareness of everything around me, which calms my panic. My body relaxes again and I continue to follow him around the dance floor hopeful he didn't observe my discomfort.

When his arm draws me close against him, I revel in the tingling that begins in my toes and expands rapidly up my body. I've never felt this way before, not with a human and not with another vampire. I purposefully kept to myself and refused to date any of my kind merely because I want my human life back. But, my desire to do more than dance with Zach saturates my mind with images I've seen only in books. I'm not ashamed to admit I'm a virgin at twenty-eight and have only desired one man in my life, the one holding me. However, any relationship with him now would end in disaster. So, I make a resolute decision.

"Oh!" I feign surprise and pull away. "I've got to run, Zach. I promised my friend, Phyllis, I'd call tonight before ten. If you'll excuse me?"

I dash back to my table before he can react, grab my purse, and run out of the gym to my rental car. I don't stop until I'm halfway back to the hotel, when I pick up that special drink to stall the fire burning in the pit of my stomach.

Tears gather in my eyes. My body, still on fire from our closeness, continues to vibrate after I'm seated in my car again. To halt the trembling, my hands clutch the steering wheel. As my head falls against the seat back, my mind wills my body into control.

It's Zach who caused this maelstrom of craving to throb in my veins. It's Zach who also created this desire to fall into bed with him, and never let go.

Why now? Why am I punished with emotions that can never be acted upon? More than ever, I want my human life back. I want to experience what all those books I read reflect—to feel that euphoric sense of oneness with the man of my dreams.

Not for the first time tonight I scoff at my life. The man I desire can never be mine. Unless I can be changed back. Will it be too late by then?

Tears of regret stream down my face when understanding grips me. No matter how much I desire him, we can never be. He'd hate me if he knew what I am, and possibly wish to destroy me. With no other way out, there's only one path left to me. I will assist the cleanup committee in the morning, then head home early. I need some serious alone time to sift through my feelings as I pressed against him. Now that I've experienced that yearning, how will I assuage it? I need to talk to someone, someone like me. I have to find a way to stop the quivering between my legs before I do something I shouldn't.

Phyllis answers after the third ring. "Emma. Are you having a good time at the reunion?"

"Not especially. I have a problem."

I slump down on the chair in my hotel room and suck down the remainder of my protein drink. It settles the trembling somewhat.

"First. Why didn't you show tonight? I thought you'd be there and was disappointed you weren't."

"Sorry. Um, problems within my circle kept me here. I'll explain later. So, tell me…"

Her voice wavers when she speaks "circle," so I give her a pass. I'll ask another time. "You remember Zach, the boy from high school I was in love with? Well, tonight he asked me to dance and I accepted."

Phyllis whistles on the other end. "Good for you, girl. Was it all you dreamed it would be?"

"No! I felt… things. My body, and I can't think of a better term, craved his. I've never experienced this reaction before, Phyllis. I've never wanted to jump into bed with anyone before, and I definitely can't with him. Not the way I am. He'd run for the hills if he knew what I was. So, tell me how to stop the quivering in my stomach, the desire to sink my teeth in his neck, and lick him all over."

"I'd say you've got it bad for this guy. So, sex is off the table? You won't try?"

"I don't want some one-night stand. It'll only break my unbreakable heart when he runs from me. And when I say run, I mean bolt—the moment my fangs extend—and never look back. He'd… he'd hate me for all eternity and possibly out me to the world. How do I live with the likelihood someone may hunt me? I'd rather die alone than face that."

Without realizing it, I'm on my feet pacing the room while my mind churns with images of being burned at the stake or worse, beheaded in front of a crowd. I must calm down. I must regain control of myself. I carry my now empty cup to the bathroom to wash out and make sure to clean the remnants from the sink, too. This simple act has the desired effect.

Phyllis breathes heavily into the phone, which captures my attention again. "It's possible he doesn't feel the same about you. Did you think that through?"

I crumble onto the bed. "No." She could be right. He said he only wanted to talk. Now I'm upset I didn't stay. "He mentioned he wanted to ask someone to prom ten years ago, but was afraid she'd say no. Why would he bring that up if I wasn't the one?" I roll onto my back and stare up at the white ceiling. Maybe he's gay. He isn't married, didn't date during senior year that I know of, and only took that Michelle person to prom because of his teammates. It's possible that's what he wants to tell me.

"Okay, do me a favor. If he shows up wherever you are tomorrow, talk with him. Maybe he's shy and doesn't know how to tell you how he feels. Maybe he has the same feelings for you and worries you don't care for him. Just listen to him, Emma. Then decide what to do next."

Sounds like Phyllis is pushing me toward this guy. Why? There's no future for me with him, especially if he's gay. On the other hand, maybe he got the message tonight and will stay away. I can leave in peace and not worry one more moment what life with him could have been like. Steph will be upset, but I'll make up some excuse about work or something and promise to return in the fall. Mom and Dad... I can deal with them. It's become too easy, actually.

"Fine. If he shows tomorrow and wants to talk, maybe I will." I roll to my side. "On another note, when I was looking at the photos hanging in the gym tonight, my enhanced memory remembered when each was taken and where I was at the time. I found it amusing."

"Honey, everything about us is enhanced. Remember that when you talk with Zach. Your senses will be on full alert. Pay close attention with *all* your senses, alright?"

When we hang up, I can't relax. My body is still in crazy mode. I do the only thing I can since I'm not at home. I change to go for a jog.

Lynne Anders

CHAPTER 5

ZACH

H aving Emma in my arms again, dancing at the reunion, is a dream come true. I have been able to stay in the shadows the past ten years because I knew someday we would be together. And now that we are? My body throbs out of control with desire. Her scent created the draw. Did she notice? The immediate connection? Thrumming begins in my toes and travels through my body urging me to couple with her. If I loved her less, I would have escorted her to my room at The Alexander to shower her with the love our kind experiences in the bedroom.

However, the shaky ground under my feet worries me. I need to tell her why I changed her ten years ago and hope she will not hate me for eternity.

So often over the past ten years, I observed her, first during her college years, and then in the Buckeye home she fashioned for herself. It is a modest home, one that still speaks of her human life. The childhood books, a couple of stuffed animals, and so many pictures of her siblings and parents. She appears to have trouble withdrawing from that life. That is one area where I will be able to assist her.

It took me little time to forget my parents and the miserable life I endured in the eighteenth century. Maybe that is why I embraced what I became. Granted, being changed at the tender age of twenty-two left me with little resources to move on.

St. Augustine, during the period Spain and Britain savagely fought over our property, became a hellhole of misery. But, I worked when and where I could, saved as much money as possible, and fought my way through warring Native American tribes all the way from Florida to Kentucky and into what became Ohio with the rest of my circle. I applied techniques learned from tribal healers along this journey to help the Native and growing immigrant population, especially after the small pox epidemic a year or so earlier.

No one, other than my maker and some members from our circle, knows my true identity or history, or that I have several medical degrees, earned from a variety of top-notch medical colleges all over the country. My degree in research, for instance. It was earned from Ohio State School of Medicine in the nineteen twenties. I returned to that alma mater fifteen years ago to work at Wexner Medical Center. I loved my work at the facility and learned more from the staff about blood and blood components than I had in class. Little did I know others' deeds would soon lead me to Emma.

Three years into my position, a couple of our circle members chose to defy Francisco's ultimate rule—hide in plain sight—and rampaged through a weekend gathering of campers, sucked a few dry of blood, left their bodies for the other campers to find, and then boasted of their victory to members within our circle. Word, of course, leaked out about the savage animals who mauled the campers. Knowing the authorities would, sooner or later, interview a survivor who witnessed the attack, Francisco insisted we immediately move the circle from Ohio to Indiana.

I was not to return to my position at Wexner. Instead, I went back to high school to hide from the authorities. My age of twenty-two was easier to camouflage if I played the role of student rather than find another position similar to the one I previously held. Others within the circle were also tasked to change their professions as well. I hate to say we were used to this process. However, this move occurred sooner than planned because of the attack.

The offenders were ordered out west in lieu of punishment. They were to report to Oceanside and wait for us to follow. When Francisco determined the authorities had given up trying to locate the beasts who ravaged the campers, we would follow.

In Indianapolis, Francisco found homes for the rest of us to live in while we waited. I integrated into high school life again without much trouble. However, my role as school jock was for show. Since I was faster both physically and mentally than the other sixteen, seventeen, and eighteen-year-olds in school, the basketball coach, who was also my gym teacher, asked me to try out for the squad. It took all of my abilities to slow myself enough to play. Some days, I hated my current existence. If it had not been for Emma...

My purpose now is one of physician. As a specialist in cardiology, I study human anatomy and find ways to extend their lives. My circle leader marvels at my ability to observe human blood when I perform surgery and not be enticed to drink from my patients. Age played a great role in that skill. I have not tasted from a human in several decades. Well, other than Emma's.

Brought back to the here and now by the beauty in my arms, I am stunned when Emma makes some silly excuse and runs from me. Dumbfounded, I stand and watch as she retrieves her bag and rushes out the door. I am too shocked to move for a few moments. Once my faculties return, I offer my goodbyes to the remaining teammates at my table and leave only minutes behind the girl I love. I know her destination and rush to intercept her.

When I arrive at the JW, she is just pulling up. Because my appearance will be unkempt due to my haste to arrive, I decide to allow her a few moments to gather herself while I do the same. However, while I sit in the reception area, I watch as she departs through the front door minutes later, walks to the front sidewalk, and makes her way to the jogging path, which tracks along behind the hotel.

My only option is to follow her. I stay in the shadows and watch as she runs along the dark Canal Walk, alone, without so much as a reflector on her wrist. How can she be so naïve? Predators lurk everywhere. Even though I know she can defend herself, why put herself in this situation? Someone could attack her. What would she do then? Fight him or her off? Use her special skills? Without any training, her fangs will drop and she will be hard pressed to stop herself from driving them into her assailant's neck. I can only hope Phyllis prepared her for this situation.

I duck into the shadows as she jogs to the path's end near Eleventh Street, circles the turnaround, and heads back toward the hotel. My head spins back along the path when my senses pick up someone near Michigan Street. Does she detect the same? I rush to the area ahead of Emma and observe from a church parking lot. He is down there, I can smell him from my vantage point, but decide to wait. If he leaves her alone, he will remain safe. If he attempts to intervene, I will instead. I will charm him into oblivion if need be.

Emma approaches the homeless man, but he makes no move to obstruct her path and I sigh with relief. Confrontation averted. I watch a moment longer. The way her body moves with each stride transfixes me. She runs with grace and strength. The expelling of each breath with the rhythm of her steps, the pump of her arms as she glides smoothly along, and the swing of her ponytail, all simple movements, but they mesmerize me. The joy I feel knowing she has acclimated to this new life overwhelms my being. I did not know how it would turn out when I took her humanity from her. I only knew I did not want to lose the girl of my dreams. Now, if I can only convince her...

Her strides become longer, her speed increases. She must not realize she moves faster than anyone around her when she runs. Maybe she has never put the pedal to the metal to see how fast she can actually move. That is another quality she will need to learn about herself.

For me, I cannot wait to join her.

I follow Emma all the way to the front door of the hotel before I relax again. She will be safe inside tonight. Tomorrow I will find a way to talk to her, instill into the vampire I love some insight about our lives, and hopefully make her mine in body.

The moment light appears in her hotel room window, I turn for The Alexander. I am a short few blocks away and can be at her side within moments, if necessary.

However, when I return to my room alone, dread settles in me. Why did she flee from me tonight? While I pace around my suite, I imagine many unpleasant scenarios, which only builds my concern. With nothing to distract me tonight, I change into my running clothes and find the hotel exercise center to work off the pent-up anxiety permeating my being. I would prefer to be engaged in romantic activity with my mate. Not for the first time tonight I claim the truth.

I am still a coward.

With a towel riding low on my hips and one held against my hair, I grab my ringing phone, hoping against hope my love somehow acquired my number. Dread fills me when I notice the picture showing on my iPhone. I take a deep breath and decide to add a ringtone to his account so I am not surprised the next time he calls.

"Good evening, Francisco. What can I do for you?"

He is going to ask. There is no doubt about it.

"My dear Zachary. You haven't checked in tonight and I was wondering if you had good news for me."

The familiar rasp of his voice knots my stomach. How did I not realize what a letch he is and find a way to leave his circle decades ago? My involvement with him during my existence proved productive the first hundred years. However, his continued persistence where Emma and I are concerned weighs heavily on me now. What is his agenda?

I decide to be as truthful as possible. "We spoke, we danced, and tomorrow she agreed to discuss our arrangement." Yes, that is a fib, but I do not want him to appear on my doorstep, or worse, hers.

"I thought I made it perfectly clear, son. Tonight was the night. Now you have another excuse. Must I remind you of our agreement?"

How I have grown to dislike the beast on the other end of the phone. "No, Francisco. You need not remind me. She will be mine tomorrow night. I apologize. It is late, and I must purchase a drink and then rest. I promise I will contact you once the deed is completed. If you have no other concern, then I will say goodnight."

I wait to see if I have pushed too far.

"Zachary, Zachary, Zachary. Why disrespect me? I only think of your future existence and the loneliness you'll experience if you do not claim what is yours. She may fall into another's hands and be lost to you forever."

His pause for effect is obvious. I allow a few seconds to expire before I speak again. "Rest assured she will never belong to anyone but me. Thank you for your concern, Francisco. We will speak again tomorrow."

This time I do not wait for him to respond. I drop the offending phone on the bed and return to my nightly routine. However, worry seeps into my consciousness. I must tell Emma to be watchful. I cannot relay the reason why, but she needs to be on full alert now. Once she accepts our commitment to each other, she will understand.

Trust and Francisco do not belong in the same sentence. If I know my leader, one assumed misstep on my part and he will travel here to take over where he believes I have failed. Actually, he may already be in town watching Emma. Instead of resting, I dress in dark clothing and stroll over to the JW Marriott. I locate a decent vantage point at the base of a tree in the shadows near the hotel, pinpoint her room, and wait. Lights currently illuminate her windows. Before I settle in for the night, I scan the area and sense no one near. Still, he may be lurking somewhere outside my area of awareness.

I look up quickly and watch as her lights extinguish. My girl should be in bed. Perfect. I stroll across the street and notice no valets outside. I push through the revolving front door and wave to the gentleman behind the reservation counter. Since the elevator doesn't require a room key to access Emma's floor, I push ten and wait while the doors sneak closed.

The empty hallway allows me to move quickly to her door. I listen for any sound or movement. It appears she is asleep. And, I detect no other scent in her room. So far, she is safe. Hoping she cannot hear me, my words tumble out. "Good night, my Emma. Allow your dreams to find me."

My palm caresses her door before I turn for the elevator again.

I return to my vantage point in the shadows and remain alert until the morning sun tips over the horizon. With a few hours before I plan to intercept her, I stroll over to White Castle on South for additional infusion.

around and places his back against the wall instead. His lips remain locked on mine, which triggers my body to quiver all over. I instinctively press against him, my hands grip strands of his hair while his arms hold me tightly, and I push one of my legs between his. All space and time cease to exist while our lips remain locked in our sensual embrace.

Desire builds hard and fast, demanding release. Even though I know this is not the time or place to continue this encounter, there's not much I can do but wait for my willpower to build until I'm strong enough to pull away. When I do, in my haste, I nick my lower lip and draw blood. I drag my body farther away and press my lips together, tight. If I don't, my fangs will be exposed.

My gaze captures his and I notice his eyes look fully dilated. Completely black, almost like the iris is... I shake my head to clear where my mind goes because his eyes are changed so drastically. *He's* not the monster. *I'm* the monster. I'm unnerved and try to rationalize. Eyes dilate when emotions are high. They're simply reflecting his obvious attraction to me—not to mention my own response. Scared he'll find out who I am or, rather, *what* I am, I back up a step and nearly stumble while everything inside me tells me to run away. With all the willpower I possess, I turn to do just that.

Before I am able to take a step away, Zach grabs my arm to stop me.

"Emma, running away will not solve anything. Please. Give me a chance to explain what is occurring. Did my kiss not spark desire in you? Did you not feel the immediate connection? Tell me you felt nothing and I promise to leave you alone. However, if you felt what I know you did, stay with me. Allow me to explain."

I can't. He doesn't know what I am and, with other humans lurking, I must keep my identity to myself. So, I have to leave. I pull away, rush around the corner of the building, and slow when I notice Steph standing beside my rental. Truth shoves its way into my mind and brings reality back.

Zach. God, I love him. The way my body responded to him left me quivering all over. But, there is no going forward with him or any human for that matter. Resolve forces me to do what I must. I continue to my friend, while the man left pressed against the building wall continues to yell for me to wait. I turn back once. He hasn't followed me. And, leaving him drops a lead weight onto my soul, but I have no choice. If he kisses me again... he'll *know*. I can't risk discovery. As I grab the keys from my friend, my mind whispers to me, *The color of his eyes... was that your imagination after all?* Again, I bury the thought.

Steph doesn't ask, but notices the set of my lips as I drive away from the parking lot. Before an awkward question soaks the air, I decide to share the encounter with my once best friend.

"He kissed me. I've never been kissed that way, Steph." I press a shaking hand against my forehead. "I definitely want more, but it *can't* happen."

Traffic isn't heavy, so I barely stop at a stop sign, then plow through without looking. Steph grabs my arm, gasps, and retracts her fingers immediately.

Damn. I forgot. My body temperature is lower than humans. I should have worn a long-sleeved sweater. "Sorry, Steph. He surprised and upset me. Guess my body hasn't recovered yet."

Lame excuses, that's all I have for her.

"Did he say anything about you two?" Steph wraps her arms against her body as if she's the one with cool skin.

"Just that we were friends once. When I attempted to explain, he kissed me." My head shakes and my lips tighten in exasperation. "It isn't in the cards for us, Steph. I live in Arizona, he lives in California. Long distance relationships never make it. And, besides, I have issues of my own to solve."

Yeah, I tell myself, like I'm a vampire who wants to be changed back.

I thought maybe if I returned to the scene of the crime, the despicable creature who did this to me would possibly make a return visit and I could ask. Guess I left too early last night for him to show. Now I don't know which way to turn. Damn, Zach. He has me turned inside out. My mind also processes he isn't gay. Not after kissing me like that, he isn't!

"You never were good with confrontations. Can't we forget about Zach and focus on the plans I've made for the rest of the week? I know Tray would love to spend time with you. And the girls want a night out without the husbands tagging along. What do you say, Emma? I promise I'll keep you entertained."

God, I want to go home. However, my reason for coming in the first place is still valid. Maybe the slime bag will show and I can finally move on with my life.

I know I'll regret it, but I reverse my decision to leave town early. "My parents invited me to dinner tomorrow evening and I can't stand them up. Plus, I have a couple of other things I need to accomplish while I'm here. Okay, you've got me the rest of the week."

When she grasps my arm this time, she doesn't pull away. "Good. Now, what are your plans for Tuesday?"

My once BFF and I discuss the remainder of the week and the activities she's mapped out. I agree to dinner at her place Tuesday and a girls' night out on Wednesday. The rest I decline. I don't need to go shopping and I really don't want to revisit some of our old haunts with her. I planned to do that myself, again hoping I'll run into the monster who changed me.

When I drop her at home after our early dinner, Steph stands outside the open car door and leans against the frame.

"You don't need to hide from me, Emma. We've been friends since freshman year. You know my secrets and I know most of yours. So, call me tomorrow evening when you get back from your parents' and tell me you're more settled. And, don't let Zach Matthews ruin your trip. He's still a dashing figure, but he hasn't made any effort to contact you at all over the years, has he?"

Her last comment soothes some of my turmoil. She's right. "No." I don't want to make excuses for the man, so I stop what I was going to say and smile. "Thanks, Steph, for being my friend. I'll see you Tuesday."

She smiles and closes the door.

Because I'm in need of a drink, my second in as many days, I step on the accelerator a bit too hard when I back out of her driveway, screeching my tires on the black asphalt. I stop immediately and laugh as I wave goodbye and call through the open window.

"Not my car! Guess I need to take it a little easier. See ya!"

From the neighborhood street, I inch the car forward. Once I'm around the corner and out of her view, I step on it again. The sun has cleared the clouds and I have to blindly dig into my purse to locate my sunglasses. Once they're on, I drive to the local Burger King for my drink. Then, as I did so often during my junior and senior years, I leisurely drive around Interstate 465 to think. Mom and Dad's constant bickering, my desire to attend college with no funds available, and worry I'd never meet Mr. Right and end up alone, led me to drive the highway's fifty-two-mile loop around Indianapolis on many Saturday afternoons.

The exit to Washington Street on the east side, as I make my third pass on the highway, comes up. Memories of my favorite family home saturate my mind. We lived in that house while I attended grade school. I slip into the right-hand lane and take the off ramp. Franklin Road is the first stoplight on Washington Street. When I turn left, I search for the old rooming house where my third-grade teacher lived. Ms. Naylor often invited her students over to work on craft projects for the classroom. Since she lived less than a block from my home, Mom didn't mind if I chose to walk over alone. She never worried I'd get abducted or lost.

The boarding house has been replaced with a Steak 'n Shake. It's sad, but progress tends to blot out memories from our past. Although I'm unhappy with this change, I don't know what condition the old wooden structure would be in if it was still standing anyway. It'd probably be unsafe to live in by now, I suppose. When my head turns to the right, the house I grew up in no longer exists, along with the next two to the south. All that remains is an asphalt parking lot for the Franklin Road Baptist Church. So… the church finally did it. They bought the property, removed the houses, and extended the church and parking lot into what used to be my home. I drive into the lot and park for a moment while I reminisce about my days growing up in that missing home.

This is where we lived when I attended Eastridge Elementary School. It's also where I met Ayres Bridges, my prom date. Even though the house was rental property, Dad converted the attic into one large room for my sister and me. The house had been a two bedroom, but we needed the extra space for the three of us kids. The entire upstairs became a "girls only" zone. My brother, begrudgingly, slept in the converted basement until our room was ready.

Memories flood me. Those were some of the best years of my life. We could play outside after dark and not fear for our lives. Unlike today, we knew all of our neighbors and they knew us kids. We'd play blind man's bluff, war, put on what we considered variety

She sips in a quick shaky breath before she speaks. "You asked me to slow my pace. Your hand is as cool as mine. You're... like me, aren't you?"

The fire in her eyes matches the tone of her voice. If I do not come clean right this minute, I will lose whatever advantage I have. With the gentleness of a cool summer breeze, my words roll out smoothly. "Yes, Emma. We are the same. Now, will you speak with me? I have much to share."

She takes a step in my direction, fury filling her eyes. "Did you do this to me? Are you the one?" Her voice grows softer but her ire rises with each word, and I am fearful someone will notice.

I reach to grasp her hand, but halt immediately. Instead, I gesture toward the elevator. "I will explain, but only out of earshot of the entire hotel."

My gaze focuses on her eyes. I will charm her if need be, but somewhere in my gut I know I will pay dearly if I do.

With a huff and a spin, she continues toward the elevators, pushes the up button, and stands rigid while she waits for one of the doors to open. I remain behind her, hopeful she will listen and then allow... Well, we will see what the night holds.

Lynne Anders

CHAPTER 8

EMMA

Damn. What if it's true? What if my best friend, my confidante, the boy I loved, did this to me? Better yet, how did he hide his identity from me, especially during the last year of high school? We were together almost every day. How did I miss it? Or, maybe like me, he was changed somewhere during the past ten years. Before the elevator door opens, I spin back to him and stare. His eyes remain unblinking. I want to ask, but decide to wait until we're alone.

The elevator door opens slowly. We wait until the few people inside escape the confines before we attempt to venture in. I purposely push against the back wall as far away from Zach as I can get. I don't trust him and I won't until he explains himself. It'd better be good.

"What floor?"

His words startle me. "Ten, please." I half expected he'd know, not only the floor, but my room number, too.

Zach remains against the opposite wall, but openly stares at me during the few moments it takes the elevator to lumber up to ten. I return his glare. If he's the one, he must know I would never ask for this life, I will never become the animal history speaks of, and I will do whatever I can to persuade him to change me back, if it's possible.

The doors slowly open on my floor. Zach motions for me to precede him, then trails me down the hall, two steps behind. Once the door to my room opens and I rush inside, he quickly follows. I close the door behind my once best friend.

"Now, if you don't mind, please explain yourself. Did you do this to me?"

Zach, for some reason, walks farther away from me. I felt certain he'd be all over me the moment the door closed. When that isn't the case, I wonder if I'm incorrect in my accusation. So, could it be he was changed after me? My ire slips a little with this possibility.

Zach perches against the desk and folds his hands in his lap. "What I have to tell you may be difficult for you to hear, Emma. Please," he gestures toward the large king-sized bed, "sit down."

"If you're telling me *you* did this to me, you're right."

Anger floods my system. How could he? How could my once best friend change me into this... this monster to live my life alone, to watch my family die off one by one? I won't have a man who will love me to distraction and provide me with children to raise. I'll have to move from place to place, recreate myself every few years so no one is the wiser. How can I do that? How can I exist knowing, or not knowing, how long I'll wander this Earth?

Before I fall down, I sit on the bed across the room from the creature before me. I no longer know who he is. I stare into his dark eyes and wish, for just one moment, I had the strength to end his existence—if I only knew how. My fingers find their way into my hair and I push its long strands back behind my ears. My eyes close while I wait to hear his explanation.

"Yes. I am responsible for your transformation." He spits the words out quickly.

I stand to run, but he's faster and grabs my arms to hold me to him. "Listen, Emma. Please. I had no choice." His insistent voice sounds laced with regret.

My struggle to free myself is in vain. I stop, shrug free of his hands, and stare into his eyes.

"*You* had a choice! You left *me* without one."

The young man I knew clasps my shoulders. "No. I. Did. Not. If I had not changed you, my maker would have, and then you would belong to him and not me."

I wiggle against his hold again and shove his chest. "What do you mean? Belong to you? I don't *belong* to anyone!"

When he releases me, I stumble. When I regain my balance, the fire in my eyes surely matches the pain in my slow-beating heart. "Why do you believe I belong to you?"

My intense stare is meant to intimidate him, but it creates the opposite effect. Amusement curls his lips and sparkles his eyes.

"Emma… I am much older than you and have the power to subdue you easily. So, if you are finished being angry, let me relay my story to you."

His relaxed stance and soft voice calms me somewhat. Also, it's a story I came back home to find out. I gingerly make my way to the bed and, still smoldering, ask him to begin.

He starts with the young man he once was in the late 1700s, and the life he led after being changed by a vampire named Francisco Navarre. The required promises and demands to live within that vampire's circle, pain me. He shares how I must also promise to fulfill my responsibility to that circle and its leader.

His promise to change me, mate with me, and immerse me within *that* lifestyle fills me with dread. I don't know if I'll ever be able to live under such a rigid structure after existing mostly alone for the past ten years.

Zach observes my reticence, but continues. "If I had not complied that night, he would have, and you currently would belong to him, living day-to-day without purpose or freedom to choose for yourself."

Is he serious? I disregard his comments as they relate to this Francisco creature and focus only on the upheaval he brings to my life. It's much the same story Phyllis relayed ten years ago regarding his so-called circle. I wasn't asked to participate, I wasn't given a chance to refuse. Damn. This is all his doing.

I swallow heavily. "Is Phyllis a member of your circle? Is that why she came to me, to fill me in on this lifestyle? Why didn't she explain about you and all this then?"

He steps closer, but not too close. Tension radiates from him and permeates my core. Maybe it's because of what he claims, that we belong to each other. Is that why desire for him infuses my body? What will happen if I touch him? I hold myself in check and attempt to listen.

"I asked Phyllis to help you through the first few months. When I was ordered to finish your change and attach you to me, I asked for some lenience because of your age. You were still a child, Emma. I could not take that away from you. I had already taken your life."

My head subtly shakes. "You took my youth, Zach. You took everything away without a second thought and left me with this cold, solitary existence I don't want. Please. Tell me you can change me back. Tell me there's hope that I'll be able to live a normal life, have kids, a family to grow old with." I close the distance between us. "There has to be a way. Who do I ask? Who do I beg to give me my life back?"

Zach steps back and turns for the desk. Maybe this isn't the best place to carry out this conversation. The empty bed draws on every fiber in me.

His eyes close for a moment. "There is no way, Emma. I would have heard of it if there was." His voice, strong before, contains a slight tremble. However, his gaze fixates on me, which causes me to quiver.

If we're not careful, one of us will cave and I'll be the loser. I cannot lose my virginity now. I want my life back first. I want to be with the man of my dreams when I give my all.

Those thoughts stall and I blink them away to clear my mind. "Someone who's ancient will know. How old is this Francisco guy? He may know and maybe I can convince him I'm no good for his circle."

"Emma." His gaze lowers. "First, I have no idea of Francisco's true age, but believe him to be more than two thousand years old. That is ancient by vampire standards. He also possesses strength I do not. As the one who demanded I change you, he will never allow you to leave his circle. I am sorry, Emma. You are in this situation because I fell in love with you."

He what? My eyelids open wide, following my mouth. "You're in love with me? Why didn't you tell me, Zach? We could have run away from him, lived our lives together, raised a family, and…"

I stop when sorrow infuses his eyes.

"All a pipe dream, I guess?"

He nods. His admission backs me up a step. While I continue to forage through all I've been told, he walks toward the door.

His hand rests on the doorknob. "I must leave or you will have to mate with me tonight since I am too strung out with desire to trust myself much longer. I do not believe you are ready and, since I have taken everything else from you, I will not take that, too. But, I need you to be watchful, Emma. Francisco's spies are everywhere. If he finds out we remain unmated, he may force the issue. I promise that is not my intent. Just be aware of people around you."

My eyes focus again. He's just admitted he loves me and he's walking out.

His fingers push his hair away from his face while I gather strength to keep my distance, but the draw intensifies.

"You have no idea how strong my desire is for you. I want to kiss you goodnight, but I fear it would lead to mating. Let me just say I will see you sometime tomorrow. Unless you want me to…"

My hand raises as if to push him away. "No. You're right. I'm not ready to, um," I peek at the bed, "just yet. I need some time to think, to figure this out… us out. Is that agreeable?"

"Of course. Well, goodnight, dear Emma. I will call upon you in the morning if that is acceptable."

"Um, not too early. I have a lot of thinking to do. And, I promised my parents I'd have dinner with them tomorrow night."

"I'll see myself out, then." With a backward glance and a wink, he closes the door behind him.

I slip out of my clothes and into my nightgown the moment I'm alone. My mind tumbles with questions like… Who is this Francisco and how does he have such a hold on Zach and, apparently, me? I am *so* not ready to live my life under the manipulations of that vampire. And, Zach. He left me alone for more than ten years. Why would he do that? But, he also said I was a child when he changed me. Was he waiting until I matured and possibly be more willing to accept my fate? With a huff, I drop on the bed and fall back to rest my head on the pillows. And, what about Zach? He changed me because of that creature. How can I even for a moment not hate him for the rest of my existence? But… he says he loves me, wants to make love to me, or in his words, "bed" me, "mate" with me. Sounds a little archaic, but that's probably due to his age. He's two hundred and fifty-what years old? How can *that* be? Phyllis told me we age one year in twenty. He'd appear to be in his mid-forties if that's the case. However, he hasn't changed much since high school. He may possess a few extra crinkles around his eyes, but everything else looks mighty fine.

My body trembles again at the mere thought of him naked before me. I close my eyes to quell it, but desire intensifies instead. An image of him standing before me in black slacks, a white shirt unbuttoned to his waist, and feet bare, much the same clothing he wore when he left me several minutes ago, consumes my thoughts. In my daydream, he strolls toward a closet door while tugging his shirt from his slacks. I watch his fingers unclasp his belt and pull the zipper down, which allows his slacks to fall. When he bends to retrieve them, his boxer-briefs-covered ass is on full display. I can almost reach out and touch him.

As if he reads my mind, his face turns back toward me, with a smile and a twinkle in his eyes that gives me pause. He stands again and saunters my way while stripping the shirt from his arms.

Zach stands at the end of my bed in nothing but the briefs, his thumbs in the waistband ready to discard his last article of clothing.

My tongue darts out to wet my parched lips as desire blooms powerfully between my legs. I squirm against the comforter and watch the black briefs hit the floor. My hands clutch the cover while he strides around the bed toward me in all his naked glory. I've never seen a man naked in person, only in pictures, and Zach's perfection puts them all to shame. How I wish he were here right now, that he truly was striding toward me with his gaze consumed in desire. Without realizing it's happening, my legs separate to welcome his embrace.

My head lolls to the side when I feel his weight on top of me. My back arches when a hand cups my breast. Fingertips persuade my head back, lips lower to mine, and pull me into a heated kiss. Instinctively, my arms surround him and we writhe together on the bed. I don't stop him when his fingers glide down my body. They remove my panties and toss them to the side. A moment later, he's nestled between my legs ready to thrust inside.

My eyelids burst open while my breast heaves in raw passion. I half expect him to be on top of me, but he's not. I scan my small room, nonetheless, and feel disappointment when I realize it was all a dream. But... I felt his weight, his lips pressed to mine. How did he do that?

I rise up and shake the cobwebs, almost sorry I stopped him before he penetrated me.

"Damn, Zach, I'd rather be present during our first time, not experience it through a dream," I declare to no one.

I slip into the bathroom, disrobe, and turn on the shower. I don't think even cold water will strip the desire from me. At least I believe I know what to expect when we do mate the first time. If it is anything like this dream, it will be epic by my mere standards.

My eyes close again while I lather my skin with bath gel. The aroma of roses saturates the air as I swirl soap around my sensitive breasts, sensitive only because his hand possessed one. Zach. His name repeats in my head while I remember the gentleness of his touch. My hands flow over my stomach and in between my legs, now aching to be touched.

As if on cue, the shower curtain rustles and Zach steps into the streaming water with me. He grabs the container of gel and rubs his hands together until they foam with the rose-scented suds. His long-fingered hands begin at my shoulders, work their way down my arms, and come to rest on my stomach. He leans in to kiss me, and I allow it. His tongue slips against my lips and fights to gain entrance into my mouth. I'm wary at first, but allow him inside with the hope he won't nick his tongue on my descending fangs.

Shivering from his nearness and the lashing of his tongue, I circle my arms around his neck to draw closer. His body slides against mine and I rise up on my toes to better align with him.

Zach's hands, cool against my skin, circle my waist and come to rest on my backside, which draws me against his erection. But, I back away again and murmur to myself, "Not in here, please."

He doesn't persist. However, one hand slides between my legs and touches my sensitive folds. No one has touched me there ever, and I reel with exhilaration as if I'm on a roller coaster ride at Disneyland when one of his fingers glides back and forth taunting me. Hungry for his touch, my legs separate to allow his exploration to continue.

His lips continue to torture me while his finger works me into a frenzy. If this is what making love with someone feels like, I'm all in.

Amidst the gentle play of his tongue and fingers, my mind hears, *"Touch me, Emma. I need you to touch me."*

Zach grasps one of my arms and coaxes my hand to his hardened length. My fingers circle around him. His body jolts when I squeeze. My hand slowly draws up and down his shaft almost with the same rhythm as his finger slides against me.

Time seems to stand still while we pleasure each other, tongues lashing and hands caressing. Suddenly, a strong desire spins through my head to sink my fangs into his body… anywhere, which surprises me. This repeat craving worries and thrills me at the same time. Can I do this in a fog-induced dream? He's not really here, he's just in my head. Right?

Before I can figure that out, my entire body quivers and trembles when my lover's finger slides inside me. My hand clasps his length harder while tingling spreads through me, and I hear a growl when cool liquid flows from his tip. I continue to squeeze until my trembling slows and his secretions subside.

My head falls to his chest. I resist the urge to bite him and kiss him instead. "Was that an orgasm?" I dare not open my eyes. He'll disappear if I do, and I want him to stay a few moments longer.

"It was." His whisper against my hair comforts me. *"You have much to learn, my Emma, and I cannot wait to teach you. Go to sleep now, and dream of me."* With a final kiss to my hair, I hear *"I love you"* fade away as his essence leaves me alone in the shower.

"I'd like to do that again."

My eyes open to no one. Disappointment floods me.

I finish my shower, dry off, and slip into bed sans nightgown this time, hoping if he decides to visit me in my dreams tonight, I'll be ready.

Sleep eludes me, though. I toss and turn, still too strung out to rest. My body hums with what I believe is hunger, or maybe craving. How can a dream invoke such feelings?

Our tryst in the shower only increased my desire for him. Maybe if I close my eyes, he'll come to me again. But, all I visualize is darkness. I try again, but it's still the same. He's either asleep himself or simply not responding to my request. With a huff of frustration, I roll over onto my side and relive the last hour in my mind. The way he cupped my breast tingles me, the touch of his lips on mine burns a fire in the pit of my stomach. And his fingers. My body writhes against the sheets one more time when the quiver spreads through me. I roll to my back and wait for my body to calm.

CHAPTER 9

ZACH

S he is still young in some ways. Frightened for her first time, but willing to try. Truth be told, I am amazed she has not indulged before. She is a beauty among women, has a strong sense of being, and appears to be passionate. How she has kept from other's favor is beyond me. Then I remember. Her essence resides in me, so she is mine and, on some level, she understands this to be true. However, it is a known fact that vampires experience sex with like-minded creatures before they connect with their life-mate. I have tasted from others in the past, but realized early on only one would capture and hold my attention. Once connected, the draw intensifies. The bond between mates surpass any other want or need, correct? It has proven true for me.

I spin back toward my bed and clench my fists. The thought of Emma in someone else's embrace... I release the rage immediately. She is still mine and, if I play it right, no one will ever know my Emma but me.

After our little escapade in her shower, I still want nothing more than to storm over to her hotel room and finally claim her body. The way she responded to my touch... she would welcome me. Still, I am hesitant. There is so much I must teach her about how our kind couples, and I do not want to scare her off before I explain. With our minds already bonded, at least that hurdle has been jumped. She was so receptive and did not fight me off when I penetrated her psyche.

I still need to explain how we communicate when we are not together. That will take practice. Tonight was a beginning, though.

Sated for the first time in what seems forever, I lower to the bed and close my eyes to visualize my love again. Her perfect body displayed no discernable scars, only cream-colored flesh in all the right places, her nipples delicate rosebuds ripe for my touch. The two marks I left on her perfect skin ten years ago are barely visible on her neck.

I am awakened from my day-dream by the irritating chime of my phone. I know whose ringtone it is, and I do not wish to speak with him. However, if I do not answer, he may show up on my doorstep.

"Good evening, Francisco. To what do I owe your precious time?" I sit up against the headboard and tug the blanket over my feet out of habit. I also close my consciousness to the girl of my dreams. I need to keep her safe from Francisco's clutches.

"Zachary, my friend. I have not heard from you and wondered how you're getting along with your mate?"

His voice, although his words are spoken softly, chills me. He is probing for information. Do I tell him I completed my conquest or tell him the truth? I decide on the truth. He probably already knows anyway because of his ring of spies and his ability to penetrate my mind.

"We are progressing well. We experienced a mind-link and she was receptive. There is still so much she must learn, Francisco, but my plan is falling into place. Before she leaves on Friday, she will belong to me completely."

"That's good to hear. Does she realize she'll be asked to leave her modest home and move in with the circle here in Oceanside?"

Now, he is challenging me. "About that. Without the benefit of a teacher these past ten years, I would like permission from the circle to live with her while she learns our ways. Once she understands her place amongst us, she will move in with me and join the circle. It should not take more than a month or two at most." This is the best plan to keep her far from his clutches. I want her fully invested in our lifestyle, too, before I subject her to the rest of Francisco's circle.

"That's something I'll need to think over, dear boy. We'll discuss it again when you return at the end of the week. In the meantime, enjoy your petite delicacy. I'm waiting patiently to formally meet her."

The sound of his voice warns me of his intent. I, more than ever, realize I must keep Emma from his control. He will take what he wants and because he is the leader of our circle and my maker, I will have no say in the matter. However, I keep my voice light when I respond.

"And, she will be delighted to make your acquaintance, too. Until later, then. Good evening, Francisco."

"Good evening, young Zachary."

Just another dig to remind me he is ancient and I am not. His decision will be absolute. Distressed by the conversation, I jump from my bed, dress quickly in dark clothing and run over to the JW. When I peer up at her window, no lights illuminate the room. She must be sleeping. I decide to throw caution to the wind and transport my psyche into her room.

I stand at the foot of her bed and watch the beautiful young woman smile. Is she dreaming of me? Will she be receptive if I lay next to her? How I want her, but I dare not try. I will not be able to control myself if she objects.

My Emma. My precious love. How do I protect her if she does not share her body with me? I cannot allow Francisco near her until she does. He will ruin her just as he has ruined other young females he brought into the circle. How his mate, Nadia, tolerates him is beyond me. However, they have existed together for centuries. There must be something that changes a vampire along the way into what those two have become. Power maybe? He has more power and control than most of the circle leaders I have encountered during my existence. Does he require more?

My only desire is to live with Emma in peace and love. No drama, no special agenda. To spend all of my days and nights loving this beautiful creature will be more than a dream come true.

My decision to withdraw from her room stalls when her body moves. Emma's legs kick at the sheet covering her and her head lolls side to side. I delve into her subconscious and grin. She is experiencing our connection, without any assistance from me. What a jewel she is. Her education will progress quickly if she is already this attuned to me.

Euphoria sweeps through me. My fingers long to touch her. But, no! It will undo me and I will be knocking on her door to allow me in to complete our mating. My hands clench at my side. I promised I would not until she was ready, so I do what I must. I disentangle from her mind, making sure no outside interference has penetrated our connection, withdraw my psyche from the room, and leave her to her dream.

Sleep avoids me, however, when I crawl into my bed again. I crave her body, our connection. Damn. How is it I slept alone for the past ten years and did not require any involvement from her? My eyes close and I fantasize about my fervent wish to be buried inside her.

Unable to rest, my mind jumps from image to image until it conjures the last evening when I had visited her in Buckeye.

She had just returned home from work. I hid in the shadows as I had done these past ten years, while remembering Francisco's incessant demands that I finish our bond. During this time, I repeatedly told him I intended to wait until she gained more maturity and became more settled within her new existence before I bound her completely to me and our circle. To bring her into our fold at eighteen or even twenty could have meant her end. Emma was nowhere near ready for that world. When I explained to Francisco the circle she found helped guide her along in this life, he settled somewhat and realized she was in capable hands. He knew of their leader from Elder Rayner, our circle's regional superior. I still worried, year after year, that he would visit her and take her himself just to speed things along. So, I also kept a watchful eye on my leader. I did not trust he would leave well enough alone for much longer.

Emma hurried inside, frantically seeking something. Two friends called while I observed her, to invite her out. She declined both, telling them she needed to complete some research. She located a volume under paperwork on her desktop. In her hand she held The Historian, written by Elizabeth Kostova. A half-smile curled one corner of my mouth. I knew the book well.

Additional vampire-themed books created stacks on her end table. I browsed the titles. It appeared Emma was obsessed with vampire folklore. That was an interesting turn of events. Having spent years of my life listening to elders within our circle expound on vampire life, the tales told within those books, in some cases, depicted how many of us used to live. Without the availability of Velvet Crimson, many more animals would have perished and humans would have been used as a renewable food source. It also meant the existence of vampires would have been widely known. Thankfully, that is not the case. We are able to exist hidden in plain sight among humans without fear of retribution or annihilation.

Zach doesn't speak again until after we've purchased our drinks and are back in the car. "I heard from Francisco last night."

"Oh? Did he ask you if we've done the deed?" I chuckle believing I'm being cute. However, the scowl on Zach's face suggests he's anything but amused.

"Yes, he did. I told him not yet, but I intended to by the end of the week."

My head spins to him. "After last night... it's all I think about now. By the way, how did that happen? How could your mind possess mine so deeply, I felt you there when I know you weren't?"

Throbbing between my legs starts slowly, but builds as I think about his finger inside me, and the way my body reacted to his touch. I reach for the radio to distract my thoughts at the same time as he does, and our fingers touch. I don't want to say a spark flew from them, but the air ignited around us.

My hand retracts and returns to the steering wheel. "What was that?" There's so much I don't know about vampires and their mating. I'm almost too scared to ask now.

The handsome creature next to me shifts in his seat and clasps my arm. "We have just fed, Emma. Our bodies have heightened awareness right now. So, before we have an accident, please pull off somewhere we can talk."

I nod and decide to find a spot around University Park. With most people at work already, we can stroll around the grounds and talk without being overheard.

Zach links our fingers and walks me into the park. A few homeless people lay across empty benches, but no one appears to be interested in us. We saunter to the fountain in the center and sit on the cool stone ledge. The cherubs that surround the center fountain appear to laugh at us as water cascades from the dish above their heads. My gaze captures the trees, the benches, and the walkways within the park as memories of days long gone filter into my mind. I love Indianapolis in the spring and summer. It isn't too hot yet and everything has already turned green from the harsh winter. Today is one of those days. A few clouds sprinkle the sky and birds chatter loudly as if wondering when someone will come along to feed them. My head swivels to the side as I overhear a couple arguing on the other side of the park, something to do with her mother meddling in their lives. I wish, for just one moment, my life was as uncomplicated as theirs. My focus redirects to the individual next to me and I study his body language. Something is brewing beneath the surface.

"Tell me why Francisco's call disturbs you."

Zach's head spins to me instantly. "How do you know it disturbs me?"

I shrug. "By the way you're deciding what, or what not, to tell me. I can't read into your mind completely, but can pick up emotions. I suppose that's all part of the enhanced business and 'me being yours' thing, right?"

"Oh, my Emma." He clasps my hands while his gaze captures and holds mine. "I have waited ten years for you to find me." He scoots closer. "Yes. In fact, you witnessed it last night. Now that our minds have bonded, we can communicate more easily. That is only the surface of our connection. As for touching you the way I did... I admit it was wrong of me to take advantage of you."

My hand withdraws from his hold and captures his cheek. "You didn't take advantage of me. I wanted you to touch me. I mean, I don't understand all the ins and outs of mating with you, but I felt your desire for me and acted on it. My only question now is when we can finish what you started. This trembling in my body needs to be quenched, Zach. I don't know how much longer I can sit still here and not... ravish you."

Zach shifts away. I want to grab him back, but he stalls me with a brooding look.

"You have plans for this evening, tomorrow night, and Wednesday. What I have to tell and show you requires much more time."

My audible swallow and wide-eyed stare changes his brood to amusement. "It is all a process, my love." His hands, once again, claim mine. "Do not be frightened there is some ritual you must pass in order to become mine. You have already proven our connection." He studies my face as if deciding something. "Your schedule has you returning home Friday morning, correct?" His voice sounds a little edgy.

I nod and allow him to continue.

"My plan was to fly out tomorrow. However, I believe I will change it to accompany you Friday morning. I will escort you home and you can decide if you want to introduce me to your area's circle. I must tell you I know most of them already."

"You do? How?" I wait for his answer, maybe already knowing.

The smile that lights his eyes and steals my heart broadcasts immediately. "I have watched you for ten years, Emma. That is why I asked Phyllis to push you toward Arizona. My circle resides in Oceanside, as does my medical practice. But, I would like to change that. If you will have me, I will move to Buckeye, date you so others will notice, and marry you after a brief courtship. The marriage is for your human friends. I would not want them to think you are a loose woman who invites strange men into your bed."

He wants to marry me? Wasn't this my dream ten years ago before he changed me into this creature?

Without warning, the desire to be changed back surges to the surface again, and I push back the emotions threatening to overwhelm my nervous system. Tears threaten. I'm about to burst his bubble and mine. My head bows as grief drenches me.

"I'd love to spend my life with you, Zach. As tempting as that sounds, I can't. Ten years ago, I would have run away with you. But, you didn't ask me ten years ago if this is a life I would have chosen for myself." My head raises and I stare deeply into his eyes. "It isn't. As much as I want *you*, I want my humanity back much more. Will you do that for me, Zach? Change me back?"

The handsome vampire drops my hands, stands, and strides away. He stands with his back to me for a few moments before he spins around again. By the look on his face, his response isn't going to be to my liking.

"I apologize for my actions ten years ago. I had a moment of self-indulgence based on my fear for you under Francisco's influence. I am sorry to have brought such agony to your young life. As for your request, I know of no one who can fulfill it, Emma."

Do I see tears in his eyes?

"Since an existence with me will cause torment for both of us through the years, I see no alternative but to grant you freedom to seek someone who will do your bidding. Check with your circle leader in Phoenix. She may be able to assist you. My only concern is Francisco. He *will* come for you. I will do my best to stop him but, as I mentioned before, you need to be watchful. His spies are all around us and he will stop at nothing to forcibly drag you into his circle."

I nod because I don't know how else to respond. He's correct, though. I must divorce myself of him now, before I'm more deeply involved. With my decision absolute, the desire I felt last night and this morning quickly dissipates. I stare into his unblinking eyes. He's withdrawing from me, too. My sigh is deep and painful. When no other option presents itself, I stand and begin the slow journey back to my car alone. The one I've loved for ten years remains behind.

As I close the car door and hang my head I can't stop my thought. *What have I done?*

CHAPTER 11

EMMA

During the drive to my parents' home, I attempt to mentally connect with Zach. His shield is up. He apparently blocked me when he withdrew from our connection this morning. My day went from wonderfully positive to downright depressive within those shared moments in University Park. As intimate as we were last night, all that's left are memories of his tantalizing thoughts and touch. Why would he believe I'd wish this life on myself? My mind tumbles through many of our conversations from senior year and finds no inkling of the man, or creature, he is—and no reason for him to believe I'd want to live forever.

That thought also brings up the possibility of how long I will live, or exist. Phyllis told me I'd age one year for every twenty of existence. Zach hasn't expanded on that stratagem with me, yet appears much younger than the forty something he'd have become. Maybe she didn't know for certain. She said *she* aged one for twenty, not me. I'll have to ask Zach, if I ever see him again.

My hands strike the steering wheel. "Damn, Zach. Why can't I get you out of my mind?"

Before I turn into my parents' street, I pull over a block away and try, once more, to connect with the man who held my heart so many years ago. To relax my mind, I sit back, close my eyes, and breathe deeply. He's just out of focus when my mind touches his. I instill how sorry I am for how I reacted this morning and ask him to contact me tonight so we can talk.

No response. I'm still ignored.

With a sad shrug, I drag my mind from the link and pull back into the street. When he does talk to me again, I promise myself I'll listen. If I'm destined to live this existence, maybe I can tolerate it if he's my guide and confidante. God, I can't stand this back and forth non-decision. I want him, I want my life. I want him, I want my family. I want him.

Mom and Dad's house sits just up the street. When I turn into their driveway, they both run from the front porch. Mom reaches the car first and opens the door, which allows me to step out into her arms.

"Welcome home, honey. My goodness, you haven't changed much since we saw you two years ago. Arizona must agree with you." Mom hugs me hard, releases me, and my dad's arms surround me next.

"Glad you could make it home, hon. Your mom's talked of nothing else the past couple of days." He releases me and looks inside the car.

"Nice rental. Does it drive well?"

My dad. Always emotionally cool. At least this time I got a hug. "Yeah, Dad. For a Chevrolet, it isn't bad."

He slams the door shut and follows my mom and me toward the house. Mom, being Mom, asks if I'm seeing someone before we're even to the front door. Do I explain about Zach when I don't know if he'll ever speak to me again? Maybe if I say the words out loud...

"I kind of have someone, Mom. We had a little tiff this morning, so I'm not sure where we stand right now. I asked him to call me later tonight to work things out."

"That's nice, dear. Someone from school or someone from Arizona?" She tugs open the screen door and allows me into the house first. When I look around, the décor is the same as it's always been: tufted dark-beige sofa with nail-head trim and a matching loveseat, a weathered barn-door designed entertainment console that matches the end tables, and pictures from my siblings and my childhood scattered on top of every piece of furniture in the room. Mom told me she kept those pictures out since I didn't live in Indiana any longer so she could still picture me running through our old neighborhood when the three of us were kids. My sentimental mom. How she'd hate me if she knew the truth about me now.

Mom's beagle, Sheba, runs up to me with her tail wagging, but suddenly turns and takes to the wind with her tail between her legs when I reach down to pet her. Last time I was home, Sheba was at the vet's due to a reaction to something she ate from Mom's garden. Perturbed by her reaction, I watch her rush out into the yard through the doggie door. Did she sense I am other than human? One more question I need an answer to.

When Mom doesn't react to Sheba's discomfort, we continue through the house while she pumps me for additional information. I respond enough so she's satisfied. Then, she begins to relate news about my brother and sister, and leaves my life alone.

We chat for an hour or so while sipping tea at the dinner table. Dad has disappeared. He's probably outside toying with his car or the lawn and garden equipment. He was never one for small talk.

Later, I follow Mom around the kitchen while she prepares dinner. Tonight's fare is roast chicken, oven-baked potatoes, fresh Indiana corn-on-the-cob, and cherry cobbler for dessert. Not what I'd consider a healthy meal, but it's Mom's home cooking I enjoy anyway.

Once we're seated around the kitchen table, Dad says grace. This family tradition has been around since my grandmother's days and, tonight, it brings tears to my eyes. I say my own little prayer and ask God to forgive my lifestyle with the hope He understands it was not my choice. As a dead creature, does He even hear or acknowledge me?

When Dad says Amen, I raise my napkin to my lips and cough to cover my sniffle, pat my eyes, and smile for my parents. Mom grabs our plates and fills them with too much food, as is her habit. I accept mine from her hand and stare at the ear of corn. This could present a problem. With my elongated incisors, I decide, instead, to cut my corn off the cob in case either of my parents notice.

Mom's silent stare holds me in place. "What are you doing, Emma? Isn't the corn cooked enough?"

She attempts to grab it from my hand when I laugh. "No, Mom. It's perfect as always. I prefer to eat it with a fork than to have butter splattered all over me. Okay?"

Mother relaxes somewhat, but eyes me throughout dinner. Does she notice something different? I'm doing my best to appear relaxed, eat slowly, and talk in measured tones. I don't need any red flags today. I want my parents to believe I'm still me.

Dinner clean-up is a breeze because Mom and I washed most of the pots and pans before the meal was served. Once we shoo Dad off to watch television, the rest of the cleanup commences. My fear surfaces the moment Mom and I reach for a bowl at the same time and our hands collide. She withdraws hers quickly, and cradles it in her other hand with concern shading her eyes.

"Emma, why is your hand so cold? Are you ill, honey?"

Worry replaces concern, which distresses me on so many levels. I want to tell her the truth, but understand she isn't strong enough to handle it. But, damn, I'm still her daughter and I need my mom. How can I tell her I'm no longer human? I've had to continue with my life without my family and watch from a distance while my siblings marry, produce grandkids, all to cover what I've become? I've used all the excuses in the world to explain why I can't come home for birthdays, or anniversaries, or weddings. If they ever found out…

My eyes blink purposely. "I've had a cold for a couple of weeks. Nothing serious. The doctor says it'll wear off soon." More lies to cover up my dilemma.

Mom recovers and carries the rest of the plates to the kitchen sink. "As long as you're taking care of yourself…"

I follow behind with the offending bowl and utensils. "The best I can, Mom."

Mom and I join my dad in the living room to watch the local news once the kitchen is cleared. I'm not interested. Not now. After my near collapse in the dining room, I really think I should leave.

"Mom, Dad…" I stand and grab my purse. "I think I'll hit the road. I want to be back in case my friend calls me. Do you mind?" I didn't relate it was Zach. Since he and I spent so much time together at my home senior year, Mom would have asked too many questions.

Mom looks up from her seat on the sofa. "Why not spend the night, Em? We have plenty of room."

How I love my mom. She'd make up my old room if I'd stay. "I didn't bring anything with me. Plus, I promised to see Steph tomorrow. I'm also returning home early. The girl they brought in to cover for me at work didn't work out and they've asked me to cut my vacation short. I told them I'd think about it." That will keep her from asking me to come home again this week.

His sideways glance and smirk don't go unnoticed. "We have sources to help us transition into a new existence. This last incarnation was created in 1998. One of these days, I will give you the list of names I have used throughout my life span."

My wide-eyed glance raises his brows.

"What was your birth name, Zach?"

He swallows audibly and announces, "Oswyn Avery Lightfoot."

The words spill from his lips and leave an anxious crease around his eyes, which also worries me. Part of his history he hasn't shared?

The elevator door opens on the tenth floor. We exit and stroll toward my room, and before I realize I'm saying it out loud, I blurt, "I'm going to need a score card."

Zach reaches for my card key and pushes me behind him. Because I trust him, I wait a few steps away from my door while he opens it and walks inside alone. My body instinctively pushes back against the hall wall to wait for the all-clear from my maker.

"You may come in." His voice booms from inside my room.

First, why did he search my room? Second, why did I allow it? I push away from the wall and join Zach inside. "Who or what did you think you'd find in here?" Once I rinse my cup and deposit it in the bathroom trash, I join Zach in the main room. He's hovering next to the desk.

"No one in particular. I was being cautious."

When his gaze captures mine, I almost swoon onto the bed. I'm not ready to succumb to his desire yet, so I divert my gaze. "Okay. So, how did you know I'd stop at White Castle?"

Zach strolls my way with his head cast down, though when his eyes glare up through his lashes, I back up and hit the side of the bed. And, just as quickly as it left, our connection returns. Was it completely gone in the first place? It certainly felt that way this morning. I swallow to hide my growing desire, and sit.

"I followed you. When I realized the path you intended to take, I swept past you and waited. If you had continued, I would have met you at the hotel."

"How did I not see you or notice your scent?" Is he faster than I am? And, I should have captured his scent.

His lips curl. "You would have… if you were paying attention."

He stops a few steps away when his phone chimes.

Lynne Anders

CHAPTER 12

ZACH

Timing. His timing could not be worse. "Good morning, Francisco. To what do I owe the honor of your call?" This had better be good. I was about to entice Emma to share her body with me.

"I've heard some rumblings, dear boy, that your sweet Emma is leaving early. Is there any truth to the matter?"

The rasp of his voice shivers my body. "Emma is with me at this moment, Francisco. Can this call be postponed until later?"

"Have I called at an inopportune time then?"

He must have delved into my subconscious and discovered my anxiety over our situation tonight. Snake. How does he expect me to proceed if he continues to interrupt me?

"Most inopportune. If you will excuse me, I will return the call later." I end the call, toss the offending piece of electronics onto the desk, and spin away from my love with clenched fists. How do I hide from Francisco? There must be a way to block him from drilling into my thoughts at a whim. I cannot second guess every decision I make because I suspect he is listening in. I cannot, especially where Emma is concerned. With my love for her and my desire to share my existence in her arms, I resolve to find a way. As that aspiration drops into another compartment of my mind to explore later, I turn back to the woman on the bed.

"Sorry. That should be the last I hear from him tonight. Now," I collapse in the desk chair primarily to keep from touching her, "you were asking about my name."

"Yeah. Um, you mentioned you had sources. How does that work?"

Emma clasps her hands and fidgets while she sits on the end of the bed. Is she anxious because of the call? Or, does she realize she will become mine in body tonight? I decide not to delve into her mind for the answer. Part of the reason I want to do this my way, without any outside interference, is because of her reactions. Emma appears to have a highly sensitive and responsive nature and I do not want her experiences to be choreographed when we mate.

With my legs crossed, I recline back in the chair and smile. "We have sources for many things. Obtaining a new identity is the easiest. Well, now, not quite as easy due to the Internet and technology. But, we manage. Some of the elders kept their names, but have only moved between two locations their entire existence. I did not wish for that reality. To experience as much of the world as I could was one of the primary reasons I have stayed with Francisco's circle all these years."

"Then you've traveled a lot?"

Zach peers out the window while toying with his bottom lip. "Not really. After promising us freedom to travel in the beginning, Francisco kept us on a tight leash most of the time."

"I sense you're making a decision that won't include him in your future."

Oh, my Emma. Are you so attuned to me already you can read my energy?

"We should table that conversation for another time."

Her nod followed by a shrug intrigues me. "What, Emma? Do you want to discuss Francisco now? Please tell me." I must keep this conversation light. Francisco may choose to drop in again.

"Not if you don't want to. I just wonder why you've stayed with him."

The lovely young woman before me shifts on the bed. Although still in her running clothes, she is the epitome of beauty. Her long graceful neck, hair pulled back in a long ponytail, and golden flecked eyes opened wide in anticipation. My gaze scans her top to toe while desire builds inside me. I will my body into control while my hands grip the arms of the desk chair to hold me in place. It is too soon. I will ruin everything if I do not take my time.

Although she is aware of this stipulation, I restate it more to convince myself. "Francisco is my maker. One of his demands is that all he creates live within his circle." My gaze stares off into space as I recount some of my story. "When Francisco found me alone, destitute, and near the end of my human existence, he asked if I wished for a better life. A life-affirming 'yes' exploded from my mouth before I thought. Little did I know what he actually meant. I have since followed him from location to location, occasionally feeding from animals. Later, rumors spread that some in his circle fed from humans. Francisco had told me it was not acceptable, but I wondered at the time if he said that to placate me, or if it was indeed true. I have been watchful since."

Emma's eyes open wider in question. "Have you ever used humans that way? I mean…" her obvious swallow and deep inhale of air fills the quiet room. "I guess what I mean is, have you killed anyone."

My frown surprises her. Do I tell her the truth, that in the early days I used humans to sustain my new life? I do not believe anyone died from my feeding, but I cannot be certain. I decide to table this issue for a later date. "No, Emma. I have never killed another human. Maybe an animal here and there, but with Velvet Crimson, there is no need."

Discussing our lifestyle appears to unsettle her. She grabs an empty water bottle from a nightstand and stands. She walks slowly back and forth at the end of her bed, stops abruptly, and spins back toward me.

"Why *me*, Zach? Why did you make me into this… this monster that requires blood? Why rob me of my life?"

Time for the truth. I rise and cross the room to stand in front of her. "You are my other half, Emma. I have known it from the first time I saw you." My thumb wipes away a tear as it spills from her eye. "The first time I passed by you, your scent drew me in. I can explain it no other way than to say something in my makeup reacted to something in yours. It is as if we were created for each other, even before I turned you. How I handled what I did holds no excuse, however. I took your human life from you without your consent to create a mate for myself and to keep you from Francisco. I apologize again for my total lack of judgment, and only wish you will accept me as your life-mate now. Neither of us have to be alone again."

Another tear leaks from her eye.

"Zach… I— I wasn't alone before. I had a family who cared deeply for me. They still do, but I don't know how much longer this charade life will satisfy them. One day, they'll notice I haven't changed. What do I do then? Abandon them all?"

My arms surround her trembling body. "No, Emma. Charming. Charming is the answer." I release my tight hold and raise her chin with my fingertips until she is looking into my eyes. "You will explain to them you are older than you appear, which will allow their minds to age you for themselves. That is one of the positive benefits for us. You do not have to live without your family, dear one. One moment of explanation and there will be no more questions."

Her subsequent release of tension indicates she possibly accepts this explanation. Happy I have provided a suitable solution, my eyelids close, my lips fall to hers, and I take full advantage of her open mouth. The water bottle hits the floor. The instant her arms circle my neck, I pull her close again. My hands caress her shoulders, flow gently down her back until I push her pelvis against mine. When she does not back away but rubs against me, tingling begins in my gums and flows throughout my body. My tongue nicks her elongated incisors and a smile lifts my lips. She desires me.

Before I claim her body, I must be certain. I end the kiss and search her eyes. "Emma. Are you ready? I promised I would not seize what is not mine to take. But, if you are willing?"

Her labored breathing and darkened pupils speak multitudes. However, I wait for her to answer me.

She licks her lips and presses her hands against my chest. "No, I'm not."

Stunned, I draw her against me willing her to change her mind. How much longer must I wait? This young creature pulls at every fiber of my being then casts me aside with three words.

Her arms circle around my back and she lays her head against my heaving chest. I whisper against her hair. "I promised I would not force you. So, we will wait."

My love pushes away from me and with her back to me, walks toward the door to her room. "Do you understand why I can't, Zach?" Her whisper is barely audible.

"Maybe."

She slowly turns to face me. "I want my life back. I want to live, Zach. I mean live. I'm happy to be faster, and stronger, and need less sleep. Oh, and I'm especially happy I don't have to watch what I eat because my body will never change." Her pupils dilate further with each word spoken. "But... my family, my mom and dad. They're, more or less, lost to me. My sister and brother, too. I live alone and confide in no one other than those in the circle I chose. I wanted so much for myself, Zach. I wanted to travel the Earth, explore cultures, and art, and music." She paces toward me with her jaw set.

"I want a family, a husband and children, and then grandchildren one day. I want what was promised to me as a little girl. So, until I know this vision of my life is all a mere pipe dream and I must live this," her hands raise to her head and outline her body down to her hips, "existence, my answer remains the same."

This lovely being expresses what I felt after my change. With my help, she will learn and prosper in this new existence.

I explain again that I know of no one who can remedy her situation, and to ask Francisco will be a death sentence for her, and possibly me since I have failed in my attempt to fully make her mine.

In one quick stride, I close the distance between us and enfold her in my arms again, my face nestling in her hair. "But, I will try to find your answer, Emma. I will enlist a few close friends in my... no, *our* attempt to resolve this predicament." While my lips caress her hair, my mind wonders, "If she can be changed back, will I be able to live with a human and be satisfied in all ways?" I admit I have not met any other vampire who fell in love with a mortal who wished to maintain his or her humanity. The individual was always receptive to living forever and longed for this life with their chosen mate. What makes Emma different?

I shrug off my worry and focus on the present. "In the meantime, you must stay close to me. Francisco must believe you are mine. Otherwise, your existence is in jeopardy. Do you understand?"

Her nod against my chest answers my appeal.

"Good. Now. You must allow me to spend the night with you."

When she pushes away with a withering look, my lips curl into a smile. "I promise I will not take advantage of the situation. I will simply retire next to you in your bed. It is all for show, Emma. If Francisco decides to drop into my subconscious, he will observe our closeness. That should appease him for now."

Her gaze scans me head to toe as if remembering our tryst in the shower. Hopefully, she is reliving the touch of my hands, the warm flow of desire she experienced, and the orgasm that captivated her body.

In answer to *her* scan, I feel a throb beneath my slacks and my body thrums in desire. How much longer must I wait? If I was not already dead, I would be dead by now. Of course, that is a mere figure of speech.

"Fine. If that suits you and your maker, then by all means sleep next to me. Just… don't try anything, alright? I want to wait until every leaf has been overturned, every avenue scoured." Her pursed lips stall before she continues. "Now, if you don't mind, I want to take a shower to wash off this day. Do whatever you want to do. I'll be out in a few minutes."

With that, the lovely brunette strides to the bathroom and closes the door behind her. I toy with the idea of joining her, but decide to leave her alone with her nightly rituals.

Once I secure the door, I discard my clothing down to my briefs, grab the remote, and turn on the television, which is a total waste of time. The news is out. Silly sitcoms as well. Tried and true dramas are my thing. I search and find years-old episodes of *Law & Order*. When the face of Lenny Briscoe appears on the screen, I settle into the bed and wait for my love.

She joins me halfway through the episode, does not utter a word, but grins and lays in bed beside me facing the opposite direction, curled into a ball. My hand reaches out to caress her, but I withdraw it before I touch her skin. I wait until her breathing is slow and rhythmic before I switch off the television and curl behind her.

CHAPTER 13

EMMA

I wake slowly and stretch my legs and arms, not surprised in the least when no resistance pushes back. I ran track in high school and my body required I stretch after each event to ward off inevitable cramps. Of course, that isn't necessary now.

My mind slowly gathers images captured from last night's run: the sights and sounds from the city I used to love. I did walk some, but only after I ran into… That's when I realize I'm not alone in my bed. My head twists quickly and glimpses the sleeping hunk next to me. I inhale deeply to quiet the panic that rises.

Zach stretches out behind me, soft black waves of hair spread haphazardly across his forehead. His full lips, slightly parted, tip upward in warm greeting. The longer I peruse his body, the deeper my breaths become. His handsome features lure me to kiss him, but I don't dare. It will lead to corrupting the one possession that's still mine alone. Until I know for certain no one can correct the dilemma I've experienced, I will hold onto hope and give myself to the man who will be with me throughout my human lifetime. Since that doesn't appear to be the man resting next to me, I turn away from him. Cold water splashed on my face should do the trick. However, before I'm able to rise, his hand grabs my forearm to stall me.

"Do I get a good morning kiss before you run away?"

"Zach, I…"

Words catch in my throat as I choke out that reply. How I want to say yes. Damn, I want him to be the man for me, but I still can't wrap my mind around what I've become. Even with all the advantages and enhancements, I've lived as me for the past ten years, except for the blood, and hold onto the hope someone can make me human again. It's all that drives me most days, and if I cave now I won't be able to forgive myself later.

Instead of succumbing to his request, I wrench my arm free and dash into the bathroom. My gaze lowers from the mirror when I clasp the counter top. I count to ten in an attempt to calm my breathing. That's supposed to work, right?

The door to the bathroom opens and I spin around as Zach marches in. "Do not run from me, Emma. I will not harm you. I promised. Remember?"

If I hadn't indulged in a Velvet Crimson last night, I would have an excuse for the tingling in my body. Is this pull his power over me? Him being my maker and all? I will my body to keep a distance from him, but the longer I stare into his eyes, the more the tingling radiates throughout me.

My chest heaves when I push away from the counter and stroll right into his arms. My fangs elongate while quivering shakes my body head to toe. I want to stop myself, but the draw is deep. Arms surround my shoulders and hold me close. I reciprocate and tug our bodies closer together until his hard abs caress my stomach through my nightgown, and the bulge in his shorts expands until it throbs against my pelvis.

My desire is strong, my willpower weak. Plus, there's something about the way his hands float up and down my back caressing me, holding me to him, that generates a thrum in my body. Oh, how easy it would be to lead him back to the bed and share the wondrous experience he's referred to.

Zach discards his briefs then bends to pick me up. My legs instinctively circle his waist which also exposes my legs. And with no underwear on, we're skin to skin when I nestle against his stomach. The cool temperature of his body puckers my folds and I draw a deep breath when a desire to sink my teeth into his neck surfaces. My nipples harden and push against the flimsy material of my nightgown, which tortures them more. When his lips connect with my neck, my head tilts to the side to allow him better access and I slurp in a heavy breath when I feel fangs scrape across the tender skin. He doesn't sink them in, he merely reminds me of the possibility.

The man holding me turns from the doorway and carries me to the bed, deposits me there, and slowly moves to cover my body with his own. Resting on his forearms, his face is only inches from mine. My gaze connects with his before his hand touches me. This is Zach. This is the man, or creature, or whatever, who I have loved for a decade. Why am I afraid to give in to him? He told me he would not take what isn't his without permission. Damn. Why can't I let him?

My eyes close. His breath across my face, while he pushes my hair back, sends shivers up and down my spine. If he doesn't touch me soon...

As if reading my mind, what feels like a finger traces circles around one of my breasts. His hand continues down my body until it grasps my nightgown hem and gently pulls it up to my waist, exposing me in all my naked glory. Zach's lips fall to mine in a sensual kiss. Longing for more, I squirm beneath him and attempt to align with his erection. I want him to take me. I've never wanted anything so much before and realize it's about to happen. However, before he pushes into me, his fingers tease my tender flesh first.

Why? What's holding him back? Isn't this what he wants? What we both want now?

My thoughts are waylaid the moment one of his fingers pushes through my folds and taps around inside me, which arcs my back from the bed.

"Zach..." my breathless retort goes unnoticed while the man on top of me pursues his exploration.

Fangs graze my neck again. His tongue whips out and gathers something moist on my skin. Did he nick me? Am I bleeding? I want to stop him and check, but I'm too far under his spell to care. My heavy swallow brings his lips back to mine in a passionate kiss. His free arm circles under me and, together, we roll until we're side by side, while his fingers continue their torture.

When my eyes open, I pull away from his chest and look at the immortal beside me. His eyes open, too, and I observe his irises have turned black Not dilated. Black. Through the fog of my need I realize I *hadn't* imagined the change in his eye color before. It signals desire.

"You must decide, Emma. Will it be now or shall I wait? It is your decision my love. I promised..."

His words, sincere in their meaning, tear away the fabric of my resistance. I want him to make love to me, I need to experience what the books I've read referred to as "euphoric." Hopefully, he'll take it easy on me since this is my first ever...

Still reluctant, my gaze scans his while I determine how best to respond. Will it really make a difference if I wait? Will the human man who might marry me care if I'm not pure? While I ponder my decision, an unexpected tear leaves my eye and drips onto the sheet.

Zach's hands stop their pursuit and he grasps my shoulders. "Emma... we do not have to do this now. I promise I can wait until you are completely sure this is what you want, that I am who you want to spend your existence with."

His blackened eyes clear to dark blue again. Do my eyes blacken, too? I've never asked. Before those words flow from my mouth, Zach pulls our bodies closer so his forehead touches mine, while I attempt to assimilate our actions.

After a deep breath, Zach pushes my hair from my face and endeavors to smile. "It is clear you are not ready. We will table all discussions of our mating until you are comfortable discussing it further. Deal?"

Another tear escapes my eye when I nod. Oh, how I want to continue. However, Zach, being the gentleman he is, wills himself to wait. He doesn't charm me, he doesn't push the issue. His love must be true if he's willing to give me all the time I need.

My face burrows against his chest and I whisper, "I'm sorry."

One of his hands strokes my hair while his breath flows across it. "I understand your dilemma. Until all rocks are overturned, until every lead has run dry. I will wait for you, my love. I will wait."

I can't help myself. I snuggle closer and am wrapped in the comfort of his arms. Time stands still for a few moments while I attempt to organize my thoughts.

"Zach, you mentioned you didn't want to live in Francisco's circle any longer. Is it because of how the others live, or is it solely because of me?"

He releases me and leisurely spins out of bed. "We need to talk, but somewhere else, Emma. I do not feel comfortable in this room. Take your shower and meet me downstairs in forty-five minutes."

I raise up on my elbow and gape at him. "Really? Why not here?"

He bends to kiss me, then reminds me. "Too many spies around. Maybe a camera or microphone hidden in your room? I do not want to take the chance." Even though whispered, I hear his words clearly.

My lips burn from his brief contact and I nod my understanding. "I'll meet you in forty-five minutes."

Zach dresses quickly and stands at my door ready to leave. "Do not be late." With a wink and an air kiss, he leaves me laying across my bed, while my desire ebbs slowly. I roll to my back and sigh.

"Decisions, decisions, decisions." Since I'm not getting anywhere laying around, I crawl to the edge of the bed, place my feet on the ground, and stand. "And, shower alone it is."

While standing under the streaming water, my mind rocks me with, *Do you really wish he'd stayed?*

As promised, Zach sits in the same chair he occupied the first time I saw him in this hotel. This time, he's dressed more casually in a long-sleeved navy-blue sweater and a pair of khakis. I'd say, "Wow," but he already knows how smitten I am with him. I've gotta say that vampire is trying to push all my buttons.

I stroll closer and catch a twinkle in his eyes when he sees me. I'm surveyed head to toe as well and tingle from the goofy grin on his face.

"Why, Mr. Matthews. How nice to see you again. Have you been waiting long?" My purse, clutched tightly in front of me, swings side to side, along with my hips, while my lips match his grin.

He stands and reaches for my hand. "Come, dear Emma. Time for breakfast."

I follow beside him and am surprised when he leads me toward a black Audi A6 with highly tinted windows.

"Is this yours?" I climb in through the opened door. It has that new car smell. After he's seated with his safety belt buckled, I watch the instrument panel light up as the vehicle roars to life.

"It is a rental, but similar to my car at home." Zach drives us away from the JW Marriott and heads northeast.

The cityscape changes to residential the farther away from downtown we travel. I look out the side window and observe tall green trees in full bloom, rustle in the morning breeze. Memories of my home and family invade my mind and torture me again. I continue to stare out the side window and force them away. I need to focus on the creature next to me right now.

Additional recollections from our high school days filter through my mind as we speed toward whatever destination he's chosen this morning. One in particular was of a day we decided to cut class and drove to one of the city parks to play tennis. Luckily, my racket was in my school locker. It was a spur of the moment decision, but I didn't care if I got caught. I was with him, the basketball player every girl in my class wished belonged to her. And he asked *me*. I'd played before, but Zach seemed proficient, so much so he helped me with my grip and swing. He stood close behind me, grasped my wrist, pulled the racket back, and followed my arm forward until the racket was over my left shoulder. He was so close, I could have kissed him. I didn't, but I wished I had.

Next, he tossed balls from the other side of the net for me to hit. After a few minutes, my swing improved, but unfortunately one return hit him in the head. He fell to the court instantly as if he'd been injured. I rushed to my instructor and, by the time I reached him, his laughter filled the air. He was so easy to please. I somehow brought sunshine and happiness into his often-somber existence. Those were the days I felt close to him, the days I cheered him up. He never discussed his sadness, but it continually flowed beneath the surface.

We had to run for the car when the clouds opened up and pelted us with rain. But it was a lovely couple of hours, especially since he held my hand while driving all the way back to school. I always wondered why we didn't formally date. We spent time together, mixed within a group or, sometimes, just the two of us. But, for some reason, he never asked me to go cruising on Friday night, or out to dinner, or even to an evening movie. Subsequently, I didn't date either. My time with him was more than enough for me.

Many long-forgotten memories of the times we studied and shared ideas throughout our senior year flow through my mind. Could I be happy existing with Zach as my instructor and lover now? Is it really possible to charm my parents enough so I can visit without threat of disgust or hate? If so, can I shove my human life into a chest, close the lid, and lock it away in order to move forward in this new existence with him? After ten years of torturing myself, maybe it's time to accept what I am, learn all I can about myself and my kind, and find a way to be happy with my decision.

If it was only that easy.

I stare at the creature driving and hope he doesn't observe my perusal of him. He's so handsome. Black hair falls in wisps across his forehead, his temple glistens in the morning sunlight, a smile curls his lips, and that long slender kissable neck. My incisors elongate while I focus on his neck where skin, hidden beneath his shirt, covers his shoulder. Desire to do more than kiss that area shoves its way into my mind again. I turn away when my breath hitches in my throat. To appease my yearning, my hand reaches across the console to caress his thigh. When his hand covers mine, a tingle begins when he flips my hand over and draws circles in my palm. It expands up my arm and then throughout my body. I should pull my hand away, but I can't or don't want to. When my head lolls against the back of the seat, my eyes close.

Ten years I've wanted nothing more than to become mortal again. Ten tortuous years living away from my family and friends, hiding what I am. Ten years… it's nothing but a drop in the bucket in the lifespan of a vampire.

His fingers curl around my hand and squeeze, which opens my eyes. I catch his quick peek in my direction and grin in return.

Is it possible, after spending four days at home and a minimal amount of time with him, I've experienced a change of heart? I almost laugh at that thought. Heart. I suppose I have one. It just doesn't operate the same way any longer. Anyway, the reason I returned was to find out who changed me and ask to be changed back. I found out who, but with no current possibility of becoming mortal again, maybe it *is* time I accepted my fate… for now. I draw a deep breath, expel my fears, and resolve to try. My focus returns to the man, or rather, creature driving. I also resolve to stay by his side, to be his life-mate, since that appears to be my destiny.

A slow smile spreads across my face in understanding. Even if I was changed back, my life would not be without pain and heartache. I could possibly fall ill with some terrible disease, or be killed in an automobile accident, or just die of old age one day, alone. What's ahead for me now is the promise of new horizons to explore, touring the world with all its wonders, and enjoy the sun on my face during the day and twinkling stars at night for centuries. My mind bubbles with excitement. I've spent the past ten years wishing my life away, waiting for a miracle to change me when my miracle sits next to me in this car.

My hand squeezes his back. His slight head turn and resulting smile comforts me.

"What?" His lips curl in amusement.

"Um... First, where are you taking me?"

"I thought I would surprise you and revisit one of our high school haunts. Remember the pancake place along Pendleton Pike?"

"Kind of. Is that where we're headed?"

"Yes." His head briefly turns toward me again. "Is that all you wanted to know? I sense something more important brewing in you."

How can he tell? Am I that easy to read?

"What do you mean?"

His lips purse. "Your mind churns with questions."

I glance at him when I remember our link. Memories of our evening in the shower burst forward and I would blush, if it were possible.

Zach chuckles. "Our minds *are* linked, Emma. I can sense your thoughts."

My brows furrow. "Can others see into my mind?"

That's frightening!

"As your maker, your blood resides in me. So, I am the only one. Not even Francisco has that ability."

Almost under my breath, I mutter, "*That's* a good thing." With a slight head shake, I turn back to Zach. "So, is that everything?" I may as well ask since he appears open to sharing information with me.

My maker's gaze stays focused on the road ahead as we maneuver through heavy traffic on our way across town. "Well, because we can charm people, if someone reacts to us in a negative way, we have the ability to alter their perception to our benefit."

My head spins toward him. "Is it that easy, this 'charming?'"

"For us, yes. It makes our lives easier, Emma. For instance, during the prom, Michelle threw a fit because I danced with you. Instead of allowing her to continue her rampage, I simply suggested we leave early." He shrugs. "You had left the gym and I wanted to find you. It was easier to take her home than deal with her tirade."

Another scare races through my mind. "Francisco can charm me too, right?"

"I am afraid so."

My head bobs. "Okay. Best if I stay away from him then." I already dislike how Zach reacts when he talks about his maker. Will I feel the same? My head turns away from the physician again and I stare out the side window, worry forcing its way into my mind.

When his hand grazes my shoulder, I'm taken by surprise and jerk in my seat.

"Just wondering where you went." His voice doesn't question why. But, I have to answer.

"Francisco. You're certain he can't read my thoughts?"

My friend blinks a couple of times stalling his reply. "Francisco changed me more than two hundred years ago. He has the ability to drop into my thoughts whenever he chooses, but it stops with me. Now. If he were to drink my blood again or if he drank from you, that would be a different story. Only then could he read yours as well. I plan to never allow him the pleasure of either scenario."

The way he speaks of his maker, the tone of his voice, the quick lick of his lips. It appears he doesn't trust him.

"Then, can I say something and ask you to think it over before you answer me?"

His gaze darts to me and back to the road in an instant. "Why are you worried?"

He's doing it again, he's reading me.

His audible sigh makes me laugh. "I'm sorry. I've never had anyone *read* me. It'll take some getting used to."

Zach turns his vehicle into the parking lot for Pete's Pancakes and pulls into an open spot. Once he turns off the car, he shifts in his seat to face me. "Sorry. It feels strange to discuss this with you." He swallows and tries again. "It is not so much that I can read your mind. Sometimes it is the way you speak, the dart of your eyes, your hands clutching at nothing in your lap."

I nod at his admission.

"So, tell me, Emma. What has you concerned this morning?"

"You. Us." I draw a deep breath to continue. "Zach. I've, ah, changed my mind."

When his brows raise up and his lips turn down, I smile to ease his anguish. "No, I'm not running away, Zach. I'm running to... you.

I've existed these past ten years striving to find someone to change me back. Someone who apparently doesn't exist. Yet here you sit, without a second thought, asking me to be your life-mate for all eternity. I realize I have much to learn, but I want to learn, Zach. From you. I want to share my existence... with you."

I barely get the last words out before he leans across the console, grasps my face in his hands, and presses his lips to mine in a passionate embrace. That mouth, the kiss... I swoon against him when the tingling erupts in my toes and flares into my core moments later.

He backs away first. When my eyes open, I see the length of his fangs for the first time up close in the daylight and wonder why my neck doesn't have large scars where he first bit me. Maybe he'll bite me again and I'll find out. The thought that maybe he'll allow me to bite him races through again.

Surprise at my thoughts drags me away from him. I've never wanted anything so much in my life than to sink my teeth into his neck, or thigh, or...

"Emma... we should go back to the hotel. I want to make you mine, my love, for all eternity."

When his eyes open, his black irises appear sinister to me. Plus, his lips curl back to expose those fangs again. However, the gentle flow of his words coax and sooth me. I gulp back the anxiety and gather strength from the understanding I am the same as him.

While I ponder this thought, my date night with Steph creeps into my mind. If what he mentioned before is true? That we should expect a couple of days to...

I spit out quickly, "I have plans for tonight, Zach. I'm dining with Steph and her son, Tray. I promised I'd be there around five, and then tomorrow night all the girls are going out, and..."

My potential lover slides back against the car door, his hand grazing the back of his neck. "When, then, Emma?"

My gaze skates through his. "I'm not leaving until Friday. We could, um, get together tomorrow night after I return from the evening out. Or?" Another thought drifts in. "Why don't we return to Arizona Thursday? When are you expected at work?"

Zach reaches for the car door, pushes it open, and strolls to my side. When he opens my door, his hand reaches for mine. "We should eat first before we discuss this further."

I step out into his arms and rest my head against his shoulder. His scent infuses me with memories from high school. Days we spent laughing, talking, studying. My arm circles his waist and we walk, side by side, into the crowded restaurant, all talk of mating left behind in the car.

Lynne Anders

CHAPTER 14

ZACH

Emma and I drive away from Phoenix Sky Harbor Airport with our bags secured in the trunk of her car, our conversation light throughout the drive between Blue Sky Parking and her home in Buckeye. The beauty next to me asked me to drive so she could rest. I imagine that is partly due to our discussion last night. Anxiety surges through me as well. Images eddy through my head of our impending coupling. I turn up the volume on the radio and listen to the local country-western station to ease the swirling visions occupying my mind. Not good. The current song playing speaks of long-lost love and taking it to the next level. Emma, already able to interpret my moods, switches it off and places her hand on my knee to relax me. Relax me! I cover her hand with mine and heave a sigh.

My thoughts turn to how I intend to pursue her in bed. My experiences have been fairly limited. However, I did have one lover, decades ago, who taught me what females desire. Sharing them with my life-mate delights and troubles me now. Will she be receptive to my techniques? Will she acclimate easily into our lifestyle? I thought I was prepared for tonight. After last night's discussion, I am not.

The decision to leave early proved to be the best solution for us. Actually, Francisco's constant badgering left me no other choice. He threatened to travel to Indianapolis and complete the task himself if I had not by the end of the week. My desire for my young vampire has grown substantially these past few days. Losing her to that monster... I cannot allow my mind to tumble with those thoughts. He could be lurking, ready to push me aside in his quest for my Emma.

Thankfully, she had already agreed. I peek toward her now and notice her head resting against the seatback with her eyes closed. Is she thinking of later and how we will proceed? My beautiful girl. This will be her first time. I must take my time to ease her into this life with me. Knowing she desires me quells some of my anxiety. It *is* half the battle.

My gaze turns toward her again. "Do we need to stop anywhere first?"

Her head turns to the side to face me and I stare into her unblinking eyes. "Um, you told me already that we, ah, utilize a lot of energy in our..." I hear her gulp.

"Mating?"

Hands folded in her lap, her head pushes against the back of the seat, and a shy smile curls her lips. "Yes. So, do we need to purchase a Velvet Crimson or two for, um, after?"

My gaze switches back to the road to hide my delight before I respond. Although she still appears embarrassed discussing our coupling ritual, she is thinking about it. Since I do not wish to add to her nervousness, I shove my desire deep inside me and answer in a composed voice.

"We will. It is thoughtful you asked. What restaurant is close to your home?" We will not actually require Velvet Crimson after we mate. I decide to withhold that piece of the puzzle for now.

Her eyes close again. When her answer is not forthcoming, I begin to worry. Does she regret her decision? She must know I can fully protect her once we become one.

"Emma?" She is much too quiet.

"I'm here. Just thinking... The best place will be the Burger King on Watson. It's close to my home."

"Is the address in your GPS?"

Emma and I drag our suitcases into her single-story home a little after eleven on Thursday morning, June fourteenth. Though I had mentioned I had met some of her circle throughout the years and also kept track of her, I pretend this is my first time inside her home. I decide to tell her later that I, more or less, stalked her for the past decade.

After we deposit our bags near the front door and place the two drinks purchased in the refrigerator, she shows me through the living areas and the first two bedrooms. Her home is decorated in true Arizona style with shades of brown encompassing everything, with a splash of burgundy in her drapes and pillows.

We walk through the door into the master suite. She has interspersed personal photos of her childhood and siblings on top of bookcases and tables to remind her of her human life.

"This is where I spend most of my time when I'm at home. I love to sit in bed to read, or watch TV, or just relax. The rest of the house is mostly for show." Her quiet laugh enthralls me.

My dear, sweet girl. You transfix me with the delicate trill of your voice. My eyes close and I inhale her scent, which further embeds her in my psyche. It is time.

I stand behind her and clutch her shoulders. "Emma." I spin her slowly to face me and draw her face up so she looks directly into my eyes. Her body trembles slightly as my fingertips trace a pattern from her shoulder to the skin of her graceful neck. Her eyes remain unblinking when I lower my lips to hers. She yields to me instantly. I slowly wrap her in my arms. She steps closer to me and does the same. How gentle her embrace.

With my eyes closed and my lips pressed into her hair, I whisper words I have kept buried inside me to the woman I intend to spend my existence with.

"Emma, I have waited almost two centuries for you. Waited an eternity for the one who completes me. My body quivers with its desire for you. Do you feel it? Feel the draw, the raw passion brewing beneath the surface?" I clasp her hand and draw it to my chest. "You must know that I cherish everything that you are. Your gentle nature, your inquisitive mind, and especially the golden flecks that sparkle your eyes, promising me the world." I lower my lips to her neck and place a gentle kiss beneath her ear. "Promise to stay with me through all this existence brings to us. Allow me to love you with reverence and compassion. Trust that I will always place you first, position your wellbeing above anything and everyone else in this life. Be mine, my Emma. For to lose you would end me."

My fingers draw her face up and I press a sweet kiss against her lips. She does not speak. However, her smile and the tears flowing gently against her cheeks speak volumes. When her head lays against my chest, I hug her to me as if there is no tomorrow.

Emma. My Emma. Is this truly happening?

After a moment or two have passed, the slow thrum of my body jolts me back from my reveries. Desire swarms through me. I need to make her mine.

My fingers locate the top of her dress and slide the zipper slowly down. The clasp of her bra snaps open when my fingers glide past. While I taste her mouth, my fingers explore her back. The texture of her skin is a soft distraction of silk. My body thrums heavily with yearning solely from the feel of her.

I must remind myself this is Emma's first experience making love with a man, let alone with a vampire. I will not rush her. I will lose her if I do. I must explain every move, and why, for her to understand the reason she must give of herself as I must give to her.

Emma draws closer to me and clasps the nape of my neck in her hands, while her mouth asks for more. I want to fulfill that need as much for myself.

Images of our coupling consumes my mind while desire floods my senses. I long to run my tongue along the peaks and valleys of her body, savoring her nectar, and take her to that exclusive mental chamber, visited only by mating vampires, while I am encased inside her. Before I completely lose control, my tongue departs her mouth and I step back to look at her. Before I have the opportunity, she pushes the cloth from her shoulders and stands before me in panties and black high-heeled shoes. Her skin is magnificent this close up. I have, of course, seen her naked. Once the night of our prom and also from across her room. Sharing the shower that night was fundamentally in black and white and did not showcase her glorious alabaster color. What I see now... my throat constricts.

My fingers flow up her arm, over her shoulder, and down to her perky breasts. She is not what I would consider overly endowed, but when I cup one in my hand, the fit is perfect. Drawn back to the here and now when she moans, her hands clasp my arms to steady her and her head lolls back, inviting me to kiss her neck. I do. However, my fangs extend fully and, if I am not careful, I could nick her. All in good time, I remind myself.

often than not and I will find it difficult to keep from pursing her at all hours of the day. I wish to relish her delicate nature while it lasts.

Her hands clutch the sheet to her chest while her gaze focuses on the place where she drank from me, which healed soon after her fangs withdrew. Her fingertips trail against that area. "I thought I damaged your skin, but it's almost invisible."

My hand grasps hers and I kiss her knuckles. "I told you we heal quickly. There will be no visible scar either."

She nods. "Good to know." Her hand retreats under the sheet again. "Before I explain, please tell me this occurs each time we... um... mate."

Glory be, how delightful her questions. She would be blushing right now if it were possible. "Yes, it does. Typically, our mating continues for hours, which allows the dreams to diverge during our connection. I decided to take it slow since this was your first time making love with a man, or a vampire as is the case. We will resume once you are ready."

Emma's hand caresses the back of my neck. Her glorious smile heats my blood. "Whenever you're ready..."

Oh, how I want to continue my pursuit of this magnificent creature. However, I wish to hear her description of the time she spent in the chamber with me.

"Soon, sweet Emma. First, please relate the memory which sought you during our coupling."

With a deep breath, she relates experiencing much the same memory as mine, only from her perspective. It heartens me to learn she felt enamored with me much the same as I was with her those first few days. A deep sigh heaves my chest.

While she recounts her thoughts in great detail, my fingertips skim her shoulder, down her arm, and across her belly. When one finger slips inside her, her eyelids flutter.

"Enough, my love. Shall we seek each other again?"

Lynne Anders

CHAPTER 15

EMMA

I awake to a dream. It must be a dream. Zach lies next to me, his eyes closed, a smile gracing his perfect lips. Light, as it filters into my bedroom through drawn drapes, illuminates his long black hair, which is pushed behind his ear permitting me to study his face in close detail. He's beautiful.

Full black eyebrows punctuate his forehead above long eyelashes, which fan his pale cheeks. High cheekbones, a chiseled nose, and those sensuous full lips I wish to devour again. He mentioned yesterday feelings of desire would escalate daily. He's correct. My body longs for his already and it's only been two hours. After two days of our bodies entwined, I'm ready for him to touch me again.

I sigh and close my eyes. I should probably rest, but I don't feel tired. However, Zach did speak of replenishing our energy. One of the side effects from our mating. We're weakened for a time and can become vulnerable to predators if we don't rest enough, especially during daylight hours. I roll to my back and conjure up one of the memories we shared, the one from a field trip we took with Mr. Scott, our teacher, during a botany class. That thought vanishes quickly and is replaced with wonder. How is it we think the same thoughts? It's another question for later today.

Sleep finally surrounds me. My last thought is I didn't call to tell Mother I made it home safely. I must remember to call when I wake.

Darkness and the smell of cinnamon assault my senses when my eyes flutter open. Also, the man of my dreams appears to have left the bed. And he didn't wake me. Is he tired of me already? I rise slowly in case my body objects and find not only am I not sore anywhere, my energy appears to have returned with gusto. I slip out of bed, locate a robe and house slippers, and saunter down the hallway toward the scrumptious aroma.

Zach turns toward me the moment I pass into the kitchen, my smile growing wider with each step I take in his direction.

"Good evening, my love. I hope I am not the reason you woke early." He pours a liquid concoction into a mug and hands it to me.

"What's this?" I sniff and recognize the cinnamon I woke to. I take a sip. It's hot, but not too hot. Umm, cinnamon tea. "You made this for me?"

He turns back for his mug. "Yes, I did. Actually, tea was the only item in your pantry. We should do a little shopping today, Emma. But... maybe not. We must leave for Oceanside, probably sometime later tonight."

"Why? We just returned home," I mention as I slip into a chair. "And, I have to work on Monday."

What's he not saying?

Zach's lips purse with frustration. "Francisco called. He wants to meet you. I believe he wants to confirm our connection." He pulls a chair from the dining table and slips into it. "It is better to get this over with now so we can continue with our lives. And, before you say it, yes, it is important to do as he bids... for now. I also plan to stay behind a few weeks while I relocate my patients to other doctors since I intend to live with you, no matter where it is."

"But, what about *my* job? I can't just run out on them, Zach, or I'll never be allowed to work in the industry again. I have bills to pay, and taxes, and insurance, and..."

"There is no need for worry. Call your supervisor and explain you have had a setback and will be in the following week. Once Francisco has met you, you will be allowed to travel home, but I must stay behind for a time. As I said, I have loose ends to clean up and also pave the way for me to live with you until my maker demands we return."

"I thought we were going to—"

Zach stops me with a glare and shakes his head. "Later." His mind immediately reaches into mine and projects we should not discuss Francisco openly. I nod my understanding.

The moment his mind dislodges from mine, I feel weak. I set my mug down, afraid it may spill if I don't. I gaze up into his dark blue eyes. "An effect from the connection?"

His nod is quick, his lips a firm straight line. "You will grow accustomed to our connection. That will end the weakness." Worry fills his eyes.

Worry about me? I want to take him in my arms and tell him all will be well. We'll work through whatever we need to and find a way to divorce ourselves from his maker once and for all, which conjures up more than one question. I decide to begin with the easiest.

"You haven't explained how we age. Phyllis told me she ages one year with each twenty. However, I haven't changed and you appear to be in your twenties as well. How is this possible?"

He seems grateful. Because I didn't pursue discussing Francisco's circle? He must know how I feel. He is my life-mate now. Whatever Zach needs or requests, I am forever attached to him and will find a way to comply. Just as he professed he'd do for me.

The "young" man of my dreams thinks for a moment and finally answers. "It depends on your maker. Francisco ages slowly. Because he does, so do I and so do you. My belief is we age possibly one year in one hundred. Francisco appears to be in his late forties. He has never divulged his age when he was turned. But, I would say he is more than two thousand years old." Zach stops for another moment. "I also believe when we reach a certain age, we age more rapidly. But, we are stronger and develop additional abilities with age as well. If we live long enough, that is."

"What does that mean?" I take another sip from my tea.

"Predators are everywhere, whether in the form of another vampire or vampire killers. We always must be watchful, Emma. No one is as innocent as they appear."

I allow his words to sink in before I rise and carry my mug to the sink and shiver in understanding. "Well," I turn to face him, "then I suppose there's more for me to learn. I'm thankful I have you as my teacher."

My instructor rises and collects me in his arms. "We will teach each other, my Emma. Now we must pack and prepare to leave tonight. I wish to be home in California before the light of day tomorrow."

Packed and ready to leave by ten thirty Saturday evening, Zach loads our bags in the trunk of my car while I close up my home. My final walkthrough has me in a tither. When I called home to speak with my mom, something felt off. I couldn't put my finger on it and when I asked, she told me I was imagining things, said she loved me, and hung up. She's never been one to talk too much, but this time it was as if she didn't want to speak with me at all. Worried she knows I'm not who I once was, I ponder my next move. A call to my dad at work on Monday will do it. Satisfied with my decision, for the time being, I finish closing the house and join Zach outside.

His arm circles my waist when he leans in to kiss me. "You look pensive. Are you already regretting accompanying me?"

I don't want to hide anything from him. He'd read it in me anyway. "I'm worried about my mom. Something's wrong and she won't tell me what."

He releases me and opens the passenger door. I slip inside and wait for him. Once we are on our way, he muses, "What do you plan to do?"

"I'm going to call my dad on Monday. He has to know what's going on."

We take the Miller Road on-ramp to I-10 West. The GPS redirects us to State Route 85, which leads to I-8, and we settle in for the four-plus-hour's drive to Oceanside. I'm anxious enough sitting next to the immortal driving the car, and jump in my seat when his hand caresses my thigh.

"Talk to me, Emma. Yes, I can read your emotions, but I would rather hear the words."

My hand covers his and I smile when he glances my way. "I don't want to talk about my mom. Can I ask more questions instead?"

"Ask me anything you wish."

First on my agenda is his ability to perform surgery on a human and not be enticed to suck the life blood from his patient. Zach's explanation wows me.

"It comes with age and my desire to heal. I learned early on, with my decision to practice medicine instilled in me, how to curtail my desire. Problems plagued me at the beginning, but it became easier over the years." He chuckles lightly. "Of course, there were those patients I would rather not help and the draw became more difficult to control. My medical oath reminds me, however, I promised to help those who seek my services."

"So, it's possible to control the urge?"

"Yes."

His one word answer stops my next question. There must be more to curtailing the urge than he wishes to explain. I get it. A subject for another time.

Zach and I spend the rest of the drive discussing his past and how I will fit into Francisco's circle. I ask why Phyllis doesn't live in California with the rest of the circle and am told she preferred to remain in Indiana when the rest left for the west coast. He believes it has something to do with her life-mate, who has since perished.

"She was never called to live with the rest of you? How did she escape Francisco's clutches especially if her mate died... again?" Maybe there's a loophole we can also use.

"Francisco's interest in her never materialized. When Thaddeus passed, she, more or less, declined Francisco's offer of security, stating her friends in Indiana would continue to protect her."

"So, you'd have to perish before I can be free of him? I don't think I like that scenario." But, maybe there's another way. I shift in my seat to face him. "When I go back home, I'm going to turn in my notice with the firm. I'll be required to give them at least thirty days to find my replacement and get that person up to speed. In the meantime, while you're with your circle, I intend to find another home for us, somewhere close but not too close to Buckeye. We can figure out where to go from there."

Zach shakes his head. "Francisco will still be able to locate us through our mind-link. He will know before we take the first step away."

"Then you have to figure out a way to block him. Has anyone ever been able to stop their maker from reading their thoughts?"

"Not that I am aware of, but I intend to search for an answer to that question. There has to be a way. And, if Francisco hears I have made those inquiries, I will simply state it has to do with your link with me."

The determination in his voice soothes my worry.

I reach out to clasp his shoulder and am gifted with a slight head turn and smile. "Since he can't read my mind, I won't tell you what I'm up to. Just know whatever I do is in our best interest."

The remainder of our journey, we work on our mental communication skills, building my ability to connect with his. By the time we reach Oceanside, I am comfortable sharing images of thoughts with him. Although it appears easy, I have to remember we're sitting next to each other, not thousands of miles apart.

Zach turns my car into a gated community of townhomes, punches in a code at the box, and rolls through the opening gate. We slowly maneuver around the community until he pulls a remote from his pants pocket, pushes it, and a garage door to the right of us slowly climbs up. Once we're secured in the garage, Zach exits the car and comes around to my side to assist me out.

"Our bags can wait. I want to show you around first."

He leads me around my car and I marvel at the dark grey A6 sitting next to it, so much like the rental in Indianapolis.

"Nice car."

Zach smiles, says nothing, but appears to be a little edgy. I hope it has nothing to do with me, other than how his maker will receive me.

The back door leads us into a utility room, which contains a white washer and dryer set situated on bases. They appear new, as if never used. Does he send all of his laundry out or is his cleaning person so thorough, she makes the appliances sparkle, too?

My question scatters when Zach grabs my hand and draws me into the kitchen, which is considerably larger than mine at home. The sterile appearance, although immaculate in its look, lacks any color with its white cabinets and crystal white granite counter top. Even the appliances and sink are stainless steel. No personal items adorn the room either, not even counter top gadgets or cookware. It appears new, as if he just moved in and hasn't unboxed his favorite utensils.

We don't stop in the kitchen. Zach drags me out through a bay-windowed eating nook and into a large family room equipped with four charcoal-colored theater chairs, with an entertainment unit centered beneath a sixty-inch, or larger, wall-mounted television. Stairs leading to the upper level stack to the right. We ascend to a loft where a full bath occupies the entire right end with three bedrooms accessible from a long hallway. The first, he explains, is a second bedroom, the second an office, and the third the master suite with its own full bath. He spirits me around the room and into the bath to show off his newly-tiled shower enclosure. When I peek inside, my hand floats to my throat. A bench seat, jet sprays on three sides of the enclosure, plus an overhead rainforest shower head conjure up thoughts of us standing in the middle engaged in all sorts of foreplay before I'm pressed against a wall. My head spins to him. Did I think those thoughts or did he place them there? Damn. How will I ever figure out where my thoughts end and his begin?

Zach doesn't acknowledge the inquisitiveness in my eyes and instead checks his watch. "It is almost four. Shall we unpack and then have a bite to eat before I contact Francisco?" He pulls me from the bathroom, strolls into his walk-in closet, and discards his shoes in favor of slippers.

"Okay, you have to explain," I mention and point toward said slippers when he returns to the bedroom.

He chuckles and looks down. "I typically go barefoot when at home. Something about the feel of the cool tile on the bottom of my feet. However, I thought you would find my behavior strange and decided to wear these."

"What I find strange, Mr. Matthews, is your living quarters. No personal belongings embellish the walls or shelves. No pictures from the past, no art collection, nothing that links you to any sort of humanity. Why is that?" I lower to the bed and wait for him to join me.

My lover sits down in a huff and clutches the side of the bed tightly. His eyes focus somewhere in front of him. "I have a storage unit in another city, a little place called Menifee. Most of my precious pieces reside there in that climate-controlled space. I have hidden them there because I believe Francisco imagines he owns all of my possessions and will come for them one day."

The grim expression on his face worries me yet again about this maker of his. How can Zach live within the circle and be afraid he'll lose everything if he stays? My circle at home doesn't put any demand on me or my things. That's the way it's supposed to work, right? He should feel confident and secure in his existence. So, if *he* feels this way, how am *I* going to fit in? And why doesn't Francisco know about this storage unit? If he dips into Zach's mind, he must have learned of it at some point. There must be more to the mind-link probe I'm not privy to yet.

I clutch his hand and draw it into mine. "We'll find a way, Zach. We'll be free from Francisco and his minions, we'll find the perfect place to live, and be accepted in a circle where we'll be considered equals."

His head slowly turns to me and a smile creeps out. "Yes, my Emma. We will find our place." He stands and draws me up with him. "Come. We should eat. Then I must take you to Francisco. He is not a patient man.

After an antipasto salad, cheese, crackers, and red wine, Zach drags our bags from the car and stows them in the utility room. In the meantime, I check my reflection in a mirror in his downstairs bathroom before our trip to meet his leader.

CHAPTER 16

ZACH

F rancisco's lascivious tone, when he inquired about Emma tonight, boiled my blood. I do not trust that vampire. Oh, he wants more than to meet her. He wants her. I feel it in my bones. However, I smile sweetly at the image of beauty who sits next to me to help her remain calm. I have shared too much on the subject of my maker and now only wish to keep her safe from his clutches.

I turn the car into the long circular driveway of Francisco's opulent home. Lights illuminate the Spanish architecture as I park near the entrance. Before I exit the car, I sit for a moment and remember the first time I experienced the grandeur. Francisco paraded me through his ten bedrooms, all of which were occupied by members of our circle, eight bathrooms, and grounds most mortals would die for. His pool alone is a full-sized Olympic hosting four swimming lanes.

I flinch when her hand graces my thigh. Absorbed in my own thoughts for a moment, I forgot the love of my life next to me.

"Sorry, Emma. I was lost in thought for a moment. Shall we?"

Her tender smile and golden-flecked eyes brim with love. "I'm yours always, Zach. Please remember that tonight."

My breath catches in my throat. My girl read my thoughts, or if not my thoughts, my mood. How is it I found my forever love in this divine creature? But, will she continue to love me once she knows of my past? If she knew I did drink from humans once upon a time when times were different and I was fostered by the brute inside this home… I must hide those images. One day, I will be obliged to relay all of my past to her, but not yet. She is still too young in this life, and knows only what I have disclosed of my past.

I grasp the hand from my thigh and bring it to my lips. "And I am yours. All of me. We should take care of business and then return home. I feel the need to ravish you tonight."

Her eyes brighten at my words. "Clever man. You read my mind." She leans across the console and kisses my cheek. "Ready, my love?"

"Yes." The word holds a promise for so much more.

Emma waits for me to open her door and together we walk the short distance to the entrance into my maker's home, arm in arm. I gaze up at the night sky, overjoyed when I remember the evening I changed her. For one moment, I thank Francisco for prodding me to do so. I clutch her tightly to me, pull her hand to my lips, and kiss her knuckles. My love's gaze meets mine showcasing her sparkling eyes and tender smile. Have I told her enough that I love her? One can never express that sentiment sufficiently.

Before we reach it, the front door swings open and my Spanish leader stands ready to welcome us in. His dark eyes glow with the reflection from the pillar lights, the grin trapped on his face, over the top. The power he exudes, however, worries me the most.

He addresses me first. "Good evening, fair Zachary. It's a pleasure to see you again."

I stand rigid with my life-mate by my side ready for a confrontation while his gaze captures me head to toe. My jaw clenches with his words. I am being reprimanded for living alone in my own home and not holed up in this palace. I have repeatedly explained I live apart from the rest because of my unconventional schedule.

"I apologize for the responsibility my profession places on my time, Francisco. Our prior discussions have been lengthy on this subject. Until I retire, I must service my patients to the best of my ability. Demand would not be so high if I were less of a physician."

"Fair point, my son. Fair point. Now..."

He turns to survey my love. The lust he attempts to hide is not lost on either of us.

"This must be Emma. Please come in, my dear. I'd enjoy showing you around my humble home."

The vampire reaches his hand to my girl, but she holds steady to my arm and almost pulls me in beside her.

"Thank you, Francisco. We'd love to see your home."

We bypass my maker as I accompany Emma inside, my hold steadfast. A heavy swallow, while waiting for his reaction, is the only indication of my concern.

Several members, who I recognize from my circle, occupy the chairs and sofas in the main living room as we close in on the steps leading down. The door closes behind us and the circle leader joins us, standing too close to Emma. When his hand raises to clasp hers, I tug her to me and traipse down the stairs while she observes the view overlooking his pool and gardens. At the bottom, he clasps her arm and almost drags her from me. "Allow me to introduce you to some of *your* family."

Emma releases her grasp on my arm in order to accompany the vampire, and I barely quell the low growl straining my throat. While he makes the circuit of the room, I follow close behind and nod toward my fellow members, while seething inside. The way he introduces my mate to the others... it appears as if she belongs to *him*. I realize the others from the circle acknowledge she is my life-mate, but does he? So as not to cause a fight, I hold my tongue, follow their progress, and watch as he leads her to the opened patio door overlooking his grounds. The ocean view from that vantage point soothes the soul. However, I had planned a particular walk with my girl along the beachfront and he is about to ruin it.

I hasten to intercept them before he leads her down the stairway into the garden. "Excuse me, Francisco. *I* wish to show Emma the beachfront."

Emma smiles sweetly at me and turns to Francisco. "Thank you for introducing me to your family, sir. I believe Zach wants to introduce me to the rest of your property. If you'll excuse us for a time?"

Francisco's grimace hides behind his squinted eyes. "Of course, my dear. Return soon so we can better acquaint ourselves." He bows and returns inside.

Emma and I, arm in arm again, traverse the stairs into the landscaped garden, past the pool, and toward sand and beach. The night air is cool with wind buzzing steadily around us. Neither of us speak. Maybe we need to put some distance between us and the creatures in the house. Or... maybe thoughts for our future consume us and we do not quite know how to express them yet. I chuckle to myself and elect option two.

"Penny for your thoughts, Ms. Christensen." We stop to remove our shoes before venturing into the sand. I tie mine together by the laces and drape them over my shoulder. I offer to carry Emma's so she will continue to hold onto my arm with both hands.

Her sigh rings loud and long. "He almost bruised my arm, Zach. His hold was much too tight for my liking."

"Well, hopefully, you will not be required to submit to his request again. I have done as he asked and brought you to meet him. That should be the end of it until you are required to live in Oceanside with me."

Emma pulls on my arm to stop me, her eyes frantic. "I don't want to live here, Zach. I thought…"

I stop her from talking by placing two fingers gently against her lips. I also shake my head to warn her.

"Once everything in Buckeye has been taken care of, yes, my dear, you will join me full time here in Oceanside. However, if Francisco agrees to some lenience, I will close down my practice for a time, then join you while we acclimate as a couple. It could take us a few weeks, maybe longer. Then we must return to my home here."

My love seems to understand the need to keep our plans to ourselves when she responds.

"You're right, Zach. I wasn't thinking. What you propose does sound appealing, I must say. So, I'll return home within the next day or two and you'll join me when possible?"

I clasp her hands in mine. "Yes. And, I will speak with Francisco before we leave and beg for his approval. Until then, shall we enjoy our stroll along this lovely beach? Then, we should prepare to leave before the sun is fully awake."

Emma and I leisurely walk through the wet sand behind Francisco's home, down toward another jetty, and back before the sun opens for the day.

We stop at the bottom of the stairs and listen as music filters down to us. The ballad is lovely. I collect Emma into my arms and slowly sway back and forth to the soft words of *Brave for You* sung by The xx. Emma lays her head against my shoulder and snuggles closer while the words penetrate our hearts.

"We have danced together twice. However, both times you ran from me. I gather you have decided not to run again, correct?"

Her hand clasps the nape of my neck and when she raises her face to me, those warm brown eyes sparkle with love. "Never again, my love, for I love you more with every breath I take. I promise I will never leave you of my own free will, and I will support and follow you, no matter the path, from this moment forward."

Complete unadulterated love from her. I drink in a quick breath at her admission. "And I, you, my one and only love. No matter the distance, I promise to always return to you."

Our lips meet to fortify our spoken words. I do not aspire to worry her, but somewhere in the back of my mind I realize Francisco will stop at nothing to possess her. She must be assured her safety is my only priority. I will find a way to maintain it, even if it means an end to my existence.

After what I take as an understanding nod, her lips turn down as worry chases through her eyes. I draw her lips to mine again, press as close to her body as possible, and speak to her with my mind. "Do not worry my love. I did not mean to distress you. I believe however, it is time we leave for home."

I sling my arm around her waist to hold her to me. When she reciprocates, it feels as if we are finally one. Our steps are small, our movement slow, as we proceed to the stairs guiding us to Francisco's home. We stop at the top to replace our shoes and to admire the early morning sky one last time before we advance to the open patio door.

When we arrive, Francisco is there to greet us and asks that I accompany him into his study, which leaves my mate alone with his minions. I notice her clenching her hands nervously, but I kiss her cheek and ask her to wait for me. Emma sits next to another female, one who greeted her kindly when introduced. Her name is Nicole, as I recall, and was brought into our circle by Oliver, one of my few friends. He is not in residence this evening and I have to wonder why. Emma nods her okay. Images of reassurance flow from my mind to my love's as I follow my maker into his study.

He closes the door behind me, saunters to the chair behind his massive oak desk, and forcefully plops down. Before I am seated in a chair in front of the desk, he steeples his fingers in front of his face and hisses. "Why did you drag her off, young Zachary? We were acquainting ourselves."

"She is naïve when it comes to the diverse group of personalities that live within this circle. I simply did not wish to intimidate her further tonight. Her circle in Arizona constitutes a few newborns, a young leader, and none have experienced the taste of human blood. At least none that I am aware of. If she is to live within this company, she must be brought in slowly, told how some of us lived decades ago, and earn her trust that we will never choose that path again."

Francisco relaxes back in his chair, his strong hands gripping the arms tightly. He appears to mock me. "You seem to forget I am the leader of this circle, Mr. Matthews, and am far better equipped to teach our fair young vampire the ways of the world than you. I won't demand you leave her in my care tonight, but I will require constant updates on your progress. If I find you lacking, you will be required to turn her over to me. Is that clear?"

His sneer and evil grimace enrage me instead of threaten. How dare he? She is my life-mate and I will never turn her over to him. Not for all eternity. I have watched as he destroyed other young vampires. He taught them the way we used to hunt humans: to feed from them, but not drain them, then force them into slavery to satisfy his hunger. Although that practice is no longer required because of Velvet Crimson, I vow never to allow that vampire to corrupt Emma in such a way. So as not to anger him further, though, I must pretend to acquiesce to his request in order to take my love home with me.

I drain my current thoughts before he reads them and inserts the desire to follow his request. "Perfectly clear, Francisco. I have already begun and wish to continue the process in a place where she feels secure." I shift and lean forward, clasp my hands, and lay out my desire to live in Phoenix with her for a time. By the time I finish, my maker appears satisfied with my plan and has relaxed his stance somewhat.

"Take the time you need to put your practice on hold. Wouldn't want any backlash from patients. You mentioned Emma returns home day after tomorrow to quit her job and that thirty days is the minimum notice she'll give. Why? Don't humans typically give a two-week notice?"

"For most positions, I suppose. However, Emma is the manager of a medical practice. She anticipates a couple of weeks to find her replacement and then a couple more to get that person up to speed. I would say by the end of August, all will be complete and we will return to Oceanside to reside in my home here. I will reopen my practice at that time and she will be prepared to join our circle."

Francisco's face troubles me. His lips form a tight straight line and his eyes are half closed with a sinister glint.

"Why two additional weeks? What requires additional time before you return to the fold, Zachary?"

His question is meant to intimidate me, but my warm smile remains. "She will be working the first four weeks, which does not allot me adequate time to teach her all she will be required to learn. That is why I am asking for seven weeks, Francisco. If it can be accomplished in less, we will return then. However, I will not rush this. She lived alone for ten years and only involved herself with her circle occasionally. We discussed this. She understands what position she will hold when she joins our circle as I am your second-in-command. Her comfort must be addressed first, though. As you know, we can be a testy bunch of vampires at times."

My maker taps his fingertips together while he decides our fate. Over his shoulder, I watch as light peaks through the marine layer across his grounds out to the ocean, which ushers in the new day. I wished to be home by now, and fear my life-mate worries about my well-being while she waits.

When Francisco makes no further comment, I stand to end this charade. "The sun is up, Francisco, and time I take Emma home. If you will excuse me?" Before he responds, I turn my back on him and begin toward the door.

Before I reach it, Francisco is up from his chair and standing in my way. His fangs extended, he sneers, "You are to return by the first week in August, *young* Zachary. If not, no excuse will suffice. Do I make myself clear?"

Threatened by the vampire who changed me, my fangs extend as well. However, I keep them hidden and merely nod.

Satisfied his point has been made, Francisco opens the study door and allows me through.

Emma stands the moment I appear in the living room and joins me on the steps leading out. I clasp her hand tightly in mine. Thankfully, she bids Francisco a good night before we exit his home.

The morning fog has yet to dissipate, which shrouds our visibility during the drive home and adds to our distress. We have not spoken. I do catch a few timid sideways glances, though. Sorry I brought her into this situation, I watch as her concern radiates in the form of shaking hands, which she wrings unfailingly.

It was my maker who pushed me until I did the unthinkable. My maker who prodded me into taking her life... Damn. Who am I kidding? I loved her from the moment I saw her and knew she would one day belong to me. Too upset to continue those thoughts, our path is clearer. We must formulate a plan in the next two days to escape this circle, which also means we could be on the run for centuries. Until I am certain Francisco is not lurking in my mind, I forestall discussing it with her.

Once inside the garage at home, we both exit the car at the same time and amble into the house, me reeling from the aftereffects of my confrontation with my maker. Emma turns into my arms once the door closes behind us.

"What took so long? I thought you were gone, Zach. I thought that... that awful creature killed you." Her words are whispered against my shirt, and when she raises her head, her worried gaze possesses mine.

"I am here, my love. I am here." I clasp her head in my hands and draw her lips to mine, our kiss fueled by the love we share.

Throughout the tender embrace, my mind stirs with elation. No one has ever worried over me before, and what is left of my heart takes flight, soaring to the heavens with joy. To have her so troubled because of me? My mind cries out, *My Emma. She's truly loves me.*

I break our connection and stare into her golden-flecked brown eyes as water pools within them. "No need for tears, dearest. We will find a way out of this dilemma."

She licks her lips and nods. My girl walks out of my arms and with shaking hands, wipes the moisture as it descends from her eyes. She takes a step and stands straighter. "We don't have as much time as we believed, do we?" When she spins to me, it's with authority.

"He wants us back in Oceanside by the first week in August." My gaze follows her as she lowers into a kitchen chair.

She chews on a fingernail. "So, he agreed to the seven weeks. I'd better get a move on." Her gaze flows to mine with determination. "When can I go home?"

The change in her demeanor is obvious. Her words discharge with no emotion whatsoever when moments ago...

"Are you so ready to leave me, my love? I had hoped we would share our bodies again before you return home."

Love shines from her eyes when she speaks. "I was planning what I need to accomplish once I'm there." She stands and reaches her hand to me. "For now, come. Take me away from all the worry and bear your soul to me."

My love and I climb the stairs and stroll arm in arm up to my bedroom.

Lynne Anders

CHAPTER 17

FRANCISCO

I watch as Zachary and Emma depart the confines of my home and chuckle to myself. The audacity of that young vampire. He can't believe the beautiful Emma belongs to him. She's mine. *I'm* the one who forced him to change her ten years ago. *I'm* the one she's meant to exist with throughout all eternity. The sooner he admits it... I won't have to have him killed if he relinquishes his control over her.

I confess when she found out he was the one who changed her, I believed she'd hate him for snatching her humanity. I also believed she'd revel in her new-found existence based upon her inquisitive nature and lust for life. How wrong I was on both counts. I am certain, once she returns to the fold, the young beauty will succumb to my charms and willingly join *me* in this life.

The moment she accepted my hand, when I escorted her through the living room introducing her to our friends, our connection sizzled. If he hadn't followed so closely behind us, Emma most certainly would have chosen to accompany me for an extended tour of my home and into the bedchamber, where we would have connected on an otherworldly plane.

Once they return in August, it will become obvious to him when she does join with me. Emma will rightly assume her place as my life-mate and, together, we will rule our circle. No one will be able to stop us. As for Nadia, she's kept to herself since I admonished her for her foul ways. If her skills diminish with each passing year, as has been foretold, I'll be required to relegate her to the under-chambers for disposal, which is all well and good since Emma will take her place beside me. All in good time, I tell myself. All in good time.

I return to the members of my circle and observe as, one by one, they kneel before me to await my inspection. The risen sun reminds us, however, it's time we rest. My gaze flows to young Nicole, who sits on the extended couch and appears deep in thought. Why is she not kneeling? One has to wonder if she recalls her duty to me. I glide over to her, clasp her chin in my hand, and raise her face to me.

"Dear, Nicole. Why show such disrespect to your leader? Has something occurred to force this impertinence?"

Her body trembles from my touch. Good. Fear separates the leaders from the followers.

"No, my lord. I was contemplating Oliver's return. Do you know when that might be?"

"All I can tell you is he is off on an errand for me and I expect his return imminently. So, if that soothes your distress, please show your leader his due respect." I release her face from my grasp and wait as she kneels before me. I pat the top of her head. "When I hear from Oliver, I will pass on your desire for his return."

"Thank you," she whispers, her head bowed.

I continue my inspection of those who live within the confines of my home as, one by one, they leave for their rooms. Most joined me centuries ago, some decades. I'm proud of the circle I created. They follow me and do my bidding without question.

As I make my way to the rear door, I sigh when the fragrance of Emma assaults my senses. Her essence permeates the air around me. I inhale deeply and close my eyes. I locate Zachary's mind and delve inside. It appears he and Emma are together in the mind chamber at his home. Not wishing to become part of their experience, I pull away and swallow back my desire for the beautiful young female.

How alike my mortal wife, Christine, she is. The same coloring, the same features, eyes that penetrate your soul. If I didn't know better, I'd say she is the reincarnation of Christine, the only woman I ever truly loved. She bore me three sons, all of whom died during the Second Punic War in Ancient Carthage against the Roman Empire. The pain I experienced during those disastrous days consumes me with hate still. Christine died in my arms, fraught with the loss of our children. With no one to console me, I wished for my life to end as well.

It did three evenings later.

I had stumbled out of a din of ill repute that evening, followed by a man who had purchased several drinks for me. I believed him to be the procurer and when he asked if I wanted a better life, I responded I'd prefer to be dead.

The moment I awoke, I knew something inside me had changed. I was no longer heartbroken for my Christine, I was desperate for food. When I surveyed the dank room, I noticed someone had left a container on the floor beside the straw mattress I slept on. I didn't think twice. I inhaled that liquid and immediately experienced a change in my overall disposition. I rose slowly and made my way to the door, ready to vacate this place. It opened into a hallway I recalled. It was the brothel I visited what I believed was the previous night. I sauntered down toward the sounds of hearty laughter and exited into the main gallery. When I searched for the way out, I saw the gentleman who offered me a better life sitting in the middle of the room surrounded by men and women of varying ages and ethnicities. It was if they worshiped this man. They, one by one, offered their hands to him and he patted each.

He looked up from the group and broadly grinned. "Welcome, Francisco. We're happy to have you join us this evening. Come, dear boy. Have another drink to quench your thirst. I will tell you of your new life."

I learned who and what I was from my maker whose name was Alfredo Bianchi. He was from Italy, brought by the Romans to fight in the war. He became a deserter when the opportunity to begin his own circle presented itself. After a time, I promised to marry his daughter, Nadia, and to learn from her the ways of his world. Saddled with a vampire wife to replace the one I lost seemed ominous at first, but I learned to accept her tutelage as well as her loving care.

My maker found his end three centuries ago when the leader of a friendly circle accused Alfredo of raping his life-mate. Justice prevailed when my maker's head was separated from his body after a short investigation. I, being the elder vampire from our circle and his son-in-law, took over the responsibility after avowing friendship with that leader, and have since grown our number to fifty. We are small in comparison but, as with all groups, the fewer the number, the less chance I'll be challenged for leadership. I prefer it this way.

There are but three members who could possibly overthrow me now. One is my young friend, Zachary. That's one vampire I need to watch closely. I chuckle at the thought of him carrying out such a deed, though.

Enough reminiscing. It's time for sleep. My body, still roused from the aroma of Emma, will require the ministrations of Nadia. Hopefully, she's willing this morning. If not, I know of one other who is.

CHAPTER 18

EMMA

The moment I drove away from Zach's home, anxiety consumed me. Seven weeks, maybe less, to find a way to leave Francisco's circle or I don't know what. Zach alluded to that monster injuring or possibly destroying him, which would leave me without my mate and maker, and most likely place me in harm's way as well. Our shared moments in the mind chamber strengthened our connection, but immediately after, I watched Zach's demeanor switch from loving and caring to watchful and pensive. When I asked, all he told me was we'd make it through this.

"What exactly does that mean, Zach? We'll make it through. Make it through and then what? Be on the run the rest of our existence waiting for that creature or his followers to find and destroy us? Isn't there a way we can live in peace without that worry?"

My love led me into his living room and asked me to sit. He lowered to the sofa beside me and clasped my hands in his. "It was not what Francisco said. It was the way he said it. He is attracted to you, Emma. I believe he wants you for himself. He, more or less, admitted that to me while we were in Indianapolis. As I mentioned before, he threatened to whisk you away and make you his if I did not complete the deed. I stalled him until we reached your home. However, if you had denied me, I have no doubt that vampire would have stolen you and completed what he threatened."

How conniving can that creature be?

"I would never go with him, Zach. He's… disgusting, if you want my true opinion. I'd rather die than become associated with him in any way."

Zach's expression changes before me. His eyes darken, his fangs elongate, and his lips curl into a sneer. "I will fight him to the death to save you. I promise you, Emma, I will never let you go."

My maker pulls me against him and kisses me with pure lust. My hand gravitates to the back of his neck to secure our intimate embrace, my lips giving as much as I get. My body quivers with need even though it has been only hours since our last tryst. Understanding this will be the last intimacy we'll share until he follows me to Buckeye, I surrender to him and allow the vampire beside me to take full advantage of me.

Pushed down onto the sofa, my panties are ripped away, my dress shoved well above my waist, and without a thought or care, Zach plunges deeply into me to my welcome relief. My back arcs at the sudden invasion and I gulp in air to steady my breaths. Our fueled desire exists on a different level this morning, though. I don't desire to bite him, I only wish to pleasure him.

With each of his strokes, my body hums with longing for our coupling to never end. I draw his face from mine and stare into the blackness of his eyes. With his mouth opened and his fangs exposed, he pants greedily.

Zach studies me for a few moments, licks his lips, and snarls, "Emma" before his eyes close and he devours my mouth again.

On the brink of an orgasm for the first time outside the mind chamber, I don't know what to expect. I sense a tingling in my lower torso. The fast thrusts from my partner force it to spread outward through my body until I feel on fire and can't hold back. The powerful surge arcs my back again, my fists clutch his shirt tightly, and at the peak, I scream his name.

Zach's rapid thrusts continue throughout my orgasm. Just before his release, his back bows, his head falls back, and his hands clasp my breasts so tightly I feel they might twist off. Thankfully, he releases both before his assault becomes too unbearable.

A smile finally surfaces on his face as we come down from the high. "I do not recall a time when all I wanted was an intimate sharing. It has always been about feeding and sex. This, my Emma, was pure pleasure. Tell me. What did you experience?"

All of our lovemaking has been new to me so I don't know how to respond at first. While his labored breathing eases, I glimpse a new side of this young immortal I'd not witnessed before. His features appear serene, his body relaxed. If I didn't know better, I'd believe he was human.

My fingers tangle in his hair and I draw his face closer to mine. "This is all new to me, Zach. I thought every time we shared this connection, we fed. I didn't feel that. Why?"

The handsome man above me lowers and rests on his arms, effectively encasing me below him. "I always thought mating led to feeding as well. This was definitely one for the ancients to explain." His lips brush against mine. "I enjoyed it. Immensely. I think, however, it is partly because we spent so many hours feeding from each other these past two days... Maybe because our bodies did not require blood this time?"

My gaze searches his. Maybe he's correct. However, something in the back of my mind tells me no, it is more than that. But, without the knowledge or explanation from others of our kind, I accept his offering and smile into his eyes.

"You're probably right." I heave a sigh. God, I don't want to leave, but... My fingers outline his swollen lips. "I have a long drive ahead of me, alone I might add, so I'd rather reach my home before the light of day, sir." I ask him to allow me up so I can reassemble my costume and be on my way.

After gazing into my eyes one last time, he pushes himself up and pulls me along with him. I replace my slightly damaged panties while he zips his slacks. My dress falls back into place and I tiptoe to the bathroom. When I come out, Zach is on the phone.

"Yes, Angela. We must assess all current patients, place those who cannot wait for my return with Dr. Bartholomew, and advise the rest my practice is on hold for one month. If anyone chooses to relocate to another doctor, so be it." Silence while he listens. "Yes, you and the rest of the staff are being asked to take a leave of absence as well. I apologize, but something important has come up that I must address immediately. I will return to the office tomorrow and promise to cover our existing appointments for the next two weeks. Any future appointments must be handled by Bartholomew." Silence while he listens again. "I have no surgeries scheduled. I will notify the hospital as well."

Zach turns to me when he hears my approach. He reaches for my hand and clasps it tightly, then returns to his call. "I will be more than happy to sign a letter of recommendation for you and any other member of our staff. I am sorry to lose you, but I also understand you need to work. Have them ready in the morning. Possibly when I return, you will reevaluate your situation."

I hug his arm to me. When his arm circles my waist, I drape my arms around him, too.

"Good evening, Angela. I will see you in the morning."

Zach closes his cell phone and places it on the counter. "Well, step one underway. Now... is your bag in the car? Do you need anything before you leave me alone to wonder how you are?"

His cheerless tone saddens me.

"You'll know every move I make, sir, just as I'll know most of yours. But tell me, Zach, why didn't you go into your office today? It is Monday after all."

"Since I was scheduled to return Thursday, I allowed myself the weekend to recuperate and the extra day just in case you returned with me. I preferred not to leave you alone after only three days."

For some reason, I don't quite buy that story. I leave it for another time, though. "Well, I guess I should be on my way. Walk me out?"

Zach and I enter his garage to say our final goodbyes. Once the car door is opened and my bag thrown in the back seat, he kisses me long and hard.

My lover pushes my hair away from my face and studies it. "Drive safely. If you have any problem, contact me. Depending on where you are, I can reach you in under two hours. Understand?"

I feel like crying, but I don't want to leave him with tears in my eyes. I don't want this to be goodbye, either. But, I also realize I have to find and hire my replacement before he joins me in a couple of weeks. So he doesn't see water build in my eyes, I quickly kiss his nose.

"I understand completely. I'll contact you as soon as I'm in the door. Miss me, Zach. I'm going to miss you every moment of every day." My lips curl into an impish smile and my eyes relay more than my words. "I enjoyed our time together."

When he snickers, I slap his arm. "For a vampire, you certainly have a one-track mind. Not just in bed, silly. All of it. The long walks, the ocean, learning my way around Oceanside. It's a beautiful place to live. Makes Arizona drab in comparison."

"Well, once you quit your position, returning becomes the next issue we must face." He pulls me closer and hugs me hard. "I will not rest until you are safe in my arms again. Promise me you will be watchful. Promise me we will talk every night." He draws back and stares unashamedly into my eyes. "I love you, Emma. More than you know."

Now, I definitely don't want to leave, but I know I must. "I love you, too, Zach."

With one final kiss, I slip into my car and begin the long drive back to Buckeye. When day turns to night, the sky does little to dispel the dread. No clouds visible, the stars should have twinkled their way into my soul to ease my dismay. When that doesn't occur, I switch on the media player and listen to one of my favorite playlists and daydream of the one I had to leave.

Early Tuesday afternoon, June nineteenth, I place a call to my office to inform them of my return. After I explain my situation to the head nurse, I am asked to contact a placement agency to commence the process and to report first thing in the morning to speak with the doctors. Her attitude leaves me in a dither. Amber was always cool toward me, but today she is downright rude. I apologize a second time and promise I'll stay long enough for my replacement to be brought up to speed. I also advise I'll be available for a few weeks after to answer any questions that arise.

With my first task handled, I decide to check the local listings for rentals in Chandler and Ahwatukee. They are approximately sixty miles from my current home. I figure we can get lost in a residential area, hopefully for a few weeks, while we decide where to go. I recall what Zach had told me about cameras and possible listening devices in my hotel room in Indianapolis. With the possibility of gadgets in my home, I change into running clothes and seek out the local library for my research.

Another area called Sun Lakes lies south of those areas. Most are fifty-five and older communities, but I locate a couple of rentals that would work for us on a short-term basis. I pull my phone from my backpack.

"My dear, this is the time of year we normally cannot rent these units. You know, because of the heat," the Realtor says. "But, since you and your husband are searching for a new location, maybe we are the best solution for you. You know, because we're centrally located. Easy access to the Valley and to Tucson. When would you like to view the unit?"

"I have a few things to take care of tomorrow, but I could come this evening if you're available." The sooner I find us a place, the better.

"Why, that'll be fine. Let me give you the address where we'll meet."

Mrs. Coates repeats the address while I jot it down. Venturing out this evening instead of during the day will restore energy I utilized jogging to the library. I thank the agent and am about to return my phone to the backpack when I notice a missed call from Zach. Do I call him back or wait until he calls me again? I wait a moment to see if he's left a message, but when none appears, I decide to call.

"Hey, handsome. Miss me already?"

"Good morning, Emma. I hope you do not *mind* my calling this early. I am checking in to see if you have given notice at your office."

His voice is flat, unemotional. Plus, the way he emphasized mind, maybe he's trying to tell me something. "Yes, I have made the call and have been asked to contact a placement agency to begin the hiring process."

"Good. I have also begun the process of closing down my office for a time. I should be able to join you in less than three weeks to begin your introduction into our circle."

While my maker retells some of what I already know, a tingling behind my eyes alerts me to impressions placed in my mind. I open to him and allow the imagery to flow freely. He's relaying Francisco has contacted him, he's being monitored by someone or something, and to not divulge anything over the phone. I send an impression of me kissing him to signal I understand.

He coughs to cover up what I'm sure is a chuckle.

"I await your visit, Zach. Please say hello to Francisco for me." I almost choke when I mention that despicable vampire's name. The more distance between us, the safer I'll feel.

With final pleasantries out of the way, my lover sends a sensuous kiss into my mind. My gasp before he hangs up brings forth another chuckle from his end. He's toying with me, the fiend. He must know my body craves our connection. Doesn't he feel the need? Damn. He didn't mention when he planned to visit me either.

Once my phone is dropped in the backpack again, a sigh escapes my lips. My body, already stressed from events I can't control, requires my lover's. Finished with my first task, I decide on a shower when I return, and a long rest before my meeting with Mrs. Coates at seven this evening.

I arrive at the home, located on Desert Vale Drive, fifteen minutes late. Thankfully, the rental agent remained and stands waiting for me near the front entrance.

"I apologize, Mrs. Coates," words rush from my mouth as I near the lady. "The drive took longer than I expected. If you still have time, I'd love to see the home." I extend my hand to her in greeting.

"I expected you may be late, Mrs. Wooten. Traffic from the west side always backs up this time of day." She grasps my fingertips instead of my hand, limply shakes them, then releases her hold.

I chuckle to myself. When I originally spoke with her, I gave her my name as Marilyn Wooten and my husband's name as Bill. If necessary, I will charm her—one of the skills Zach taught me last week—when she prepares our lease to keep her from asking for a background check. I also figure cash speaks loudly. If I pay three month's rent and the deposit with cash, maybe she won't delve into our backgrounds. No matter where we live, we must hide our true identities.

Mrs. Coates opens the door and spends thirty minutes reveling in the amenities of the two-story home. It's much too large for my taste, but it is hidden behind closed gates, which offers some security, except from vampires, I remind myself.

When we reach the front entrance again, I offer to lease the home for three months, August through October. I also ask if, when my husband arrives, she will show the home to him before we sign the lease. Of course, with the promise of a three-month lease during the hottest period in Arizona, she happily agrees.

We part ways outside. I watch from my car as she locks the front door and then deposits the key in a lockbox. My final wave is returned as I drive off toward my home. The sun has set and it is time for me to go on a long run.

CHAPTER 19

EMMA

I escape the confines of the medical office and rush to the parking lot, tears on the verge of escaping. The doctors, not happy with my decision at first, changed their minds when I informed them I plan to marry in the near future. Happy I shared this information with them, they congratulated me on my decision to finally start a family. Family. I hid my chuckle. But... I'll never have a family. Not unless...

Just like that, questions on whether or not to remain an immortal torture me again. Have I made the wrong decision? Can one remark from people I've worked with for four years corrupt my resolution? Do I want my life back? If so, why am I going through this charade, leaving a great job to follow Zach around? I'm torn again between existing in his world and the one I dream of living. My hands shake while I push the contents of my purse around to locate my sunglasses. The few days I shared with him melt into oblivion in the hot Arizona sun when the reasons for my dismay assault my mind.

My time with Zach has been both out of this world wonderful and calamitous. Out of this world because I thought I found my happily ever after with the man—no, make that *creature*—I fell in love with in high school. I've never experienced love, not like the love he's shown me. The promise of immortality... all the places we can visit, the history and culture available to us, witnessing the world progress beyond its limits again, and its people creating new technology to prolong the life of this planet. I'd miss that, but more than the world changes, I'd miss *him* more than I can imagine.

Flip the coin... calamitous because, when he changed me into this freak who requires blood to exist, he also threw me to the wolves because of his maker. If I remain a vampire, I will be on the run from that monster my entire existence. Is that any way to live? Are we destined to be hunted for all eternity and if captured, destroyed?

Flip the coin back... if I regain my humanity, won't that monster still pursue me? Will I fall under his spell, be changed back by him this time, and live out my existence watching Zach's empty stare?

As much as I love the one who created me, I did not choose this life. Tears fall steadily and blur my vision as I drive away from the stucco and stone structure. The draw to live as a mortal grows with each block I pass, even with all the pitfalls of being human. I'd be subjected to heartache, diseases, and later death, but happiness, too, and a family of my own experiencing the love of one man. My relationship with my siblings could be strengthened, my children would grow up knowing their cousins... I could be happy, couldn't I?

My promise to live with and then marry Zach tears me in two. I love him. How can I walk away after we've shared so much these past few days? On the other hand, how can I continue to exist with him when I so vehemently want my life back and a family of my own? Those needs were shut away before we left Indianapolis, me believing I could exist with him in this life. I had myself convinced I would be happy as long as Zach remained my partner. However, one comment from the doctors to the contrary challenged my decision.

While I continue my drive on I-10 West toward Buckeye, my mind drifts with how to explain my feelings to the one I'm destined to injure. Part of me wants him, but the way he used to be. Well, at least how I thought he used to be. However, after meeting Francisco, how can he even for a moment think I'd enjoy living under his threat for all eternity? Even though he's hundreds of miles away, his presence creeps into my psyche and shivers my back.

Before I finish my drive, I stop at Burger King for my drink. See? This is why I don't want to be what I am. I have to remember to drink blood every so often or I'll possibly kill an animal or a human to survive. I'd rather have my existence terminated than to constantly require blood.

Stress from the morning meeting zapped my energy enough that my gums tingle while I pay ten dollars to the cashier at the drive-up window. She nods with a recognizing smile. I do my best to return the gesture, but my heart isn't in it. My fake smile lasts until I'm on the drive home.

My phone rings while I exit the car. When I look, I see Zach's face. "Good morning. How are you?"

How do I tell him? What can I possibly say to explain my dilemma?

"I sense something brewing, Emma. Are you having a problem at work?" Worry paints his words.

"Um, the doctors are not thrilled I'm leaving. They did wish me well and were happy I decided to marry and start a *family*." Do my words sound harsh? I don't wish to antagonize him, but we need to talk in person. "How soon can you join me?"

"I can visit this weekend, but I need to return for appointments on Monday. What is wrong?"

"Zach, I…" I can't continue. With all I promised this past week, I now must renege on my assurances. "Just come here as soon as you can, please? We need to talk."

"Is there something I can help you with now?"

Anxiety forces its way into my voice. "This life, Zach. I'm not cut out to be…"

"Stop right there. I will join you this evening around seven."

The call drops the moment I open the door into the kitchen. I guess it's better to get this over with before we commit to a move.

Instead of worrying myself silly, I distract myself by settling in my office to log into the placement agency's website to review potential candidates. Even if my wish comes true and I become mortal again, I must continue my search for a replacement, since I've given my notice.

Three qualified individuals are listed in our account, one who appears more qualified than the others. I focus on Jan McDermott's resume first, then jot down all three individuals' references, and once all documents are printed, I place the first call.

Following the last conversation, I write a review for each candidate and forward my email to the doctors suggesting each be brought in to interview. Once I hit send, I relax back in my office chair and contemplate how to begin the gut-wrenching conversation with my maker. He isn't going to enjoy listening while I attempt to explain. I need to stay strong, though. I don't wish to be charmed into believing immortality holds the best scenario for me. An intelligent conversation, no emotions or theatrics, is what I need. I pray he'll listen and understand.

With little more than two hours before Zach's arrival, I decide on Panda Express for dinner. I slip into my shoes and drive the short distance to the restaurant. When I walk in, a young boy stands against the front window holding his hand while an elderly woman, maybe his grandmother, wraps a napkin around his thumb. Tears cover his face, but he is being brave and not crying out loud. When I walk past them, I notice blood seeping through the napkin. The woman applies another paper to keep the fluid from dropping to the floor.

Without warning, my body tenses, my vision blurs, and I grab a chair back to keep upright. My fangs extend and I'm near passing out when I realize my dilemma. The draw is immediate. I was told I would not crave human blood if I kept my body infused with Velvet Crimson. That is so not the case today.

To keep myself from doing the unimaginable, I find strength to leave the building before I claim my first human victim. I climb into my car and drive out of the parking lot, all the while desiring what my body craves. Once I've driven around for ten minutes, I'm settled enough to try another restaurant. I pull into the drive-through lane at McDonalds, order my meal, and take it home with me, still shaking from my near miss.

The tasteless fish sandwich and fries do little to quench my hunger. I'm still shaken, but believe ingesting another Velvet Crimson could help. I toss the remnants of my dinner into the trash, pick up my purse, but flinch when my doorbell rings. It has to be Zach.

He stands, waiting, when I pull open my front door. The moment he steps inside, I fall into his arms, which surround and comfort me.

My body shakes with fear. "I wanted to kill a little boy today, Zach. His thumb was bleeding and his grandmother was doing her best to stop the flow, but all that blood. I wanted to push the grandmother aside and sink my fangs into his neck, Zach. I wanted to suck the life out of him. Why? I had a Velvet Crimson maybe three hours before. Why would I feel the need to kill that little boy? I don't understand!"

My hands twist his shirt in my fists. My eyes squeeze closed when I visualize the little boy again. How can I live like this?

"Shush, Emma. We all experience that craving once in a while. Frankly, I am surprised you work in a medical office and have not been subjected to a craving." He pulls away, draws my head up, and looks deeply into my now opened eyes. "I am also very proud of you. You were able to walk away. That should prove you had control over the situation."

"*No!* I wanted to sink my fangs in him, Zach. I wanted it, even if it meant spending the rest of my existence behind bars or being killed because I took his life. It took all of my willpower to walk out of there." I crumble into a chair. "I only hope no one noticed my fangs or watched me stagger out."

His light laugh does little to qualm my fear.

"They would have thought the sight of blood made you ill and you responded the way you did based on *that* fear. Look, no one followed you out, did they? Everyone was concerned for the child. I would be surprised if anyone noticed you at all."

I swallow back my worry and nod. "Maybe."

I rise and pad into the kitchen. Zach follows, but not too close. Does he sense how the desire to be changed back consumes me? Maybe if I bring it up now, he'll accept my choice.

I turn toward him with my arms folded across my chest. "I can't continue to live this life, Zach. Today proved it to me. As much as I love you, I can't live like this. Always wondering if I'll kill someone, needing blood to exist, living within Francisco's circle. Everything became complicated when you entered my life again. If you had just left me alone to wander this Earth by myself..." I spin away and walk toward the back window, looking at anything but the regret in his eyes.

"If I can't be changed back, I still don't think I can live always on the run, looking over my shoulder, wondering when we'll be found. I'm not cut out to be a vampire. And, before you say it, yes,

I still held out hope I would somehow be able to regain my human life and live with whatever pitfalls and promises came to me."

When he doesn't respond, I peek back and observe Zach's expression, which rips me in two. "Say something. Please. Tell me you hate me, tell me I'm foolish, tell me I lied to you. Just tell me, Zach!"

He approaches, but doesn't touch me. "I apologize for bringing such pain and misery into your existence. Truth is I am the selfish one. I am the one who changed you, created you if you will, to be my life-mate. If your choice is to part with me, I must accept it. But, I warn you. Francisco will come after you once he learns we are no longer a couple."

I clutch the counter in front of me when Zach's body presses against me. His fingertips glide slowly down my arm. My body, already strung out from the episode today, responds as I'm sure he intends. My eyes close and my head lolls to the side in answer to his caress. Damn him!

My eyes slowly blink open when tingling begins its journey from my toes up into my core.

Zach leans in and kisses my shoulder. "Allow me to taste of you once more, my love. I promise it will be the last time, if that is your wish." His whispered words drift across my bare shoulder.

His hand draws my hair from the side of my face and he kisses my neck, my earlobe, and down my jaw. Pent-up anxiety, stress, and craving swirl around inside me and I cave under the influence of his touch. I spin to face him, press my body against his, and kiss him long and hard. My fangs extend when desire floods me. My tongue forces its way into his mouth to caress his extended incisors.

With our lips locked, Zach picks me up, carries me to the bedroom, and within seconds we're naked on the bed, exploring each other's bodies. Moans of desire escape my mouth when his fingers tease my folds. One finger dives inside me which arches my back off the bed. When he inserts the second, I cry out as an orgasm rips me apart. It's been only two days since we made love in his home. Why is it I crave his touch so desperately?

While my body calms, Zach positions himself at my entrance and slowly dips inside me. Just the tip at first, as if he's waiting for my objection, which is the furthest thing from my mind at the moment.

He continues in and my eyelids open to his blackened eyes, full of desire. He stalls movement when my hand cups his cheek.

"I love you." A tear slides from my eye and lands on the pillow beneath my head when it hits me this will be our last experience in the mind chamber. My eyes close when his lips converge with mine again and I smile when the creature I love picks up his pace and pummels into me, hard and fast, as we taste of each other.

I'm transported to that day in Indianapolis when I decided I could live this life as long as he was my instructor and confidante. Our bodies writhe against each other in our passion and, when I feel the next orgasm spin through me, I also intercept a thought from him. He has a way to block Francisco from future mind probes. My mind requests he tell me more, but I feel, rather than hear, *Later.*

Absorbed in our love, I close that thought from my mind and spend the next two hours ravishing the vampire whose body catapults mine into another realm. Colors of every hue swirl around me. I'm dancing in a field of wildflowers on a bright sunny day, laughing at nothing except the feel of his hand in mine. We're both barefoot, his jeans rolled up to his knees, my full skirt captured by the breeze floats up in a draft and covers my eyes, exposing my legs and pale blue panties. Zach pulls me to a stop and draws me close to kiss me.

Suddenly, the day darkens, the colors fade, and Zach surrounds my shoulders with his arms. Someone has found us. Someone is after us. Zach grasps my hand and we run like the wind away from the dark figure that approaches.

We locate a path into a forest and continue through, scampering over bushes and fallen trees in our effort to escape the ominous creature at our heels. We delve deeper into the woods. However, when no opening presents itself, Zach forces me to stop, places me behind him, and turns to face our pursuer. The moment Francisco's face with snarled lips, nostrils flared, and eyes squinted, becomes visible, I pull myself awake from this dreamlike trance and clutch Zach to me in desperation.

His arms clutch me to him as if to keep me safe from the vampire's grasp. I repeat to myself this was only a dream, a dream, only a dream, while Zach attempts to calm me with soft caresses down my back. When my body shivers with fear, my lover covers us with a blanket, but does not relinquish his hold on me.

"Don't ever leave me, Zach. He will take me if you do. Please promise me, Zach. Please." My pleas wrench straight from my heart.

My life-mate kisses my temple to stall my distress. "I will never leave you, my Emma. I will protect you from anyone who wishes you harm, even if you become human again. You have my solemn promise."

I nod, pull the comforter closer, and draw his arm around my waist when he spoons me. My life course changes, yet again, in knowing that vampire will stop at nothing to make me his.

As if reading my mind, Zach's words calm me. "Rest now, my love. I must leave in a couple of hours. Forget today and continue with our plans. I will explain what I relayed to you once I return again. Just understand I have found a way."

No words comfort me tonight. I'm destined to remain a vampire. And, my thought Francisco would help me find someone to change me back dispels with each breath I take.

Zach wakes me near midnight with a kiss to my neck. "Wake, dear Emma. I must return home."

I roll over into his arms. "I'm sorry about earlier. After what I witnessed in the mind chamber, I understand my place is with you. I promise never to leave your side."

His brows raise and his lips purse. "What did you experience? Did I miss something?"

He didn't experience that dream with me? "You didn't run in the meadow with me? Or bolt through the forest to escape Francisco's clutches?"

"I was in the meadow with you, but did not run from anyone. We danced through the field, then fell to the ground and made love. Please, recreate the rest of your dream."

I do. I leave no detail out including the sneer on Francisco's face when he caught us. "You didn't share this dream with me? How can it be?"

Zach pulls away, climbs out of bed, and begins dressing, irritation obvious in the way his hands jerk his slacks into place and the scowl marring his beautiful face. "He found a way into your mind through mine. This must stop," he spits. "I will confront him today and tell him to keep his distance."

"I didn't think he could read my mind."

"He cannot read it, per se, but evidently he can intimidate you through me. What I do not understand is how." Zach sits on the bed, stock still. His eyes tighten as he slams his fist against the comforter. "If he wishes to own you, why frighten you?"

Zach pulls on his socks while I crawl over to him. "Then stop him from exploring your mind, Zach. You said you knew how. Implement it. Keep that evil twisted beast from your thoughts."

Zach stops and stares straight ahead as if making a decision. "I have one more week to work, Emma. I must allow him access until I leave Oceanside. Once I am here for good, I will shut him down, but only enough so he is not the wiser." Zach continues to dress, but his fingers refuse to cooperate in buttoning his shirt. He allows his arms to hang loose, shakes them, and begins again.

When he finally finishes, he stands and reaches for my hand. "Walk me to the door, my love. I will not see you for a few days and I want to kiss you so you will remember how much I love you."

We stand at my front door, share a sensuous kiss, and draw back to stare into each other's eyes. I do have one more question I must ask before he leaves me.

"Zach, how can I train myself to walk away from human blood? Is there any special technique you can pass on which will stall my desire to taste it? I don't want a repeat of today's situation, should one arise."

He kisses my forehead. "It comes with age. You handled yourself extremely well for experiencing that situation alone. Trust yourself, Emma. You wish no human harm. Remind yourself of that when, and if, the situation presents itself in the future."

I nod but think to myself, if it were only that easy. "Will you call me tomorrow night to check in, please?"

"Of course. Until then, my love."

After another quick kiss to my lips, Zach opens my front door, looks around briefly, then disappears into the night. I have to wonder. Did he charm me tonight, entice me to stay with him? Or did I make up my own mind? Somehow, I don't think I'll ever know the answer to that question.

Lynne Anders

CHAPTER 20

ZACH

That fiend. What does he gain by frightening my life-mate? Did he truly believe she would be a willing companion if he pursued her while she romped with me in the meadow? All images Emma portrayed scamper through my mind while I rush toward Oceanside. Thankfully, the dark starry night infuses me with enough energy, I am able to reach my home in less than two hours without lingering aftereffects from our lovemaking.

I ponder my next step: blocking Francisco from my mind. Phyllis, still my close friend and confidante, discussed this process with me at length on the phone after Emma left Tuesday. We spoke in generalities in case Francisco delved into my mind while we conversed. Grateful for her insight, I now possess the ability to shut that vampire out.

Phyllis and I had worked tirelessly for three hours until I was able to corral the area of my brain susceptible to Francisco's. The solution is basically mind over matter. She taught me how to recognize Francisco's interference, channel my own thoughts when I experience his intrusion, and stop whatever I am working on or discussing if it relates to the new life Emma and I have planned.

As I wander around my empty home, I review the details of our conversation in my mind, so I do not forget any important points.

"Where did you learn this technique, Phyllis?" I recall asking.

Her chuckle had curled my lips, too. Obviously, I am missing something.

"Zachary. You're getting senile, even for a vampire." Her melodic laugh offered comfort and peace. "Thaddeus was an elder. His knowledge of our kind met or surpassed even Francisco's. He taught me many tricks during our time together, but only after I promised I'd never disclose any which would harm another being. In your case, I'll teach you all I know if it will help protect anyone from your master."

Her sudden silence had worried me.

"When his life was ended, I wondered, at the time, who had a hand in it. Unless I find proof, I can't act on my suspicions." She cleared her throat. "Anyway…"

"You suspect Francisco was a partner to…" If that is true, he is not just a beast, he is a cold-blooded monster who will stop at nothing to obtain whatever goal he chooses.

"Let's not discuss this until you're certain you can block him. I wouldn't want to be the cause of your death, too."

"Phyllis. Why say that?"

"Again, another time, please? Look, my friend, I must run. It's time for my evening Pilates class. It helps me relax. Keeps me in line."

"Thank you, Phyllis. I thank the powers above that Thaddeus brought you into my life. If I can assist you in any way, ever, please do not hesitate to ask."

"Keep her safe, Zach. That's all I want. We all were young once, searching for our path through this existence. Help her understand who and what we are. Maybe it will settle her some to know she will grow to appreciate this life. Right now, though, she still has family and wishes to be reunited with them. Allow her to visit as often as possible. Thaddeus granted me that favor. I loved him more because of it. Also remind her she isn't alone. I'm always available to talk."

"You seem to like my life-mate quite a bit."

"I do. I grew to care for her while she was my student ten years ago. She's definitely one for the ages."

"Thank you, Phyllis. I believe she has special qualities as well. Um, I believe I have a visitor. I will let you know how this works."

Once I had ended the call, the connection grew. Francisco was, indeed, probing my mind. I went about my business as if all was right with the world. I changed clothes, showered and, once reading became too unsettling because of his lingering presence, I turned on

160

the television. By half past eleven, he had left my mind. Possibly he thought I would have called to speak with Emma.

Since I already had spoken with her earlier in the day, my decision to speak with Phyllis had been the correct step. I would not allow my mind to be invaded by that creep again without my knowledge or permission.

Tonight, all thoughts of Francisco's invasions filter away. I am prepared for any ambush he brings. I lower into my recliner holding an empty Velvet Crimson container. Relaxing, I close my eyes and visualize my Emma. Her long light-brown hair bounces against her back and, when she turns to capture my gaze, a smile gently plays on her lips. We continue our romp together in the sun...

I bolt upright when images from her dream parade through my mind: Francisco chasing her, teeth bared, fangs extended, ready to take what is mine.

He will not! I will give my life, if I must, to salvage her from that beast. I will locate a place she feels safe and hide her there, then come back to finish what I should have ten years ago.

Fury rages through me until I have no recourse but to recline in my chair and drag images of Emma in high school through my mind to quiet it.

Hours pass. When Francisco does not attempt to invade my thoughts again tonight, I close my eyes and delve into Emma's mind. She appears to be resting, thank goodness. I stand at the foot of her bed and watch her sleep, the quick rise and fall of her chest, the sweet smile displayed on her luscious lips, and the outline of her body, curled as if we are spooning, beneath the pale pink blanket. I count the days until she is in my arms again.

Satisfied no danger lurks near her, I leave her to her sleep and climb the stairs to my bedroom. Tomorrow I must work. I must plan my exit and leave, hoping never to return to this residence. At least not until the fanatic is out of the picture.

Friday morning appointments are light. The several clients I treat inform me they will wait for my return, but will see Dr. Bartholomew until my practice reopens. I thank each one, knowing that will never be the case. I do not plan to revive this practice in the future. When I do open a new practice, I will have a new identity and credentials anyway.

During my lunch break, I contact Emma to ask how her day is faring. "Have you interviewed anyone yet?"

"It's been the best morning. The first young lady arrived early and I must say she'd be perfect for this office. I set up an appointment next Monday for her to meet with the doctors. They have the final say. The second interviewee should arrive in a few minutes. His background and references impressed me as well. And, the third comes in at three. Not as impressive a background, but a possibility."

"Sounds as if your morning is off to a perfect start. What would you say to your boyfriend's request to visit you again. Say, once the sun sets?"

"Really? You can come back tonight? Oh, Zach. That'd be the icing on the cake. Now I can't wait for the day to be over with. What shall we do this weekend?"

As if she has a choice, I chuckle to myself. I plan to drag her into bed and not allow her out until I must leave Sunday night.

"Hmmm. We shall find *something* to do, most certainly." I can almost picture her lips curled in a playful smile and her eyes mischievously twinkling.

"We do have one item to cross off our agenda. Mrs. Coates contacted me and wants to know what time to expect us tomorrow."

This will throw a damper on our two-day liaison.

She sighs. "Saturday evening. Maybe seven? We'll have most of Saturday that way." The pitch of her voice confirms she's thought the same. "Then, maybe I can show you around that area a bit on our way home. It's grown so much in the few years I've lived here. Then we can resume our— Oh, my one o'clock just walked in. I've got to run. See you tonight?"

"Yes, my love. Until then, be well. I love you, Emma."

"I love you, Zach. Bye."

The rest of my day repeats from the morning. I promise my clients I will return, but they are in good hands with the cardiologist who shares my space. We are not partners in practice, just two who split costs.

With my last patient's progress noted in the laptop, I clean off my desk then check the digital clock on the wall. Half past five. Not bad for a Friday afternoon. If lucky, I will be in Emma's arms no later than nine this evening. I do have a few errands to complete before I leave.

I grab my jacket off the back of my office chair and round the desk buttoning the last button when my phone vibrates in my pocket. Believing it to be Emma, I grab it and push open before I notice the picture on the screen.

"Are you anticipating my arrival, my love?"

"Only if you promise to bring chocolates. Good afternoon, young Zachary. Have I caught you at a bad time?"

My feet stop moving at the sound of his voice. Chills run up and down my spine from wondering what he wants now.

"I was on my way out to visit my life-mate. What can I do for you, Francisco?" I wait to open the door into the waiting room. I do not wish my employees to overhear this conversation.

"I was wondering at your sudden departure the other night. I also wish an update on Emma's progress. Any news there?"

I return to my desk and lower into my chair. His intrusion has yet to penetrate my mind, but I do not put it past him to try.

"She interviewed three individuals today. I believe the doctors interview them next."

"Good progress then. Possibly you will return faster than expected."

His pause for effect worries me.

"I have a request for you, Zachary. I wish you to accompany me to a gathering this evening. As my second-in-command, I would enjoy introducing you to more of our leaders. Please arrive at my home before eight. We will journey to the meeting together."

He knew I planned to see Emma this evening. How? I felt no interference from him yesterday or today, other than... A sudden realization hits me. One of his spies works in my office. She must have overheard my conversation with Emma this morning. With a heavy heart, knowing I will disappoint my love, I agree to my maker's request.

"Of course. But, as soon as the event ends, I must leave for Buckeye to see Emma."

"I ask nothing more from you after your participation tonight. Oh, it's black tie. Wear your Tom Ford single-vented jacket. It fits your body type."

And now he is dressing me? "Whatever you say. I will arrive at the estate around eight. Good afternoon, Francisco."

My head rests against my hand while I ponder my call to Emma. Hopeful my arrival is not much past two in the morning, I place the call and wait for her to answer. I would share this information through our mind-link, but decide she should hear the reason directly from me.

The forty-mile drive takes under an hour, which is unusual for Friday night traffic. Francisco ushers me through the door into the three-story mansion along the Coast Highway near Laguna Beach. It belongs to the syndicate that rules the west coast vampire world. I stop inside and wait while Francisco shrugs out of an overcoat. When I arrived at his home this evening, he was already wearing the coat, which I found strange at the time. First, our bodies do not recognize heat or cold, unless excessive. And second, it is late June. His tux jacket would have been sufficient.

What is revealed beneath is a crimson tuxedo jacket with back trim above black slacks. Is this the look of the leaders? I scan the area and notice a few others with the same outfit. I scoff. Is the color meant to intimidate or only to identify the circle leaders? Unfettered by his display, I follow a step behind, as any underling would, into the open room. The guests include many of our kind. Most surround their circle's leader, while several others in red stand off to the side observing.

Francisco joins that group and introduces me as his second. I have met several of them at Francisco's home over the decades, but a few are new to me. I sense a difference in their demeanor tonight, however. While his gaze wanders the room, Francisco licks his lips as if tasting something utterly exquisite.

With permission from my maker, I travel the room to pay my respects to others from our circle and vampires I have met while attending previous gatherings. By the time I return to Francisco's side, the crowd has become anxious in anticipation of some sort of display. I attempt to listen to the conversations, but only pick up, "It's about time he got his due," from the mumblings.

The patio doors swing open, which allows the cool summer breeze to flicker the lighted candles displayed throughout the room. As if on cue, participants separate from the opened doors and create a pathway leading into the center of the hall. The leaders form a single line on one side, while I step behind Francisco out of view. A young man I recognize as a member of our circle is dragged through the throng. I wish to rush to his aid, but dare not move in fear of retribution. He is a friend of Oliver's. Nicole's mate and this friend ran errands for Francisco. What does this mean for Oliver?

I step closer to Francisco and whisper, "Cassander and Oliver performed as directed by you. Why is he being subjected to this disrespect?"

Francisco holds up his hand to stall me. "Watch and learn, young Zachary."

Cassander, covered in blood and dirt, is tossed onto the floor in the center of the room while the leaders create a circle around his tattered body.

Elder Rayner, one of the vampire leaders for our region, speaks for the others. "Cassander, you have defied your leader. You were found consorting with other immortals in an attempt to overthrow Francisco. What do you say to this charge?"

The grungy vampire on the floor raises his head and searches for an ally. When his gaze falls on mine, he subtly shakes his head to warn me off. I nod discretely to let him know I understand. If I can be of assistance later, I will do what I can to clear his name.

His gaze continues through the crowd and falls upon a young female, who steps forward. "I will speak for Cassander."

The Elder stops her with a pinned stare. "He must answer the charge first."

She sniffles and steps back.

Cassander swallows heavily and gains momentary authority to speak. "My actions were executed at the request of Francisco. At no time did I entertain a possible overthrow of his regime. He is my leader and I respect him. The charges are false, sir. No one has allowed me to explain."

Chatter arises amongst the attendees, stalling Rayner's comment. His face contorts into a grimace when he yells, "Quiet!"

Within a moment, the room once again falls silent.

Rayner's sneer when he speaks twists my insides. "You have been given several opportunities to explain yourself, Cassander. However, nothing you have said indemnifies you from what we found during our investigation. Since you apparently have no other light to shed on the charges, the Court of Elders finds you guilty of high treason against your maker, and you are hereby sentenced to death."

The silent crowd erupts into disparate gasps and cheering. Do some truly wish to witness his death tonight?

I watch Francisco closely and wonder. Did he bring me along tonight to observe what will happen to me if I dare defy him where Emma is concerned?

Since I want no part of this business, I step back a pace or two while the rest converge on Cassander. The young female, who spoke up for him, falls to the ground near him and tries to touch him. The crowd pushes her back and, as one, falls upon the condemned vampire, each sinking their fangs into his body any place open to them.

The sight is hideous. Most enjoy sucking the poor young man's essence from him despite his continual shrieks. Francisco does not participate, but from the twisted grin forcing his lips into a sinister sneer, he is more than tempted.

Sickened by the unfolding scene, I distance myself from all who enjoy killing this vampire.

After the collective drains Cassander, his lifeless body is dragged from the room onto the back patio where another wields a sword. The body, torn to shreds by the mass inside, is placed on a long platform with his head lolling off the end. The crowd pushes outside and as it surrounds the platform, the vampire raises the sword above his head and strikes it against the neck of the lifeless body, severing it from the torso. The crowd, giddy from their participation and infused with vampire blood, cheers while the young female runs back into the mansion. My gaze follows the teary-eyed vampire until the front door closes behind her.

A bonfire burns brightly against the night sky out near the thirty-foot drop-off to the beach below.

Elder Rayner, stimulated by the night's activities, bares his fangs and directs those closest. "Remove the body and head, and place them on the fire."

To more cheers, a few of the participants collect what remains of Cassander, carry the pieces to the fire, and toss them on top. The rest of the ugly crowd follows along behind and watches while what remains of Cassander turns to ash before them.

My gaze searches the area behind this mansion and locates no observers other than our congregation. I am thankful the local police will not be called to intervene.

Since I have no desire to participate in the fury outside, I reenter the open room to wait for my leader's return while wondering when I became sensitive to the horror provided tonight. I admit I have witnessed and occasionally participated in such brutalization's during my two hundred plus years, but confusion runs rampant through my mind. When did my desire diminish? Is it because I feel required to protect someone? Is that what changed me?

With the display over, the group begins their return into the mansion, and out the front door with thanks to their host for a most enjoyable evening. I stand to the side to wait for the monster I call my leader. How could he allow this travesty of justice? What evidence proved that young vampire proposed an overthrow? Now I wonder about Oliver. Is he imprisoned somewhere, too? Should I alert Nicole of the possibility? Could she be another of Francisco's possible conquests?

When I perceive his presence enter my mind, I shut down those thoughts and change to the opulence of this home. Thankful he did not pick up on my previous ponderings, I search the room for the beast and find him walking my way from the back door.

"Time for us to head home, young Zachary. The evening's entertainment is complete."

Instead of responding, I nod and follow my maker to the front door. He offers his thanks to the leaders grouped there, grabs his overcoat, bids each goodnight, and together we exit into the night.

Once settled in his car for the ride back, he voices his opinion of the night's activity. "Cassander proved himself to be a traitor to our circle. I'm not certain of Oliver's culpability, but I assure you I will get to the bottom of this."

Okay, he opened the door. I walk through it. "What proof was presented against Cassander?"

"The documents are only for the Elders' eyes, young Zachary. The proof, however, overwhelmed me. If not found out, I'm certain he would have proceeded with his plan to topple my regime. The punishment was just."

I nod, but stare out the side window. He refuses to disclose the charges, citing exclusivity. Fine. I will not dredge up Oliver's name in case he is implicated as well. That being said, no additional words are spoken during the remainder of the ride home.

Back in Oceanside by one in the morning, I bid my maker goodnight and advise him I will be with Emma until Sunday evening.

"Stop by Monday. I may have additional news to report by then. In the meantime, enjoy your weekend."

I rush home to change, grab a small carrier, and begin my run to Emma's. I mentally send her a thought of my impending arrival. When I receive no return response, I chalk it up to the time. Of course. She is resting.

CHAPTER 21

ZACH

H er house is dark when I knock on the front door. No answer. I pace around the front perimeter while my mind attempts to contact her again, but there is no response. It is as if she has disconnected from me. Why? She knew I would come as quickly as possible. I am here later than I anticipated. But, where is Emma?

I search for and find, next to the garage, the hide-a-key in the flower pot which should open her front door. Since few humans roam the streets at this hour, I am inside, undetected, within moments.

I race to the bedroom first. Empty. I run to the utility room door, which opens into the garage, and find her car is gone. I slowly close the door and wonder. Why would she leave without communicating with me? Maybe she left a note. The door closes with a thud while I begin my quest. Even though my eyesight is perfect in the darkness, I switch the overhead lights on and search each room. Again, nothing. No note, no sign she has even been home. Where could she have gone? And, why leave when we have so little time together this weekend?

I stop in my tracks when my body reacts to a strange scent. It is not Emma's. Could it be a friend or circle member of hers showed up unexpectedly and she has taken her or him out for a drink? I check my watch again and notice it is nearly four o'clock.

My mind hits overdrive. Where is she? Even though we have not been together that long, I know her well enough to know she would leave some sign, some evidence, where she has gone. First, I search her bedroom for her purse. She usually keeps it on her desk chair. It is not there. Okay, she has her purse. Next, I search her bathroom for her makeup kit. Hmm. It sits under the sink so she is not planning to spend time away. So... what else does a woman take with her when she leaves home? A coat or jacket? Since the temperature outside does not affect us, that seemed to be a silly thought, unless it was for show. When I tug open the coat closet door, I admonish myself. I have no idea if anything is missing. The door slams shut from my frustration.

I must compose myself. I cannot lose control. I have to find her, and that means I have to think calmly. I plop down on her sofa and survey the room. What am I missing? What am I *missing*? My hands thread through my hair and grasp its ends. I try our mind-link again, but it feels as if I am searching the universe for one little pebble. Nothing.

I feel hopeless. I rise from the sofa, my hands ball into fists. Frantic to locate her, I stride back and forth in her living room while worry and anger burn inside me. Where are you, Emma? Where are you? I am so on edge I grab a chair and am about to toss it out her front window when I remember where I am. Luckily, I stop myself in time and gently set the chair back in its place.

Damn. She must be in trouble if she has shut me out this long. I recklessly rummage through all of her drawers, the cabinets, and the garage in my search for a clue. I know my Emma. There must be evidence somewhere. But, I find nothing.

I plop down on a kitchen chair and rub my eyes with the heels of my hands. We have an appointment with that Mrs. Coates to see the rental this evening. This is our first step away from the circle, which is important to both of us. She must return before then.

The circle. I bolt upright. Has Francisco found out about our plans? Could he have orchestrated Emma's disappearance? Even though my mind tells me he would not go that far, I only half believe it.

That monster. If he did anything to harm her...

I immediately reinforce the area that observes his intrusions. I felt it earlier, but was not in the mood to allow him to see my distress. If that beast had anything to do with her disappearance... My lips curl into a grimace and I snarl at the thought. Is that why he requested I join him tonight? To keep me occupied while one of his minions kidnapped Emma? Did he want to instill his authority over me so I will understand what will happen if I demand what is mine? How could I be so foolish to believe he was prepping me to be his second-in-command. He has Nadia. That is all the command that evil beast requires. My hands ball into fists and I growl long and low. I will kill him if she is injured in any manner.

Emma. My Emma. You have only belonged to me for three weeks. How is it I miss you as if we had spent our lives together? After a deep sigh, I release the pent-up anger and focus on ways to find her. If she is in his possession, my options will be few. I lower into a chair again. To further calm myself, I rest my forearms on my thighs and clasp my hands together, my eyes close as I begin to breathe evenly again. When my eyes open, they catch something on the floor. A cone-shaped, clear, plastic object lays beneath the next chair. I am on my hands and knees within seconds to retrieve the inch-long object. My eyes open wide to a syringe needle cover. What is it doing in Emma's kitchen, specifically on the floor? She does work in a medical office. However, she is not involved with treatments of any kind, only administrative work. So, where did this come from?

My fist closes around the offending article. Francisco! That fiend. I must return to Oceanside. She *is* there somewhere. I feel it.

My frustration calms as reason takes control. In case one of Francisco's minions returns for any reason, I decide to leave a note on her kitchen table wishing her well and apologize to her since it did not work out. I also plant this image in my memory for Francisco to find. I do not want him to know I am on to him. I hurry through Emma's house and straighten what I ransacked. Before I leave for home, I walk each room, turn off the lights, and secure the door into the house from the garage. I decide to keep the key with me in case I need to gain quick entrance again.

Locking the front door fills me with regret. You must have had a moment or two to contact me, Emma, before...

The sun splatters reds and yellows across the valley as it rises. I search the area for activity and watch a few teenagers with backpacks stroll down the sidewalk across the street. Instead of a quick exit, I trudge along in the opposite direction, worrying about my life-mate. Once I am out of their sight, I take off running. If I am lucky, I will reach Oceanside within two hours. But, then I will require rest from my journey. Perfect. It will allot me time to prepare for my confrontation with the monster who stole my life-mate.

My body, drained from the long, high-speed journey back in the sunlight, drops onto my bed the moment my clothes are discarded and piled on the floor next to the chair. Pent-up worry invades my thoughts. I must recruit someone to assist me in my quest to recapture Emma from our leader. But, who? As tired and as muddled as my mind is, the only name that materializes is Phyllis. I cannot trust anyone who lives here. Francisco can read their thoughts and will discover my plan long before it has been implemented.

Since Nadia is still in the picture, I do not expect Emma to be in any immediate danger. I have witnessed this leader after previous pursuits and know for certain Francisco will take care to keep Emma hidden somewhere until he rids himself of his current mate. Where he has her is a mystery, though. I must locate her quickly. I cannot think about what will happen if I do not.

I lay back on my pillow to rest before I contact my friend. I need my wits about me, especially when I am in Francisco's company the next time or communicating through our thoughts. I do not plan to alert him of my return yet. Once I do, he will request an immediate audience, which must appear as agony for me when I relate Emma has left me.

My eyes open two hours later to a bright summer day. My shutters, although closed, allow streams of light into the bedroom through the slits. I am not ready to rise, but bolt upright when Francisco's thoughts tug at my mind. I am prepared and allow him in. However, all I permit him to see is my quest to locate Emma. I picture me standing in her living room, staring out at the residential street. I am forlorn and contemplating my crestfallen return. The instant his mind separates from mine, my phone chimes with his ringtone.

I prepare myself. "Hello, Francisco. To what do I owe your time?" Hopefully, my voice sounds despondent enough.

"Do I detect a problem, young Zachary? Something feels off with you, my boy."

I huff before I respond. "Emma. She appears to have left me. She was not here when I arrived last night. She left no note, her car is gone, and I cannot reach her with our mind-link. I possibly pushed too hard the past couple of weeks in my attempt to immerse her into our world. Any suggestions, Francisco?"

Let me see what he has to say.

"Well, dear boy, it's possible she's off thinking things over. Give her another day, then return home and, if she still hasn't contacted you, we'll locate her for you. We can't allow one of our young female vampires off on her own, now can we?"

"She is not alone, Francisco. She has the circle she has been a part of the past ten years. It is possible she sought to confide in one of them. I will contact their leader. She may have an inkling where Emma may be." I allow a moment before I utter, "I suppose it is possible she returned to Indianapolis. If that is the case, there is no more I can do from here. I will return home if she does not show by nightfall."

This is all a distraction. Why would he call me tonight knowing full well I intended to spend the weekend in her arms?

"Whatever you feel you should do, my boy. In the meantime, if I can be of assistance, please ask. I have a network of friends who are more than willing to help. Just say the word."

His network. I protect my thoughts. Is that how he stole my girl? That beast.

"Thank you for offering. I will contact you once I have returned. Have a good day, Francisco."

The phone drops to my bed as my anger rises. He is not as concerned as he should be. He offers help, but for later. And, he more or less asked me to wait another twenty-four hours before I return. Damn. He has her. I am positive. But, where?

Lynne Anders

CHAPTER 22

FRANCISCO

I close my phone while standing in my open-door front entryway observing the morning sky. Zachary has no clue. Imbecile! All went as planned last night and the young female now resides in the chambers below ground. I must check, however, to verify she is still sleeping off the drugs.

The front door closes with a thump. I stroll into the library and push the hidden button on the fake *Interview with a Vampire* book, which unlocks the secret doorway to the underground. It creaks open slowly. When I pass through, the button on the opposite wall closes the hole in the wall, and I begin my journey down the shadowy spiral stairway toward my goal.

I stop at the bottom and survey the area. Diffused light from the Davy lamps hung from the stone-covered ceiling filters down the long cavernous walkway and casts rainbow slices of color against the age-old walls. This passage once led to an adjacent home, which has since been torn down. The wall that encloses the large cell at the end blocks the long-ago escape route. I stroll down the corridor, alone in the cascade of light except for two heartbeats, one faint.

Several empty chambers line the passage on my way to that being. I asked to have the girl placed in the large compartment at the end. It is the best, after all, and directly beneath the kitchen. The connected dumbwaiter avails us the ability to send blood to my charge as often as necessary without anyone being the wiser. Plus, the new technology installed avails me a look into the chamber through the image-enhancing cameras, and the motion-sensitive light beam will repress any escape attempt.

My pace slows as I approach the cell with caution. The opening in the door, encased with steel-reinforced bars, offers me a glimpse into the chamber. I observe her asleep on the twin bed, covered by a quilted comforter. Well, not quite asleep, drugged. I couldn't take the chance she'd attempt to contact Zachary when Alexander intercepted her. In the meantime, she's safe and out of the clutches of the young vampire who changed her at my bidding. Although their connection appears strong, once I claim Emma as my own, her allegiance will adjust the moment she accepts my promise of protection. She'll also occupy her place of authority by my side for all eternity, which will be a blessing. First, though, I must deal with Nadia.

The display panel on the wall next to the door indicates the electronic beam is active. Should Emma wake early and attempt to escape, a high intensity light beam will score her skin. I don't wish her harm, but she must learn her place is with me. The sooner the better for all.

Satisfied she's resting peacefully, I turn from the chamber, absorbed with thoughts of my mate, Nadia, and the shame she's brought to our members.

Our circle reaped favor from the five West Coast Elders, who have ruled our region for centuries, until recently. The problem began when Nadia schemed with several members of our circle to convert mortals with muddled histories—most including aggravated assault charges, arson, and burglary—into immortals. They were thugs during their mortal lives, and continued their ways after being changed. I have spent many hours cleaning up their messes, attempting to keep law enforcement away from our circle. These hoodlums of hers altered our dynamic, thereby creating chaos. I brought this allegation to her attention one afternoon and she laughed at the absurdity of my accusation. Knowing full well this practice would continue, I had no alternative but to assert my position and promise she'd be imprisoned if she enticed another member to prolong this program.

The Elders, after learning of the disparity between Nadia and me, became disappointed with how we managed our circle. They admonished me for *her* conduct, I was cast aside, and not afforded my rightful place on their council until the bedlam was cleaned up.

This was all Nadia's fault. I promised Elder Rayner tonight I would work doggedly to regain the council's respect again. Maybe with the help of Emma, that task will become easier.

When I reach the top of the stairs, I listen before opening the secret door. There are only three vampires who know of this chamber and I want to keep it that way. Unfortunately, Nadia is one of them.

I perceive no sound from the adjacent room, press the button, which springs the door open, and walk back into the library. The room is vast, with countless ancient books shelved floor to ceiling. Most of the works I've collected over my lifespan, though some were presented as gifts. I've read them all, have my favorite authors, of course, but find little time these days to read. My existence has become more complicated and allots little time for my favorite dalliance.

Speaking of dalliances, my property is in need of inspection. I fear, since I was away last evening, there may be some blood-letting on the beach now, as has been the case lately. I walk back to the hidden door, verify it is secure, then proceed through the lower level of my home to the back patio. The door opens to sunlight dancing on the smooth surface of the pool, which creates an iridescent ripple. How lovely. What I wouldn't give to share myself with Emma in this very pool one evening soon. My eyes close when I picture the shimmer of her soft skin against the backdrop of the mature fern pines that line the pathway to the ocean. She'll be in my arms, caressing my face, asking me to join our bodies. What a perfect night it will be.

My attention is redirected by commotion near the beach. I speed toward the sound and watch as two from my circle engage a young mortal male in a heated exchange, circling him, ready to pounce. This will end badly, I have no doubt. Before one of the youngsters goes too far, I decide to intervene.

"Good morning, Casper, Stuart. I see you've brought a friend home to enjoy our beach." I turn my attention to the frightened male. "May I offer to show you around, sir?"

"Um, no thank you. I... ah, think I should get going."

His face, tanned from the sun, pales when he observes my extended fangs. It's the only way I know to keep him from the harm those two could employ. To charm him, I force my will on him. "It is a beautiful morning. However, I understand your need to retire. You will not remember accompanying Casper or Stuart to our property and will leave by the path next door. Have a pleasant rest of your day."

The young man slowly nods and creeps back toward the sand path leading to the street in front. He doesn't look back, thankfully.

"Now, what did I tell you about playing with your food on my property?"

I bid them both to follow me inside. Being the dutiful little younglings they are, they trail behind me without question or complaint. Once I'm out of earshot of our neighbors, I tear into them.

I barely contain my contempt. "The next time I catch you harassing a guest, you will be placed behind bars and not allowed to feed until you accept my rules! Do I make myself clear?"

They respond in unison. "Yes, sir."

"You're despicable. You two will ruin this circle for all eternity with your careless ways. Go to your chambers. I don't wish to lay my eyes on you until tomorrow evening."

As one, they rush up the stairs without a word. I listen until both doors close before I leave to continue my patrol.

My head shakes. What has Nadia done?

My patrol ends without additional fanfare just as the sun crests overhead. I stand for a few moments and stare out across the vast ocean.

"Poor, poor Zachary. He must be out of his mind with worry." My smile spreads while I stand in the wet sand attempting to read into his thoughts. For some reason, I cannot seem to register with him. Hmmm. That's not like him. Usually, all it takes is a moment.

I spin back toward my home and watch the sun creep through the cloudless sky. I can't worry about young Zachary now. It's time for my rest. It was a challenging night, after all. First the Elders, the death of Cassander, Zachary's departure, Emma's capture, and those two youngsters. I can't think any more. I need sleep.

I climb the stairs to my chamber, drop my clothing on the closest chair, and crawl under the sheet. With my head resting against my crossed arms on the pillow, Emma's image forces its way into my mind again. The lovely Emma.

"Soon you will belong to me, my dear. Just think of the possibilities." My eyes close when Emma's smile and golden-flecked eyes pierce my lifeless heart. So young. So vulnerable. So ripe for the taking.

CHAPTER 23

EMMA

I wake slowly, lick my dry lips, and wonder where Zach is. However, when my hand reaches behind me, that side of the bed is empty. He was supposed to arrive last night. I don't remember if he did. In fact, I don't remember going to bed. I roll over to check his pillow just in case he rose early to make me breakfast. My gaze lands on dark stone instead of the wallpaper on my bedroom wall. I sit up, grasp my head, and sway from vertigo. A headache throbs against my temples, my stomach churns, and my gums tingle with need. My eyes close involuntarily. What is wrong with me? I'm a vampire. I'm not supposed to suffer illness.

When I open my eyes again, I scan the space I'm in. It's dark, made of concrete and stone, has a heavy wooden entrance door with bars inset over an opening, and contains possibly a bathroom inside the enclosure adjacent to the bed. What in the world? How did I get *here*?

Lucidity clears my mind. After I returned home from work last night... was it last night? I opened my door to a vampire I met when Zach took me to Francisco's. He had a message from my life-mate, or so he said. I invited him in, wondering why Zach hadn't contacted me himself, but waved it off believing something important arose that he couldn't convey to me directly. We sat in my living room for a few moments and discussed Oceanside and Francisco's home when I realized I hadn't offered him a drink.

"You've come a long way..." I waited until he told me his name.

"Alexander."

"I remember now. Yes, Alexander. May I offer you a drink?" I scanned him head to toe. Something felt off, but I decided to keep an open mind since Zach sent him.

"I have a Velvet Crimson in the refrigerator if you'd like."

Alexander stood when I did and followed me into the kitchen. When I reached for the refrigerator door, he came up behind me and covered my nose and mouth with a cloth. I vaguely remember a pinprick on my skin before I clutched at a chair, then fell against him.

My focus restores when I realize my predicament. I drop my legs off the side of the bed and attempt to stand. Although I'm weak, I find strength to pull myself up. I notice I have on the same dress I wore to work yesterday. Was it yesterday? Cautiously, I walk toward the door, but stop abruptly when a hot spear of light pierces my arm. I back up, rub the spot, which begins to heal immediately, and return to the bed. Tears form in my eyes. Why imprison me? Why would Zach wish me harm?

Weak and afraid, I'm near the end of my strength when a small door opens on the wall to the left of the cell door. I slowly make my way there, watchful, afraid I'll be struck again with the light beam. When I arrive without injury, I reach inside the opening and draw out a glass filled with what appears to be blood. Thankful for the drink, I chug it down without testing it first, lick the rim of the glass, and replace it on the empty shelf. I'm not certain what I drank, but it definitely wasn't a Velvet Crimson. My body responds to this liquid in a manner I've never experienced before. It's as if raw energy surges throughout me. My fangs extend, my headache disappears, the spot on my arm that was healing is gone, and strength gushes through me from head to toe. Could it be human blood? Is this what human blood does for a vampire? It's as if I've been granted a new existence. Interesting. I wonder how long the surge will linger?

I step away when the small door closes and whoever sent the drink down recalls the dumbwaiter. However, infused with new energy, I decide to try to figure out where I am.

Although the cell appears large, by cell standards, it only requires four steps to walk from the bed to the enclosed bathroom. I step around the corner and see a bathtub, a toilet, and a sink. At least I'm allowed some necessities when and if I require them. My body already feels grungy from the musty air, so a shower or bath might perk me up. Damn. I'd better be released before that's required, though.

I step away from the bathroom wall and scan the ceiling to see if I can locate any cameras, hidden or not. There is a red dot above the door, which could be some kind of visual aid for whoever incarcerated me. It must be how he or she knew I was awake and required blood.

I spin around and notice the bed, which consists of a mattress and frame. It is the only furniture inside this chamber. No dresser for clothes, no place to hang anything. Just the bathroom and bedroom area. I return to the bed, lower to it, and attempt to reach Zach to no avail. Has he shut me out? Does he know I'm here? But, where is here?

The only light available shines in through the barred opening in the cell door. I don't know if that door is locked since I can't get close enough to check without that beam of light burning my skin. But, possibly I'm more resilient right now. I stand and move one step at a time, until the beam crosses in front of me when my hand extends into that area. It hurts, but it doesn't feel as intense this time. However, when I cross that plane and it hits my body, I have to back up. The pain is excruciating.

Angered someone wishes me harm and enjoys watching, I pull myself together and scream toward the light, "Hey! That hurts. Quit torturing me." Maybe whoever is monitoring the camera will stop. Even though the burn mark on my arm disappears within seconds, it still smarts when that beam scorches my skin. So, with no other recourse, I continue my tirade.

"When can I get out of here? Is anyone listening? Do you hear me? I want out!" I focus on the red light, hoping someone with any clout will tell whoever imprisoned me to grant me my freedom. Geez. Why am I even here?

Instead of continuing my harassment toward the red spot, which obviously is getting me nowhere, I return to the bed and sit down. I sigh a few times, hoping my captor will get the hint and come to check on me.

But... where is Zach? Why hasn't he contacted me through our mind-link? Is he being held somewhere too? The question that swirled through my head earlier returns. Who would do this to me and why? The better question is *why*? None of this makes any sense. Unless...

I try to reach Zach again, but all I sense is black, empty, nothing.

My gaze focuses on the spot a moment later and notice the light has gone out. Does that mean whoever is holding me doesn't wish to watch me any longer? I'm sunk.

The sound of footsteps on stairs reaches me. Maybe I'm being rescued. I stand, straighten my dress, and wait. I don't move. I don't wish to be burned again.

The door to the room opens inward. Francisco, along with Alexander, stride inside and quickly close the door again. They both stay close to the door.

"My dear Emma. How lovely to see you again. I must apologize for your meager accommodations. However, since I'm certain you will attempt to contact Zachary should I release you, you must remain in here for the time being."

"Why *am* I here, Francisco? What happened to the plan? I'm supposed to be in Arizona training my replacement. Then Zachary and I were to return to acclimate me into your circle. What changed?"

"I didn't wish to wait, my dear. I wanted you here sooner. So, I sent Alexander," he motions toward his companion, "for you last night. I surmise he did you no harm?"

Alexander stands next to my jailor with his feet separated and hands clasped together. He's an imposing figure, one meant to intimidate, I'm certain. Since I'm still reeling from the aftereffects of drinking what I assume was human blood, I don't feel the least bit threatened. However, I intend to keep that little tidbit to myself.

"He stuck me with something. I remember clutching the back of a chair to keep from falling. Then I wake up in this dingy, dirty jail cell confused why anyone would wish me harm, only to find out it's all on you, Francisco. And, where's Zach? Where's my life-mate? Have you done something to him as well?"

Rage and worry drives my words. He'd better not have messed with Zach!

His hand reaches out to me in some sort of kind gesture. I refuse to accept it and back away. When the back of my knees hit the edge of the bed, I flop down. Damn, he has some explaining to do and he'd better get on with it.

"Young Zachary presently resides in your home, my dear. He promised to return here tonight, if you don't show up by then. Of course, you won't. However, I cannot allow you to let him know you are here. That's why you're in the safety of this chamber. These stones," he gestures around us, "hinder reception."

He steps forward. "You've consumed human blood, Emma, for the first time I assume. Your powers have increased because of it. If not for the light beam, which is motion sensitive, you would have escaped. I cannot allow that. You see, Emma, you were changed to become *my* life-mate. It was not my intention for you and Zachary to become a couple. You were supposed to hate him for changing you. However, when that didn't occur," he shrugs, "I made it a point to bring you here anyway, on my terms."

My eyelids fly open. No way am I going to allow that monster to take me.

Francisco observes my upset. "The time will come, sweet child, when you'll beg me to share my body with you. Especially since I control when and how much to feed you."

My fangs extend inside my mouth with his words. I must control myself. I must not allow him to have the upper hand. At least, while I can prevent it.

"Do as you wish with me, Francisco. Feed me or not. I belong to Zachary, and only Zachary. Unless…"

"What, my dear?" His eyes open wide in anticipation.

"Unless there is a way to change me back, to grant me my humanity again. I've asked Zach over and over to find someone who has the ability to reverse this curse. That's the only reason he and I are together. I don't love him, Francisco. I've used him to find a way to be restored to my human life."

I certainly hope Zach can't hear my words. He may believe them, especially with all my yo-yo decisions.

Francisco steps closer. "And, what has he told you in answer to your quest?"

"There is no one capable. I'm doomed to live my existence as a vampire. So, you see: feed me, don't feed me. I don't care. If I can't be changed back, I'd rather die sooner anyway."

"Emma, my sweet Emma. You shouldn't speak of ending your existence. Why, once you and I are joined, you will become the queen of all I possess. You will want for nothing. You and I will reign over the circle together, enjoy the benefits the Elders grant us, and we'll live together for centuries as one. Doesn't that appeal to you?"

If I pretend to care, maybe I can find a way out of this hellhole. "You have a mate, Francisco. What about her? Would I be required to fight her to the death or something?"

His eyes shine with amusement. "No, of course not. Nadia will be dealt with in time. However, until I'm certain you truly wish to mate with me... well, let's discuss this matter then. Hmm?"

My stomach churns. He's despicable. Zachary told me he and Nadia had been together for centuries. What has she done to gain his wrath? I tighten my hold on my emotions and attempt to smile.

"I'd like to shower and have a change of clothes." I want him out of my sight.

Francisco advances toward me. Before his hands touch me, I speed to the far wall. He's faster and reaches me before I can move again. His grasp is cold and clammy. It's the sneer on his lips that quivers my body, though. It's the same sneer that pierced my thoughts during the last trip I made into the mind chamber with Zach. I reel with fear.

"Do not run from me again. Do I make myself clear, Emma?"

His lips open enough for me to observe his extended fangs while his fingers grip my arms tightly. If I were a mere mortal, I'm certain bones would be crushed.

Scared he wishes to drink from me, I say the first thing that possess my mind. "I apologize. I didn't know what you intended. I will not run from you, Francisco, if you promise not to take me against my will."

Lips, once curled in an evil grimace, soften. "I promise."

My mind blurts, *Sure, that and a nickel will buy nothing.* How thankful I am that he can't read my thoughts. I regain my composure. "Thank you."

Alexander, still waiting in front of the cell door, clears his throat. "Sir, you have a meeting with the Elders to discuss the two younglings."

Francisco, gaze focused on mine, relinquishes his hold on my arms and steps back one pace. "I will see to it that you have a change of clothing before you shower. All the necessities in the bathroom are at your disposal. Until later..."

Francisco bows, turns, and follows Alexander out the cell door. When it's closed, I look up and see the red dot blinking again. That's creepy. I rub the areas on my arms where Francisco's fingers bit into my skin, stagger back to the bed, and lower onto it.

Tears from stress form in my eyes. Where is Zach? Doesn't he know I'd never leave him without a word? Hopefully, he'll figure out this fiend has me locked away. But, what can he do? Francisco is his maker, is stronger, has his army of followers who do his bidding, and for some reason wants me. If I knew the truth behind his desire, maybe I could play it against him. Until I know, I'll have to participate in this charade to exist.

Not for the first time, my mind screams, "Please, Zach. Find me soon."

While I wonder how to pretend to care for that monster, my mind focuses on why Zach didn't tell me the effects human blood has on a vampire. All these years, no one mentioned the added strength or cognitive value. What other side effects does it possess? Maybe if I can persuade Francisco to allow me out of this cell, I can research ways to use that strength against him. Ten year olds have nowhere near the capabilities of a, what, two-thousand-year-old creature? But…

I remember something Zach mentioned. Vampires judgement changes with age. If Francisco is an elder, possibly his reasoning capacity has diminished. Can I find a way out if I outsmart that evil brute? I must develop a plan. I have to escape this musty dirty cell and soon. If I don't, I fear Francisco will charm me into becoming his.

Damn, Zach. Where are you?

Lynne Anders

CHAPTER 24

ZACH

irst things first. I attempt to locate Emma through our mind-link again. I almost feel her, but lose the connection a moment later. She must be close, but her mind is out of reach. What blocks it now?

I pace around my house, eyes frenetic and my mind in turmoil. Francisco has my life-mate. How do I find her when I am unable to lock onto her thoughts? If I show up on his doorstep now, he will realize I know and force her into submission without a second thought. Damn. Every moment she spends with him... My fist punches my home-office door producing a gaping hole. I cannot allow her to spend time with that evil being. But, without help, I have no choice. His powers surpass even Nadia's.

I spin in place and ball my fists at my sides. An uncontrolled high-pitched scream raises my face to the heavens. I suck in a breath and scream one more time, "Emma!"

Without a plan and nowhere to turn, I must control my rage and ask for help. Phyllis mentioned she had been in that house with her mate once upon a time. Maybe she is privy to information I am not.

The call is quick and to the point. "Yes, I am certain, Phyllis. Do not ask me how I know. I just do. Will you help me?"

"If you promise to keep me away from the house, then yes, I will." The timber of her voice distresses me.

"Why do you not wish to enter the house?"

"It isn't Francisco that worries me." She inhales deeply. "It's his mate. Listen, Zach. If Emma is being kept against her will, it may be because of Nadia."

"Please explain." Why would Nadia want Emma?

"The circle has fallen from favor with the Elders. Everyone close to that circle knows this to be true. The reason for the rejection stems from allegations Nadia attempted to create a band of violent thugs to overthrow Rayner and his disciples, and force her way onto the West Coast Council. She is one power-hungry vampire."

"Rumors are typically rumors. Why place confidence in them?"

"The thugs are real, Zach. They aren't a rumor. Look, if Emma is stashed somewhere on that property, you'll be hard-pressed to find her. Francisco had state-of-the-art surveillance equipment installed two years ago. I only know this because Thaddeus was instrumental in the planning stages."

My love. My empty hand balls into a fist again. If he harms one hair on her head...

"If he has surveillance equipment, maybe he has technology to deflect our mind-link, possibly more. Damn." This is my fault. I was too busy watching over Emma during my free time the past decade, I neglected following my maker and his actions. I would have known about the upgrades if I had paid closer attention.

"Did Thaddeus share with you any hiding places, somewhere Francisco could hold Emma?" I bite my lip while I wait.

"No, I'm sorry, Zach. He didn't share any of the real particulars with me. I do believe he was killed because he knew too much, which threatened Francisco or maybe Nadia."

"I am sorry to involve you in this, then, Phyllis. Forget I called." I am about to end the call when her voice implores me.

"Don't hang up on me, Zach. If I can help you fight off those two evil beings, it'll be my pleasure. I'll hop a plane and be there in the morning. Pick me up in San Diego?"

"Are you sure?"

"I'm positive. Now. Relax if you can today. We have a lot of planning to do, my friend. We need our A-game minds in place if we're to outwit Francisco and Nadia."

"I will never be able to repay your generosity. Thank you, Phyllis."

Her chuckle warms my dark soul. "Don't thank me yet. We haven't accomplished a thing."

We end the call, and hope fills my mind for the first time in two days. However, before I attempt anything else, I hide these thoughts deep down where Francisco cannot find them, utilizing Phyllis' technique. Satisfied they are hidden, I place a call to my maker to check in as he asked.

"Good morning, Francisco. I have returned home without Emma. She did not return and has not contacted me. My only recourse is to wait to hear from her leader."

"Don't fret, dear boy. She'll surface. When she does, prepare yourself for changes she'll have made. I don't doubt she's frightened, conceivably of you. Before you lay blame where it doesn't exist, welcome her home, but listen to her reasons for abandoning you. It may surprise you to find out others' influence brought her back."

That sneaky beast. He is making his intentions vividly clear.

Unfortunately, I allow anger to cloud my words. "She belongs to me, Francisco. She is my life-mate. I changed her and I will fight anyone who says differently."

"Calm down, young Zachary. No one has implied otherwise. However, you must allow your charge to decide for herself who holds her alliance. You must prepare yourself for that eventuality."

The underlying calm in his voice rips me in two. It is his attempt to subtly charm me. I am well aware of his methods, so I do not fall under that spell any longer. The implication is crystal clear, though.

"Once she returns, *we* will decide where she belongs. She and *I* will discuss her issues at length, as a couple, to determine her choices in the matter. Now. If you will excuse me, Francisco, I have work to attend to this morning."

Running over to his house is out of the question, but it is my first inclination. I drop my phone in my pants pocket and pace around again. Where is she? Why is my attempt to contact her thwarted? I refuse to stop trying. I stop, close my eyes, and give it a go again. I reach deep down inside me and search for her mind. As if on cue, her mind opens to me. We connect for only a moment. I relay I am looking for her and not to give up. Her response is to hurry before the link ends.

At least she is unharmed at this point, and she knows I am searching for her. Damn. I should have asked her where she was. The next time we connect, I will.

After a quick check of my watch, I dash into the bedroom, change into work clothes, grab a Velvet Crimson to ward off the stress from this morning, and leave for my office. Only a few more patients require my attention before I close up shop. Even though Emma is lost to me at this point, I intend to follow through with our plan. I must find a way to rid us of Francisco and his circle of deviants. The sad part is, I was one of them once upon a time.

Tuesday morning, June twenty-sixth, I race to San Diego International Airport through the perpetual morning marine layer surrounding San Diego to retrieve Phyllis Megalos. Her flight arrived at seven thirty and I am late. I replied to her questioning text promising I would be there within ten minutes.

Phyllis, always one to dress with a little flair, stands alone at the curb outfitted in a yellow, green, and blue-print maxi dress. Her arms are covered to her wrists and her feet are adorned with ankle-strapped sandals. She appears to have stepped off a fashion show runway with dark sunglasses perched low on her nose and an oversized straw handbag draped over her arm. If she wanted to draw more attention, she would be standing there with her fangs extended licking her bright red lips. Before I am able to exit the car to open the door for her, she grabs the handle, tosses her bag in the back seat, and flops down next to me. She drops her glasses and with a quick head-turn toward me, exclaims, "It's about time. My gums are tingling. Can we stop along the way for a drink, please?"

"And, good morning to you, too." I hide my disheartened chuckle as my car inches forward with the rest of the arrival traffic until I am on Interstate 5 heading north. As we begin to pick up speed, I relax against the seatback. "I have plenty at the house. Can you wait an hour while we stop somewhere we can speak in private?"

Her eyes squint. "We can't speak privately at your home?"

"Francisco installed surveillance devices in his home. I am fearful mine has them as well. That creature will stop at nothing."

She gazes out the windshield. "What about our conversation yesterday? Do you think he overheard?"

"I have no way of knowing, Phyllis. All I know is I no longer feel secure in my own home. I would rather speak in private somewhere. Not my office and not my home."

"What about in your car?"

Would he? "Possible, I suppose."

We share a knowing glance. "I know of a place in Del Mar, on the beach and out of the way, that serves the best breakfast." I decide not to mention the name, just in case.

We arrive in under an hour, are shown to a remote table on the back deck, order meals and our drinks, and settle in for a long discussion.

Phyllis shares her observances from her past explorations of Francisco's estate. "I'm surprised you haven't been granted the grand tour. Doesn't Francisco consider you to be his second-in-command?"

"He reminded me the other night." Unsettled by the graphic display I was forced to witness, I shift in my chair to explain.

"Rayner accused one of our members, Cassander, of plans to overthrow Francisco. They tortured him, Phyllis, then severed his head and tossed the remnants on a burning pyre. In all my years, I have never witnessed anything as gruesome, and I have seen plenty. Most of the attending vampires wished to participate in his death. It appalled me and also troubled me. Being a vampire, I should have wished to participate."

Phyllis stares at me while struggling to find words. Her lips close into a smooth line before she responds. "Emma has changed you."

Confusion draws my brows together. This is what I thought to be true that terrible night. However, I want to hear her explanation. "What do you mean?"

"She's reminded you of your humanity, Zach." Phyllis grasps my arm. "Francisco's influence over you has changed throughout the centuries. And, now that Emma has shared her body with you, you are evolving more. You aren't the same despot you once were."

Despot? "I behaved as Francisco wished for years after he changed me, I admit. However, once I was introduced to Velvet Crimson, I no longer sought out humans for sustenance. That drink saved me from a life of destruction and eventual death."

"Don't you see, Zach? Vampires choose their existence. Francisco rules his circle with an iron fist. Do as he says and you'll survive. However, step one pace away and you're considered a threat. You will be disposed of the same way Cassander was if you're not careful. Mark my words. He doesn't trust anyone, especially those he considers a threat to his power."

"I have no desire to rule his circle. Far from it. I prefer existing under the radar of all mortals. And, as long as Emma is with me, peace will follow along as well."

My friend stares out across the water while she rubs her arms as if she were cold. "Now you know why I won't join that circle. Thaddeus warned me years ago about that maniac *and* his mate. Neither are competent to govern any circle. With all the stories that have circulated about them... I worry for you, my friend."

"Concern for me is unnecessary. I know when to hold my tongue." I take a sip of warm coffee and hail our waitress. "Leaving that circle does present a problem, but Emma and I will do anything to accomplish it. Now, how do we activate our plan?"

Our waitress pours hot coffee into our cups and over the next two hours, Phyllis and I discuss who amongst the circle can be trusted to help, unknowingly of course. Once Emma is freed, the final leg of our plan will be implemented. Now. Where has he imprisoned her?

Phyllis' insight spins my head. "Before his death, Thaddeus spoke of secret passageways throughout the house. Francisco disappears from one room and reappears in another without being detected. You don't suppose there are secret rooms as well, do you?"

I shift my chair closer to the table and clasp my hands on top while I visualize the interior. "I have never paid close attention before. But... I do recall a day before I left for the reunion. Stuart and I were seated in the living room talking and Francisco suddenly appeared as if out of thin air. At the time, I felt we were too engrossed in our conversation to notice our maker enter. Now that you mention it, though, he strode in from the patio door. He seemed as surprised as we were at the time, too, as though he did not know we were in the house." My head turns toward Phyllis. "How did he enter without us knowing since we have enhanced senses?"

Her lips curl. "He didn't. There must be a secret passage or doorway near the patio door. It's the only explanation."

With this knowledge, Phyllis and I discuss our plan for another hour, pile back into my car, and finish the drive to my home in Oceanside. Francisco has not attempted to read my thoughts yet today, but I worry when he will try. I must maintain my vigilance, however. Too much is at stake.

The cloud cover dissipates during our journey and brings forth a breezy sunny afternoon. I welcome Phyllis into my home and deposit her into the second bedroom. Since listening devices may be planted in my home, rest is on the agenda for the remainder of the afternoon. I plan to visit Francisco this evening. I want a better look around his home. Maybe I can detect Emma if I am there.

When Francisco has not contacted me by early evening, I place a call to his cell phone. "Zachary. To what do I owe this pleasure?"

"I require your advice."

"By all means, dear boy."

The soothing tone of his voice chokes me and I must swallow back my desire to kill him. "I would rather not discuss this over the phone. May I come over instead?"

When a welcoming reply is not immediate, I assume he is pondering me in the house with Emma somewhere nearby. "I will only stay a few moments, Francisco. You must know this is vital to me."

"Please make it quick then. I must leave within the hour, Zachary."

"Thank you." I end the call before he can object, and turn to Phyllis.

"Stay inside. Someone may be watching the house. I did not detect anyone earlier, but that does not mean they are not there. And, by all means, do not speak with anyone." I huff and run a hand through my hair. "I must sound paranoid."

"Yes. It means you're concerned. Go. Get it over with so we'll have a better idea where we stand. If you need me, I'm right here." My friend grasps my arm and fixes me with her gaze. "We'll get her out, Zach. I promise."

My weary chuckle and downcast gaze worries even me. "We can hear a pin drop, smell a rose a mile off, and run faster than an airplane at its peak. How is it, with all the attributes and extraordinary senses available to us as vampires, we cannot locate one small woman?"

"You forget, Zach. He is elder. His powers surpass ours combined. Nadia's, too. You must hold onto hope you'll find a crack in his armor tonight. Something that confirms where Emma is held. Keep your eyes open, but don't show your emotions. He'll be on to you if you do. Look around quickly then return home. We'll find a way in."

A nod is all I can muster. "Again, please stay inside and do not answer the door to anyone. I will be back within the hour."

With no other plan than to look for hidden passageways and doorways, I climb in my car and drive the short distance to Francisco's estate pondering how to proceed.

CHAPTER 25

FRANCISCO

If he wishes to look around my house, I may as well allow it. He won't find her. With the many safeguards installed throughout the home and grounds, he doesn't stand a chance. I stop to ponder the next idea that presents itself. What if he not only finds Emma, but she rejects him? I toss my head back and laugh out loud. That scene will destroy the boy. "You'll play into my hands, young sir, and you will lose everything."

I must act quickly. He'll will be here within a few minutes. I pull my phone from my pocket and send a quick text to Casper outlining what I want from him. I then rush toward the patio door, draw the curtain aside, and push the button which opens the secret door into the stairway. From the living room, the doorway appears as a floor-to-ceiling window with a view of the patio. I chuckle as I trot down the stairs. It's all done with mirrors. The mirrors conceal the entrance perfectly.

The door into her cell opens with a creak and as I close it, I watch her approach but not far enough to be stunned by the burning beam.

"What do you want, Francisco? Come to torture me again?"

My hand waves to the vampire observing from above and I watch as the red light above disappears. It's safe to venture forward. "Emma, my dear." I reach for her, but she shies away. "Don't retreat from me, my sweet. I come with news of your Zachary."

At the mere mention of his name, her eyes open wide and her lips part in question. When her hand clasps her stomach, I walk closer and force my presence into her mind.

"Yes, my love. He has come to bid you goodbye."

She visibly slumps before me. Good girl. She's prepared.

"When you see him, you will thank him for his concern, but relate you've had a change of heart and wish to learn from me instead of him. Don't forget to thank him for bringing you this far. Do you understand, Emma?"

Her nod proves she's under my spell. "Now. Let's clean you up and prepare for his arrival."

When I open the door to the cell, Casper stands before me with clothing I purchased for this occasion. She must appear for my underling as though she's been treated like the queen she will become. He also must accept her decision and then disappear from her life if she is to become mine completely. His interference will only hamper the completion of my plan.

"Change into these, Emma. I will return in a few minutes for you."

The door closes soundly behind me. I wait a moment, but decide to allow her to change without observing eyes. While I wait, I stroll down the long corridor to check on the other occupant on this level. He's been exceptionally quiet the few times I've visited, and I want to verify he's still alive. After the commotion with Cassander, I worry he'll not consume any blood and will perish before I have the answers I require.

I stop before the door and peer inside. Oliver squats in a corner of his cell, knees to his chest, arms wrapped tightly around them. His head is cradled against his arms, but raises slowly when he perceives me.

"What do you want, Francisco?" His voice hisses through clenched teeth.

"Oliver, why disrespect me so? If you'd provide answers to my questions, you would be out of here. Cassander has been released. Why not follow suit and regale me with the truth as well?"

The vampire before me reaches behind him to push himself up, steadying against the wall at his back. It's only then the chains that hold him in place become visible. "Me? Disrespect you?" He rattles the shackles securing his arms. "You starve me, which deprives me of my strength, chain me like a slave, and wonder why I disrespect *you*? You already have the truth, you idiot. Cassander and I did not desire to overthrow you. You are our leader. We respected you. It's your mate, Nadia, who placed those thoughts in your head. *She* wants to control the circle. Not us. Don't you see the writing on the wall?

By destroying those who follow you, worship you, she's removing all who would assist you when she decides to overthrow *you*."

I've heard enough. "Nadia is satisfied with our existence and circle. Furthermore, she has no desire to rule. Why would she? She has everything she could ever want or need now. You are grossly mistaken, dear Oliver. It's you who has planned my demise. It's you who will remain in that cell until you bear witness to your actions."

Oliver turns his back on me and lowers to the floor again. I huff and spin back toward Emma's cell hoping she's prepared for her audience with Zachary. He's the other vampire in my circle who wishes me harm. I may have to resort to confining him in a chamber one day as well.

I peer inside her cell, hoping she's refreshed herself and dressed in the gown I chose. My exhale of breath hisses against the corridor walls while I study the vision before me. She's tied her hair back into a long low ponytail, which lays against the full-length linen frock. She spins my way. It's no wonder Zachary fell for this one. Her beauty is flawless.

The chamber door pushes open. I walk through and stop. Have my eyes deceived me? The image of my human wife stands before me. From her hair to the shoes she wears, Emma is the woman I married more than two thousand years ago.

I rush to her in greeting, take her into my arms, and place my lips gently against hers. "Christine, my dear. I have missed you." I whisper into her ear.

The girl staggers away and brushes the taste of my lips from hers. "I am not Christine. My name is Emma Christensen."

Reality forces my mind open with an image of my wife dead in my arms. My gaze refocuses on the girl in front of me, so much like my Christine.

Christine. Can this lovely creature replace my one and only love? I stare openly at her. Yes, it is possible. But, first, I'll grant her this moment of resistance. I'll also need to further charm her into believing she's in love with me so she'll carry out the charade upstairs. And, after that's completed...

"Of course, my dear. You took me by surprise. You see, your appearance resembles my wife from long ago. Please forgive my impertinence." I step closer and capture her focus once more. "You do belong to me, Emma. Do you agree?"

Her head nods while her pupils dilate slightly.

"When we meet with Zachary in a few minutes, you will not spurn my advances. Do I make myself clear?"

Again, a quick head nod and she's under my control.

"Let us greet our guest, shall we?"

I offer my arm to the beauty, who grasps it to follow me out of her chamber. We take the stairway up to the library in case my charge has already arrived. Emma doesn't make a sound while I open the secret door then close it behind us. She stands with her hands clasped waiting for my instructions.

I perceive Zachary's presence in the living room and ask Emma to greet him first. I follow behind to ascertain if she follows my instructions. I'm treading on unknown ground. I believe she's under my influence, but will intercede if I'm incorrect in that assumption.

Zachary rushes to his mate, clasps her to him, and kisses her cheek. "Emma. Where have you been? I have been searching for you." He draws away and peers into her eyes. "Are you alright? Please tell me why you left and have not contacted me."

Her lips tremble slightly. I fear she may blurt out the truth, so I intervene. "Emma came to me, Zachary. She feels you've taught her all you can and wishes to learn from me now. Isn't that correct, my dear?"

Emma stands erect, but with her back to me. I slowly approach the two lovers and watch her closely to assure myself she's fully charmed. When she turns to face me, I notice the resistance. However, her lips purse when she refocuses on Zachary.

"Yes, Francisco. It is time for me to assimilate into your circle."

She blinks twice, then continues. "Thank you, Zachary, for teaching me your ways. Now, it's time for me to advance my learning. I look to Francisco for my future."

Zach stares in disbelief. He subtly shakes her and begs, "You are my life-mate, Emma. We have bonded, shared our bodies and blood. You belong with me. Why throw away all we planned? Do you not realize how much I love you? How much I gave up for you?"

Emma steps away and clasps my arm. "I thought I loved you as well, Zachary. However, Francisco promises more. This is where I belong now. Please forgive me and... forget me."

Shunned by his life-mate, Zachary staggers back, turns, and almost runs out the front door. However, the moment the door closes,

Emma drops to the floor. She's fainted. I kneel beside her and help her sit. It takes a few moments for her to gain control of her senses.

"Emma, my sweet. You should take better care of yourself."

Still not completely cognizant of her surroundings, she surveys the area in disbelief. "Why am I here?" Her head spins to me. The fright in her eyes, while not unexpected, answers my question before I must ask.

"You escaped your chamber, Emma. Come. It's time to return."

Weak from the charm, she readily accepts my assistance and stands. Together we traverse the living room and back into the library. However, to keep her from watching how to open and close the secret doorway, I ask her to turn away while I blindfold her.

"Once we're inside your chamber, I will remove the mask. Come, sweet girl. I will assist you."

With my arm slung around her waist, Emma and I pass through the opening door. Once it's closed from the other side, I scoop her up in my arms and carry her down the spiral stairway to the underground passageway floor, where I release her to stand on her own.

Still blindfolded, I lead her toward her chamber. However, when we near the cell Oliver is chained in, the vampire utters a high-pitched shriek. Surprised by the scream, Emma jerks away from me and bangs her head against the opposite wall. Luckily, I catch her before she falls to the ground again.

Scooped in my arms, I turn and curse Oliver. "One more sound out of you… it will be your last. Do you hear me, Oliver?"

"I'm dead already. Your threats hold no significance to me anymore, Francisco. Do what you will with me. Just get it over with."

His voice fades the farther away we trod toward her chamber. Once inside, I lay the young vampire on the bed, wishing she were awake and beckoning me to join her.

"All in due time, my dear. Soon you will belong to me and you'll have forgotten the young vampire who changed you." I remove the ribbon which holds her ponytail in place and allow her long light-brown hair to cascade over the pillow. I bend to kiss her inviting lips, but stall inches away, fearful I won't be able to stop.

"Until later, my dear. Rest now. I will come to you later in the night."

I pull her door closed, stroll down the long hallway, and climb the stairs to the library without further fanfare from Oliver. He's getting on my nerves and must be dealt with soon. However, without confirmation he and Cassander plotted against me, I must decide how best to rid my circle of this once-devoted fanatic.

While I slowly meander out of the library, an idea formulates in my mind. I can rid myself of both. It's time to call upon my mate. I will make it a priority to deposit this idea into her thoughts so she'll believe the plan is hers. Before I ascend the stairs to the second floor and her suite, I remember to contact the security office and ask that Emma's cell be armed again in case my charm has worn off. I mustn't allow any contact between her and Zachary. It will jeopardize everything.

Chapter 26

Emma

My head pounds when I wake, but it dissipates shortly after my eyes open. For once, I'm happy I'm a vampire. My joy fades when I recall the scream, which frightened me and caused me to quickly back away from that cell. My fingers probe the tender bump on my head while I wonder if I suffered a concussion. My head did hit the rock wall rather hard. When I roll over to place my feet on the ground, one other memory storms through. Zach. He was here, but I asked him to leave. Why? I love him. Why would I tell him I wished Francisco to complete my training? What happened to our plan to leave this circle? And, more importantly, why didn't I try to mind-link with him? He stood right in front of me. I could have assured him I was here under duress.

Another memory floods my mind. Francisco. His eyes, the velvet texture of his voice. I take a chance and bolt to my feet anyway. He charmed me! I'm about to voice my protest, but remember someone watches this cell from above. Instead, I enter the bathroom, which is hidden from prying eyes.

I attempt to contact my love. My eyes close and I visualize him vividly. I pray he perceives my thoughts. For a moment, he enters my mind and I internally rejoice he responded to me. I send a thought of Francisco, and charming, and relay I love him with my entire being. The impression he sends is, *"Where?"* I try to capture the rock walls encasing me. However, I'm shut down the moment that thought formulates. Damn. Hopefully, he seized the prior images.

I pretend to wash and dry my hands for those above, change out of the garments I'm in, and re-dress in my dirty two-day-old garb. Something about the linen dress disturbed me. Rid of it, I toss the garment into the corner, also wishing I had other clothes to wear. With my hair tied up in a high ponytail again, I exit the stall and return to the bed.

I look above the door and notice the red light shines again. Was it before? I didn't look up, so I'm uncertain. Is that why I was able to contact Zach? If so, something in that light or setup shields my thoughts, too. Next time Francisco chooses to visit me, I'll watch for the light to disappear then try to reach Zach.

In the meantime, my gums tingle from lack of blood. I focus on the light and cry out, "I need blood. Will someone please send some down for me? And, food, too. I'm hungry."

With nothing else to do, I recline on the bed to wait. When I close my eyes, my mind focuses on the staff in my office at home. They must believe I've run out on them. Damn. I didn't want my tenure to end this way. I wanted to train my replacement and leave on good terms. Not knowing what the future holds, I may require a job again and I'd like to call upon them for an endorsement.

"That's out of the question now," I mention to no one. I roll onto my side and huff. Why am I concerned with finding a job? I may never get out of here and, even if I do, I'll be on the run with Zach forever unless we rid ourselves of Francisco and his circle.

What about my mom? I didn't find out what troubled her either. I need to talk with my dad to find out if she's okay. I've just *got* to escape this place. But how?

Sound from the dumbwaiter catches my attention. Hopeful someone heard my plea, I rise and slowly maneuver toward the opening, still afraid I'll be struck by the light beam if I move too quickly. When I reach the dumbwaiter, I notice a small glass of blood and what appears to be raw meat on a plate.

"You've got to be kidding me, right?" I snatch the glass and drink the liquid quickly. My fangs extend and my body hums with energy a moment later. When I place the empty glass back where it came from, I stare at the uncooked piece of meat. Nope. Not even going to try it. I can't wrap my mind around raw meat. Blood, yes. But, that? No way!

Instead, I enter the bathroom and attempt to contact Zach again. All I get is blackness, as predicted. To cover up my endeavor, I wash and dry my hands again. When I exit the stall, I look up above the cell door. The red light glows.

Infused with energy, I try but can't sit still. I pace around the space thinking of a way I can escape my captor. If that beam of light was turned off, I'd stand a chance.

Footsteps echo outside my chamber, but when I look above the door the red light still shines. Whoever it is doesn't plan to enter my cell, evidently. I step toward the door, but stop well short of the light that burns my skin. A woman dressed in black, which matches her long hair, stands in front of another door. Is that the one we were passing when I heard the gut-wrenching scream? It sounded like whoever is incarcerated in there was being tortured. Maybe she's come to check.

Even with my enhanced vampire hearing, the words shared down the hallway are muffled. I want to creep closer to the door, but must stay back to keep from harm's way. When the female turns as if to leave, I cry out, "Please! Help me!"

She spins my way and slowly saunters toward my chamber. I don't recall meeting her before. However, something inside me cringes when her gaze converges on mine. Does she know *me*? I stand my ground and wait until she's outside the door before I speak again.

"My name is Emma Christensen. I've been abducted and placed in here by Francisco. Can you help me escape? I want to return to my life-mate, Zachary Matthews. Do you know him?"

Her hideous laugh backs me up. She steps closer to the bars of my cage before speaking. "So, *you're* the one. I was told he abducted you, but I didn't believe my confidantes." She surveys me from head to toe. "I admit, you do resemble Christine. But, you most definitely are not her. She was weak and chose to die instead of live beside her husband."

I gulp my words as I speak. "Who is Christine?" I survey the woman standing outside my cell while waiting for her reply. Realization dawns on me when she bares her fangs. My body jolts. If I'm correct, in front of me stands the mate of evil personified.

She surveys me again and turns from the door. "Actually, she's none of your business. Oh, and by the way, my name is Nadia. I'm Francisco's mate."

She continues to walk away until she turns a corner and moves out of my sight. Thankfully, she doesn't utter another word. But, fear overtakes me. She could harm me without Francisco being the wiser. Why did I call out to someone I didn't know? How stupid!

I sit down and return my thoughts to Zach and the days we spent together. I long for his touch, the pleasing scent of him after we've mated, the taste of his blood on my lips, the gentleness of his character. My eyes close as I recall the shape of his body that first night undressing in his room while I watched from mine. The moment his fingers touched me for the first time in the shower.

My body quivers with need. Is the blood I consumed opening my mind to his? Excited and hoping he is able to understand me, images of the cell, the hallway, and Nadia as she stood in front of my cell pour out of me. Just as quickly, a flash image he understands invades my mind. I want to rejoice, but stall my voice in case someone is listening. Instead, tears of joy roll down my cheeks. My Zachary. He'll find a way to get me out of here. He just has to. Between Francisco and Nadia… I'm in jeopardy, no matter which one comes for me.

My eyes blink open and I peek above the door. The red dot is absent. So, it wasn't the blood. Someone turned it off. I spring from the bed, quickly reach the door, and gently pull it open. It isn't locked. Before I reason why, I make it down the hallway to what appears to be a medieval arched stone opening on the left side, which leads to a circular rock and stone stairway. I bound up in seconds and search for a way to open the door in front of me.

Before I locate a way out, voices raised in anger reach me from the other side. I listen to the heated exchange. It sounds like Francisco and possibly Nadia discussing what to do with Oliver. Could that be Nicole's Oliver? Is he the one imprisoned below? Why?

I don't have long to ponder his situation when I catch my name shouted by the female voice. I miss most of his response, except "…on my way to see her now." Since my escape through this doorway is rendered impossible, I retrace my steps, but stop at the cell door where I saw Nadia earlier.

I peer inside. "Are you Oliver?" The creature inside huddles against the back wall in dirty days-old clothing. Their stench reaches my nose and I back up a step, but not before noticing his cell is much smaller and does not have a bathroom suite like mine.

At the sound of my voice, his head raises. His appearance backs me up. His teeth are bared and his fangs are extended. "Who are you and what do you want?" his voice hisses.

"I met Nicole a few days ago. If you're Oliver, she's worried sick about you. Francisco told her you were on a mission for him."

He stands and walks as far as his chains allow. "Who are you?"

"My name is Emma Christensen. I am Zachary Matthew's life-mate. He was told to bring me here to meet his maker, Francisco, and that I was to become part of his circle. However, I awoke a couple of days ago inside the cell down the hall when I'm supposed to be in Arizona training my replacement at work." My head shakes. "I'm getting ahead of myself."

He pins me with a stare. "You belong to Zach? You're the one?"

Confused, my lips pucker. "I'm the one what?"

"You must be careful. If I'm correct, Francisco plans to do away with *her* and make *you* his life-mate. It's Nadia you must be wary of. She's on to him and will come after you."

"But... I belong to Zach."

Noise from above catches my attention. My head turns toward the sound and observes light cascading down the stairwell.

"I've got to go. If they catch me out..." Without further explanation, I rush into my cell, push the door closed, and sit down on my bed. When I look up, the red light is still absent, maybe because Nadia stopped Francisco before he could make his way downstairs? I decide to pretend to be asleep in case someone should peek inside the cell. Thankful for once I don't have a discernable heartbeat, I turn from the door and curl my arms under my head. If anyone were to look in, they'd believe me to be resting.

Two voices carry down the long stairway and into the corridor. The argument I overheard continues as they close on my cell. I stay on my side and listen to footfalls as they approach.

"She holds no interest to me, my sweet," Francisco coos to his mate. "You are my one true love, Nadia."

"Do you believe me to be a fool, Francisco? She's the spitting image of your human wife." Nadia's sharp tone transmits her obvious wrath.

I lay still and hope those two bypass my chamber. No such luck. When the door opens, I spring from the bed and press my back to the far wall. I peek up and see no red light above the door and momentarily consider attempting an escape. However, if Zach is coming for me, maybe I should stay put for now.

Francisco steps nearer. "Don't be afraid, my dear. We've come only to check on you." His eyes glint black when his lips curl into a malicious smile. "Nadia tells me you asked to be released from your accommodations. Is that correct?"

Does he intend to harm me if I speak the truth? I decide to repeat what I asked of his mate. "You had me abducted, Francisco. Of course, I want out of this dirty cell."

Menacing eyes focus on mine. "I see my charm didn't last long." He closes the space between us. "You have more power than I expected, dear Emma. Maybe I should try again."

I'm about to protest when Nadia intervenes. "As long as she remains inside this cell, you have nothing to fear from her, Francisco. Leave this dirty reincarnate of your deceased wife alone. I can take care of her later if you'd rather. Besides, we have more pressing matters to attend to."

The circle leader glares at his life-mate. "No, Nadia, your assistance is not required nor requested. Leave the young creature to me. I do believe it's time to shower Oliver with our kindness. Shall we visit him instead?"

Without another word, the two evil vampires exit my cell. I stride quickly toward the door only to be burned by the light hitting my shoulder. I look up and see the red dot above the door as I rub the tender skin. So, when someone intends to visit me, the light or beam is turned off. I intend to put that to good use next time.

But... where is Zach? I figured he'd be here by now. Does he not know how to access this level of the home? He's been here countless times. He should know.

My attention is diverted when cries of pain emanate from down the hallway. I step as close to the door as I dare and watch as Oliver is dragged out of the cell, around the corner, and probably up those stairs. I recognize Alexander as one of the two vampires manhandling the prisoner. The other I've never seen before. Francisco and Nadia follow closely behind.

Before he turns the corner, Francisco spins his head my way. Is it a challenge to remain quiet or a reminder that my fate remains his to do with as he pleases?

I shiver and step away. My arms wrap around my body as I return to the bed. I don't wish to draw any additional attention from that pair. I jump when a door closes and I realize I'm alone again in this dank level of the estate.

Even though the red light shines from above the door, I attempt to contact Zach. It's fruitless. Darkness surrounds me completely. For the first time since becoming vampire, fear grips me.

"Where are you, Zach? I'm afraid."

Lynne Anders

CHAPTER 27

ZACH

She is being held hostage in some dark cellar at Francisco's. How can that be? I thought I had been on every level, in every room of his estate. Since he has repeatedly informed me I am his second-in- command, why is it I do not know anything about this... this dungeon? And, more importantly, who else is, or has been, imprisoned within those walls?

"You have some heavy explaining to do, Francisco." I mutter to myself as I pace around my kitchen deciding my course of action. I must act soon. Her vision portrayed desperation.

Phyllis strides in through the back door, her body glowing with the sheen of exercise, and tosses her empty water bottle into the trash bin. She stands with hands on her hips, her breath completely normal. "What's up?"

"We need to get Emma. She was able to send me a message a few moments ago about a rock-encased room where she is being held. Someone will die if we wait much longer."

"What's your plan?"

"To find access to that dungeon, extract her somehow, and continue with the plan we devised. We need to get her out of there *now*. There is no telling who will do her harm."

Phyllis paces around the kitchen. "I told you, Zach, I will not step foot inside that house again. Too many memories of despicable acts committed there haunt me. I will not open my psyche to them again."

My desperate gaze focuses on her. "Please. I cannot do this alone."

Phyllis rubs her forehead as she processes my request. "Fine." She shakes a finger at me. "But, you'll owe me big time, mister. Give me five minutes to change."

She rushes up to the second bedroom and returns dressed in khaki and white. "Well, what are we waiting for? Let's go rescue Emma."

Walking with purpose, she strides toward the utility room door leaving me to follow in her wake. My mind allows me one moment to thank her internally while we pile into my car and drive the short distance to Francisco and Nadia's residence.

All seems quiet when we pull up, but loud voices radiate from the back. Believing Emma to be involved, I rush around to the patio, deserting Phyllis without a backward glance. The scene before me shows Alexander dropping Oliver onto the deck where Casper holds a blade high above his head. Francisco and Nadia look on.

Before I can stop myself, I yell, "Stop!"

Everyone's head swivels toward my shout.

Phyllis has chosen not to join me. I quickly determine it may be more opportune if I attempt this alone anyway. I continue to the people on the deck and stare in disbelief.

"What are you doing, Francisco? Oliver has always been a trusted member of our circle. What charge has been applied to cause *his* death?"

"Treason, Zachary, and this is none of your concern. I must ask you to leave immediately, or…" he leisurely turns my way, "are you complicit as well?"

"Complicit in what treason? I have done nothing but your bidding all these years. And when, pray tell, did Oliver and Cassander attempt this treason you suggest? They have pursued your incessant errands the past three months. *Your* errands, Francisco. Yet the congregation at Elder Rayner's home devoured and destroyed a valued member of our circle. Tell me what proof you have and tell me now. Or must I contact the Elders and ask for a hearing myself?"

Francisco hisses. His fangs elongate, his eyes blacken, and he glowers at me from the back of the deck.

"You should remember your place, *young* Zachary. You forget your life-mate is in my care. One step out of line and she will face the consequences. Do I make myself clear?"

210

"You always make yourself clear, Francisco. I wish to speak with Emma. Bring her to me now. I want to ask her why she has chosen to leave me and asked you to guide her."

My comments have the desired effect on Nadia. She strides closer to Casper and holds her hand out to stop the blade. Her lips move against his ear, but she speaks much too quietly for me or Francisco to understand.

She returns her malicious gaze to her mate. "What is this, Francisco? I knew you desired the young female. I didn't know she has chosen *you* to guide her through this life."

Her eyes glaze over. She stands rigid before him, her jaw clenches, and a growl escapes her mouth. The wrath of Nadia is not to be toyed with. I stand my ground, anyway, and wait while Francisco negotiates a path out of the hole he's dug.

His blazing stare matches hers. He lunges toward her and grasps her wrists. "*I* am the ruler of this circle, Nadia. My law prevails. If you are unhappy in this life with me, you may take your leave... *now!*" He violently tosses her arms from his hands. Red ridges ring her wrists where his nails etched her skin. "Who I choose to share this existence with is *my* business. I fought for centuries to create this circle. We were the favored circle amongst many until you found it necessary to divide our members with the addition of those freaks you consider worthy. Now, the Elders consider us no more than the heathens you created. This lenience toward you and your hoodlums has gone on far too long. It stops now."

Francisco turns my way and addresses me. "You have overstepped your position as well, Mr. Matthews. The young vampire living in my home came to *me* with questions concerning our kind, questions you were unable to answer. Her allegiance to me came as a surprise, but since she has made this overture, if I were you, I'd walk away."

"Then why hold her prisoner in your estate if she came to you of her own volition?" My fangs descend. I will *not* walk away. I stand straighter and concentrate on the evil before me. "You are not me and I have no intention of leaving until I speak with Emma. Have her brought here, Francisco. I want to hear from her myself." I am out on a limb here, but I will not back down. If he charmed her before, he will not have time to accomplish that again now.

Casper no longer stands next to Oliver wielding the blade. In fact, he has left the patio altogether. It is Alexander who stands vigil in his place. I do not understand the implications until I hear her voice.

"Zach! Zach, here I am."

I spin in the direction of Emma's voice and watch her rush out through the patio doors and into my arms. I also catch a glimpse of Casper near the drapes. At whose bidding did he release my mate? My answer comes immediately.

Francisco sneers at Nadia and lurches toward her. Before she can react, he holds her neck in his hand, effectively choking her. "So, your little minion brought her to him, Nadia. How did he find her?"

Her evil laugh sputters as she replies. "You fool! *I* changed Casper. You know what that means, Francisco. He may show allegiance to you occasionally, but he does my bidding, not yours."

Francisco lifts her from the deck, his hold tightening around her throat. "You will pay for this, my dear."

I do not wait for the outcome. I hold Emma tightly to me and dash toward the front of the house, where Phyllis—thankfully—waits with the car running. As our driver speeds away from the estate, I watch for someone to follow us, but sigh in relief when no one appears.

We race to I-5, then south.

"Block him now, Zach. I don't want him to find us."

"Already done. Where are we going??"

"As far away as we can get today. Once we're certain he hasn't followed us, we'll implement the rest of our plan. But, first, how are you, Emma? Did he…"

"No." Her lips part as if she wishes to say more, but then immediately close. She peers into my eyes. "He won't stop, Zach. He'll hunt us down and kill us. He's evil. And, so is she. How in the world have they been allowed to control your circle when they're crazy?"

I hold my mate close to me and inhale her scent. There is definitely a difference, but underneath is still Emma. For the first time in three days, my body relaxes.

"I intend to report their behavior to the Elders. Hopefully, our leadership will change."

My gaze fills the rearview mirror. "What is our destination, Phyllis?" My lips graze the top of Emma's head, thankful I am able to kiss her again.

"Nashville. I figure we'll be close enough to Indianapolis, but not too close. Francisco is certain to send his thugs there once he realizes you've left California and are not in Arizona. Tell me the name of your bank. Once you've cleared out your account, we can proceed with step two."

"Bank of America. Stop at the one closest to the airport."

Phyllis asks the Waze GPS to locate Bank of America, sets in the desired location, and continues down I-5.

"I just love technology," she muses.

Emma nestles her face against my neck. "Thank you for rescuing me. I thought that vampire was taking me to Francisco until I heard your voice."

My lips kiss the top of her head again. "I had no hand in your release. It was Nadia. Casper is one of her goons. She did it because I mentioned in front of her that you were taken by Francisco."

Emma raises her face to me. "Actually, I told her that earlier. She visited my cell, Zach, after she checked on Oliver. I sort of met him. He's been kept in that cell for a long time by the looks of his clothes."

Her body shivers. "I couldn't contact you, Zach. I was terrified you'd never find me and I'd end up with that..."

"Shush. He will never possess you again. You are my life-mate. I will die to protect you. Focus on our future. Ours and Phyllis' because I do not believe she will be able to return home either, once that fiend learns she helped us escape."

Phyllis catches my glance in the rearview mirror. "He has no idea I was there. He also has no hold on me. I'm safe. It's the two of you who concern me."

"Since he can only read my thoughts and I have the ability to block him, thanks to you, I think we stand a chance of escaping his clutches."

Once my funds are secure in my body belt, we depart the bank in search of new papers. Phyllis, having time to kill while the bank closed my accounts, contacted a local artist who will create new identities on the spot for us, identities just to get us out of town. We do not require them to be professional grade, just enough to fool airline personnel, and possibly car rental agents.

The three of us exit the dilapidated two-story apartment building while Emma and I stuff our new passports, drivers' licenses, and birth certificates into our individual backpacks. Phyllis chose to keep her name intact, so was not involved with the forger at all. She said until Francisco connected the dots, she felt safe.

I wondered how long it will take Francisco to locate this individual and extort our new information from him. Hopefully, I paid him enough to allow us a few days' head start.

The authenticity of the paperwork impressed me. I remove the documents from my backpack and stare at the names again. I am Everly Sanders, my wife's name is Terra Sanders. The marriage certificate I hold proves she *is* my wife. My mind drifts to making it legal, but not until we are safe from Francisco's clutches. I replace the forms in my backpack and sit back. Step one done.

Our next stop is the Verizon store for new phones.

Emma grips my hand tightly as the three of us walk toward our gates. The first flight out of San Diego flies Emma and me to Ft. Lauderdale. From there, we will catch another flight, mid-morning tomorrow, to Atlanta. Phyllis booked a flight later in the afternoon that flies directly to Nashville. She will spend the night there and wait while we drive the rest of the way from Atlanta, hoping to further throw Francisco off our scent.

"Do you have any idea where we should stay, Zach?" Emma relaxes in the passenger seat while we continue the drive into Nashville with Phyllis. We'd picked up our friend from the Hampton

Inn at the airport, where she spent the night, and now she sat in the back seat.

"I still can't use that new name. It doesn't feel right."

Emma recites her new name a couple of times, trying it out. When it spills from her mouth the third time, my body tingles from visions created by the marriage license. My wife! We discussed it once. Will she still be receptive?

Even with all the worry that surrounds us, I have to smile. But, she asked me a question and I must refocus on our escape plans. "Maybe around Vanderbilt University. With so much student housing available in that area, we could get lost in plain sight. Plus, Interstate 440 provides a great escape route if we require it." I reach over and cup her knee in my palm. "We *are* safe for a while. Please stop worrying."

The lovely vampire beside me glances out her side window and does not respond at first. "I need a drink, Zach. Do you know where we can pick one up?" Her voice sounds off. Hopefully, after we purchase our Velvet Crimsons we all will feel better.

Phyllis calls out from the back. "The Pancake Pantry on 21st Street is closest. Want the address?"

Phyllis rattles it off and Emma adds it to Waze. Closer than we thought, the next turn off from I-440 is 21st.

Limited parking behind the restaurant forces us to locate a spot on the street. Fortunately, a car leaving opens a space as we drive past.

When I come around to open the door for Emma, she steps out, stumbles, and falls against me.

"Would you rather wait in the car?"

She seems out of sorts. If she would rather wait, I will ask Phyllis to remain with her.

She gently smiles and shakes her head. "No, I think I need to walk. I was cooped up in that cell, then on two airplanes, and in this car for the past several days. The stress from all of this... well, my energy should return once I've had my fix."

Hoping that is the truth of it, the three of us walk into a packed student-filled breakfast place a little after one o'clock on Monday, July 2nd. I did not expect the large crowd, but overhear conversations discussing the first summer session finals later in the week. I grip Emma's hand tightly when we approach the check-in podium.

A young female eyes us suspiciously. "How many?" Her clean, crisp burgundy uniform suggests she just began her shift. When she looks over her shoulder toward the restaurant for a table, her long brown ponytail slashes the air as her head quickly swivels back.

My grin is immediate. "Three, please."

With menus in hand, she leads us to a table near the back of the room where we can consume our drinks and speak privately. Once we are seated, she asks for our drink order.

My life-mate answers quickly. "A Velvet Crimson please and a glass of water."

I watch for any objection. When her smile appears, my previous judgement proves sound. "The same for me."

Phyllis orders the third.

Our waitress leaves while adding notes on her tablet. We look at each other as if questioning what to do next. "I suggest we spend the night in a hotel close by. We can contact a management company tomorrow to locate a more permanent location."

Phyllis clasps the menu in her hands tightly. "I'm going to rent a car and drive home, if that's alright with you two."

Surprised by her statement, Emma and I openly stare at her.

Emma speaks first. "What if he's waiting for you there?"

Phyllis shrugs. "My circle will protect me."

I want to tell her once Francisco links her to us, he will stop at nothing to do away with the three of us. However, I do not voice my concern. She knows her circle members. If she wishes to return home, we will not stand in her way.

Emma clasps our friend's arm. "Yes, but…" Emma stops before she voices her concern when she sees the set of Phyllis' eyes "Of course, if you feel comfortable returning home, you should. Can I ask a favor, though, when you have time?"

She stalls her question when our waitress returns with our drinks. I watch my love chug hers halfway down, then set the container on the table with a little more force than necessary.

"Whoa, girl. Strength return already?" I chuckle and clasp her free hand.

The waitress, still at our table, points toward her glass. "Careful. Wouldn't want you to spill any of that here." She checks the area around us. "Not all would understand. Now, can I bring you something to eat? Our specialty pancakes are out of this world. That is, if you consume something other than those." She points her pen toward our drinks.

Emma places an order for cakes as does Phyllis. I settle for typical bacon and eggs. Our waitress winks before she walks away.

Phyllis turns to her high school friend. "What favor, Emma?"

"Will you check on my mom and dad for me? Something was off when I spoke with my mom a couple of weeks ago. I meant to call my dad, but got kidnapped before I got the chance. I'll give you their address in Muncie if you don't feel it's a problem."

"Sure thing. I'll go when I feel no threat has followed me home. It may take a few days, but I'll call you and give you the low down."

"Thank you, Phyllis. It means the world to me."

Phyllis' smile is sweet. "If I can help in any other capacity, you will let me know, right?"

Emma and I nod in unison.

We consume our meals slowly, discuss our future plans, and relax from our two-day escape from California. Dread filters into my mind when Francisco tries to intercept my thoughts. He has tried several times over the past two days, but I have not mentioned this to either of my companions. I do not wish to further worry them. I must be resilient, though. That fiend will stop at nothing to locate us.

We drop Phyllis at the car rental lot at the Nashville International Airport, bid her a safe journey, and drive off toward the west side of town after she promises to call when she has safely returned home.

Nashville's heat and humidity forces most humans indoors today. With little to no effect on me or Emma, we roll the car windows down to inhale the sweet smell of summer. Emma lays her head back against the seat and appears to be resting while we cruise the neighborhood. I still have not asked about the kidnapping or what she experienced while in Francisco's dungeon. If she wishes to relate her experience, I intend to listen. But, I will not prod her into reliving anything unpleasant.

I peek sideways with a glance and notice her closed eyes. Is she asleep or resting? My heart soars with love for the young vampire next to me. Our escape is far from over, but at least she is with me again.

When it appears I have passed the district with hotels or motels, I decide to take the next turn off Interstate 40. Old Hickory appears on the overhead sign, and I take the off ramp and turn south. The countryside in west Nashville is green with lush foliage, too. It reminds me of my home in Indianapolis, except for the corn fields. My mind drifts to Phyllis. I am anxious to hear from her. *I* placed her in harm's way. It is me who will suffer if anything happens to her.

I pull to the side of the road when convenient to search Waze for a hotel. The first to pop up is the Brentwood Hilton, approximately thirty miles away. Without knowing the area and hoping this is our best choice, I set our course and resume the drive.

I shake Emma awake after I have pulled into a parking spot. "We're here."

She sits up and blinks a couple of times. "Where's here?"

I chuckle because I am not sure either. "Somewhere south of Nashville. Come on, sleepyhead. We need to rest for a while. Then I will take you shopping for some clothing."

My sweet looks down at the garments covering her. "You mean I can't stay in this getup any longer? That's a real shame."

Her tentative laugh worries me. I grasp her hand and will her to explain. When she does not, I let it go.

All in good time.

CHAPTER 28

EMMA

Zach and I leave Target with several large bags. We've loaded them in the trunk when I notice his grimace.

"What's wrong?" I grab his shoulder and turn him toward me.

His head shakes. "Francisco," he whispers. "He has found a way to antagonize me through my thoughts. I have kept him out so far."

"So far? How often, and don't sugarcoat it."

That evil twisted vampire. Even though he's far away, he's found a way to intimidate my mate.

"I will tell you more once we get back to the hotel, okay?"

We climb into the car and return to the hotel. Once inside the room, he starts.

"He began lurking two days ago right after we landed in Atlanta. He has not gained access, but I have to be careful."

The bags are tossed on the bed to sort through, but I'm hurt Zach didn't share this information with me before I pressed him.

"Okay, so tell me what I can do to help. We need a plan, Zach, a way to assure ourselves he doesn't locate us." I flop down on the king-sized bed. "I knew we'd be on the run the rest of our existence." Something he mentioned when we left Francisco's home pops into my mind. "What about contacting the Elders? Tell them of Francisco and Nadia's devious undertakings. Make them understand how unstable they truly are. It wouldn't hurt, would it?"

My mate lowers to the bed next to me. "They could tell Francisco where we are. I will not jeopardize our location yet. Besides, we need to relax after the stress we both experienced."

Zach's jaw clenches. "I could use another Crimson. How about you?"

"Two in one day. That must be a record. Fine, but let's wait until this evening before we venture out again. What do you say to some additional rest and relaxation after we hang up the clothes we purchased?"

His arm surrounds my shoulder and he leans in to nuzzle my neck, pain and worry set aside for now. "I like the way you think, Mrs. Sanders."

"Yeah, about that." My body squirms with need. In a low breathy voice, I utter, "Who said I wished to be married to you, sir?"

"Too late now." His lips lock on mine.

Days of anxiety and fear give way to our desires. Bags are tossed to the floor along with our clothing. I'm glad to be rid of mine since they represent a time and place I wish to forget.

Zach pulls back the comforter, lays me on my back, and climbs in on his hands and knees while speaking softly. "I thought I had lost you, Emma. I was terrified I would never hold you in my arms again. I do not wish to experience those feelings ever again. So, today I am making you a solemn vow. I promise never to allow another being take you from me even if it means the end of my existence. I will protect you with all I am." He plants a soft kiss against my temple. "Marry me, really marry me, Emma. Even though it changes nothing, I need that promise of forever from you."

My arms circle his neck while a tear leaks from my eye. All thoughts of becoming human die a quick death while I'm encased in his arms. Somehow, a cloud also lifts from my heart. "I'm yours, Zach. I never want to leave you again. So, yes, I'll marry you."

Lips collide, tongues lash, fangs extend, and bodies writhe on the bed while the creature I promised to spend my existence with and I share our blood. I long for the mind chamber and am not disappointed when images of walking along a white sand-covered beach in a red bikini and floral shawl draped at my waist filter in. Zach, clad only in navy blue swim trunks, holds my hand, then picks me up and twirls me in the air. The sun shines down on us and casts shadows of our spinning bodies against the sand while we laugh and dance into the warm water.

I'm pulled from our dream when a second orgasm, much stronger than the first, shudders my body. My fangs withdraw from his shoulder and I relinquish my hold on my mate as the sensations spiral down. My eyes open and focus on Zach. His staccato breathing keeps his head from rising at first. When his face appears, he's already above me resting on his elbows. His fangs, still elongated, are covered in blood. Drawn to the color, I lick my lips and then his incisors. The taste is foreign. Why don't I taste like me? I will ask, but not until I'm finished with him.

Zach's eyes, still black with lust, stare down into mine. A transformation occurs right in front of me. His lips curl into what appears to be an evil grin, his features contort, and he snarls low and long. Hair on my arms and legs stand at attention from the sound. I push him off of me and crawl to the other side of the bed.

My mate's fists ball and he rises to his hands and knees, eyes still black and menacing, his breathing heavy. Fear moves me farther away from him, against the headboard. Does he mean me harm? I know I'm strong, but he has the ability and speed to do me in.

Zach struggles but holds himself in place, shakes his head as if to clear cobwebs, and turns toward me. "What were you fed?" His voice sounds gruff and angry.

A few moments pass before his eyes slowly transform to dark blue and his fangs retreat.

"That's your first question? You snarled at me, Zach! What was that all about?" The comforter, clutched tight at my chest, provides my only defense. I'll run if I must, but possibly he has an explanation I'll accept.

His hand pushes hair from his forehead while he attempts to control his breathing. "I am sorry I snarled at you. Come back here, Emma. Please. Your body is shaking."

I watch his eyes and his lips for any change, then decide to take a chance and crawl back to him. "You scared me. We were romping in the water on that white sandy beach. When I wake from that lovely moment, you snarl at me. And, Zach? While your fangs were still extended, I licked my blood from them as I often do. I know I don't taste the same as you, but my blood didn't taste the same as the last time."

His brows close together and he asks again. "What were you fed?"

I don't know what difference it makes... "I believe it was human blood." I crawl into his lap when the memory surfaces of how that blood infused me. "I had super energy for a while, felt I could conquer the world. Is that what human blood does for a vampire?"

Zach holds me close and exhales heavily. "He did that on purpose."

"Did what on purpose?"

My mate turns me so I'm leaning back against his chest, drags the comforter from my clutches to cover us both, and wraps his arms around my waist. Doesn't he want me to watch his expressions?

"Human blood. Once you have been introduced, it becomes difficult to walk away from a situation like you experienced in Buckeye. He intended to turn you into a monster like he is, and like I used to be."

My breath stalls in my throat. "You... what?"

His chin rests on top of my head and his arms hold me tighter. He doesn't want me to witness his emotions.

"When I was a young vampire, I did Francisco's bidding. All of it. Our circle used humans for nourishment, drained them almost to death, then charmed them, and sent them on their way. Velvet Crimson was not around to sustain us back then." He huffs then draws a deep breath. "It was a long time ago, Emma. A time I am not proud of or approve of. However, I do not believe I have killed a human to save my life. I came close in my early days, but learned when to stop drinking when their heartrate slowed."

I hate to interrupt, but I have a burning question. "Why... um, human blood..." This is more difficult than I expected. I gather my thoughts and try again. "By tasting human blood, I'm now going to risk my existence in order to sample it again? Why didn't someone explain this to me? And, why did you snarl at me?"

"Because your blood is now mixed with human blood. Just as my blood is mixed with yours and yours mine. Francisco changed your dynamics, which fosters desire to drink from humans. Have you felt the pull yet? A need to quench your thirst?"

"We've been on the run for two days. I haven't thought of anything other than escaping that vampire and his mate."

"Even while we sat in the restaurant? You did not search out a specific human or desire to attack one?"

I spin to face him on my knees. "Are you telling me I will?"

Zach licks his lips and fixes me with his stare. "Maybe. However, the fact that you did not could possibly mean you are stronger than he or I realize."

I don't wish to become *that* vampire. But, stronger? "How do you mean stronger?"

My mate spins me back around so I'm nestled against his chest again. I do feel safe wrapped in his arms. My hips wiggle when I encounter his erection.

"Are you always, um, erect?" I'm still a little shy when we're undressed in the daylight. I thought maybe by now I'd have shaken those reactions and become a wonton vampire, one whose sole purpose is to devour her man, or vampire lover, if you will. When his chest rumbles with laughter, I turn my head to rest against his shoulder.

"Emma, my love, when I am in your presence, this is *always* the case. Have you not figured that out yet?"

"No, I haven't." I wiggle my ass against him because I can. I want to pick up where we just left off, but defer to my question... for now. "Now, tell me about being stronger."

My love and I spend an hour discussing ways I could possibly be stronger than other vampires my age. The significant difference is my mental capability. I already proved I could walk away from blood a few days ago, which is not the norm for one not inducted into this world by others of her kind. The fact I lived alone for ten years and only joined with others in my circle in Buckeye occasionally still baffles Zach. He mentions one of them should have brought me under his or her wing and shared their knowledge about existing as a vampire in this world.

I credit Phyllis with what I've learned. She may not have explained all the gory details, but I didn't know what to ask either. I gather she wished me to experience something first and fill in the blanks after. Our relationship was built on that premise at the start. And, now with Zach as my instructor, he should complete the process for me.

He is still discussing my mental acuity when I refocus on his words. My mind has always been open to challenging myself. If I don't have an answer, I search until I do. Is that why I defied what I became? Since I'm determined, more than ever, to stay with the vampire I love, and find a way to escape the clutches of his maker, it no longer matters.

Our discussion over for now, Zach and I shower together, change into clothing we purchased today, and leave the confines of our room to share a meal. It's great to be outside in the warm, humid air. Crickets chirp, lightening bugs chase the breeze, and the wind whips the fragrance of magnolia through the air. It's a fresh scent, one which reminds me of a family vacation in the Smokey Mountains many years ago.

Thoughts of my parents permeate my mind as we drive to the Waffle House, which is almost across the street. Should I call Phyllis to check in? I decide to wait. She was gone from her home for a few days. She'll call Zach when she has news.

My life-mate and I sit in a small booth and wait for the server. When she arrives, she takes one look at us and grins. "A couple of Velvet Crimsons? What else can I fetch for ya?"

I want to ask how she knows, but leave well enough alone. "Ah, we don't require Velvet Crimsons, but I'd love a pecan waffle dark, and warm the syrup please. Oh, add a side of crispy bacon, too. Thanks."

Zach orders the same and winks at me.

We listen as another waitress calls in an order using "smothered and covered" every other word. My laugh is spontaneous. I've missed living in the Midwest.

I search the restaurant and notice everyone has a cup of coffee in front of them. I whisper, "Coffee too please so we don't stand out?"

The waitress reply is immediate. "Sure thing, honey." Cups are placed in front of us and hot steaming coffee pours into each from a full pot.

After the waitress retreats to take an order from two at the counter, I direct my attention to my mate again. "What are the plans for tomorrow?"

He grasps my hands on the table and squeezes. "I thought, in the morning, we could drive out to Center Hill Lake to relax. Maybe rent some jet skis, or visit the falls, hike the state park. Take our minds off what we have been through and focus on us for a change. Then, once we hear from Phyllis, we can begin to formalize our next move. What do you think?"

"I think I love you, Mr. Matthews. Unless it rains, your plan sounds perfect."

Our waitress delivers our meals, and after we've consumed all and paid the bill, Zach and I return to the car for the short drive back to the hotel.

When we're seated inside, he grabs his head with both hands and rests against the seatback. "Leave me alone!" His tone rings with frustration.

I remain quiet hoping Francisco departs his mind quickly when he can't break through. Zach appears to be struggling, though. What in the world can that vampire do to cause such a disturbance?

A few moments pass before my mate's hands drop to his sides and he exhales loudly. He shakes his head as if to clear it and starts the car without a word.

I grab his arm to stall him. "Tell me."

His head turns toward me. His eyes appear a bit glazed over. "We should get back first. I will be able to assimilate it all by that time."

His weak smile hurts me inside and out. I smile in return and leave my maker to himself. It must be horrific if he doesn't want to discuss it now.

The drive takes only five minutes, but it's the hardest five minutes of my existence. To see him this traumatized, this distressed, wounds me as well. I don't wait for him to help me out of the car and we stride into the hotel through a little drizzle. When he doesn't clasp my hand, I grab his to offer strength.

Once inside our room, I watch as he strides toward the desk against the back wall, aggressively tugging his jacket from his arms. He stands with his back to me at first, takes a deep breath, and finally rotates to face me.

"Images. Images of you shackled in chains in that dungeon while he…he…" Zach balls his hands into fists while I rush to his side.

"He didn't do anything to me, Zach. Please believe me. Some light beam scored my arm a couple of times, but that's the extent of it."

"No, Emma. The images are of what he intends to do once he has you again. He will drink your blood, take your body, and make me watch while he destroys you, which will also destroy me."

Zach… "My darling, he won't find us. We escaped and no one knows where we are except Phyllis. I don't intend to seek out my family even though we're close to my home. So, until that evil twisted inhuman fiend has a reason to give up, we'll keep our heads down, we won't draw attention to anything, and if we have to, we'll leave the country. His network of spies can't be everywhere."

I draw my pretend husband into my arms and hold on tight. He reciprocates, nestles his face into my hair, and draws a deep breath.

"I did not want to tell you how difficult it had become keeping him from my thoughts. My fear is he will find a way to break through. I want to be ready when that happens."

"Ready? How?"

"We… begin by formulating a list of grievances and present it to the West Coast Elders, through a surrogate of course. Since Francisco's circle is out of favor, the Elders may listen. Next, we enlist Phyllis' help. She is with her circle because of Francisco. Maybe there are others who have been wrongly accused by him or Nadia and suffered their consequences. It may be too late for Oliver, but I am certain Nicole, and Cassander's mate, will attest to the false claims made behind their deaths." Zach huffs audibly. "Francisco's goons will locate us soon, so we need to put some sort of plan in place. It is possible to fight them off, but I would rather utilize the bureaucracy of our world before creating a situation where we become known to humans."

"Where do we start?" It sounds like a good plan, and Phyllis hopefully will agree to assist us.

"I will allow Phyllis another day before I call her. I hope we do not bring trouble into her life by requesting her assistance again."

My nod against his chest also brings worry. How far will Francisco go to steal me away again? My guess is to the moon and back.

CHAPTER 29

FRANCISCO

The audacity of that vampire! What does he think he can accomplish by hiding her from me? I am his maker. I am the leader of his circle. He owes me! I storm into the house followed by Nadia, who, with anger distorting her features, grabs my arm and spins me around.

"I am your mate, Francisco. I rule this circle in the same capacity as you, you fool! That was our bargain those many years ago when you were but a youngster in this world. You and your 'poor, poor pitiful me' existence. My father saved you from a fate worse than death, helped train you for the role you play today, and your promise to always respect and care for me has not been lost these hundreds of years. That you still crave your dead human wife sickens me. Have I meant nothing to you?"

I clench my fists and glare at my mate. "It's you who has created the issues we now face with the Elders." I pace closer. "It's you who spread rumors Oliver and Cassander were attempting to overthrow me." And yet closer. "It's also you who reunited Emma with her mate, which has seriously damaged my plans for our future."

In the back of my mind, I conclude, plans which do not include you.

Nadia, sensing my rage increasing, backs up and blinks her violet eyes to distract me. This worked centuries ago. No longer, dear one.

"The problem is, Francisco, you do not include me when you plan your strategies. So, I make assumptions when I have nothing else to go on. I suppose some of my reactions and responses haven't been to your liking. However, dear husband, I will not take all the blame. My spies did overhear a conversation between those two fools plotting your overthrow. I feel no remorse over Cassander's demise."

Her words calm me a degree, but one question needs to be addressed. "Was my young charge also involved in Cassander and Oliver's strategies?"

Her huff isn't what I expect either. "I have no proof he was involved. His name was not mentioned during the discussion my spies overheard."

Her ire seems to have dissipated somewhat, but I watch my mate closely. She hides her true thoughts behind those beautiful ever-watchful eyes.

"Why do you care so much for that unappreciative vampire? He owes his existence to you, but ignores his responsibility to our circle. In my opinion, he should be turned over to the Elders for disciplinary action."

Nadia walks toward the back patio, arms crossed against her chest. Her mind must be churning with ways to divorce ourselves from Zachary and his mate. However, until Emma is under my control again, I promise myself to keep an open mind about the youngster. What is that saying... Keep your friends close, your enemies closer? Although my mate has appealed to my sensibility, I do not intend to allow her influence over some of our circle to destroy what I've built. She must learn her place, which will be in the same chamber Emma occupied. Once the young vampire returns, she will assume her rightful position by my side.

"All in good time, my dear. All in good time." I must contact Zachary, first to alert him of Nadia's beliefs, and second to bring them back. While Nadia stares out the back door, I retire to my bedchamber and attempt to mind-lock with my second-in-command. All I receive is darkness. How is that possible? Maybe he and Emma are sharing their bodies. Although the thought sickens me, it's possible... I spin in place. My fangs bare and I hiss loudly. No! It isn't conceivable! He's learned of a way to block me! While I question who would dare risk their life to thwart me, I grab my cell phone and place a call to his. My call drops immediately to voice mail. The offending instrument suffers a blow against the far wall while anger sweeps my body. My fists clench so tightly in my hands, blood seeps from the wounds my nails carve. Fear I'm losing control of my circle permeates my being. I must put a stop to this insubordination immediately for fear of losing it all. I race to my car. It's time to pay Zachary a quick visit. Alexander told me they had not returned, but his home is the logical place for them to hole up.

The house is dark when I pull into his short driveway five minutes later. I don't sense him inside or Emma, either, for that matter. His hidden key under the urn at the front door grants me access when no one answers my repeated knocks. No one is in residence. Damn, he and Emma have fled.

I walk through the living room and into the kitchen searching for clues. As I pass the stairway to the upstairs, I catch a whiff of a strange scent, someone other than the two lovebirds. Another vampire occupied this home with Zachary! But who? I follow the odor up the stairs and into the extra bedroom. The scent is stronger here. It is known to me! Phyllis Megalos, Thaddeus' life-mate. What was she doing here? And, could she be involved teaching Zachary how to block my mind probes? I discount that idea the moment it possesses me. She's but a youngling herself and not familiar with ancient ways. She must have been here reassuring Zachary after Emma disappeared. I will contact my ring of spies in Indiana to verify she played no part in Zachary and Emma's sudden disappearance, nonetheless.

From all appearances, Zachary departed his home with no baggage. My conclusion, based on what I've seen here, is that he and Emma are, indeed, traveling to Phoenix. When I return home, I intend to send two of my trusted allies to locate them there.

And, what about Oliver? He must be dealt with. Nadia must not be allowed the upper hand where he is concerned. She avowed to his deceit personally. So, why would she stop his sentence from being carried out this morning?

As I travel back home, my mind churns with more questions than I have answers. Before I'm able to reconcile Nadia and her reasoning, I must locate Emma and Zachary. Until my young love returns, I must tolerate Nadia and her antics.

Throughout the day, I deal with issues as they arise. Once my desk is cleared, I send Alexander to Phoenix in search of the missing two and call upon two spies in Noblesville to verify Phyllis is at home. I'm told that task may take a couple of days since I do not have her current address. I allow them three days to report back to me before I send my goon squad.

I locate Nadia on the patio, pacing back and forth. Her thoughts are a jumbled mess. It's been decades since I've been able to read them, which worries me today, but I can't be sidetracked by her games. The Elders delivered a message while I was away requiring an update on our circle and the misfits. Now, I must develop a plan to terminate five of her vampires. Removing them, however, only places a Band-Aid over a larger wound. The Elders promised to reevaluate my circle once termination of the freaks has been certified, which means one or more of them wishes to be present. Uncertain how Nadia will respond when two of her closest minions are ended, I decide to send her on an errand when the deed has been scheduled. In the meantime, I must keep their demise under wraps.

Late in the afternoon, I attempt to mind lock with Zachary again. His barricade, although fierce, shrugs under my badgering. I am not able to gain access, but I leave behind images which will repeat in his head for hours. Sooner or later, he will succumb to my invasion.

Satisfied with my level of infiltration, I contact Alexander in the hope he's located the missing vampires. His report, although thorough, has me seething in moments.

"What do you mean they aren't there? Where else would they go?" I draw open one of the French doors to my office balcony and stand in the afternoon glare. They've run away? Doesn't Zachary realize my network of spies engulfs this country? They stand no chance of escape. "I want you to track them down, Alexander. Leave no stone unturned, no idea discarded. You must find them."

"Yes, my lord. Where do you suggest I begin?"

Dutiful Alexander. Once I place a suggestion within his mind, he will not accept failure. "When I visited Zachary's home, I inhaled a fragrance I'm familiar with, as you would be as well. Phyllis Megalos was there. You recall her mate, Thaddeus, I assume?"

"Of course. The one who knew too much."

"Yes. I believe she has visited Zachary within the past few days and she wouldn't run all the way from Indiana. Check the airlines for flights. Find out when she arrived and when she left. Also ascertain if the other two traveled out with her. Report back to me with any forthcoming information. It's paramount to our circle that you succeed, Alexander. We are counting on you."

"I will not disappoint you, my lord."

"I will expect your first report later this evening."

With the phone now tucked in my pocket, I stroll to the edge of the balcony and tightly grip the wrought iron handrail and will my anger to subside. My eyes close while I inhale the salty fragrance of the sea and sand. My eyes open to the pool beneath me, which shimmers in the afternoon sun. I long for a swim, but will wait until the sun has set. I need all the energy I can accumulate today to maintain my balance.

When I peer around the vast grounds, my mind lingers on the evening Emma spent here. I can still envision her walking the sandy beach with young Zachary. How I wish she could share such a moment with me.

"Ah, my lovely Emma, you will in time."

I turn from the relaxing view when my duties as leader invade my thoughts again. How is it possible enemies were able to infiltrate our circle to overthrow me? My system of checks and balances maintained the stability of this group for centuries. Have I neglected my duties in some way? Or is it I'm reaching an age when the daily struggles surpass my talents? I scoff at that idea. Alfredo was well into his third millennium before he was struck down, and that was his own doing. I recently celebrated my two thousand, two hundred, and tenth year as a vampire, and have no desire to step down.

I lower into my desk chair when I recall the day I was glorified into the world of vampires. My wife and sons had perished, my world collapsing around me. I was old at thirty, and ready to die, when Alfredo rescued me from that existence. As I survey the office, I remind myself of the many struggles I experienced along my chosen path. Thankful for the conveniences of this modern world, I lean back and close my eyes to the world of yesterday and focus on the challenges of tomorrow. With a new modern mate by my side, I will explore new concepts, new technologies, and create a stronger army of followers. Yes, my dear Emma. Christine has been reborn in you. There will be no one who can hold us back.

Lynne Anders

CHAPTER 30

ZACH

E mma rests against me, her mind deep in thought. I admonish myself for not being prepared when, deep down, I knew Francisco wanted more than for me to change her. If I could turn back the clocks to 2008 again, I would. I would never have taken her life, I would have loved her from afar, and she would be safe in the arms of another.

Who am I kidding? Francisco would have changed her himself, and I would now be standing on the outside watching as he destroyed the only creature I have ever loved.

But, how do I explain my reaction to her new mixture of blood? It infused me with energy, I longed for the days when I sucked humans to near death and discarded them without a second thought. Those days were supposed to be behind me. How can one taste of comingled human blood within her conjure up those heightened feelings again? I have to wonder if something else was added to that drink.

My thoughts return to Francisco and I scowl. He must be stopped. He has gone too far this time. I promise I will be ever watchful of Emma so she does not follow in my old footsteps. Truth be told, it will require more than a couple of glasses of that concoction to change my mate.

Before she drifts off, I must ask. "Emma? Were you offered anything else to drink while you were in Francisco's dungeon?"

Her sigh is heavy. "The last time there was a piece of red meat on a platter." Her hand clutches my arm. "Why would uncooked meat appeal to me, Zach?" She spins to look into my eyes. Hers glow with amusement. "Can we use our fake names? I mean, it's a real turn-on to believe you're someone new I get to devour."

My lovely mate. I push away strands of her hair that has fallen across her eyes and lower my lips to hers.

"You wish to cast me aside so soon? I am crestfallen. On the other hand, if I pretend to be another vampire in love with you who wishes to overpower you, promise not to fight back?"

Emma's legs straddle my hips, her breasts flatten against my chest, and she coaxes my lips apart with her tongue. The words, "Oh, yeah, Mr. Sanders" mix with a guttural moan when our bodies writhe against each other again. Consumed by the beauty before me, I flip her onto her back, clasp her hands at the side of her head, and push into her without so much as a howdy-do. High on Emma, we ride out the remainder of the night making love. We do not drink from each other and there is no visit to the mind chamber. I imagine this is the way mortals spend their evenings enjoying each other's bodies. However, in our case, our energy does not wane after the first, second, or third orgasm. And, in answer to her desire for new and different, we make love against the wall, on top of the desk, the floor on hands and knees, and end up sitting in the overstuffed chair.

When night fades to morning light, my life-mate jumps from the chair and rushes into the bathroom to shower, still full of energy. She giggles when she calls over her shoulder, "Care for a romp in the water, Mr. Sanders?"

I am on my feet behind her in moments. Our escapade ends when Francisco intrudes again and leaves behind additional visions of Emma tortured in a dark chamber. Knowing that will never occur, I still hold her to me until the images fade somewhat. The visions still run rampant, but I am able to compartmentalize them so they become less intense.

When my voice returns, it is with regret. "He is closer to breaking me, Emma. He may be tracking my mind for all I know. We should leave here today and find another place to hide."

"Let's return that rental, purchase airline tickets somewhere, and then not get on the plane. It'd take him a while to find out, right? And, I still don't want to head north. He may be watching Phyllis. He knows she helped you all those years ago, so I don't want to lead

My love for this divine creature continues to grow, too. What was I thinking earlier? I add calm under pressure to her list of many attributes.

"We should pack up and plan our next step. I believe we need to include Phyllis again, though. Since we have not heard from her regarding your parents, I believe heading north is our best option. We may run into one of Francisco's goons, but I would rather help shelter Phyllis than leave her on her own."

Her immediate nod confirms she agrees with my request.

I sense her readjusting to our shifted dynamic, as do I. We are equal now, in all things, even though our ages are centuries apart, but I welcome the relief. I no longer must look around every corner before I allow her to follow me. I grab her hand and kiss each knuckle. "Time to go, Mrs. Sanders?"

Her smile is immediate. "When do you plan to make that a reality, Mr. Sanders?"

"Soon. Very soon. Come along, my dear. Time is wasting."

We rush to our room, throw all of our clothes into the duffels, and use the room phone to call the front desk. She tells them I had a migraine and we are leaving for a hospital in Nashville.

The desk clerk delays her from ending the call. "Ah, someone called earlier looking for a young couple with your description. Their names were Zachary Matthews and Emma Christensen. I mentioned that no one by that name was a current guest here." After a short pause, he mutters, "I understand your situation perfectly."

I overhear the conversation and wonder. Could he be a vampire? Or one of Francisco's spies? Since I do not trust anyone at the moment, I push Emma to hurry.

She replies, "Since we don't know a Zachary Christensen or an Emma Matthews, or whoever… doesn't matter. We'll be on our way."

I hear, "Safe travels" while Emma drops the receiver into the cradle. We rush out to the car, bags in hand, and head west to I-65. It will be a five-hour trip, so we settle in and take it slow. No need for an accident.

Emma places a call to Phyllis' cell phone, but has to leave a message. Her look speaks for itself. What if Francisco or his goons already have Phyllis in their custody? We may be walking into a trap.

Lynne Anders

CHAPTER 31

EMMA

Zach drives past by Phyllis' home once, turns right at the next corner, and pulls to the curb. Her home is dark; no sign of activity. He turns off the engine and we listen. The neighborhood is too quiet, as if all living creatures have fled. I expected to hear wings fluttering as birds settled in for the evening, crickets chirping calling their mates, and the rustle of bushes when small rodents gather their families together. No sound whatsoever. I peek at my mate and observe the same expression on his face.

"This is a set-up, you know that, right?" His words are whispered in case someone is listening.

My nod confirms I heard. Through our mind-link, I relay a plan to drive farther away, park the car, and come back on foot.

Zach's hand reaches for the start button, but his car door is ripped away, as is mine, and two thugs drag us from the rental in the dusk of the evening. We surrender to ten vampires, all whose fangs are extended, eyes black, and stand formidably as one. I look at each face and recognize only one. Alexander, Francisco's head goon, the one who kidnapped me from Buckeye.

I decide not to show fear and take a step in his direction. "So, he sent you again, did he? Think you've done your leader a favor by capturing his second-in-command and his life-mate? We've contacted Elder Rayner, Alexander, and registered our complaint with him. So, please, take us back to Oceanside. I can't wait to hear what Francisco's punishment will be."

The tall, raven-haired vampire with the looks of a young John Travolta, although his body belongs to someone quite larger, sneers at me. "You won't get away this time, little miss. I've been given free range to do with you as I please." He peers over his shoulder and commands, "Lock them both in chains. Prepare to transport them immediately, and don't forget the other one held at the house."

Zach, quiet until now, grabs my hand, pulls me behind him, and snarls at the crowd. "If any of you harms so much as one hair on her head, I will end you. You have my solemn promise. Especially you, Alexander. Once the Elders have passed judgement on Francisco, you will be next. Do I make myself clear?"

I notice two of the goons shrug slightly away. They aren't fully on board with Alexander's plan, it seems. I memorize their faces in case we need one to help later in our escape, then pull closer to my mate. I want to tell him about the two, but I'm certain all of the thugs will hear. I start to mind-link, but decide to wait. Francisco may be intercepting his thoughts.

Zach and I, manacled at the neck, waist, and ankle by heavy chain and shackles, follow toward Phyllis' home as quickly as possible behind half of the army of goons. The guards didn't do their due-diligence, however. If they had and searched Zach, they would have located his money belt. Now, when we're able to escape, he'll have the means to provide a speedy exit for all three of us.

No neighbor peeks out their window, no one appears to be at home at all down the overgrown tree-lined country lane where Phyllis' home is located. Did this army of creeps see to that? Did they send the residents off on some errand for them or, like her, are they being held against their will somewhere? Phyllis told me once these neighbors make up most of her circle. How did Francisco coerce the local leader to restrain them?

One of the goons opens the back door and we all pile into her kitchen. Some overflow into her living room. I don't sense her near, however, and I worry about our friend.

"Where's Phyllis? What have you done with her?"

Alexander chuckles evilly. "She's being detained in another location. It's a shame you weren't around for her capture. On the other hand, I predict your fate will proceed much the same way. Now, sit down!" he says gruffly. "The van should be here momentarily."

I grasp Zach's hand while tears form in my eyes. If she's been harmed because she helped us... I vow to myself to retaliate on her behalf no matter how long it takes.

I lower into the nearest kitchen chair. Zach follows and sits in the chair next to mine. The goons speak amongst themselves, discussing the trip back to California and ways to control us to thwart an escape. My mind is focused on how to destroy Alexander. I assume he was directed by Francisco to locate us and our friend. I will stop at nothing to finish him.

Zach squeezes my hand to draw my attention. I sneak a peek at him and capture a couple of images from his mind. He senses Phyllis close by. He squeezes my hand again to stall my exuberance. I reciprocate, thankful he's beside me and will do all he can to protect me and Phyllis. But, we need a plan. A better plan than Alexander concocted.

The Fourth of July holiday is tomorrow. I know from past experience mortals take to their cars for vacation spots all across the nation. If we're traveling by van to mix in with the general population, our journey will exceed three days, if the drive is nonstop. This van of theirs must run on gasoline and will have to stop occasionally for fuel. Plus, Zach and I will require Velvet Crimson to maintain our stamina, unless they wish to starve us. If they require blood also... my mind begins to churn with possibilities. One thing is clear. Somehow, we must escape and get a message to the west coast.

For once, I'm thankful Zach agreed with me about the Elders. While he drove us to Indianapolis from Smithville, I contacted Elder Rayner on his behalf and explained our situation in great detail. Because Francisco's circle is out of favor, he listened. He didn't promise much, but indicated if we showed him proof of our allegations, he and the rest of the Elders may sanction Francisco and his wife. Uncertain what proof we can present, I thanked him anyway and hung up. To gather proof may be a task we cannot complete. However, I decide to begin a journal of what I endured in that hellhole. Oliver's plight should be addressed as well. However, Zach explained Cassander's decimation to me and believed the Elders would feel the same about his supposed partner in crime.

"Leave Oliver out of it for now. Nadia kept him from death the morning you were rescued. She must have her own reasons for keeping him alive."

"I'll add a note or two. If they ask, I can relay what I heard."

The remainder of our drive was virtually quiet. Zach nudged my mind a couple of times to share a thought, but our concern remained on getting to Phyllis.

Zach tugs my hand to draw me from my contemplations. Alexander's loud voice booms from the other room.

"All set. Get those two to the van and secure them in back. We'll pick up little miss sharp tongue on the way."

Phyllis? Little miss sharp tongue? I can almost hear her rant against that goon. Since laughing at him won't help our situation, I remain quiet, but share a wry smile with Zach.

While the rest of the assailants depart with Alexander, one of the two goons remaining in the kitchen grabs my shoulder and hoists me from the chair. I am forced to relinquish my hold on my mate. He is lifted up by another member of the squad. When he doesn't move quickly enough, he is hit from behind and forced to the floor. Even though still chained, he jumps up and snarls at the vampire who dealt the blow.

"You will pay for that."

I stop and turn back to help my mate, if possible. I should have known better. His fangs extend, his eyes turn black as night, and his hands ball into fists. I've never before witnessed the expression that possesses his face in a fighting moment. The curl of his lips is sinister, those squinted black orbs are menacing, and the snarl from his open mouth chills even me. Zach portrays a true ruthless vampire in front of me for the first time. His appearance is similar to what happened back in our hotel room, but this version... God help the being in his path.

My guard attempts to pull me along, but I stand my ground in the living room to observe Zach's next move. In less time than it takes to blink your eyes, he breaks free of the chains, grabs the neck of the idiot who pushed him down, and shoves him against the kitchen stove. A knife caddie sits next to the appliance. Zach grabs the largest one and swiftly slices through the offender's neck, severing his head. Thick dark blood gushes from the incision while his dead body falls to the floor. Zach drops the head on his way to me. With no time to respond, my guard attempts to use me to block my mate, but I'm pushed aside. Using the same knife and with one stroke, he severs the head of that vampire as well. I look on in horror, not knowing the fiend before me.

"Zach?" I whisper his name while he gulps air and I observe the second vampire perish at my feet.

My mate's features calm somewhat, but his anger does not.

Since they were the only two remaining goons in the house, Zach breaks my chains, which rattle noisily to the floor, grabs my hand, and growls, "Come with me. *Now!*"

I run with him, but pull against his tight grip to free my hand.

"What about Phyllis?"

"She is in no immediate danger." His snarl takes me by surprise.

"Why are you angry with me?"

Zach doesn't respond.

Our run through the shadows doesn't slow or stop until cornfields give way to residential areas. Zach slows our pace, sniffs the area for followers and, once satisfied we've outrun our captors, stops next to a road sign directing traffic to Cincinnati.

"We may be in luck. Alexander focused on the van while the other vampires piled into a couple of cars and left before we escaped. He may not have had the resources to chase after us."

"That's all well and good, Zach. But you snarled at me. Why?" Even though I love him with all of my being, he needs to explain the snarl and why he went to such lengths to subdue those two thugs.

My mate walks away from me with his hands on his hips and head down. When he stops, his head rises. He's back to me in a moment. "You have the ability to charm our abductors, Emma. Why not use it?"

"I'm able to charm mortals because their minds are overtly susceptible to suggestion. I only used it the one time to keep us out of trouble. Vampires are another species altogether, Zach." I watch for traffic along the interstate and worry while we stand arguing. We could have been followed.

Zach grabs for my hand, but I withdraw it from his reach. He's blaming me for those two deaths?

Not my fault.

"We should continue toward Cincinnati. Maybe we can catch a plane for the west coast and beat those idiots there." His countenance is relaxed again.

Angered by his remarks, I stand rigid in front of him and begin my tirade. "Not until you apologize. I'm still new at this vampire stuff, Zach. I had no formal training when I was changed, thank you very much. And, I was left on my own for ten years. Oh, except for an occasional call to Phyllis. I don't know how to act sometimes, or even the extent of the powers I possess. I just follow along beside you hoping for scraps." My anger explodes around me like the Fourth of July fireworks. "And, while we're on the subject, why didn't you break free of those chains earlier? You knew you could, yet you allowed those creeps to hold us hostage."

Zach grabs my hand and halls me deeper into the shadows along the shoulder of the street. "Because. I did not know if you were able to break yours. I decided to wait until the most opportune time, Emma. Damn."

Love for this creature consumes me, but my ire draws anger, too. He blames me for the deaths, but did nothing to escape before it was necessary to kill them.

His fangs extend and his eyes turn black. I wonder what he intends to do, but am stalled by his sinister grin. "And there is the vampire I created. I wish you had a mirror, Emma. Your appearance fits the stereotype now."

"*What* do you mean?"

"He grabs my hand and places it on my face. "Your incisors have completely extended, your eyes are black as coal, and not from lust. Plus, your beautiful lips are curled in a frightful grimace. I do not think I have loved you as much as I do at this moment."

His lips fall to mine in a searing embrace. I fight off my desire to sink my teeth into his neck and pull away instead.

"You'll have to explain how this happened one day, Zach. But, first, I need blood and soon."

Zach's breathing escalates. He won't relinquish his hold on me either. I stare into his eyes and wish we were somewhere other than the side of the road, running for our lives, and in need of sustenance. If left up to me, we'd be naked knee deep in the bushes, pleasuring each other, which would definitely allow our captors to find us.

"It *is* who you are, Emma. When overtly angered, your true identity appears. It is both a blessing and a burden. A blessing to chase away potential attackers and a burden when... well, you can guess at that reasoning."

"So... if I'm angered and out of control, I turn into a beast? I don't think I like this scenario."

Zach grasps my hand to calm me. "It is a defense mechanism. When necessary."

I nod my understanding, but don't continue with the questions that now float through my mind. Even though I'm wound up, he caresses my back. My mate steps back and I watch as he wills his body to calm. It appears effortless for him. All those questions... Will I ever know everything about myself?

"Cincinnati is a few miles away. If we make it before daylight, we may stand a chance. Come. We will locate our drink as soon as I am sure we have not been followed."

Zach looks around us, sniffs the air again, and satisfied we're still safe, grasps my hand and runs southeast toward the city. We continue to hide in the darkness and race through the night, emerging from the shadows only when necessary.

We reach the outskirts of Cincinnati long before sunup, and slow our pace so as not to call attention to ourselves. We appear as two lovers on a morning stroll.

Our first stop is a twenty-four-hour White Castle on the northwest side of town. Before we enter, however, we stop to check our appearance.

Zach smooths my hair from my face and grins. "Beautiful as ever. How am I?"

"Good enough to eat." My voice, though weak from hunger, suggests what I want. I push his hair from his face and sigh. "You're fine and I'm starving."

The creature in front of me grins and pulls me in through the open door.

Lynne Anders

CHAPTER 32

ZACH

The Uber driver drops us at the departure entrance at Cincinnati/Northern Kentucky International Airport a few minutes after eight in the morning on July fourth. The driver snorts when his car stops. We listened to his bickering during the entire drive and hesitate to provide a tip for his service. On the other hand, it is a holiday and he probably *should* be at home with his family. Instead of leaving the tip on the account, I hand the gentleman a one-hundred-dollar bill. "Thank you. Enjoy your day." We exit his car. For the first time today, he is speechless.

Once again, we are traveling without suitcases or any carryon at this point. However, while I book our flight, Emma chooses to shop. I agree to meet her in the food court in an hour after doling out a few hundred dollars to her for whatever she finds.

The first available flight out is scheduled to leave within the hour. I purchase our tickets and rush to hunt down my mate. My attempt to locate her through our mind-link finally succeeds and we meet at the entrance to a clothing store. She twirls in her new outfit.

"Nice and sunny, don't you think?"

Her red, white, and blue paisley dress, which fits the holiday, reminds me of the style Phyllis wore when I picked her up last week. Has it only been a week? With all we have been through, it feels like a year. I hide my concern behind shielded eyes and smile while she twirls, then grab her hand when she stops. She is still so young in many ways. I love that she displays exuberance even while we face the enormous task ahead. But, behind those expectant eyes, I also observe a hesitancy and fear of what is to come. I do not wish to dampen her spirits. Maybe I can add to it.

"You are *charming*, Mrs. Sanders." I say in jest. "Your sense of style enhances your beauty." I pull her close and kiss her cheek. "What about me? Did you find suitable clothing for me, as well?"

Emma's eyes sparkle when she points across the walkway. "They're holding a few things for you, *Mr. Sanders*."

Okay, is that a reminder of my promise, or is she being cute, too? Since we are running out of time, I decide to pursue that issue later.

"Oh, and I purchased a new cell phone. Actually, it's one of those things where you purchase time, which expires in a month." She holds it up for my inspection.

"A burner cell? Good thinking."

How I love this immortal! I cannot wait until we have all the time in the world to... Enough sappy feelings. We need to focus. Too much is at risk to waste time right now.

"There is no time for me to try anything on. Our plane leaves in less than an hour. Do you have all you need?"

"Just one other bag. I'll grab it while you pay for yours." Emma trots off while I stride across to the store against the opposite wall. Before I step through the entrance, the first call for our flight resonates over the loud speaker. I hurriedly pay for the items and, by the time I layer all she chose for me into a new suitcase, it is time to make our way toward our gate.

I paid a hefty price for first class. It was well worth it for the separation from the rest of the passengers. Still not convinced no one followed us, I did a little reconnaissance before sitting and watched the remaining passengers as they entered. No one appeared to show any interest in us. Once we have taken flight, I finally settle back and relax.

Emma pulls a book from her new purse and pretends to read. However, her foot continuously taps softly against the floor and she jumps in her seat when the flight attendant offers us champagne. When I place the glass in her hand, I intend to charm her, but notice the set of her lips. Instead, I ask, "What do you require, my dear?"

Without answering verbally, her lips curl and her eyes slip closed as she places image after image in my mind of the two of us engaged in sex, which also reminds me we recently ingested a Velvet Crimson. My little minx is horny.

My reply image suffers in translation, but hopefully she gets the point. I forward an image of us dancing in the moonlight the night I introduced her to Francisco. My message states, yes, I want to be in your arms, but we must be vigilant where my maker is concerned.

He has not entered my mind since Alexander captured us and I wonder if that troll has relayed he has also lost us. If he has reported his failure, Francisco is certain to try to intimidate me again. Although I have restored my block, it is possible Francisco developed another way in.

Emma's foot stops tapping. She now stares out the window. Although I know I should ask, I leave her to her thoughts, settle against the seat back, and drink from the glass of champagne. I am weary from our latest adventure and need rest. I offer my empty glass to the flight attendant, clasp Emma's knee, and close my eyes.

I am startled awake when our plane bumps along the runway as it lands in Burbank. My eyes blink open to find Emma's sweet face inches from mine.

"Welcome back, Zach." Her beautiful golden-flecked brown eyes smile with warmth.

"I slept the entire time?"

Her lips curl in a smirk. "Yes, and when I tried to use the ladies room, you wouldn't release your hold on me. We'll need to stop on the way out, please."

The warm California sun welcomes us home as we descend the rolled-out walkway. We check in at the National Car Rental desk to secure a vehicle to take us to Laguna Beach, home of Elder Rayner. Unsure what awaits us, we are hopeful we will not require the vehicle to escape.

We are on the road before noon and stop long enough to call the Elder to ask if we can visit with him today. After I explain the circumstances surrounding our return, I also ask a favor.

"I wish to ascertain if Phyllis Megalos has been imprisoned within Francisco and Nadia's home. She had been at home in Indianapolis before Alexander kidnapped us and delivered us to her residence. She has been my friend for years, Elder. I would hate for her to be harmed because of our relationship."

"I will see what I can find out. In the meantime, my home awaits your return, Zachary."

"Thank you. We should arrive late afternoon."

When I end the call, Emma stares openly at me. "Why late afternoon? We're only an hour, maybe two, away."

"We should relax for a while somewhere, and devise a plan if all does not go as expected. Alright?"

Instead of continuing along I-5 south, we drop off, find our way to the Coast Highway, and settle in for the remainder of the drive with the ocean on our right. Emma rolls down her window to inhale the salty mixture of seawater and sand.

"Can we buy a boat, Zach? A sailboat? I've always wondered what it would feel like to be out there with nothing but water surrounding me. You know, a little isolation from the world?"

Her hair blows gently in the wind from the open window and when she turns her face to the front, I notice her closed eyes and relaxed smile. Alone on a boat with my life-mate? My body thrums with desire from the thought alone.

"Yes, and we will take lessons to learn how to operate our boat. Once all this is settled, that is."

Her eyes bolt open and her smile fades. "Of course." And, in one short moment, I have fouled her peaceful mood.

My mind remains on what we may face when we arrive. This could be a turning point for us. If the Elders listen to our story, they may agree to remove Francisco and Nadia from power. If I have my way, they will be banished from our circle for all eternity. I do not wish to assume their position, but I would rather it were me than to live under their threats for the remainder of my existence. Emma's, too. Possibly the Elders have someone in mind to accept the responsibility, which will allow Emma and me to travel together, and maybe purchase that sailboat.

We pull into a Starbucks parking lot two hours later to relax before our visit. While seated at a table in the back of the café, I remind Emma she still has not spoken to her mom or dad. I am sorry I brought it up the moment worry consumes her features. She digs into her new purse, fidgets with the burner cell in her hand as if deciding whether to place the call or not, and finally punches the buttons. I do my best not to listen, but I capture most of their conversation, which is not a happy one for my life-mate.

She closes the phone and drops the offending piece of technology into her purse. If looks could break my heart, hers would have mine.

I grasp her hand and bend to kiss her knuckles. "We will finish here and hurry back to Indianapolis. There is nothing that has to be done immediately. Like your mom said, there are tests first, and several doctors to meet with before surgery is scheduled. If you would like, I will vet the doctors in her insurance plan and offer my suggestions. I do know something about breast cancer, Em. She is stage one. That is the best she can hope for. And, probably no chemotherapy, only radiation, which, depending on her tumor and a few other identifiers, will dictate how many treatments she will be required to take. If you feel it necessary to move her to another facility for treatment, I will pay for any out-of-pocket expenses for her. I promise."

Tears flood her eyes. "See, Zach? This is why I wanted my humanity back, for a situation just like this. I should be at home helping my dad deal with all of this. He must be devastated." She chews her bottom lip to stall tears from falling.

"Darling, you will be by her side in no time. I promise. And, if you wish to live there again, we will sell both of our homes and relocate close to Phyllis. I will go wherever you want to go, my sweet Emma. We will find a way."

Her sad smile fills me with remorse. She is right. If I had not changed her ten years ago, she would be sitting next to her mom and dad right now, not worrying about Francisco or Nadia or any other issue I have made her a part of.

Who am I kidding? Francisco would have changed her anyway. So, no matter what fate brought to her, she is much better off with me than with that destructive vampire and his mate.

My latte and her tea are consumed in silence. I want to offer my assistance again, but choose to wait for her to ask. Instead, I ask for the phone and place several calls to friends in the area. Once I explain the situation, each promises to respond when called upon.

Downing the last drop from my paper cup, I rise and drop it into the trash bin. It is a little after four o'clock and time to face the music.

Emma rises, grasps my upper arm, and together we exit for the final leg of this trip.

Emma and I stand at Elder Rayner's front door, hands clasped tightly, while we wait for someone to open it. I discern no activity inside, but sense beings close by. I knock again and wait. Nothing. This is unusual. Elder Rayner expected us. "Stay put, Emma. I will be right back." I decide to walk around to the back, but alone. If all is safe, I will ask her to join me.

She follows me off the porch. "Not on your life."

The estate sits high upon a cliff overlooking the sea. As we round the right end, Emma gasps at the panorama of the Pacific Ocean with its white caps and peaceful sound of breaking waves against the beach below. I grab her hand to slow her so she can enjoy this one moment of tranquility.

A stand of palm trees, near the cliff, shelters the home from any others' view and, as we continue to the back, terraced gardens and a swimming pool more lavish than Francisco's stops my mate in her tracks.

Her body tenses a moment later as does mine. We are no longer alone. I spin back and watch Alexander and three of his goons round the corner of the home and charge toward us, fangs extended, black orbs large and intimidating. More than one creature enters my field of awareness at the back of the home, too. I drag Emma behind me and rush to the back hoping to find help. What we encounter instead is Elder Rayner, Francisco, and Nadia standing under the covered patio, waiting for our arrival.

I quickly survey the area hoping for an escape route. When one does not present itself, I squeeze my mate's hand and continue forward.

"I might have known you would believe this despicable vampire over the likes of me. What does he have on you, Elder Rayner? Is that the reason you allowed Cassander to be decimated? If so, you are no better than he is."

While my confrontation with the three in front of us continues, Alexander and his goons surround us.

Emma drops my hand and turns to him, "Where is Phyllis? What have you done with our friend?"

Alexander does not respond, Francisco does. "She's safe, little one. She will join us shortly."

Francisco casually strolls to the end of the patio and turns to face us. "Now. About your complaints, young Zachary."

The intense heat of the afternoon sun bears down on Emma and me while the three older vampires remain under the shade of the patio. Maybe they believe we are at a disadvantage because of the brightness. However, they do not know we ingested our drink while we sped through Cincinnati this morning. The sun creates no ill consequence for us… yet.

Francisco steps back across the tiled slab to a formal dining table, pulls out a chair, and lowers into it as if he had no care in the world. I watch Elder Rayner for his reaction to this barbaric creature, but observe no disquiet or irritation. Nadia, on the other hand, appears agitated, constantly tapping her foot, clenching and unclenching her fists, with eyes that dart from us, to Francisco, the goons, and back to her mate. What is that all about?

I attempt to listen to my maker's voice, but the more I watch Nadia and her increased anxiety, the more I recognize a storm brews beneath her surface.

While Francisco sputters on about respect and retributions, I grasp Emma's hand and squeeze tightly hoping to relay an image to her without the others noticing anxiety building within me.

Her quick intake of breath notifies me she understands. In her palm, I count with the tap of my finger: 1… 2…

Before I get to three, Alexander and his goons are upon us. He drags me away from Emma and one of the other creeps secures Emma in chains. Before I am hauled off, I glance at her and notice a smirk against her lips and a quick wink from her eye. The message she mentally sends me is, "Got this." I stop struggling and allow the oversized vampire to lug me onto the patio while Emma is transported into the house.

This farce seizure, this comical exhibition of power is Nadia's doing, her undertaking. She has forced her way in with the Elders somehow. What part does Francisco play? I stand before Nadia, who is joined by Francisco, to hear what disciplinary action they intend to take against me. With my arms stretched perpendicular to my body by two of Alexander's thugs, I have no doubt I will be relieved of both appendages should I attempt any movement whatsoever. I stand before my leader and attempt to fathom Nadia's function.

Emma, in the meantime, disappears from my sight the moment she steps foot across the back threshold, and I have yet to receive further communication from her. I have no worry for me. I am able to fend for myself. But, Emma... I worry her bravado earlier was simply for show.

Worry creeps into my mind while I study the scene before me. Elder Rayner appears to be satisfied with the current situation and reclines in a chair across the patio. Francisco, angered by our deception, changes before me into a ghoul with long extended fangs, furled brow, a wicked grimace, and fists which turn into claws. Fear for my mate consumes me. I turn toward the back door hoping to ascertain where in the house she has been taken. When I escape these goons, I will need to locate her quickly.

I had not noticed Nadia close the distance between us until she grasps my neck in her hand and while she lifts me into the air, she squeezes, which cuts off my airway.

"How dare you contact Elder Rayner directly to conspire against your leaders with those appalling allegations, which further disparage our circle in his eyes!"

Dressed in a long black billowing gown, her violet eyes are obscured with black in a moment as her fury rises. Uncovered extended fangs glisten in the afternoon sun while long strands of her raven hair rise with the wind creating an ominous foreboding inside of me. She intends to end me.

I am near the end of my capacity to restrain myself, but power through my emotions while I wait for my life-mate to contact me that she is safe and away from this place. I must stall Francisco's mate, if only for a few more moments.

"What do you and Francisco have on Rayner to exercise such power over him?" I croak. "He is one of the West Coast Elders and rules *you*, Nadia. Not the other way around."

Emma touches my mind with a smile and a picture of the open front door. I hide my joy, though. Nadia may read my expression and realize half of their plan failed. To have my life-mate removed from this situation, though, calms me significantly.

Nadia has yet to respond to my current charge and while I wait, additional goons surround the patio with a show of force. I notice the two who questioned Alexander's directives back in Indiana and hope they remain reluctant to participate in this farce. They could still prove useful.

My gaze is torn away from the patio when the wind begins to beat against the delicate annuals planted in the urns near the swimming pool. Clouds, dark with rain, accumulate in the western sky and billow high. I hide my smile. This could provide the perfect distraction if it makes it to land. I refocus on the lady in black, who sets me on my feet again and releases her hold.

Nadia flicks a look at the two goons who have me trapped. They release my arms, but stand next to me in case I try to bolt. Since help is assuredly on the way, I attempt to induce Francisco into this farce.

"You have insisted throughout this decade that Emma belongs to you, Francisco. You have made it clear your intent was to push Nadia aside and place Emma in that position of power. I would like to hear Nadia's response." I turn my attention to Francisco's mate. "Do you intend to relinquish your position within the circle and allow our leader to replace you after centuries together?"

Nadia first glares at Francisco, then back toward me. Her evil chuckle answers part of my question at least. Her head shakes, her eyes close, and it appears she has made a decision.

She parades up and down the patio striking a pose every so often for effect. I follow her choreographed display and wonder when the dam will burst. The wait is not long.

She spins back slowly and eyes every member of the group gathered around the patio. "My father was Alfredo Bianchi, the oldest and most powerful vampire the world has ever known. I was groomed to lead our circle, to unify the regional leaders, and to form a vastly independent nation of vampires who will ultimately rule this world. I was *not* raised to be the mate of a pathetic weakling such as the one standing over there. My father must be sorely disappointed in his choice of mate for me."

Nadia's head bows and when she raises it, her twisted lips bear a malicious smirk. "I intend to correct that." The foul vampire stalks back to me. "All unfinished business will be attended to soon, but mark my words, *young Zachary*. You and your mate will never destroy what has been built these past few years." Her wild black eyes focus on my face while raven hair violently circles her features in the harsh afternoon breeze.

Francisco scowls and strolls over to Elder Rayner. His anger precedes him when he spins back to Nadia.

"You have been a thorn in my side all these centuries. Your father assured me, during many conversations, *I* was to lead our circle, after ending those who stood in my way, and that included you as well, my dear."

Fearful this confrontation is about to explode, I send a message to Emma and wait.

CHAPTER 33

ZACH

E lation soars through me. Emma, although tossing herself back into the fray along with a host of circle members, alerts me she is close. The crew surrounding the patio and those beside me luckily do not appear to have a clue. But, why not? The three vampires before me possess superior powers and should sense them if my rescuers are near. Is it possible the circle leaders believe the group converging could be additional reinforcements for them? I study each, but perceive none are distracted by this news.

The heated discussion concerning who rules our circle continues while Oliver saunters out the back door carrying a tray of what appears to be blood-filled goblets. I assume it is human blood since Francisco and his mate ingest nothing else. Upon closer inspection, my friend's eyes appear glazed over as though he is heavily charmed. It is better than the previous alternative.

Oliver joins Rayner, Francisco, and Nadia and offers each a glass, then continues around the patio and presents each vampire the same concoction. When he offers the two goons beside me a glass, I catch a quick glance in my direction. So, not as charmed as he appears. When he presents the tray to me, I decline. "I do not require blood at this time."

He turns from me and continues his deliveries. I wish I could somehow alert him help is close, but I will not for fear I would alert the others to our rescue.

Francisco and Nadia continue their face-off surrounding control of the circle. Their angry words escalate in intensity until the racket enflames the pool of vampires surrounding the patio. As one, their posture becomes fraught with tension. Mumblings of who they will follow rise until the two goons who stand next to me argue over who has more power.

While the first one states Nadia should be the chosen one, the second one asserts Francisco *was* the chosen one and should remain in power. Their discussion grows in force until the one on my left reaches around me and shoves the other. I watch as, one by one, each of the vampires surrounding the patio pushes, shoves, or claws at the one next to him or her. With my escape made possible by their infighting, I step back a pace to run, but observe Elder Rayner's grin as he watches the chaos. He created this clash! But, how?

The Elder has not noticed I am no longer standing next to the two goons who had me restrained. I continue to back away, but keep my focus on the rising combat.

The forceful wind captures my attention again. It appears the fury of the vampires is stimulated by the intensifying gale. Does he control the weather? Is he that powerful?

I brush my hair from my face and rush toward the back door in the hope my mate will arrive soon with our army of colleagues, while the ongoing fray accelerates.

Oliver greets me the moment I pass through. I grab him and smile for the first time in what feels like forever. "It is great to see you alive and well, my friend. How did you manage to escape Francisco's charm?"

Nervous I have been followed, I spin toward the door, but no one appears interested.

My friend's eyes smile with pure happiness, matching the lopsided grin on his face. "Nadia removed the spell the moment she could, but asked me to play along. She said the night was going to be a marathon."

"Does Nicole know you are alive?"

"No." He walks away suddenly as if my speaking her name caused him pain.

I follow closely behind. "Oliver. What is going on? Why have you decided against communicating with your mate?"

He spins back to me in a flash. "I had no choice. In order to regain my freedom from the idiot Nadia's tied to, I promised to devote myself to her wishes. That meant leaving behind my life-mate, much

260

the same way Francisco wished to take Emma from you. I warn you, Zachary. You are in a no-win scenario with Francisco. He will take her no matter what. He's powerful, as is his current mate."

My one-time friend does not realize the line he has stepped over. That being will never possess her. My fists ball. "He must kill me first."

Oliver shakes his head. "That's the intention, my friend. Why else do you believe you're here?"

While I reinforce my belief Emma will remain mine, the noise level from the brawl outside reaches malevolent proportions. We stride toward the back door and watch as a chair crashes against the glass and wood enclosur,e sending shards of both across the living room floor.

"It sounds as if the world is about to explode around us." Oliver backs away from the door after observing the approaching storm and vampires pent on tearing each other apart. He turns to me, his lips set in a thin line. I am about to advise him this all started after he delivered the blood. But, we both turn when the front door bursts open.

I expect my mate to bound through, but am surprised to see Elders Jacob, Timothy, Akila, and Mumbi, the four remaining West Coast Elders. A thunderclap blasts through the door with them, and now I wonder if the building storm is their doing.

Having never met them, I had heard over the centuries about the abilities the West Coast Elders possessed. I thought them to be fictional stories told simply to ensure the members abided by their circle leaders' rules. Having never been included or involved in any dispute with anyone other than Francisco, I had never witnessed their powers first-hand and still believed the rumors to be overstated.

Elder Mumbi, the sanctioned leader of the West Coast Elders, strides toward Oliver and me wearing colorful robes from her native country of South Africa. She is an imposing figure standing more than six feet tall.

"Where is Rayner? We were told our presence was required to decide the fate of a powerful creature." Her attention focuses on the fracas outside. "Why are those creatures fighting one another?"

Elder Akila joins Mumbi. Her Italian heritage speaks loudly through her contemporary Gucci pantsuit and heels, a stark opposite of Mumbi and her homeland attire. However, it is her heavy accent that captures my attention.

"Call off the dogs, Jacob. I have no time for these imbeciles."

Jacob and Timothy join the two women, who appear to be in charge. Jacob, I had learned, is from eastern Europe while Timothy first lived in Canada. Their areas of responsibility range from Alaska to the north all along the coast through Latin America to the south, and as far east as the Rockies. I believe four sets of Elders rule North and Central America. Since moving to California, our circle falls under the four standing a few feet from me and the one outside enjoying the commotion.

Jacob continues out through the patio door and strides to Elder Rayner, who stands beside Nadia and Francisco. All appear to be enjoying the spectacle before them. Timothy follows close behind, but stands in front of the demolished door to observe the massacre from that vantage point.

"Stop injuring each other this moment. There is no need for such violence." Timothy's words, spoken in a calm soothing voice, implores each vampire to end their attacks. The fighting stops immediately. It is as if they have been charmed. The overhead brewing storm also dissipates within moments, changing the sky above Elder Rayner's home to blue again.

Oliver and I stand mostly unnoticed by the Elders. We watch, however, as Elder Rayner, Francisco, and Nadia, taken by surprise by this turn of events, rush to the back door.

Rayner stops and inclines his head to the three Elders in the doorway. "Good afternoon, fellow Elders. I apologize for the status of my home and grounds. We were," he points toward Francisco and Nadia, "cleansing his circle of a few despicable creatures. To what do I owe this special visit?"

Does he actually think the Elders believe his inept words? My desire to sink my fangs in *his* neck and drink until he is no longer, grips me hard.

Oliver restrains me before I am able to move. "Not worth it, my friend."

I nod my thanks and contain my craving. But, while Rayner continues a rather lackluster explanation of the current events, my mind wanders to my life-mate. Where is Emma? Her message she was close appeared in my mind too many minutes ago. I close my eyes and attempt to send her a communication.

What astonishes me is who replies. Her accent repeats from earlier. "She's been detained, but do not worry."

My gaze flicks to Akila, who smiles briefly before she engages with the others again.

The Elders appear to finally take notice of my friend and me. Elder Mumbi nods our way and dismisses us, asking that we wait on the couch in the living room while they interrogate Nadia, Francisco, and Elder Rayner. As one, the four Elders exit the home and stop in the middle of the patio, waiting for Rayner and his colleagues to join them.

After lowering to the sofa, the distraction I require is in the questions I have for Oliver.

"How did you escape being beheaded that afternoon, Oliver? Casper was ready to drop the sword on your neck." Even though my words are whispered, I am also certain the Elders perceive every word, which is my intent.

"Nadia. As I told you, she intended to replace Francisco with me as her mate."

"What about Nicole? You have shared blood, you have lived centuries together, you even mentioned you were from the same nomad tribe in the Sahara Desert. And, like me, Francisco changed you and asked you to change Nicole so you would not be alone."

He sits forward on the sofa and clasps his hands. His head drops. "Nadia convinced me, almost a year ago, that Nicole had been unfaithful to me with Alexander. Instead of questioning her myself, I believed the allegations. I was stupid, naïve maybe, and shared blood with Nadia to return the favor. When Nicole found out, I waited for her to admit her philandering. Instead, I learned the truth. Nadia. She's one evil vampire hell bent on destroying anything and anyone in her path."

So, I am not alone in being the target of a vampire's attempt to rob a mate.

"Much like Francisco and my Emma. Damn, Oliver. You should have known better. Look, work it out with Nicole. She was heartsick when I saw her a few weeks ago."

"If I get the chance."

The heated conversation between the Elders, Francisco, and Nadia intensifies the longer Oliver and I remain in the living room. The storm that dispersed just a few minutes ago also returns with gusto. Wind whips furniture on the patio around, spray from the beach thirty feet below reaches the palm trees out on the cliff, and rain pours from black clouds above the home. Darkness blankets the interior of the building. Oliver and I, concerned for our circle members, venture toward the windows to scrutinize the disturbance and watch the four Elders admonish the three before them.

A shield of some sort surrounds Elders Akila and Mumbi, thus keeping the elements from disturbing them or their attire. I marvel at their powers again, while Oliver and I observe from the living room. In all my decades, I have never witnessed a display such as the one before me. Their powers appear limitless, but there is no vengeance in their actions. To rule, you must listen and understand your flock, not pretend to have their best interests at heart and do what you wish anyway. Humans leaders act comparably. From what I have read lately, their world is under attack, but not from immortals like me.

I shift away from the window as the confrontation outside continues. Nadia and Francisco appear to be the only ones answering the Elders' questions. Francisco has not yet attempted a mind-link with me, which also surprises me. Oliver, on the other hand, fists his hands at his sides as if restraining himself.

"What is happening, Oliver?"

His lips curl in an evil grimace. "Nadia. She's threatening my mate. Why did I ever believe her? I've placed Nicole in danger."

"Maybe not. The Elders appear to have control over them now. We should wait and see what is decided."

I also watch Nadia. She appears to be distancing herself from Francisco moving closer to Rayner. Before I realize I am speaking out loud, I mutter, "Why did I not understand her insane desire to eliminate *him* and thereby anoint herself our circle leader?"

Oliver's chuckle reaches my ears a moment later. "*Now* you figure it out!"

My head shakes. The Elders will not allow that to occur. I stand and continue to watch the ordeal before us, which appears to be nearly over.

Elder Mumbi requests that Jacob and Timothy grab the three major participants from the chaos, then turns and gracefully walks into the living room with Elder Akila beside her. As one, the offenders are dragged inside and lined up against a living room wall.

Timothy calls over his shoulder once Rayner is secured beside Nadia, "The remainder of you... stay put."

It is more of a command than a suggestion. However, the minions stand tensely around the patio, as if waiting for their next instruction. Timothy mumbles about asking someone something when suddenly, and as one, the group stands slack against the raging winds. Timothy grins at the collection of circle members, then refocuses on the captors.

Elder Mumbi slowly paces in front of the three detainees. "Your answers outside were not sufficient. We wish to know who started this brawl and why. And before you speak again, choose your words carefully."

Rayner looks to Francisco first, who is already signaling Nadia to keep quiet. When none of the three are forthcoming, Oliver steps forward.

"Excuse me, Elders. I am Oliver Younger. I have…"

Francisco attempts to intervene, but he is told to remain quiet while Oliver speaks.

Elder Mumbi refocuses on my friend. "Yes, Oliver, we have knowledge of you. What light can you shed on this situation?"

Oliver discloses how Francisco charmed him earlier to do his bidding. "Nadia released me from his charm, but asked me to deliver a glass of blood to each vampire on the patio this afternoon. While Nadia poured liquid into each globe, Francisco, with Rayner tailing, came behind and added a few drops of something from a small bottle he later placed in his pants pocket. The only vampire who did not receive the tainted blood is Zachary Matthews. As you can see, he was not affected in any form. Neither were the three of them." Oliver motions toward the captives. "Their glasses did not contain the additive either."

Elder Akila turns toward me. "Why did you not consume the blood, Zachary? Were you aware of the plot?"

"*No!* I had no need of blood since my mate and I consumed a Velvet Crimson earlier today. We walked into this plot, as you call it, and were taken prisoner by Francisco and Nadia because I informed Elder Rayner of their deceit where my mate and I are concerned."

Elder Mumbi glides my way. "You are the life-mate of Emma Christensen, is that correct?"

How does she know my Emma?

"I am."

"And, Emma was changed by you against her will ten years ago?"

Where is she going with this? "Yes, that is unfortunately correct."

"Your mate has repeatedly requested to regain her humanity, is that also the truth?"

What?

"Yes." This Elder has firsthand knowledge of my mate's desire. How is that possible? Unless... I opt to say no more.

"Timothy, allow the three females inside. I wish them to become part of this discussion."

Oliver and I share a glance while the Elder strides to the front door and disappears for a few seconds. When he returns, he is followed by Emma, Phyllis, and Nicole.

Nicole does not wait for an invitation to join her mate. She rushes into his arms and holds on for dear life. Their embrace is just short of erotic.

Emma slowly walks toward me, takes my hand, and kisses my cheek. My gaze focuses on her red-rimmed eyes and quivering lips. I want to ask what is going on, but instead I cup her cheek in my hand. Elder Mumbi's earlier words echo through me. Worry seeps in. Does she still wish to be changed back and, in effect, leave me?

I turn my attention to the vampire who follows behind my life-mate. Phyllis stops just short of me and nods.

"Phyllis. We were worried you had become a prisoner. I am happy to see you here and unharmed."

Our friend surveys the room, taking in the scene with Francisco, Nadia, and Rayner standing together against the wall. "I owe my escape to, I believe his name is Casper. He must have been called to assist someone here. All I know is the locked door on my chamber opened. I dashed out and followed him here from Oceanside. When Emma ran from the house alone, I followed her instead, and, well... here we are."

I reach for her hand and grip it while I attempt to smile. "This should all be over soon. Please say you will stay with us in Oceanside for a few days before you return home. I think we all could use a break."

Before she answers, my attention is diverted when Nadia hisses. Her fangs extend and her eyes blacken while Oliver and Nicole's romantic display continues. Francisco's mate reaches her arms toward the couple, but she is pushed back against the wall by a command from Elder Akila. It appears she has had enough of the three.

Elder Akila taps her foot against the tile floor. "Can we settle this soon? I do have important responsibilities to attend to."

"We're almost finished. Now. Nadia, what knowledge did you have of your mate's decision to drug your circle members, which caused the fracas outside? And, don't tell me you had no idea what he had planned. You two are like two peas in a pod. How you've kept this circle from annihilation before now is beyond me." Elder Mumbi's hushed tones speak volumes.

Nadia looks questioningly at Oliver. It appears she truly believes his alliance is with her. When Oliver offers no support, she clasps her hands, refocuses on Elder Mumbi, and opens her mouth to speak, but is stalled by Francisco.

His gaze focuses openly on my mate while Nadia collects herself. Does he truly believe she would rather become his than stay with me? Or is something else happening?

His gaze switches to me. "You have no idea of her power, do you *young* Zachary?"

Emma's hand grabs mine and squeezes. Her mind whispers to mine, "I love you."

I squeeze back and send the same message to her.

Francisco seethes. "Do you know why those idiots outside stopped fighting? Your mate told them to from the street. Your mate is capable of charming an army of vampires to do her bidding. Do you realize what influence that power brings to our circle? We could rule thousands of vampires with Emma by my side."

"And, now the only vampire you will rule is yourself." Elder Mumbi strolls to our circle leader, stands two feet from him, and states, "You and your mate have caused a rift in our once-calm community. You both have killed indiscriminately without trial or truthful information. You both have imprisoned innocents, you did not feed them or allow them any comfort while stuck in that dungeon at your home, and used both for your own personal ambitions. I'd enjoy your beheadings. However, I have a more appropriate punishment for you."

The four Elders stand together before Rayner, Francisco, and Nadia. Elder Mumbi continues. "It is the judgement of the West Coast Elders that you be stripped of your titles of Circle Leaders and become incarcerated inside the Santa Ana, El Salvador, prison for a minimum of five hundred years. You will give up your worldly possessions. Your estate and all its furnishings will be forfeited as well. Once your sentence has been served, it will be up to the Council to decide what the remainder of your existence will look like. In the meantime, Elder Rayner will accompany you to oversee your continued good health."

Rayner opens his mouth to object, but shuts it when Akila taps her foot again against the marble floor.

"And, you, Elder Rayner, will also be divested of your title since you were a significant partner in what transpired where these two are concerned."

Elder Mumbi backs up and turns to face Oliver and Nicole. "Now. There is some consideration due this young vampire. We understand Francisco held you captive in his dungeon, you were almost beheaded, but saved by his mate, all because he believed you plotted against him to overthrow his position within your circle."

Oliver nods and swallows heavily, unable to speak, and his chocolate brown eyes open as wide as possible while he waits for their directive. Nicole holds onto his arm for dear life.

"It is time for a new circle leader to be appointed. However, we will leave it up to you and Zachary to decide who is best suited to rule."

Elder Mumbi turns her attention on Emma and me. "You have a decision to make, Emma. You requested, almost from the day you became a vampire, to be given your human body again. Is that something you still wish?"

I grasp her hand tightly. Her quick intake of breath worries me, but if it is possible and she still wishes it to be so, I will not do anything to stop her wish from becoming reality.

"I'd like some time with Zach before I give you my decision. May I have a day, please?"

For the first time today, Elder Mumbi smiles. "Of course you may, child. Contact Elder Jacob when you've made your decision. And as for you, Zachary. You should be punished for changing her in the first place. However, I realize your leader coerced you to do so and, if not, he would have taken her life for himself. Also, Emma did not suffer at your hands. You care deeply for the young vampire. It shows in your connection today. However, if she feels compelled to regain her humanity, it is our desire she be afforded that option. What happens with the two of you after is up to her."

If I had a heart, it would be breaking. My Emma. She will be lost to me when she regains her humanity, her mind blanked of our connection. On the other hand, this is what she wished for all along. How can I deny her when she has suffered loneliness and solitude for ten years due to my actions? If Elder Jacob can restore her humanity, I will not stand in her way.

Elder Akila taps her Louboutin lace pump against the marble again. "Now?"

Elder Mumbi grasps her arm. "In a moment." She spins toward the three hostages. "Elder Timothy will escort you to your new home. I have a few words for you before you leave, however. Learn from your mistakes. Do not forget your Elders know everything you do. If you prove to us you can be productive in our world again, your sentence may decrease substantially. However, do not attempt to fool us. Our eyes will be upon you every moment of every day."

With a final nod, Timothy and Jacob, charm and chain the three, and escort them into the garage. When the garage door opens, we watch a black Lexus GX back out and drive off.

Elder Mumbi has parting words for Oliver and me. "Decide between you who should rule, and make it soon. Those idiots out back need guidance. Contact us with your decision. Oh, and Emma, release the children. Tell them to go home."

Emma nods while Elders Akila and Mumbi saunter out the front door and disappear into the afternoon sun. She squirms out of my hold and walks a few feet away.

I watch in awe as her communication, completely through her mind, disburses the crowd outside.

When she turns back to me, her eyes impel me to stay where I am. "I need some time before I make my final decision, Zach. Can I stay at your home for the rest of today and tomorrow while I think?"

I suppose Phyllis and I can stay here. "Sure, Emma. Unless you want to tell me now you have already made your decision." Before I allow her to answer, I have other questions first. I walk toward her. "How did you contact the Elders? How did you find them? Even I do not know how."

Her shy smile, which captivated me from that first day, saddens me now.

"Somehow they heard of my power to charm a group of people. After Oliver set me free, I ran into Phyllis outside and then right into Timothy. He looked into my eyes and knew I was that vampire. From what he told me, he had been asked to check on Elder Rayner pertaining to the quick storm that arose during that first fray. He asked why I was running away and, I don't know, all of what Francisco put us through gushed out of me. Phyllis had found me by then. So, he took us to a safe location and asked the other three to join him here. I also let it slip that I wanted my humanity back and why. I didn't mean to get you into trouble, Zach. But, after all we've been through the past weeks, I want nothing more than to forget it all and go home to my mom." She shrugs and her smile disappears.

I grasp her hands in mine and stare into her beautiful golden-flecked brown eyes. "You deserve your humanity back, my Emma. I will not stand in your way."

I kiss her knuckles then drop her hands and walk toward Phyllis, who has joined Oliver and Nicole. When I spin back, my love has already left.

CHAPTER 34

EMMA

Mom's first radiation treatment is today. I promised I'd drive her since Dad can't take any more time off. Since I didn't make it home in time for her surgery, I'm glad I can help out now.

The IU Health Ball Memorial Cancer Center located at the hospital is fifteen minutes from my parents' home. Five weeks from surgery, Mom is still a little wobbly on her legs. I decide to drop her near the entrance and park the car so she doesn't have to walk too far. I grab my purse, lock my car, and slip inside the medical building. She's seated against the left wall when I locate her, waiting to be called.

"Can I come back with you, Mom? I promise not to get in the way." I lift her purse from her lap and place it next to mine, just in case.

"We can ask the technician. I know there's a small waiting room back there, but let's ask first. Is that alright?"

I sense her fear. My mom. I wish I could heal her, I wish she didn't have to deal with all this mess. But, she's strong. She raised me, after all, didn't she? I grasp her hand, which is cold as ice, like mine. "Of course. Wouldn't want to get in bad with the people healing my mom, now would I?" I try to make light of the situation. For some reason, I'm not getting through.

"If it'll make you feel better, I'll wait out here. I have a book to read. I'll make due. Then you don't have to worry about anything. Okay?"

My gaze focuses on her face. Her tight downturned lips give her away. "Or, I will go as far as they'll allow me and wait for you there. Whatever you want, Mom. I'm here for you."

She's ready with words on her lips when a door opens and a nice young man with black hair, a narrow beard and mustache, and deep chocolate brown eyes calls, "Mrs. Christensen? Are you ready?" I assume he's her technician.

Mom stands instantly and takes a step. "Can my daughter come with me?"

His lips curl. "Of course! She can wait in our small lounge while you receive your treatment."

That's my cue. I stand, grab her hand again, and together we follow the young man to the rear of the building.

His head turns to me. "My name is David. I am one of three technicians in the radiology department. We also have Melanie and Rafael. We're all in this together, right Mrs. Christensen?"

Mom finally finds her smile. "Yes, we are. Thank you, David."

And just like that, her fear diminishes.

David directs her to the changing room. "The robes are in that cabinet. After you've changed, wait out here. One of us will come to get you when we're ready."

Mom nods, David leaves, and I lower into one of four chairs in the small room. I pull my iPad from my purse and open Kindle while I wait for Mom to reappear from the dressing room. The book I'm reading appears on the screen and I try to concentrate on the words. But, I can't. I'm more nervous than she is. I'm sitting in a cancer treatment facility, radiation a few feet away, and my mom is preparing to receive a treatment I know nothing about. Life is so mixed up right now. My eyes move from the book to a picture on the wall depicting sand and water. My mind drifts back to Oceanside and the creature I love.

Zach promised to be with me today, but his plans stalled when the buyer for his home requested additional time to close. Soon, he told me last night and this morning. My eyes fade to the side and close when a memory of just four weeks ago penetrates my mind.

I had a decision to make. I left Elder Rayner's home and ran to Zach's place in Oceanside. Upon entering, I immediately ran upstairs to the bedroom we'd shared and flopped down on top of the comforter. That's where he found me four hours later. I asked him to give me until the next day to make my decision, but Zach being who he is, knew I planned to be changed back.

My memory is disrupted when Mom joins me. "Guess it won't be long now."

"Mom, you've got this. The hard part is over. All you have to do is fifteen treatments and you're done. Easy peasy! And after today's, let's go to Dairy Queen for ice cream. Okay?"

She mutters her agreement and smiles.

A female technician, obvious by her uniform, stands at the doorway. "We're ready, Anna."

My smile spreads when I recognize what she is. She's a vampire working amongst all the medical staff. "I'll be right here, Mom. See you in a few minutes." I say the words more relaxed than I've been in days.

Mom dutifully follows the technician, who I assume is Melanie. They disappear from view and my anxiety grows. I attempt to read again, but I can't focus. Instead, I pull the memory again to relive my last few hours as a vampire.

I was angry, at first, that he hadn't abided by my wishes. "You promised, Zach. How can I think straight when you're standing in front of me?"

He stalked closer. "Because I intend to change your mind. I love you, Emma. I do not wish to exist in this world without you by my side."

"What am I supposed to do? You tell *me*! Ever since you showed up at the reunion, I've been on the run. With you, but still, this isn't a life I'd wish to lead. I need normalcy, I need structure, I want children, a family of my own. I want to spend holidays with my family. I haven't seen my sister or brother for years. All because you couldn't live without me. Well, I want to see what it's like to live without *you* for a change. Now that Francisco and Nadia are imprisoned somewhere in El Salvador, I can finally close my eyes and not worry when something goes bump in the night. Don't you see? I'm not cut out to be a vampire. I'm still me," words I spoke many weeks ago erupt, "just enhanced."

He stepped closer. I watch his eyes change before me from dark blue to black. His fangs extend. The center of my body recognizes the draw to be in his arms. Damn him. He's pulling out all the stops to push me over the edge. After the last few days, I'd been ready to fall but, for the time being, held my ground.

"Please don't, Zach. I'm having a tough time right now and as much as I'd love to be in your arms, I can't."

"Must I charm you to stay with me? Must I resort to those tactics? I need you, Emma, as much as I need blood to exist. So, if you leave, please rip my heart out. You will be taking it with you anyway."

The creature I adore stopped a mere few inches from me, but I was already lost to his desire. I needed him as much as I needed blood to drink, too.

Our final union exploded into a feeding frenzy. I craved his body, his blood, the mind chamber. Our link served to remind me of the pitfalls of human life. The agony of loss, days and nights spent alone without the caress of the creature who held me, darkness with no light. Tears escaped my eyes when a vision of him standing before me faded into thin air. I clung to Zach, begged him to ramp up his thrusts, and closed my mind to everything but the feel of his body coupled with mine. The orgasm that ripped me apart shattered my mind into shreds. Could I give this up, give him up?

We drifted down from our dream, lay side-by-side on his bed, and held onto each other realizing this may be the last time we'd make love.

A gentle caress to my face opened my eyes. "I will follow you wherever you go, Emma. I must know you are in no danger. Ever."

I snuggled closer. "I will always love you, Zach."

He left me alone after we showered together one last time, and returned to what was Elder Rayner's home to discuss with Oliver who should be the new circle leader. I had my suspicions, but didn't wish to pile anything further on his plate.

Mom enters the small waiting room and smiles. "All done for today. It was really easy, Em. I laid there, they adjusted me on that bed, and left to run the machine. And, I didn't feel anything either. No heat, no pain. It was as if this big blue machine just moved over me and took pictures. It was that easy."

I turn my head when a tear threatens to leak out. "Great, mom. Change and we'll go to Dairy Queen for a blizzard."

Mom and I walk through the door and into the waiting room where we first were seated. I casually look over the individuals there and notice someone from my past.

"Ayres? Is that you?"

274

"Emma? Oh, my goodness. Fancy running into you here. How are you? You aren't... you don't..."

I grab my mom's hand. "No. Mom just finished her first radiation treatment. Mom, you remember Ayres Bridges. He escorted me to my senior prom."

Mom's eyes narrow while she surveys my high school friend. "It has been ten years, Emma. You do look familiar, so I'll take my daughter's word for it. Are you here for treatment, Ayres?"

His eyes travel to the opposite side of the waiting room. "My grandmother. She's receiving her third round of chemo today. Mom was busy so I offered to sit with her."

His gaze transfers back to me. "I'm glad I did. Otherwise, I wouldn't have run into you again. Emma. So... what have you been up to since the reunion?"

Mom shifts her weight from one foot to the other. I need to get her home.

"Engaged actually to Zach. We reconnected a while back and, well, one thing led to another and..." My shoulders rise and fall. "We've decided to move back to Indiana, too. Isn't that something?"

My friend's gaze glows with happiness. "I'm glad for you, Emma. Really, for both of you. Look, I see your mom needs to go. Let's promise to have lunch or something soon, okay? God, Emma. You look great. You sure haven't changed since high school."

Afraid my friend may wish to inquire further, I stop him there. "You look amazing yourself. So, can we plan to get together?"

My high school buddy stops his pursuit. "Sure. I'd love to see Zach, too. No excuses, okay?"

"None." Thankful he didn't ask anything I couldn't answer, I smile sweetly. "Zach will love it."

"See ya, Emma."

Ayres nods while Mom and I walk toward the front entrance.

What a nice encounter. I'll have to call him in a few days. And, isn't his wedding sometime next spring?

It's late afternoon when we return home. I ask Mom to relax while I begin dinner. Dad should arrive somewhere after five. He'll want all the details from Mom, so I'd better have dinner well underway when he shows.

A knock on the front door drags me from a simmering pot of marinara and meat sauce. I dry my hands on my apron as I walk into the living room. Before I open the door, I peek out.

"Zach!" The door opens in a flash and he's in my arms. "How did you get here so quickly? I thought you said the closing was delayed."

The creature of my dreams walks me backward into the living room. "I can sign everything electronically. Hi. How are you?"

"Much better now." I grab his hand and lead him into the kitchen. "Mom had her first treatment today. Guess what." I spin to look him in the eyes.

"Tell me." Zach draws me close and stares unashamedly at me as his eyes turn black.

I check to assure myself no one is near before I whisper, "One of her technicians is a vampire."

"Did that worry you?" His lips lower to my forehead.

"No. I just thought it was interesting."

A light kiss touches my cheek.

My body thrums with recognition. "Later. I have to finish dinner."

My life-mate backs up a step. "Promises. Always promises. Alright, I will leave you alone to prepare dinner. Think I will visit Phyllis. Maybe she will walk to our new house with me."

Teasing me. He's always teasing me. "Fine. Just return by six thirty. Mom and Dad will want to see you."

"I cannot promise to eat dinner with you, but I will be here. Where are they, anyway?"

"Mom's lying down and Dad hasn't gotten home yet," I say as I stir the sauce.

With a final kiss to the back of my neck, Zach saunters off and leaves the way he entered. I sigh and continue to stir the sauce while thinking about my reasons for remaining the creature he created.

It all came down to family. Yes, I wished for one of my own. I wanted children to love, a husband to give them to me and also love me, and I wanted my own family in my life again. When I sat down and thought about it, I had most of that now. Zach and Phyllis already taught me how to charm my parents into believing I was older than I looked. I intend to use that technique on my siblings, too. I hate messing with their kids' minds, but when it becomes necessary, I'll do it.

But, children of my own? I decided I could pamper my nieces and nephews, which would almost feel as if they were mine. It's not quite the same, but...

The Elders assured me neither Francisco nor Nadia will ever come near me again. I believe them. I must. I don't want to feel the need to run away ever again.

When Oliver and Zach discussed who best fit the role of leader, Zach, realizing I would be leaving for Indiana soon, opted to relinquish his position and gladly handed total responsibility for the circle over to Oliver. From what he told me, Oliver was taken by surprise, but grateful for the endorsement. A small ceremony took place at Francisco's home—which now belongs to Oliver and Nicole—with all four West Coast Elders in attendance. I was sorry to miss it, but Zach relayed my good wishes for me.

Phyllis left California for home two days after I made my final decision, although I had yet to share it with anyone other than Elder Jacob. Her wise counsel and advice served me well, though. From the first day she told me what I was until she arrived at Elder Rayner's home asking how she could help, Phyllis is someone I know I can always count on if and when a problem arises.

And, as for my life-mate and me? The time I took tore me into two beings: one who wanted my human existence back and one who wished to remain with my current life-mate and live a life free from disease or harm. I weighed both against each other. When I tossed out the "Francisco Factor," my decision followed. Yes, I wanted all the human experiences I'd miss. Yes, I wanted my family in my life. And, yes, I needed stability in order to find myself again.

The other hand, although similar, added more than I'd give up. I had my life-mate, one who loved me to distraction and would never allow anyone or anything to harm me. I had added freedom to learn. If I wished to become a doctor or a lawyer or an architect, time presented no problem. Zach promised he'd hire me to run his business while I attended whichever university I chose. I told him I didn't need his handouts, but if it works for us both, who am I to challenge that vampire?

My final decision did hurt. I realized I'd have days when I regretted my decision, but more days, and years, and centuries I'd have to spend with the one who changed me ten years ago. After all we've been through together, how could I turn my back on him now? Learning of my ability to charm groups also played a factor. I could be a major help to my new community. So, although I spent years wishing for my humanity, I found reasons why remaining vampire suited me best. Was I growing up finally, accepting responsibility for my life instead of wishing it away?

I called Elder Jacob the next morning to relay my decision. "Yes, I've decided to remain vampire. I've been running away from the reality of it and didn't wish to accept the life I could make for myself. With centuries of time on my hands, I can make a difference if I apply myself."

His chuckle curled my lips. "I sensed your conflict, Emma. I also knew your decision before you did. One only had to witness your attachment to Zachary to realize he is, indeed, your chosen life-mate. One you will never leave."

"How did you know?" This creature spent little time with me. How in the world?

"I'm a seer, Emma. I perceive the future. That's how I knew. Your goal four weeks ago was to save your mate any way possible. You put yourself in harm's way for the one who changed you even after you protested against this life. If you had wished to become human and leave this world behind, you wouldn't have cared if Zach lived or perished."

"Maybe that's because of the person I was or am? I don't wish death to any creature, whether human, vampire, werewolf, or demon. I don't believe becoming a vampire changed my true nature."

"No, it did not. However, your resourcefulness acquiring the band of circle members to save the others proved to the Elders the leader you will become."

"I... don't wish to be a leader."

"There are many ways to lead, dear Emma. In time, you will understand."

"If you say so. I, ah, need to go home, Jacob. My mom is ill..."

"And her treatments begin soon."

"Do you also know the outcome?"

"Trust the doctors."

"Thank you. Please tell the other Elders thank you for me. I'd enjoy talking with them someday, especially Elder Mumbi. She's formidable."

"I'll pass on your request. Goodbye, Emma. Continue to be brave."

The moment my phone call ended, I dashed into the garage with my suitcase and drove home to Buckeye. Zach would have to wait. I wanted to put my home on the market and pack the items I'd ship to Mom's.

Zach arrived at my house early the following morning. Overjoyed with my decision, we traveled together to Indianapolis. He planned to stay with Phyllis and look for a home for us while I did my daughterly duty and live with the parents while Mom prepared for her treatments.

Phyllis welcomed us with open arms. She introduced us to her circle the following night, which is now our circle, too. We feel at home for the first time, maybe ever.

While Zach holds my hand, Phyllis slides her arm around my waist as we exit the Elks Lodge in Noblesville, where the circle congregates to catch up and welcome new members.

Phyllis glances up at the night sky and sighs. "Get used to being treated like family here. This is the way a circle is supposed to work. Right? Now you'll understand how a community of vampires works together to protect its own."

My free arm circles her waist. "I like this group as much as I did the circle you found for me in Phoenix."

My mind drifts back to those first few weeks I lived alone in the brittle heat of Arizona. "Thank you, Phyllis. I never could have assimilated into this life without you. Just tell me one thing."

Our friend stops in her tracks thus pausing me and Zach. "What?"

"Has Zach's speech always been archaic?"

Phyllis roars with laugher. "Yes! His speech has never evolved to match the time." She spins to my love. "Why is that, Zachary? Too New-World for you?"

He looks between us in surprise. "You wish me to change my speech patterns?"

We simultaneously yell, "Yes!"

His fingers rub at his chin. "I suppose I could learn. If you will teach me."

I bump his hip with mine. "Okay. Repeat after me: if *you'll* teach me."

The love of my life responds with the words as I dictated them to him. My eyes shine with love. "Okay. That's a start."

We resume walking arm in arm toward our respective cars as I think, *This is going to be fun.*

Zach contacted the Indiana State Medical Board to obtain his license to practice in this state, made more feasible because his current license in California is active. It will take some doing, but he wants to feel useful again. I applaud his decision. We all need a regimen to follow daily. He'll require a suitable office, but I know when he puts his mind to something, it happens.

The home he found for us is located close to my parents, but private, too. You know, part of something, but off the grid. It sits alone in the middle of a forest, trees surrounding the home and estate. It's the perfect fit.

And me? I rise every morning, look over at the creature who will become my husband in a few weeks, and marvel at our existence. We enjoy a simple life, we don't draw attention to ourselves, and we participate in our community as much as time allows. Life, or death if you will, couldn't be easier. With my studies beginning in the fall, who knows where this existence will lead us?

I love hearing from my readers.
Please consider jotting a review about it on the
Lynne Anders book page at Amazon.com.

Lynne Anders

EXCERPT FROM

FOREVER
LOVE

Watch for this new Lynne Anders release on Amazon and Kindle.

Lynne Anders

CHAPTER 1

The moment my foot leaves the sidewalk and hits the parking lot, a gust of wind swirls around me and steals the papers loosely held to my chest. Damn the wind! I'm already late for class. I rush after the frolicking pages to reclaim what's mine, while the fall wind rustles my hair, blinding me in my search for the lost sheets.

I gather them up, one by one, and stamp my foot on the last escapee.

"Gotcha!" I cuddle the pages to me, turn to stand while checking my watch again, and am instantly knocked off balance. My papers once again scatter to the high heavens while my hands and knees scrape against the parking lot asphalt.

"I'm sorry! I didn't see you. Here, let me help…"

The perpetrator who caused my tumble bends to help me up, but not before I notice his polished black loafers. He's so not a student. I'm tugged to my feet and wobble for a moment while I regain my balance. I turn my hands over to reveal scrapes and a little blood, which collects in my palms. However, when I check both knees, one is bloodied and requires tending.

"Damn. I'm already late." My remark, meant only for me, is answered by a smooth, deep, sexy-as-hell male voice.

"Let me take you to the clinic. You can text your professor from there."

My now-benefactor stands with his back to me after collecting my pages again. When he turns toward me, I don't feel half as bad as I did a moment ago. "No, that's okay. I can make it on my own."

His eyes... I stand mesmerized by dark-gray penetrating irises which host hints of blue. I can't speak. When he clears his throat, I subtly shake my head to clear the vision my mind created of this stranger pulling me close and kissing me thoroughly. Damn. I must stop reading those romance novels. My voice finally returns. "Sorry. My name is Mira Lawrie." I offer my scuffed-up hand.

My wayward pages are placed in my palm. "Weston Benjamin. Wes to my friends. Nice to meet you, but sorry I caused you to be even later."

I fold the documents into my portfolio and clutch it tightly to my chest. "It's... fine. Well, see you around campus."

Weston catches my arm before I walk away. "Can I buy you coffee after your last class today? I'd really like to apologize."

"Thanks anyway, but I can't. I have a job." Still in need of a clean-up, I scamper off to the nearest clinic. I turn back once to watch him walk away while those wayward thoughts run rampant through my head. With a heavy sigh, I enter the medical clinic in search of treatment.

While I'm attended to, I send a text to my professor and ask him to forward today's assignment to me. I'm too close to finals and need all the help I can elicit in my Food Chemistry class.

My next lecture starts in twenty minutes. I limp out of the clinic with one bandaged knee, salve on the other, and palms which didn't require treatment except washing. I strap my backpack in place and head off to the Social Sciences and Humanities building, hoping I won't be late.

The classroom is near to full when I find my seat. Once my backpack is stowed on the floor next to my feet, I open my laptop to take notes. Absorbed in thoughts of the tall stranger, I barely overhear a couple of the ladies around me whisper something about our professor. My gaze rises from my computer and what I see before me causes my breath to catch in my throat. The culprit who knocked me over earlier stands next to Professor Matsumura's podium. I nudge my friend, Constanza Perez, the classmate next to me, and nod toward the front.

"Good afternoon, class. My name is Weston Benjamin. Your professor asked me to fill in today in her absence." He flips open the Principles of Macroeconomics book and begins his dissertation.

I type a few words into my computer while trying to forget the gray eyes which created the mental image of his lips locking with mine. If I didn't have to work at the coffee shop this afternoon, I'd be hard pressed *not* to accept his invitation. Maybe...

My chin rests in my palm while I listen to his voice, my gaze fixed on the movement of his lips while he elaborates on the subject at hand. However, I'm pulled from my musing by Connie.

"Don't get too dreamy-eyed over that guy. I've heard rumors."

Her lips move but I barely hear her speech. "I'm not dreamy-eyed over him. I'm trying to listen." My head shakes and I close my eyes. Was that too loud? If so, my voice would have carried to the front of the room from this second row. How embarrassing!

"Well, just so you know, he's a player. Not interested in committed relationships, only fast cars and faster women." Her whispered voice hardly reaches me.

I whisper back. "Don't worry. I'm not interested." When my gaze spins back to the front of the room, his gawk confounds me. So... not as quiet as I'd wished.

"Do you have something to add, Ms. Lawrie?"

A blush creeps up from my neck and turns my face, I'm certain, a brilliant beet red. I've never been able to control blushing. Now, I wish I was dead. "No, Mr. Benjamin, I do not."

The instructor nods and continues to teach while I bury my face behind the lid of my laptop, but not before I slap Connie's arm. She started this!

Thankful when the class ends, I load my book and laptop into my backpack and stand to follow the rest in my row out the door. Mr. Benjamin, I notice, collects his book and notes, and stops beside the open door as I near. Expecting him to scold me for talking in class, I allow the students behind me to pass by. Connie nudges my back when she passes, I suppose in warning. When the last pupil exits, I slip my backpack over my shoulders and wait for his criticism.

"My offer stands, Ms. Lawrie. A quick cup of coffee won't kill you and I'd enjoy getting to know you. What do you say?"

Taken aback by his words, I fumble before I utter, "Thank you, but no thank you, Mr. Benjamin."

"Wes."

"Wes. And now I'll be late for my next class. Have a good rest of your day... again." I escape as quickly as possible and run on my injured knees to my next class.

I don my black apron and walk through the coffee shop cleaning up from the few students who left their cups and plates on the tables. Although I don't particularly enjoy the continual tidying, the job I have provides me with hands-on experience for when I own a similar café one day. That's my goal after graduation: to own and operate a boutique coffee shop in Auburn, California, my hometown. Starbucks will be a fierce competitor, but I plan to expand my services to capture loyalty from the locals.

My schedule at school doesn't afford me much time to work, but my employer, Nancy Franklin, took me on last year after I pleaded and committed to work as many hours as she required. She told me her evening shift tended to be the most difficult since students come in late to study and occupy most of her seats, leaving little for the surrounding community. I mentioned I'm a student as well and would enjoy creating a schedule for the study groups on specific nights, which would allow time for her local clientele.

"Your coffee shop is popular because the library doesn't offer coffee and pastries. What if you set aside three evenings a week for study groups? That will leave three nights for the locals. I think everyone would be appreciate knowing what to expect when they walk in."

Nancy laughed out loud. "Now, why haven't I thought of that before? That's a great idea. And, you're hired!"

We shook on it and I started the next night. She allowed me two weeks to wrangle the student groups into control, and it's been a smooth run since. As I look around the near empty café now, I remind myself the three groups scheduled tonight should arrive in a few minutes, mine included. Practice for the future, I mentally congratulate myself.

My relationship with the owner, once I divulged my future plans, developed into more of a mentorship. Over time, she allowed me to help process her inventory order and also learn how she creates her homemade pastries. That's the most fun. From muffins, to scones, to small cakes and pies, cookies, and her famous cinnamon rolls... my hands are involved in it all to some degree.

Over last summer, she added sandwiches for the lunch crowd. I haven't delved into that aspect yet. I'm still learning how to bake without burning the place down. Nancy is the perfect instructor, though. If I had more time, I'm certain my learning curve would improve.

A lull in traffic allows me time to read through the notes I took in Macroeconomics class this morning. I stop after a few minutes and remember the tenor of Wes's voice and his formal posture as he paraded across Professor Matsumura's stage spouting on about the principles of our current economy. Even though I have no time for a casual relationship this semester, I almost wish I'd accepted his offer.

"So not meant to be," I muse as I stow away my laptop when the evening crowd begins to stagger through the front door. I recognize students from two of the study groups scheduled tonight. I staff register two while Nancy creates their drink orders. Once they're completed, I'll step away and Nancy will manage both the register and the orders since I'll be on break to involve myself with my group. If she needs help, she knows she can call on me. That's our deal.

One by one, each student places their order, stands off to the side to wait while it's created, and then joins the rest at their assigned table in the back room. The chaos subsides after a few minutes and the noise level lessens to a sharing of ideas and note taking.

My peers have not arrived yet and I wonder if I've missed a change in time. I check my phone for any missing message, but find none. I assume they're a little late.

The last warmed pastry is plated and handed off to an older student who was in my public speaking class a year ago. I believe his name is Andrew something. Since he must not remember me, I decide to just smile when he grasps the plate. My gaze follows him to his table while wishing I had time to date someone... anyone... this semester.

An explosion of voices cascades through the café, turning heads, when the door opens again. My head shakes. Connie and the other four members of our study group push into the shop discussing their upcoming vacations, which occur in three weeks' time. My straight-lipped stare is captured by my best friend.

She shushes the others, stands at the register, and grins. "Um, sorry."

The rest of the girls voice their apology as one.

"What can I start for you?" Ready to add her order to the register, I peek up and smile.

"I'm going all out tonight. A large black coffee and one of Nancy's cinnamon rolls."

"Is that all?"

"Yup."

"May I have a name for your coffee, please?"

"Quit fooling around, Mira. You know my name almost as well as you know yours." My friend laughs, taps her phone against the reader, and stands aside for the next student.

When all have placed their orders, I point toward the back room. "Our table awaits. Take your drinks in and I'll be right behind you with your pastries."

Connie waits behind for a moment. "Are you sure you won't come with me to Chicago for the holidays? Mom and Dad would love to meet you."

"And leave my parents and brothers? No way! You enjoy the snow. I'm staying put."

Connie follows the group into the student-filled room. "Don't say I didn't ask!"

I take one quick walk around the café cleaning what I can before I follow my friends into our study cave.

My Apple Watch beeps later that night, showing "10:45." I rise slowly, stretch my arms above my head, then stuff my schoolwork into my backpack.

"Time for me to turn back into a pumpkin, ladies. Don't bother cleaning up. It's late. I'll take care of it. Thanks for a great session. I feel much better about our nutrition class now."

The five prepare to leave, each talking over the other, as they close books and computers, sling their packs over their shoulders, and carry what they can to the trash bins out front. My boss has already wiped down the empty tables in the larger room and smiles when I emerge from the back.

"If you handle the rest, I'll start closing down the register."

"Sure thing." I turn to my friends. "See you in class tomorrow. And, be careful walking back to the dorm. Night all."

I grab a tub and gather the remaining dishes from the tables in back. After all are placed into the dishwasher, I wipe down all tables and chairs with our disinfecting spray and cloth while Nancy closes out the cash register and deposits the cash drawer into the safe in her office. Used towels and cloth napkins accumulated are placed in a bag to be taken home for washing. I turn out the lights in the study room while Nancy clears the counters and places all food items from inside the display case in the large fridge in back. With one final look around, I sigh with relief. Time for bed.

"Good night, Nancy. See you tomorrow evening."

"Thanks for your help, Mira."

With a final wave, I sling my backpack over my shoulder, cross to the door, switch the Open sign to Closed, and step out into the cold fall night. The wind whips down the dark almost-deserted street, so I pull my scarf from my pocket and drape it around my neck. I haven't taken four steps when I bump into someone. This just isn't my day. At least my schoolwork in safe inside my backpack this time.

"Excuse me," I utter as I turn toward the individual I walked into. I stop immediately. "Are you following me?"

Wes Benjamin grins broadly. "No, not really. I finished copying a thesis next door and was headed home. I can actually ask the same of you. And, by the way, what are you doing out this late on a school night, young lady?"

So, he's forgotten my name. "Mira. My name is Mira. And I just got off work at Just Coffee." I point back toward the sign. "I work here four nights a week."

I'm getting cold and it's already late. I have an early class, so I continue on my way. "Good night, Weston."

He turns as if to follow me. "Wait! Can I give you a ride back to your house or dorm?"

"Nope. Thanks anyway." I call over my shoulder. I have too much to do and I need sleep. Also, I don't want him to know where

I live. If Connie is correct in her accusations about this guy, I don't want to invest any time with him.

When the tall dark handsome man doesn't follow me, I chalk it up to me not being his type. I am not one to become involved with a once-and-done situation. I'm looking for the forever guy who wants many of the same things as I do: a quiet life, not extravagant, but filled with love and devotion, kids, and a home in the trees of Auburn where we can get lost from the rest of the world.

So, why am I obsessing all over *this* guy? Maybe it's because I haven't been on a real date since… I have to think. Last summer? Damn. My pace increases. I'm chilled to the bone from the wind. "Doesn't matter, Mr. Gray Eyes. I'm not interested."

It's a little before midnight when I reach my dorm. I almost admonish myself for not taking Mr. Benjamin up on his offer of a ride home. I'd already be in bed.

ABOUT THE AUTHOR

Lynne Anders is a relatively new author who lives in the heat of Arizona most of the year with her husband and friends, and plays with her grandchildren whenever possible.

She began her writing career at a very early age when she created a simple poem and was asked to read it before her school assembly. The writing bug possessed her from that one magic moment on. However, the need to earn a living pulled her away from serious writing. Instead of creating characters, she spent years in the accounting and property management industry, and wrote poems only on occasion. However, after she retired, she decided it was time to return to her first love. The outcome of that desire can be found on Amazon.

Lynne enjoys writing about small-town America, possibly because of her Midwestern background, and believes friendships and lasting relationships weather the storm more easily when the pace and distractions from large cities are not part of the equation.

You can find Lynne here:

Website: LynneAnders.com
Instagram: AuthorAnders
Facebook: LynneAnders
Email: Author_la@lynneanders.com

Happy reading!

Made in the USA
Las Vegas, NV
11 February 2022